Danielle Ramsay

Danielle Ramsay is a proud Scot living in a small seaside town in north-east England. Always a storyteller, it was only after pursuing an academic career in literature that she found her place in life and began to write creatively full time after being shortlisted for the CWA Debut Dagger in 2009 and 2010. She is the author of three previous Jack Brady crime novels, *Blind Alley*, *Broken Silence* and *Vanishing Point*.

Always on the go, always passionate in what she is doing, Danielle fills her days with horse-riding, running and murder by proxy.

DANIELLE RAMSAY

Blood Reckoning

MULHOLLAND
BOOKS
HODDER

First published in Great Britain in 2015 by Mulholland Books
An imprint of Hodder & Stoughton
An Hachette UK company

1

A CIP catalogue record for this title is available from the British Library

Paperback ISBN 978 1 444 75484 1
eBook ISBN 978 1 444 75485 8

Printed and bound by CPI Group (UK) Ltd, Croydon, CR0 4YY

Hodder & Stoughton policy is to use papers that are natural, renewable
and recyclable products and made from wood grown in sustainable
forests. The logging and manufacturing processes are expected to
conform to the environmental regulations of the country of origin.

Hodder & Stoughton Ltd
338 Euston Road
London NW1 3BH

www.hodder.co.uk

To the memory of Stan Ramsay.

'No mortal can keep a secret. If his lips are silent, he chatters with his fingertips; betrayal oozes out of him at every pore.'

Sigmund Freud

SATURDAY

Chapter One

He checked the time on his mobile. He was starting to get pissed off now. No text – nothing.

He didn't want to be here. Shaking his head, he tried to get rid of the doubts that had started to creep in. He couldn't put his finger on what it was about tonight's arrangements that made him feel so . . . so uneasy. They'd been meeting like this for months now. Discretion was everything. He more than anyone understood the need for anonymity, but he was still at a loss.

Why here, of all places?

He needed a drink. That would calm him down. Maybe it was just the fact that it was a different rendezvous than usual. Not as upmarket as he liked, and definitely not in a location he would have chosen. He was used to boutique hotels like Malmaison on Newcastle's trendy quayside. This place couldn't have been more different. It left him bemused. It added to the feeling that something about the set-up was wrong.

What's taking you so long?

The silence was making him nervous. Jumpy even. His mobile suddenly bleeped. He had a text. Relief kicked in. But it was short-lived.

Shit!

I'm really sorry. Please ring me. Please. Just give me a chance to make it right x

It was his girlfriend – again. She had been calling repeatedly, but he hadn't answered. In this situation silence was the best tactic. He'd tell her that his phone had run out of power. An easy excuse that negated the need for elaborate lies that could trip him up.

Before he left he had deliberately started an argument. One that quickly escalated. His way of creating an 'out' for tonight. Reverse psychology. He had accused her of causing problems in their relationship. Started having a real go at her. Told her to be careful. That she was suffocating him. That she had turned into a controlling, suspicious, psycho bitch.

Not that he felt good about it. She had every right to be paranoid. The regular late nights and furtive phone calls and texts were more than enough. When questioned about his unexplained absences, he would use the same old corny excuse every time – work. He was nearing the end of his Masters and had repeatedly used the pretext that he was working on his final dissertation. He was focused on his career and knew exactly where he wanted to be in ten years' time. That took devotion. And not necessarily in the way she imagined.

He scrolled through his other messages in case he had missed one. Nothing. He had sent a text when he had checked into the hotel. Same as always. But this time there had been no reply. It didn't make sense. The feeling of unease crept back.

For fuck's sake, it's Saturday night, Alex! What the hell are you doing in some crap seaside hotel waiting . . . waiting for what, exactly?

The answer wasn't one he particularly liked.

SEX – sordid and hard. The kind of sex that costs.

He checked his mobile again: nothing. He always got a text if there was a hold-up. A slither of fear edged its way in. What if someone had found out?

Fuck!

He contemplated texting but decided against it. He knew the rules; apart from when he checked in, texting was out. Suddenly his phone bleeped again. Hopeful, he read the new message.

Why won't you answer your phone? Alex please. I love you
x

He felt a sudden stab of shame. It quickly evaporated, replaced by irritation. Right now she was the least of his problems.

He got up off the bed and walked over to the window, trying to shake his darkening mood. The hotel room was pitifully pedestrian. Magnolia walls, beige carpet and cheap brown MDF furniture. It didn't even have a mini-bar. The view did little to improve his spirits. It was dominated by a black expanse of sea. Bleak and miserable. Directly below was the Promenade, illuminated by a hazy yellow glow which added to the seediness of the place. Explosions of drunken laughter and taunts drifted up to the second floor.

It was a Saturday night – what else did he expect?

He watched as a group of loud-mouthed pissheads lurched past towards the lure of the gaudy lights and pulsating music that spoke of girls with glazed eyes, fake tans and even faker smiles. They all shared one discernible trait – young men looking for a good time. Regardless of the cost. Getting pissed and laid, in that order. Didn't matter whether that included a night sobering up in the police cells. It was all part of the weekend. It would inevitably end with them getting in someone's face. Fighting or shagging amounted to pretty much the same thing; they were too fucked to care. That was all they aspired to, unlike him. He had plans. Big plans. Tonight was just another step towards securing his career.

Alexander De Bernier looked at his stark reflection against the blackness of the night outside. He was naked – as instructed. Twenty-two years old and in his prime; six foot two, muscular, broad-shouldered, with well-defined abs leading down to a narrow waist and then . . . He looked down at himself. Pleasingly well-endowed, to say the least. He'd first realised his luck in the communal showers at his all-boys school. His deep, dark brown eyes lingered over his reflection. He smiled.

He had a lot to be proud of and he was damned sure he

wasn't going to put it to waste. He had often been accused of suffering from 'only child syndrome' – selfish, opinionated, egotistical and hugely narcissistic. But he would be the first to agree that he was all of the above.

And he detested being kept waiting.

As if on cue, the low, deep growl of an approaching car interrupted his thoughts. He watched as the white Audi R8 sports car pulled into the car park below.

Seconds later, a text arrived. Excitement coursed through him. He knew the game. Knew what was expected. But tonight was going to be different. He needed to talk. Straighten out what was in it for him. By now he would have expected more from these clandestine meetings. Sex first, of course. Then they would discuss his burgeoning career. After all, why have powerful contacts like this one and not use it?

He walked over to the king-size bed and picked up his phone.

FIRST RULE – NO TALKING
SECOND RULE – BLINDFOLD YOURSELF
THIRD RULE – FACE-DOWN READY TO BE BOUND AND GAGGED

He hesitated. This was a new trait, one he didn't recognise. He had always been in control. The one who dominated.

But this was . . .

He dispelled the thoughts hurtling through his mind.

You're being ridiculous. What's the worst that could happen?

He didn't have time to analyse the new rules. The last thing he wanted to do was disappoint. He needed to get ready. He looked around the bland hotel room for a blindfold, spotted his tie hanging in the open wardrobe. Good enough.

He didn't have to bother leaving the hotel door ajar. He had left the duplicate room key card hidden as usual. Discretion was crucial. Both of them had too much to lose.

★   ★   ★

He had done as instructed. He was blindfolded, prostrate on the bed with his arms obediently clasped behind his back – the willing victim.

His breath quickened when he heard the door open.

He instantly recognised the cologne; expensive and subtle. He liked the older man's taste. It spoke of money and power – everything that Alex coveted. He could feel the excitement stirring within him, reaching down to his loins, and shifted his weight slightly to accommodate his growing hardness.

He resisted the urge to speak or pull the blindfold down and turn round. He so wanted to see the look on the older man's face at the sight spread before him. But he remained perfectly still. He was good at obeying orders. For now.

Silence.

The urge to move was starting to become intolerable, but he fought it. Still nothing. He reassured himself that the older man was simply enjoying this new game. He was certain that he was appreciating Alex's honed body in front of him. He was obediently waiting . . . waiting to be taken.

Filled with anticipation, he held his breath as he heard the other man move towards the bed. He felt his ankles being bound together by rope – then his hands. The bindings around his wrists were twisted tight. Too tight. He could feel the rope burning his flesh.

Shit!

His girlfriend came to mind.

He had one rule – no physical marks on his body.

Before he had a chance to object, his head was roughly jerked back and his mouth gagged with duct tape.

What the . . . ?

The duct tape was wound firmly over his mouth and around the back of his head.

This was too full-on. Too extreme for a sex game. The older man had never shown any interest in sadism before. Alex hoped that he was just getting excited, too enthusiastic with his newfound dominance. But that didn't mean he was just going to lie here and accept it. He attempted to protest but all that he managed was a frustrated muffled sound. Alex shook his head. He needed him to know that he wasn't comfortable with this.

But his stifled objections were ignored.

Alex could feel panic stirring in his stomach and tried to keep calm, to reassure himself it was nothing more than a game. The other man was much older and physically weaker than him. And crucially, he had more to lose than Alex – a lot more. If he went too far, then Alex had enough to destroy him.

But that didn't quell the disquiet he felt. This wasn't what he had agreed to. He twisted his wrists in an attempt to loosen the knots, but the more he pulled against it, the deeper the rope cut into his flesh.

He tried to scream in anger and frustration. Nothing. His shouts were deadened by the tape.

Alex wanted this to end. Now.

Every inch of him was telling him that he should do something – anything. He struggled in desperation. It didn't work. His hands felt sticky from his exertions and he realised it was blood. The rope was slicing into his wrists. Now furious, instinct made him attempt to shout out. But again, nothing.

You fucking old cunt! I'll have you once this is over!

He thrashed his body around. It was futile.

Fuck . . . fuck . . . fuck!

Something was wrong. Very wrong. Alex tried not to panic but he was gagged, bound and blinded. Unable to move or talk. He was completely at the other man's mercy. But why? Why was he doing this to him?

My wrists are fucking bleeding, you bastard!

Alex was suddenly winded as a heavy weight crushed his lower back. Enraged, he realised the man had straddled him.

He hadn't anticipated the next move – the rope against his throat. Deceitful and totally unexpected. Blood pummelled through his veins and roared in his ears as the rope dug deep into his skin.

He couldn't breathe.

An unexpected pleasurable sensation shot like an electric current to his groin as more pressure was applied. It was a few moments before his sexual excitement dissipated, replaced by pure alarm.

It's tight . . . too fucking tight . . .

Shit! I can't breathe . . .

His legs jerked as the rope squeezed even harder, ramming his Adam's apple up towards his skull. He struggled to stay conscious as the blood vessels in his eyes ruptured, releasing an explosion of white flecks.

Fuck . . . fuck . . . fuck . . .

The rope twisted even tighter. He couldn't think straight. Nothing made sense. The deafening shriek of his body dulled his sense of reality. All he was aware of was burning – as if petrol had been doused down his throat and then set alight.

Alex felt himself slipping into unconsciousness and welcomed it.

Seconds . . . or was it minutes later? He wasn't sure. All he knew was that the black nothingness had been replaced by crippling pain.

His head was yanked back and the duct tape ripped off. He gasped air. Slow, shallow and raspy snatches of air. But it was enough.

He tried to make his mind play catch up, but his thoughts were dulled by the blackness that had temporarily taken him.

Without warning, he was rolled onto his back.

Shit!

Something cold and metallic touched his face, teasingly. It took him a few moments to realise that it was a knife. He felt the chill of the blade as it traced its way up his cheek until it reached the makeshift blindfold covering his eyes. A second later, and he was squinting in surprise at the sudden glare of light.

He didn't have time to understand.

His brain felt sluggish, his body in too much pain for him to make sense of anything.

9

He felt a firm hand around him – massaging . . . squeezing . . . trying to make him hard. His body didn't feel like his own. It felt numb. Paralysed, he watched, tried to blink back the tears. He felt pathetic. He was pathetic. It all made sense. He could see that now.

You stupid bastard, Alex . . . You fucking stupid bastard . . .

He felt the cold tip of the blade as it seared his flesh. It took his damaged senses a moment to comprehend. His eyes widened in terror.

Fuck! No . . . Not that . . . Anything but that . . .

Chapter Two

Saturday: 11:52 p.m.

The cool air was a welcome relief as he walked through the streets of Whitley Bay. He smiled as he indulged himself in memories. He had waited so long. Too long. Delight played on the corners of his lips. He did not register the old, homeless man huddled in the doorway of the B&M store, speaking gibberish as he clutched a bottle of something lethal. He was inconsequential. As were the taxis speeding towards the bars and clubs along South Parade and the Promenade, and the drunken people lurching across the road, laughing and singing.

His mind was caught up on earlier events. Flashes of blood-drenched scenes consumed him. He had savoured every minute detail, stored the images with the others; cataloguing them for when the desire arose to peruse them. The heady aroma of kebabs and curries that dominated the town centre was lost to him – all he could smell was fear; pungent and acrid. He breathed it in.

He felt calm. The unrest that plagued him for so long had been silenced – temporarily. But it was enough. Until next time.

For there would definitely be a next time.

'Spare any money, mate?' the huddled figure suddenly called out at him, hopefully.

The whining, croaky voice brought him back to the seedy reality of Whitley Bay on a Saturday night.

'Just a quid, eh?' the old man asked as he weakly held up a trembling hand.

He turned and looked down at the homeless man.

Startled, the old man shuffled back away from him and shivered involuntarily, despite the warmth of the dirty old quilt wrapped around his body.

'Sorry mate . . . don't matter,' he mumbled as he pressed his body back against the door.

There was something about those eyes that terrified him. They were devoid of anything. No feeling. No empathy. The homeless man felt like he was staring into the eyes of something that was not human.

He clung onto the half-full bottle of scotch and waited for him to move on.

When he did, the old man breathed out slowly, watching as the tall, suited figure crossed over towards Whitley Road. He wasn't sure who he had just accosted for money, but he knew that he was lucky not to have had his hands smashed to smithereens to prevent him from ever begging again. He had lived on the streets for too long not to recognise the signs. Out here you lived by instinct and wit alone and you learned the hard way who to avoid. And the ones, like the man who had just passed him, who were simply wired differently from the rest of society. Dangerously so. He unscrewed the cap on his scotch and took a much-needed glug. The warm raw liquid slipped effortlessly down the back of his throat, but it did not have the desired numbing effect. He realised his hand was still trembling as he screwed the cap on. And he knew why. It was the man's eyes. Cold and menacing, with a hunger in them. A hunger to kill.

The old man scanned Whitley Road for any sign of him, but he was gone. He snatched up the bottle, took another gulp and then wiped his mouth with the back of his blackened, rheumatoid hand. He tucked the bottle safely in an inside pocket and, struggling, staggered to his feet.

He had a bad feeling – and living on the streets, he had seen enough to know when it was time to disappear.

SUNDAY

Chapter Three

'James? Where the hell have you been?' Ronnie demanded when Macintosh walked through the door. He was really pissed off. He had been delaying calling the police for the past hour, just on the off-chance that Macintosh showed.

James David Macintosh smiled apologetically and shrugged. 'I'm really sorry, Ronnie. I . . . I don't know what to say. Time just eluded me.'

'You better bloody think of something to say. It's after midnight for Christ's sake. You've been missing for over five hours! Curfew's seven p.m. You know that!' He ran a shaking hand absentmindedly over his shaven head as he gave Macintosh the once-over. He was immaculate, as always. Dressed in a dark charcoal suit, with a crisp white shirt open at the neck. No tie. He was in his late fifties, yet seemed younger and fitter than a lot of blokes in their mid-forties – including Ronnie. He looked as he always did; exceptionally smart, with a professional air about him, one that spoke of a Cambridge education and a career as a doctor. However, James David Macintosh's career had been cut short. He'd only made it past his third year as a medical student before his personal life got in the way.

Ronnie watched as Macintosh logged himself in. 'Make sure you put the time down,' he ordered.

Macintosh nodded as he scrawled his signature.

'You been drinking then?' Ronnie asked, his voice raw with irritation.

'No,' Macintosh replied as he pushed the log book back towards Ronnie. 'I don't drink.' It was the first time Ronnie had witnessed an edge to Macintosh's voice – he was ordinarily charming and easy-going. But Ronnie didn't argue. It was clear that he hadn't been drinking. He had worked the job long enough to be able to tell when a resident was high from drugs, drunk, or both. Macintosh was neither.

'So, do you want to tell me where you've been for the past five hours?' he asked. He pushed thoughts of Macintosh's criminal history to the back of his mind. It wasn't his concern. Macintosh had returned – in one piece, which was always an added bonus. It was someone else's problem to figure out whether he should remain on parole.

Macintosh shrugged apologetically as he looked at Ronnie. His blue eyes held Ronnie's probing gaze. 'I simply went for a walk and lost track of time. When I realised how late it was I made my way straight here.'

Ronnie shook his head. 'Why, James? You've just been paroled. Why fuck it up?'

'You don't think they'll put me back, do you?' Macintosh asked, his eyes filled with concern.

'I dunno. You know what they're like. Rules are rules and curfew's one of those rules that you can't break,' Ronnie answered, glancing at the monitor on the reception desk. The screen showed various security cameras set up around the grounds of Ashley House.

Macintosh was more than aware of the surveillance cameras that followed every one of the residents' movements. The cameras were located in the communal rooms and hallways and around the exterior of the large Victorian building. There was no way in or out without being detected. The reason – twenty paroled serious offenders. All Category Three. Violent, volatile and dangerous, but all having been given a second chance at rehabilitation. Some managed to make the adjustment. Most just blew it, unable to cope with being in charge of their own pathetic, useless lives.

'Is someone out there?' Macintosh asked as his eyes followed Ronnie's.

For a brief moment he wondered if someone had followed him.

Could someone have recognised me after all this time? It was possible . . .

Ronnie shook his head. 'Nah. It's that damned ginger cat again. Why it can't shit in its own back garden I don't know.' He turned his attention back to Macintosh. 'Go on. Get upstairs. I'll let Jonathan know in the morning. It's his call what happens.'

Macintosh nodded, grateful that Ronnie was not going to report him. If he did, he would be back inside come Monday. No explanations or apologies. But his probation officer, Jonathan Edwards, was a soft touch. He knew that Jonathan would not want to be the one responsible for returning him to prison. Not after he had been banged up for thirty-seven years. After all, Jonathan had become more to him than his probation officer. Much more.

'Thanks, Ronnie,' Macintosh said.

'What for?' Ronnie questioned.

'For not reporting me.'

'Like I said, it's Jonathan's call.'

Macintosh left it at that. He turned and walked out of the office and down the corridor. A flicker of a smile played at the edge of his lips. Everything had gone according to plan. Even Ronnie's blasé attitude. Ronnie had obviously just been relieved that he had finally shown up, but he didn't want to know the details. And that had suited Macintosh perfectly. By the time the police were called, it would be too late. He would be gone – for good. And this time, they wouldn't find him. His eyes shone fervently as he thought of what he had planned.

Tonight was just the beginning.

He had to bide his time. A few more days and then . . .

Chapter Four

The cleaner knocked on the door for a third time. No answer. The 'Do Not Disturb' sign was still hanging on the handle. She double-checked her clipboard. The room was down to be stripped and cleaned ready for the new guests this afternoon.

Irritated that she was behind schedule, she knocked again, louder this time, to be sure they knew she meant business. She had better things to do than wait around for other people to get their act together.

Nothing. If they were still inside then that was their problem. They were supposed to have vacated the room over an hour ago.

She didn't know what it was – sixth sense – but she knew there was still someone in there. She had seen plenty in this job. If she had been naïve before she started, she certainly wasn't any more. She'd walked in on couples in various compromising acts. Threesomes. Foursomes. Two men together. Nothing shocked her. After all, this was a stag and hen party destination. They usually had a couple of coachloads every other weekend. It kept her in a job. Busy, but better that than scratting around on the dole.

If she won the lottery, she would quit. No hesitation. No working out her notice. One call to her boss to tell him where to stuff his hotel and the rude dirty buggers who made her life difficult. Then she would get on a plane to Spain. She'd buy some coastal property. Trade Whitley Bay beach for an equivalent in Mallorca, but with sunshine.

A sudden gloom took hold. She shook it off. She'd buy herself a scratch card after work. That would cheer her up. Take her and Harold one step closer to Mallorca. Even just for a holiday. She wasn't greedy.

Her face lit up at the thought as she swiped her key in the door.

The smell hit her first. It was a hard punch. Her smile fell as the dank, dour odour that accompanied death assaulted her senses.

She had been wrong if she had thought she had seen it all before.

Blood – dark, discoloured – saturated the sheets. Soaked into the mattress. Splattered the wall behind . . . *him?*

She couldn't be sure. She didn't want to look. Not again. But for some reason she couldn't turn away.

It . . . the body. Lifeless. Skin mottled. Ankles tied. Head, faceless. Black, thick tape. Mutilated. Flesh open. Gaping.

Screaming.

The mess. This was wrong. It was so wrong.

Chapter Five

Macintosh forced himself to smile. To look relaxed, despite feeling anything but. He wanted to get up and walk out of this claustrophobic pale blue office with its threadbare beige carpet and stale, desperate air. But he knew he couldn't. The game had already started and he needed to see it through to the end, no matter how tiresome it was proving. He had to be careful.

But first he had to convince his probation officer not to revoke his parole. He laid his hands out on the table, as a sign that he had nothing to hide. He trusted himself not to give anything away. No nervous tremors or ticks or sweat patches which could suggest he was lying. Ironically, it was Jonathan Edwards' forehead that was glistening with perspiration. Dark, damp circles also spread out from under the armpits of his black polo shirt. Not surprising; the heat in the small room was unbearable. For some reason the old, antiquated heating system was still sluggishly gurgling its way through the large Victorian pipes that snaked their way around the house.

'Look, James, this is difficult for me,' Edwards continued, sighing. He took off his designer glasses and polished them on his polo shirt.

Macintosh looked at him with an expression of embarrassment for all the fuss he was causing. As he did, he couldn't help but notice that Edwards' insipid blue eyes were smaller than he expected. His face was unremarkable in every sense of the word. Except for the severe acne scars. Thirty-one years old, five foot ten and overweight. Even his short blond hair had started to thin and recede. Macintosh knew it caused him anguish. It aged him. By the time he was thirty-five he would look well into his fifties. He didn't have a lot to look forward to. That was why Macintosh had taken such a personal interest in him. Why he was sitting here listening to the bilge coming out of Edwards' mouth.

He waited while Edwards replaced his glasses. His puffy, red-rimmed eyes spoke of weeks of sleep deprivation.

'You just walked?' Edwards continued, frowning.

'Yes. I know it sounds crazy. I don't know if I would believe it myself,' he said.

Edwards waited. It was clear he wanted more.

Macintosh leaned in towards him: 'If I'm honest, Jonathan, I'm struggling in here. It's difficult with the others . . .' He faltered as his eyes searched Edwards' face for some kind of understanding.

It was in that moment that he knew he had him. There was a flicker of understanding. And why not? Edwards knew what kind of men inhabited this bail house. Sick, depraved animals. The lowest of the low. Sex offenders of all kinds: from Tom, the clichéd dirty old man in Room 4 with his penchant for twelve-year-old schoolgirls – preferably in uniform – to the occupant of Room 9 who had been convicted of sexually abusing a three-month-old baby. Then there were the rapists and women abusers. Men who had murdered their wives and girlfriends, or who had left their victims wishing they were dead when they had finished with them. Macintosh knew that there was a panic button on the probation officer's side of the desk. Press it, and the other four members of staff would come running. Pull it out and the alarm would inform Whitley Bay police that there was a 'situation'. But Edwards hadn't flinched when Macintosh moved his body towards him. He had gained his trust. His confidence. Edwards clearly did not associate him with the murderer that he had been.

After all, he wasn't like the other paroled offenders. People liked him. They trusted him.

They allowed him to tie them up and gag them and . . .

Macintosh held back his smile as he savoured the feeling of control that he'd had over his victims. All willing participants in their own torture – and ultimately, their own murders.

'Look . . . I know it's tough. You were inside for thirty-seven years. It's a lot to expect you to come out and just fit back into society. Not after so long,' Edwards replied.

Macintosh nodded. He understood better than his probation officer could ever imagine.

'What can I do to make the transition easier for you?'

'Exactly what you're doing now. Rather than assuming the worst, you're taking the time to listen to me. To help me . . .' Macintosh paused.

Edwards smiled reassuringly at him. 'And that's what I'm here for. The last thing I want is you being returned to prison. So, all you did was walk about last night? You didn't meet up with anyone? Talk to anyone?'

Macintosh shook his head. He made a point of looking contrite. An acknowledgement that he had been foolish. Reckless even, and that he would never make the same mistake twice.

'OK. I'll tell you what we'll do, let's arrange a meeting at my office on Monday and we'll talk about it further then,' Edwards suggested.

'Thanks, Jonathan. I really appreciate it,' Macintosh replied, his voice filled with gratitude.

'No problem. And look, the next time it's really getting to you, call me. That's what I'm here for.'

Macintosh nodded. 'I'm really sorry for disturbing your Sunday with your family.'

Edwards stood up to go. 'Just make sure you don't break the curfew again.'

'I won't. I promise,' Macintosh said as he stood up. He stuck his hand out to shake Edwards', and his probation officer obliged without thinking. 'You can trust me.'

Edwards smiled at him. 'I know I can, James. I wouldn't be here on my day off if I didn't.'

Macintosh knew he looked more professional than his probation officer. His exceptionally handsome face and benign manner fooled people. They found it difficult to believe that someone so good-looking and affable was capable of committing the atrocities that had got him locked up in a maximum-security prison for thirty-seven years.

Macintosh knew that Edwards saw him as a decent human being with the misfortune to be living in a bail hostel with nineteen paroled serious offenders. After all, Edwards was a nice bloke. A man who believed in his job. He sincerely wanted to help Macintosh rehabilitate back into society. To give him a second chance. And that was precisely what Macintosh wanted too.

Macintosh stood at his pitiful bedroom window. It was an original Victorian one, which may have looked charming but was far from practical. Not only did the cold air find its way in, but so did the rain. The result was black, ugly mould covering the damp, high walls. He was worried that if he didn't get out in time the spores would burrow their way into his lungs and under his skin. He had complained to Ronnie and the other key workers, but nobody listened. He was expected to be grateful that he had a bedroom of his own – regardless of how small and basic it was. And dirty. Even though it had been repainted, tell-tale signs of the previous residents clung persistently to the room. That smell. It still lingered, despite his attempts to get rid of it.

He tried to block out all thoughts of the men who had inhabited this room before him. Debased animals who didn't deserve to breathe the same air as him, let alone lie in the same bed. It drove Macintosh insane to think of them lying there.

23

He heard a door slam and looked down as Edwards started his metallic blue Volvo V40. It was a family car. Edwards was very much a family man. Two children under the age of three. Macintosh liked his probation officer. Enough to take an interest in his personal life.

He had a faultless memory. Every droplet of information that Edwards had casually let out had been caught by him. He had memorised it and then extracted more – carefully, so as not to attract suspicion. Edwards had been more than willing on occasion to digress and discuss his personal life. Not that he had ever been really aware of it. Macintosh had a way of ingratiating himself, gaining enough trust to exact small details that seemed nothing at the time. But when you placed them all together, the result was breathtaking. It was someone's life.

Edwards interested him. Reminded Macintosh of his first kill. The ones afterwards had paled into insignificance. Nothing could ever match the high he had first felt. He had tried. Tried to rediscover that all-consuming feeling of euphoria that had immortalised him. But nothing had come close.

He decided not to reopen old wounds. He had taught himself to stop the self-destructive thoughts. Even when they bombarded his brain he had trained himself to look the other way, to focus on something else.

Jonathan Edwards: probation officer, thirty-one years old, five foot ten, married with two children and current resident of Whitley Bay. Receding blond hair, short-sighted blue eyes, doughy, pockmarked skin – nothing to write home about. But he was different from the rest. He was hiding something which made him very interesting. Macintosh could smell it on him. It secreted from his pores. Betraying him.

He had guessed the moment he met him. Whether Edwards knew that he knew didn't matter. What was important was what he was going to do about it. Inside prison, he was powerless to act. But now he was out.

Yesterday evening he had wandered the streets of Whitley Bay looking for him. Searching for his new Volvo V40. And he had found it. Along with the four-bedroomed semi-detached house in Queens Road. Exquisite location. Splendid house. Then again, the couple were both professionals. He was sure the Edwards could afford it. He had seen both children. The baby. And Annabel. Petite, with Nordic white-blond hair that cascaded in perfectly formed ringlets. Eyes as bright as shiny black buttons, dominating a perfect porcelain face. He liked her – a lot. She reminded him of *her*. He had failed then. But now, he had a second chance.

Chapter Six

Sunday: 1:39 p.m.

Brady stood in the doorway, watching her. She was asleep on his couch. Faded patchwork quilt covering her as she slept with her back facing the world, curled up in a foetal position. That had been her tactic for the past five or so months. She had turned her back on the world and on him.

He crept over, making a mental note to avoid the loose wooden floorboard that protested too loudly if he dared step on it. He placed the fresh black coffee on the floor, at arm's length away from the couch. Beside it, he laid down the *Observer* and a plate with a bacon sandwich on it. The two things she would want when she decided to wake up were coffee and the paper. The bacon sandwich was wishful thinking on his part. A longing to return to normality.

He wasn't sure if she was really asleep. He knew she pretended, to avoid talking to him. Not wanting to face him, or to deal with what had happened to her – to them – all those months ago. To face the fact that someone had brutally murdered her boyfriend and then come after her. He could only imagine what they had done to her. Claudia had never talked about it. Like him, she had refused counselling at the time. But he was stronger than her. Brady had had a childhood of pain and abuse that had prepared him for a life that could kick the shit out of you and barely leave you breathing. But still, you breathed. Still, you lived. At least, he did. As for Claudia, she simply breathed. It was the living part she had given up. The one thing she could control. Her problem was that she had never really known anything bad. She had never wanted for anything as a child, nor as an adult. Loved and adored by all. Admittedly, he had given her good cause to walk out on their marriage when she did. But apart from that, she had had a blessed life – until now.

Who could blame her for attempting to block it out? Pretend that it hadn't happened?

But he knew that she was drowning in self-denial. That her way of dealing with it – or not – was slowly killing her; and in turn, killing him. Brady sat down carefully on the floor beside her. Careful, for two reasons. He didn't want to wake her, if she really was asleep. And his body still ached from the violence that had been enacted upon it. His left knee had been shattered beyond comprehension. His right hand and fingers had turned to mash under the weight of a crowbar. Then there was the bullet to his chest that had somehow missed his lung and spared his life.

He allowed himself this moment as the afternoon sun stabbed through the partially open curtains. He needed it. He needed her. He wanted her back. The old Claudia. The one who would attack him with words that startled him. A constant reminder that she was from a different background and class to him. She was well-educated. He wasn't. She was everything to him. He was nothing to her. Without her, he was empty. Purposeless. Her refusal to let him in, to let him save her, was killing him.

He had already saved her once. Trading his life for hers without hesitation. Over five months ago she had been held hostage by two Eastern European gangsters known as the Dabkunas brothers. They had wanted Brady's brother, Nick. He had infiltrated their organisation and betrayed them. It was simple maths. Someone had to pay. So they had taken Claudia hostage in the hope that Brady would trade. And they were right. Not that he would ever reveal his brother's whereabouts. Instead, he willingly exchanged his life for his ex-wife. He owed her. He loved her.

27

But she was punishing him. He didn't need to be a psychologist to understand that much. Her boyfriend DCI Davidson had died at the hands of these men and their accomplices. Claudia had lived. Simple roll of the die. But she had taken it personally. And here she was living like a ghost, clinging more and more to the shadows in his house – their old marital home – refusing to leave Brady and yet refusing to acknowledge him. It was a living death. The house, a mental asylum. The two of them, the only inmates. She only stayed with him because he understood. He had been there. So she stayed within reach. Not that he could touch her. But she was there. And slowly and surely, she was poisoning both of them. Worse still, he was willing to take it.

Her red unruly hair fell in knotted curls across her shoulders and back. It was longer and significantly wilder than it had ever been. Feral, even. Just like her. She had regressed to a state where she could barely cope. Even eating seemed to pain her.

Brady watched as she breathed in and out. Her shoulders, delicate and fragile, moving ever so slightly. He didn't know how to fix her. All he could do was watch and wait. And hope.

Ironically, as she got weaker, he got stronger. With his body crippled, he had had no choice but to work out. Refusing to allow the bastards to defeat him. Physiotherapy had been the start. Then he had joined the YMCA in Shields. The gym was basic and unpretentious. The members worked out – hard. It was North Shields after all. No one had money to throw around or the lifestyle that went with it. The gym was there for one reason only – an out from their shit lives. A quick fix of endorphins; a natural high rather than buying it from the dealer on the street corner outside. Whether they were there with a prescription note after a stroke or they needed to work out their frustrations and disillusions, no one cared or noticed. And that suited Brady. No testosterone-fuelled guerrillas looking to prove themselves or Barbie-doll lookalikes. Just real people, trying to reclaim some control over their otherwise pointless lives.

Claudia had taken a different approach. She had made the unspoken decision to disappear. Fade into nothing. She now slept through the day – or at least pretended to. At night she danced to the cruel tune of insomnia. He would hear her wandering around from room to room, checking the windows and the doors. Then the white noise of the TV in an attempt to drown out her pain. She would not allow him entry into this netherworld. It was her domain.

He wanted her back so badly. But he didn't know how to reach her. He felt like Orpheus. She was his Eurydice. And he had lost her. He had had one chance to get her back. And he had done everything he could. But *his* Claudia hadn't come back to him. She was lost somewhere. Slowly and silently drowning in survivor's guilt.

He could feel the threat of tears and blinked them back. Not now. Not here. He knew he had to be strong for her. He had a decision to make. He had done nothing but think about it for the past month.

Brady watched as she gave out a low, wounded moan. More animal than human. He resisted the urge to touch her, to reassure her that she wasn't alone. But he knew that was the last thing she wanted. Right now she wanted to be on her own. Without him.

His phone flashed. He read the message. It was time to make the decision.

One question still plagued him – *could he leave her? And if he did, what then?*

Brady realised that he had been guarding her. Throughout all these days, weeks and months, he had been holding her captive. Scared to let her go. His fear of losing her was as crippling as her fear of what she had lost.

It was time for him to get his life back on track. For her . . . for Claudia.

He had left a note for her in the folded-up newspaper. Hoped that she would understand. He looked back down at his BlackBerry. Texted a reply. He had made the decision.

It was time to move forward.

Conrad was waiting for him outside. His engine idling. Nervous. Unsure.

Brady climbed in.

It was hard not to notice that Conrad had upgraded his Saab.

'Sir.'

His voice sounded strange to Brady. Unfamiliar.

'How's tricks?' It felt awkward. He felt awkward. Brady would never ordinarily come out with such an inane comment. But to be fair, it was his first day back on duty. And if he was brutally honest, he didn't know how he would cope. Or if he could cope.

Conrad knew it, which was why he didn't bother answering him. A non-committal shrug was the best he could offer his boss.

They both felt the strain. It would take time to slip back into their old routine.

Conrad's face was tense, jaw locked. Steel-grey eyes set on the road ahead.

'You OK? You look like shit!'

It broke the ice. This was the Brady they both knew.

'Five months of Adamson.'

'That explains it.'

DI Adamson was a Class A Wanker. Not just in Brady's books. Anyone with a grain of common sense knew it. He was grovelling bastard. Especially when it came to DCI Gates. Adamson would do anything to get ahead. Conrad couldn't stomach him either. Conrad had spent his first two years of training at Ponteland headquarters with Adamson, so knew him of old. But something had happened. Conrad had never told Brady about it, but he knew that it was serious enough for

Conrad, once they had graduated, to swear he would have nothing more to do with Adamson.

Brady watched as Conrad pulled out. He deserved better than working under the likes of Adamson. Conrad was dependable and loyal; everything that Brady aspired to be, but failed, miserably. Conrad had been his deputy for a good few years now. Brady found it difficult – impossible – to work with anyone else. He knew, without it being said, that Conrad felt the same way. It worked. It wasn't that long ago that Brady thought he had lost Conrad. He had been shot while on duty. Brady still blamed himself. For a brief, agonising moment, he had believed that Conrad was dead.

Conrad was only in his early thirties and had the potential of making it to chief superintendent. Unlike Brady. At five foot eleven, he was stocky but muscular, clean-shaven, with short blond hair and a handsome enough face when he relaxed – which wasn't often. His wardrobe was impeccable; dark tailored suits, crisp white shirts, cufflinks, Italian silk ties and expensive handmade English leather brogues. He put Brady to shame. Then there was his background. It couldn't have been more different from Brady's. It was as far removed from a run-down, problem council estate as physically possible. Even though he never mentioned his past, Brady knew he had studied at Cambridge. He was part of the police's fast-tracked postgraduate scheme. Soon enough it would be Conrad kicking Brady around. But not yet.

What had brought Conrad up to the north-east of England, let alone Whitley Bay, was beyond Brady. Conrad had never offered the information, and he knew not to ask. There was a lot about Conrad that Brady didn't know. Yet Conrad knew about Brady's personal life. *Who didn't?* His life was a car crash. A hundred-and-twenty-mile car crash at that. It was a write-off. He was terrified that he wouldn't cut it at work. That after what had happened to him, he had lost his nerve. Brady breathed out. It was all too much.

He didn't know what Claudia would do when she realised he wasn't there. Her only companion. Her only witness to her self-destruction. He realised he was an enabler. Who bought the alcohol she knocked back so readily? Who protected her from the outside world? Brady did. Why? Because he knew he couldn't live without her. Not again. Rather this than lose her forever. He knew her parents blamed him. Hated him. If they had their way, Claudia would have been in London with them months ago. But he had succeeded at keeping them at a distance.

But he knew what he had to do. Had known it for some time now. He just didn't want to face the reality of his situation – her situation – just yet. He was hoping that by some chance of the gods that without him there, the old Claudia would come back. Self-reliant, intelligent, witty, scathing and so goddamned beautiful.

The irony for Brady was that he dealt with victims of crime on a daily basis. He would interview them, take statements and then he would go to work. He would track the assailants down. If successful, he would close the investigation. Be assigned another case; a new crime. Not that he ever forgot the victims. But they would be replaced. He would move on. They, however, would never move on. Not really. And that was Brady's problem. He wasn't used to dealing with the victim after the case was closed. Ordinarily he didn't have to see the damage left behind. He didn't want to. For him, it was about resolution. End of story.

And that was why he was at such a loss with Claudia. Her attackers were dead. Northumbria's Armed Response Unit had made sure of that. Case closed. But it wasn't. For her, there was no resolution. Or if there was, she refused to accept it. He didn't know what she wanted. Didn't understand why his actions weren't enough.

Brady took in the spotless interior of Conrad's Saab. The leather seats. The immaculate dashboard. The low, seductive growl of the sports car as it accelerated. Anything to block out the thoughts tormenting him.

'So . . . New promotion?'

'No, sir,' Conrad answered, bemused. Then it hit him. 'The car?'

'What do you think, Sherlock? How the fuck can you afford this on a DS's salary?'

'It's not new. 2006 model, sir.'

'Right! That explains it then. A 2006 Aero X Concept Saab must cost . . . What, exactly?'

Conrad shrugged. 'Enough.'

Brady was aware that the 2006 Aero X had not gone into mass production. He could only assume that Conrad had somehow got his hands on one of the rare prototypes. 'You a bent copper all of a sudden?'

Conrad didn't reply. Instead he focused on driving.

But Brady knew he had got to him. His set jaw said it all.

Conrad never disclosed his private life to anyone. Not even to Brady. No matter how much Brady goaded him, he knew that Conrad would not explain himself.

A minute passed in silence behind a gridlock of traffic. Conrad hadn't even managed to turn the car in the right direction towards Whitley Bay. The roads were heaving both ways. Sunday afternoon drivers with nothing better to do than crawl by the coast.

Brady lived on the periphery of Cullercoats – a small boating village and acclaimed artists' retreat. It was an idyllic refuge with old-fashioned tea rooms, ice-cream parlours and trendy bistros. His house was a five-bedroomed Victorian terrace in a sought-after location, Southcliff; a cliff with a single row of houses that jutted out over Brown's Bay. He both hated and loved it simultaneously. It had been Claudia's choice. Now he was left living in it. He had been planning on selling up before his run-in with the Dabkunas brothers. Now that Claudia had moved back in, Brady had let the idea of selling it slip. He wasn't sure what was going to happen.

Conrad was the first to break the awkward lull. 'What do you think of it, sir?'

Brady gave the sports car another consideration. 'Yeah. Can't go wrong with metallic silver. Good conservative choice.'

'The Royal Hotel?'

Brady remained silent. Non-committal.

A call had come in over an hour ago. The Royal Hotel was where they were heading. The place was familiar to Brady. Too familiar, some might say. As was the owner – Martin Madley. Childhood friend and the man Brady owed his life to. But it wasn't just his life; he was indebted to Madley for saving Claudia too, and Nicoletta, a sex-trafficked woman enslaved by the Dabkunas brothers. She had been in protective custody and somehow the Eastern European gangsters had managed to kidnap her again. It was Martin Madley who had saved the day. Not that he had received any recognition for it. That was his way. Everything he did was under the radar.

For one good reason – Madley was rumoured to be a notorious gangster. The police had been after him for years but he was elusive. It was believed by the likes of North Shields CID's DI Bentley that he was the drugs baron and mafia lord of the North East. Not that he had any evidence. On the contrary, Madley was clean. He owned the Blue Lagoon nightclub and the Royal Hotel adjacent to it, as well as most of the bars in Whitley Bay and a few nightclubs in Newcastle. He was expanding. Buying up properties and converting them. Brady had lost track of what he did and didn't own. Not that Brady was interested. Madley kept himself out of trouble. That was as much information as Brady wanted. That, and he was a loyal friend. Whatever doubts Brady might have had – given the fact he was a copper – he had chosen to ignore them. Brady owed him. It was that simple.

He had known Madley since their childhood together in the war-torn, crime-infested streets of the Ridges. Located on the edge of North Shields, it was a no-man's land. A place that mercilessly sucked you dry and spat you back out into the vermin-ridden back lanes. Any aspirations were stolen by heroin, alcohol and a life of petty crime. Never knowing where the next meal was coming from after the dole cheque had run out. That had been Brady's upbringing. That was, until his old man had ended up doing time. It was Madley who had looked out for Brady and Nick. After all, there was no one else. A string of foster homes across North Tyneside, a mother six feet under and an old man doing time for putting her there. Without Madley, Brady wouldn't be here.

'Sir?' Conrad prompted, breaking Brady's thoughts.

'I won't know until I get there.'

Conrad simply nodded.

Before Brady knew it, Conrad saw his chance and put his foot to the floor as he swung the Saab out into the oncoming traffic. Tyres screeched to a halt, followed by a cacophony of horns beeping in retaliation.

'Sorry about that,' Conrad said. 'I had to take my chance, or we would have been there for hours.'

'I'll live,' Brady answered. But his leg had kicked off. A reaction to his body being slammed against the passenger door. The pain was a constant reminder that his left leg and right hand were now comprised of metal pins, screws, nails, rods and plates.

It was at times like this that Brady missed smoking. The hard hit of nicotine would numb the white pain. Even the puckered flesh where the bullet had gone through was on fire. He had been trying to give up before his unfortunate run-in with the Dabkunas brothers' henchmen. But it was his long stint in hospital that had been the final nail in the coffin for his nicotine addiction. He sorely missed it. Craved the kick that came from the first one of the day. Black coffee and a cigarette – pure hedonism.

Suddenly, the urge to smoke was overwhelming. Brady clenched his hands. He watched as Conrad drove, politely ignoring the gesticulating drivers who were giving him the 'V' sign. Including two elderly blue-rinsed ladies in a Nissan Micra.

Not that long ago Brady would have found it comical. Would have ribbed Conrad about his so-called advanced police driving technique. Now . . . it just seemed sad. Pathetic. That everyone was in a rush to get somewhere. Anywhere. As long as they didn't stand still. Stop for too long, then the reality of life – your life – might catch up with you.

Brady needed a distraction. He turned and looked out at the North Sea. It was a shimmering crystal blue. As was the sky. It was unusually warm for March. It brought with it the allure of summer. Hot and heady days under a blistering sun. At least that was the prognosis for the summer ahead – weather forecasters had predicted a heatwave, reminiscent of the ones that had melted tarmac in the Seventies. The Promenade was crowded. In its heyday, the Victorians had claimed Whitley Bay as a sought-after seaside resort. This followed through into the Fifties and Sixties, even into the Eighties when it was still a family holiday destination. Scots would travel down to Feathers caravan site or the many B&Bs along the seafront during the Dundee fortnight.

Then it changed. First the Spanish City was pulled down. An outdoors funfair with an old-fashioned wooden rollercoaster, it was a key attraction to families holidaying or the day visitor travelling down from Newcastle. Next, the recession had hit. It was a hard, ugly punch. The small town was left a ghost of its former self. Charity shops dominated the town centre, along with pawnshops and, crucially, bars. South Parade attracted a new type of punter – the stag and hen type. Out for a good weekend in a town that could accommodate their every need. No questions asked.

Brady's eyes scanned the Promenade. Couples ambled along, arm in arm, laughing, kissing. Oblivious to whatever abomination had taken place nearby. Kids shrieked as they hurtled round and round in circles. Groups of lads and lasses shouted, vying for attention. Dogs ran barking, excited by the fresh air and the thrill of life.

He breathed it in, knowing it would be short-lived. On the second floor of Martin Madley's hotel, an unidentified white male had been murdered.

From what had been called in, it was a gruesome death. Every murder was brutal – savage. Unfair. But some murders were worse than others.

And this one happened to be one of those.

Brady was no fool. He knew that people did the unthinkable. Committed unspeakable acts. And they would do it again. And again. Until people like Brady stopped them.

Chapter Seven

Blue and white police tape cordoned off the road from the seafront bar known as 42nd Street to the residential block of houses on the corner of Brook Street.

'You sorted this?'

'Yes, sir. I wasn't sure whether you would make it in today. Adamson and DCI Gates are attending a conference at the Met this weekend, so I was left to coordinate.'

It was a fair comment. Up until twenty minutes ago, Brady hadn't been so sure he would make it into work.

Conrad had done a good job. It was clear from the amount of uniforms milling around and unmarked police cars parked up that extra help had been called in from other Area Commands. It wasn't every day that someone was found murdered in a Whitley Bay hotel – at least, not in this manner.

Brady could see from the two large white Mobile Incident vans that Ainsworth and his forensic team were here too.

Conrad slowed down as the car approached two uniformed officers blocking the entrance into the road.

Brady buzzed his window down, ignoring the ghoulish crowds jostling one another, too close to the police tape, hoping for news of what had happened. Soon enough journalists and TV crews would be there, shoving microphones under bystanders' noses in the vague hope of sniffing out a story.

'DS Conrad and DI Brady. SIO in charge of—' He let it

hang. First day back and he was the Senior Investigating Officer in charge of a grisly murder.

The uniform holding the crime scene log checked them off against the list.

The log list would stay active until the last person left, which would usually be Ainsworth, the Crime Scene Manager. How long the body would remain at the crime scene was down to Ainsworth and his team. But given the unnatural warmth to the day, Brady imagined they would be working all out to get it bagged up and put on ice. It would be taken to the morgue at Rake Lane hospital where it would wait to be seen by the Home Office pathologist. Brady imagined the post-mortem would be expedited – despite the fact it was a Sunday.

Brady noticed the officer trying to sneak a look at his right hand. He'd obviously heard it had been obliterated by a crowbar. He didn't know what the officer was expecting to see. Blood? Gore? A gnarled stump where his hand should be?

It was going to be one of those days when everyone would be looking for some sign of what had happened to him. It wasn't just the public that had a ghoulish appetite – police could be the worst buggers of all.

'Finished?'

'Sorry, sir?' the officer asked. Then he realised what Brady had meant. His face flushed scarlet as he quickly averted his gaze.

'Tell me I'm not going to have this all bloody day, Conrad?'

'People find it hard to believe you're back so soon after what happened,' Conrad replied, matter of fact.

'What? I've had over five months on the sick. How long do they expect me to take?' Brady could hear himself starting to sound irascible. He willed himself to swallow it down.

'It's not so much the physical damage. It's more the psychological effects. What they did to you and to—' Conrad couldn't say it. Claudia's unspoken name hung in the air between them. A bomb ready to detonate.

39

'If anyone wants to know, the police shrink said I'm good to go. No Post Traumatic Stress Disorder. Zilch.'

But Brady was lying. His voice had faltered. Cracked.

Brady had had to undergo psychological evaluation. Same deal as eighteen months earlier, when Dr Amelia Jenkins had tried to get inside his head. Back then he had been shot in the thigh – too close to his balls for comfort – on an undercover drugs bust. But that wasn't the real reason. Coming round from surgery, Claudia had been there as expected. But the news she had delivered had been completely unexpected. She was divorcing him. She knew he had cheated. Had walked in on him in a compromising position *in their bed* with a junior colleague, DC Simone Henderson. She had stayed in the hospital long enough to make sure he was compos mentis and then left – for good. No going back or second chances with Claudia. That was what had sent him straight to the bottle for a bleary-eyed, head-pounding six months. During the alcohol-induced haze, Dr Amelia Jenkins, then the police shrink, had stepped into the rescue. But he had clammed up. Hit the bottle instead. Drowned himself in it.

But not now. Now he knew the game. He had wanted to come back. Didn't know who or what he was without the job. Without DI in front of his name, there was no Jack Brady. At least he acknowledged it. So he had walked a tightrope of lies. When asked leading questions, he had answered. And the fifty-something, humourless shrink had seemed satisfied. Brady had ticked all the boxes of normality and conformity – good to go. And so here he was, trying to convince Conrad that he was of sound mind.

'We need to make a move, or the party will be over before we get there.' A nod to drop the personal talk and get back to what really mattered – the job.

Conrad waited until the uniformed officers moved the police tape, giving him access. He edged forward slowly, looking for a parking spot amongst the unmarked police vehicles and patrol cars. Finding a spot, in one move he effortlessly reverse-parked.

Conrad killed the engine and turned to his boss.

'Sir?'

His eyes unnerved Brady. Cold, dark, impenetrable. Unfamiliar. He knew that Conrad wouldn't let it go. He could be like that at times; tenacious and bloody minded – as could Brady. He accepted that Conrad had been around him too long.

'Spit it out before it chokes you.'

'Claudia . . . I . . . I haven't seen or spoken to her in some time now.'

Brady waited.

'I just wanted to check she's all right. From all accounts she's not back at work and they don't seem to know when she'll return.'

Brady could feel his temper flaring. Ready to challenge Conrad. Fight first, think later. That had always been his problem. Somehow, he managed to rein it in. But it choked him.

'Jack?' It was unprecedented for Conrad to use Brady's first name. But he needed to get through to his boss. He'd heard the talk. The rumours that had spread out like an oil slick, contaminating everything in its wake. Conrad just needed to know from the one person who could tell him that Claudia was all right – was going to be all right. After all, he'd stayed in contact with her when she'd left Brady after his marital indiscretion. Or to be blunt – monumental marital fuck-up. But now she had all but disappeared. In his mind she needed professional help. More than Brady could offer.

'She's fine.' Brady sounded like the words choked him. He got out of the car and slammed the door behind him.

Conrad watched his boss head towards the Royal Hotel. He had presence. Conrad couldn't knock that. He was unconventional for a copper. And for a Detective Inspector. Six foot two, slender yet muscled, and dark with a permanent five o'clock shadow. Or designer stubble, as some people would call it. But whatever it was, he could pull it off. Women found him attractive. Dangerously so. His swarthy complexion and dark brown eyes spoke of foreign lands far removed from the harsh Ridges where he had grown up. But his clothes were still the same: a beat-up jacket that had seen better days, skinny black jeans and heavy, black leather boots. A dress code that adhered to the old school of policing. The antithesis of the new face of CID. That hadn't changed. Neither had his attitude. He refused to be compromised. Either by the clothes he wore, or the way he conducted an investigation. Not even DCI Gates could manage to get Brady to do things by the book. His saving grace was the fact that he was good at what he did – at times, too good. And it had cost Brady. Conrad could see that.

For now there was an unspoken air of melancholy about him.

Conrad waited until he disappeared from view. His jaw was clenched against the blatant lie that Brady had delivered. It was then he decided to do what he'd been putting off. He needed to call Claudia's parents. He needed them to know his concerns. Something was wrong. He felt it. But he knew how Brady worked. If he had a problem, he'd keep it to himself. Work through it alone. He was known for his maverick ways. But this was different. This wasn't some case he could crack. It was personal. Too personal. Brady had lost sight of that. Blinded by loyalty, devotion, and above all guilt.

Conrad knew that he ran the risk of damaging their relationship. But it was a risk he was prepared to take.

Chapter Eight

The stench was unbearable, even out in the hotel corridor. Brady could feel himself gagging. He and Conrad were dressed in matching Tyvek white forensic suits, blue latex gloves and shoe covers. They were ready to go.

He waited as two of Ainsworth's SOCOs came out the room. They avoided Brady's eyes. Silent, diligent and respectful. Not because the SIO in charge of the investigation had finally arrived. Their reverent air was because of the carnage exacted upon a life in the room behind them. He could see the sweat running down their faces as their hair, damp and matted, clung to their clammy foreheads.

The heat was intolerable. For some unfathomable reason, the old-fashioned cast-iron radiators were belting out a temperature more suited to conditions in Siberia.

'Has anyone thought to get the heating turned off?' Brady snapped. He could feel his skin crawling as if red ants were running over his body; prickly and irritating as hell.

Conrad didn't have a chance to answer.

'What the bloody hell do you think? Nearly two hours I've been here sweating my bollocks off. You think I'm bloody stupid? The thermostat's bloody broken.'

The response was caustic and familiar. The irritable voice belonged to Ainsworth, the Crime Scene Manager, standing in the doorway of the hotel room looking as if he was about to throttle someone. Probably Brady.

'And you two! Don't take all day,' Ainsworth shouted after the two SOCOs who had just left.

Both officers automatically broke into a fast trot to appease their boss.

'Bloody slackers! The lot of them. University graduates, my arse. You can keep the lot of them. Bloody nose starts running and they need me to wipe it! What happened to the good old days of policing, eh? When it was normal to go for a drink at the end of your shift. Stuff your namby-pamby therapy. Wouldn't surprise me if some members of my team put in for counselling after mopping up that poor sod in there!' Ainsworth stopped as he gestured at the crime scene behind him. 'Tell me, when did getting bladdered with your colleagues not count as a form of counselling? You could get it off your chest over a couple of pints and a bloody good laugh. Not sniffling into a box of Kleenex tissues saying how bad your job is. Can't cope, shouldn't sign up for it. Useless lot of over-educated prissy buggers.'

Brady did his best not to crack a smile at the short, portly but still formidable figure. Ainsworth was on a roll. But Brady knew he was right. Coppers and SOCOs were both offered counselling if a crime scene was particularly gruesome. To Brady's knowledge, most got it out their system by adopting a hard, macabre sense of humour and a healthy thirst. But there was a new breed coming through the force. One that didn't drink. Didn't socialise after the end of a shift. Instead, they would go home and check their targets and statistics, ready for the next day's onslaught.

Brady couldn't help but notice that Ainsworth looked like a man on the verge of an aneurysm. He was clearly having a bad day. If Brady made light of his diatribe Ainsworth was guaranteed to reach new heights of rage. He was a cantankerous, sour-faced old sod at the best of times, but Brady could see that the unbearable working conditions weren't helping his mood. Beads of sweat edged down from his receding head of damp, curly, ditchwater-grey hair. He swiped irritably at his forehead with the back of his latex-gloved hand as if besieged by flies, and scowled at Brady as if it was all his fault. Being civil looked like the last thing on his mind.

Ainsworth claimed his Gaelic roots were the cause of his acerbic tongue. But Brady knew it had nothing to do with his roots, he was just a bad-tempered old get who had succeeded in getting away with it.

'Well, what you waiting for, Jack? A bloody brass band?' The voice may have been raspy but the words were as sharp as a razor. 'Mind, warn your lad there that he might need counselling after he sees this little party piece!'

Brady gave him a good-humoured smile. 'And it's good to be back. Thanks for asking.' He made a point of ignoring the jibe directed at Conrad, but Ainsworth had clearly just started. His scowl was now fixed on Conrad.

'You up to this, son?' Ainsworth demanded, his voice laden with scorn.

Conrad didn't look so sure. His face had a greyish pallor about it, the blood completely drained. Brady didn't know whether it was the smell that had caused him to look as if he was about to introduce his lunch to everyone or Ainsworth's presence. For some unfathomable reason Ainsworth had taken an instant dislike to Conrad the moment he had set eyes on him. A few years on, and he still treated him with the same candid disdain.

However, Brady put Conrad's shaky countenance down to the stomach-curdling odour that hung in the air. Even Ainsworth's snarling was no match. The scent of a dead body was something that could make even the hardest copper retch. Death had an indomitable presence; something you never forgot. Brady knew as soon as he walked into the crime scene that the odour would seep its way into him. His eyes would start watering as it burned its way down into his lungs. The smell would stay with him long after he had left the scene. Every time he breathed, it would hit him. It would place itself, silent and unseen, on and around him; claiming his hair, skin and clothes.

45

He could tell even from outside the room that the victim had shit himself. He also smelt the acrid tell-tale stench of urine. Most bodily fluids tended to leak out after death. If it was a particularly nasty case, then the victim would lose control before they died. There was no dignity in death. And for some, no dignity in the type of death they suffered.

Brady thought of the victim. Deceased; his body bare for all to pick over. Scavengers, hoping to find something, anything that would tie the murderer to the crime scene. It was the inhumanity that got to him. The victim had been chosen. Targeted. Then killed. And now it was the turn of Ainsworth and his team to dehumanise the body. Treat it as evidence. Not get emotional and wonder who *he* was and how *he* had arrived at this dead end. No. That was Brady's job. To speculate. To ask: *Who are you? What made you so interesting that someone wanted to kill you?*

It came down to victimology. Know the victim, then you know your killer. In the majority of murder cases they were connected. It was up to Brady and his team to find that link. That one small lead which would unravel the reason why a young man had ended up dead in a seaside hotel. Then there was the choice of hotel. Why the Royal? From the moment Brady had heard where the murder victim had been found, he had been trying to keep thoughts of Madley at bay. But it was proving difficult. Was there a connection?

He didn't know. Not yet. And he hoped there wasn't. After all, Brady owed Madley his life. And Claudia's. He was indebted to him. He knew that much.

'If I didn't know you, Jack Brady, I would have said you were stalling,' Ainsworth said, as his small, black beady eyes scrutinised him.

'Come on, then. Show me what you've got,' Brady replied, his tone resolute. He just wanted to get it over with. To get rid of the sour taste in his mouth and the sickly, sweet odour of putrefying meat.

'If you think he smells bad out here, just wait until you meet him. I reckon he's been cooking in there all night.'

Brady knew that if Conrad hadn't told him the seriousness of the situation, then he wouldn't be here. He wasn't officially due back until tomorrow. But Conrad had called him. Better that than getting a DI from another Area Command. If Brady hadn't turned up, Conrad would have had to request DI Bentley's expertise. And, given Bentley's conviction that Martin Madley was the drugs baron of the North East, Brady had no choice but to show up. The murder had taken place in Madley's hotel. Enough ammunition for Bentley to come in with all guns blazing. He would have spun the murder for his own ends. Claiming that Madley's *questionable* business dealings had to be linked to the crime. Whether the victim was known or unknown to Madley, Bentley would see to it that there was a connection – no matter how tenuous.

But there was more to Brady's return than not wanting Bentley to head the investigation. The details of the murder had disturbed him. Made him start to ask questions. But he had to see for himself first-hand before he jumped to any conclusions. He didn't want to call DCI Gates unless he had to. His childhood Catholicism had kicked in and he found himself praying that he wouldn't have to contact Gates. That the similarities of this murder were just a coincidence. Nothing more.

Before he followed Ainsworth, he turned to Conrad. He knew Ainsworth was right – he was stalling. 'Reckon you'll be able to keep your lunch down?'

Conrad nodded. 'It's just the smell getting to me.'

Brady held his breath, walked in, then stopped – dead. He had no idea if Conrad was behind him or was bent over, throwing up. Because that was what he wanted to do – turn around and vomit.

In that moment he knew that he'd be contacting Gates. Telling him they had a situation. That he might want to leave the conference in London and return to Whitley Bay.

Because Brady was certain of one fact: as soon as the press got hold of the details of the murder there would be mass hysteria. Just as there had been in the summer of '77.

'Aye, not a pretty sight, is he?' Ainsworth said. 'And I'm talking about your lad there. If you're going to spew don't do it anywhere near my bloody crime scene!'

It was a good distraction and Brady needed it. He needed a moment to get a handle on the situation. Conrad hadn't realised just how serious this was, or the ramifications of it. He was too young. That and he hadn't grown up in the North East. The summer of '77 had lingered on in most peoples' minds for years after. Fearful, ever vigilant. Because back then there had been no real resolution. Nobody had been arrested. Instead, *he* became the bogeyman. The one that would snatch you and . . . Brady stopped himself.

He had grown up in the Eighties with the horror stories. The scaremongering. The kids that would dare you to say *his* name out loud. The dare came with a caveat of course. It had to be carried out in the dark, on your own, in the old derelict house where it was rumoured the first victim had been mutilated. Inevitably, the poor kid would be scared shitless. Brady knew. Because he had done it.

Brady looked at Conrad. If he felt sick, then Conrad definitely looked sick. In fact he looked as if he was going to throw up any second now.

'Listen, why don't you check on what's happening downstairs,' Brady suggested. It was hard not to hear the commotion below them. He imagined there were a few irate guests wanting to get back to their rooms. The second floor had been cordoned off, for obvious reasons.

Brady watched Conrad take one last glance at the victim. Curiosity, perhaps, or just downright shock. Then he turned and legged it down the corridor to the nearest toilet.

'Useless bloody bugger. Wants to man up. And you reckon

he'll make Detective Chief Superintendent one day? My hairy arse he will!'

Brady didn't respond. He could feel his mouth watering; a tell-tale prelude to being sick. He swallowed. He didn't want to follow suit. But he could feel the bile, slick and threatening at the back of his throat. In his head he counted to ten. Took a moment to compose himself. Remind himself he could deal with this – had seen worse. *Or had he?*

The heat in the room wasn't helping. He looked at the window. Closed. He had to give Ainsworth and his team their due. Brady only had to have a cursory look at the scene. Get a feel for what had happened. But this was their office. They were the ones responsible for collecting any trace evidence that might have been left behind. Forensic science was developing at a phenomenal rate. The techniques used now meant that getting away with murder would soon be impossible. If Brady found a suspect, then the SOCOs' findings would be crucial. It was Brady's job to get them to court – and it was Ainsworth's job to nail them with the forensic evidence in court.

The SOCOs would be searching for physical and biological evidence. The physical would come from fingerprints, foot-prints and fibres left behind by the killer. The biological evidence included bloodstains and DNA. Ainsworth's acumen and eye for the slightest detail could make all the difference. Blood or fibres might be found; an unintentional calling card left by the killer. Or blood, hair, other biological samples picked up from the body might be on the killer. After all, he had spent time with his victim.

Everything depended on Ainsworth and his team gathering all the evidence so that Brady could use it. But Brady had to catch the guy first.

Ainsworth frowned. 'You all right?'

Brady nodded. 'Just the heat getting to me.'

'You sure that's all it is? Because this looks uncannily like—' Ainsworth stopped himself. He could not articulate it. He remembered the Seventies well. Unlike Brady, he was old enough to have actually lived through the events of that summer.

Brady looked at Ainsworth. They both knew it. But neither one wanted to say the name – not yet. Brady tried to clear his head. He needed to be objective. But it was difficult. Especially with the suffocating heat and overwhelming stench.

The two SOCOs who had left returned with a forensic case. They both looked at Brady, standing there like some gobsmacked new copper. First day on the job and not a clue about how to go about it. It was enough to shake him. Stop him procrastinating.

Making sure he stepped on the forensic platforms, there to protect any evidence left on the carpet, he crossed over to the king-size bed. Lights had been set up over the victim, illuminating the body to a ghoulish level.

He could feel Ainsworth watching him. His eyes boring into the back of his neck, making his skin prickle under the intense scrutiny. But he knew that Ainsworth was waiting. Waiting for him to finish his sentence. To say: *Yes. It's him. He's back.*

Focus. Look for details. Anything . . . rather than this mind-numbing paralysis.

A sudden thought hit him. It hit hard. Maybe he wasn't up to the job anymore? Had what happened to him broken him? Brady shook it off. It was first day nerves. That was all. And he had been thrown in at the deep end. He went to take a deep breath to steady himself. Clear his head. But thought better of it. He blocked out the SOCOs, even Ainsworth, as he set to work.

He looked at the victim.

Looked hard and long. Fought the urge to retch. Pushed it down and kept it there.

Young white male. Early twenties. Six foot to six foot two. Physically fit.

Brady hazarded a guess that he had been dead for over twelve hours. Once dead, the body would immediately start turning cold – known as algor mortis or the death chill. He knew that with each hour the body temperature dropped by 1.5 degrees until it reached room temperature. Not that he was an expert. But he had spent too long listening to Wolfe, the Home Office pathologist, and some of his jargon had actually sunk in. Blood had already pooled in the victim's back and the back of the legs. This meant that liver mortis had set in. The parts of the body in direct contact with the bed had a distinctive bluish-purple discoloration caused by hypostasis, the accumulation of blood due to gravity. This in itself suggested that the victim had died at the scene and in this position. Rigor mortis, or stiffening of the body, sets in about two to six hours after death. After twenty-four hours the stiffness dissipates. To be certain, Brady touched the victim's leg.

Cold. Stiff. Very dead.

The victim was still in a state of rigor mortis, which confirmed in his mind he'd been murdered somewhere between Saturday evening and the early hours of Sunday morning. But he would need a pathologist to determine a time of death. Not that they could give the precise time, but it would be good enough.

He assumed the pathologist had already attended the scene and called time of death. As Ainsworth had pointed out in his usual acerbic way, Brady had shown up late.

He focused back on the victim, ignoring the snatches of conversation floating around him as the SOCOs continued with their jobs. To them, death was an everyday occurrence. They simply broke it down; dissected it into bodily secretions: prints, hairs, skin tissue and clothing fabric. They would then add their own gallows humour into the mix. It made the impact of death, the gruesome, ugly thing it was, easier to look at. Brady was certain he heard one of the SOCOs joke about the victim. About his gruesome injuries. Ghoulish speculations were now being bandied around; each one worse than the previous sick sugges-tion. Small ripples of laughter hit him like poisonous darts. He wanted to turn and tell them all to shut up. But he knew he was over-reacting. He blocked out the casual banter tossed so easily between them. Once over the gruesome shock of the murder, it was just another day to them. Another crime scene. Another murdered body. But the identity of this body would hit someone. Hard. Their life or lives would never be the same again. Because the killer hadn't just murdered the man on the bed – they had tortured him. Rope had been used. Hands bound behind his back. Ankles tied together.

Brady looked for any evidence that showed the victim had fought his assailant. That he had been overpowered and subsequently tied up. It would have taken a lot to overpower him. But Brady could see nothing that told him that he had been tied up against his will.

Had he willingly allowed himself to be restrained?

Brady put the thought to the back of his mind. It didn't make any sense at this point.

He noted the ligature damage around the victim's severely mottled and swollen throat. It looked to him as if the marks were consistent with rope burns. He wasn't sure. But he had been asphyxiated. Brady would have to wait for the autopsy report to know whether that was the cause of death. He already knew from the other injury that the assailant had wanted him to suffer. Had wanted him to understand exactly what was happening to him. Had wanted to torture him. Both physically and psychologically.

Just like the others . . . No. He wouldn't entertain it. *Not yet.*

Brady could see that strangling the victim to death wouldn't have been enough. It hadn't been the end goal. It wasn't what this murder was about.

He let his eyes move up from the bloated, bruised throat to the head – black, faceless. Duct tape had been wound around the head. This was how he had died. Smothered to death.

Don't jump to conclusions.

As if on cue, Ainsworth spoke. 'Are you thinking what I'm thinking?'

Brady nodded. He couldn't stop himself. It was the first thing he'd thought when he saw the victim.

His eyes drifted down to the carnage on the victim's body. The carnage below the midriff. To the mutilated groin. Blood covered the mattress. The carpet. The body. Even the wall behind.

Brady assumed that the victim's penis had been fully erect when it had been cut off. The blood loss accounted for that. Erect, it guaranteed blood flow. Even after the engorged member had been hacked off. However, there was no 'projected blood' as Ainsworth would call it, here: the result of an artery being cut and the heart continuing to pump roughly eight litres a minute. An adult had between four to five litres of blood. The maths was simple; you bled out in less than forty seconds. This wasn't the case here. The blood supplied to the groin came from small arteries that fed down from the abdomen. Consequently the blood loss was significant but he could have survived the mutilation. Others had.

Shit!

Looking at the exposed tissue and flesh where the penis should have been made Brady's stomach contract. His testicles shrivelled up even more – if that were possible – at the gruesome unnaturalness of it. The retching sensation was threatening to return. He understood that this was what had driven Conrad from the crime scene to bury his head in a toilet bowl.

Was it a bloke thing? He didn't know. But he was certain that every man in the room felt the same abject horror. His attention returned to the black shape that was the head. 'Has the pathologist been?'

'An hour back. Called out of a meeting for this,' Ainsworth answered. 'Wasn't best pleased.'

Brady knew exactly who Ainsworth was talking about – Wolfe. And the meeting would have been his lunchtime pint, or two, followed by a whisky chaser in the Stuffed Dog.

'And you've got all the photographs of the body in situ?'

'And film.'

'Wolfe got a good look at him?'

'I gather so,' Ainsworth answered.

Brady nodded.

Ainsworth's eyes were sharp as an eagle's. He knew where Brady was going with his questions.

'Can you help me turn him over?'

'You really think—'

Brady cut him off. 'I don't know.'

If this really is him . . . Then . . .

Brady couldn't think straight. First, he had to check the body – the hands.

Together, they rolled the heavy, stiff body over. Brady looked at the hands tied behind his back. He could see that the victim had struggled. Had tried to undo the knots. His wrists were bruised and the flesh had been cut open from rope burns.

No surprise. The panic, let alone pain . . . Brady stopped himself.

He tried to block out thoughts of his own pain. His panic when he had been tied to a chair and tortured. His rage when they had thrown her at his feet. Dragged and kicked like a dog. Beaten, and so terribly damaged. He didn't recognise her. Not at first. Not his Claudia. And he knew that they were going to kill her. Then they would kill him.

'Is it there?' Ainsworth asked, his rough voice sounding excited.

Brady nodded. He could feel the sweat building up on his forehead.

He could see it – just. Pressed between the victim's palms. Hands trembling, Brady somehow managed to extricate it from the victim's grasp.

Suddenly everything in the room faded. Brady couldn't hear Ainsworth repeating the same question. Or the comments from the SOCOs, curious about what they were looking for – and why.

It felt as if his heart had stopped. But the rapid pounding in his ears told him it had gone into overdrive. Adrenalised by shock.

Fucking shit . . . shit . . .

Brady stared at it. It was a playing card. But it was no ordinary card. It was from a Waddington's deck of cards. Vintage – 1960s. The Joker card.

This was HIS signature. His trademark. His personal touch.

Then there was the torture he carried out on his victims. It had never deviated from one victim to another. Always the same. *Even now.*

The Modus Operandi – the methodology of the crime – was different. But the signature was the same. The Joker card. The disfigurement – details too gruesome to have ever been released to the press. No one knew. No one – apart from the police and the killer.

'Bloody hell, Jack! I . . . I kept thinking it. But . . . I mean, how? How could it be possible?'

Brady didn't comment. He didn't know how. It just was.

'You're sure?'

Brady nodded. He tried to swallow, but failed. His mouth was too dry.

He'd read up about this case. Seven victims in a matter of months. The killing frenzy had taken place during one of the hottest summers ever recorded. The victims – all male – had been mutilated and then left to bloat in the suffocating heat. The crime scene photographs had nearly made him sick.

The tabloids had called the killer *The Joker.* That was the only detail about the case that had ever been released to the public. The genital mutilation – never. Too horrifying for the public. It had been the 1970s after all. The appetite for visceral details had not existed. Unlike now.

Brady looked at Ainsworth. He had no choice. *Fuck protocol.*

'We need to remove the tape.'

Ainsworth's eyes darted to the body.

Brady could see that Ainsworth was equally familiar with the Seventies murders. He, like Brady, knew the reason the killer had bound the victim's head in this manner. The final trademark of the Seventies killer – if it was him – would be under the duct tape.

Brady watched as Ainsworth cut through the thick black tape. As did the four forensic officers, fascinated by the proceedings. One, already ahead of the game, was photographing each step. Another, filming.

'You sure?' Ainsworth asked, before he pulled the tape back.

'Yes,' Brady answered, despite himself. He didn't want to look, but knew he had to. He had to see whether this was the same killer. He'd figure out *how* it was possible later.

Paralysed, he watched as Ainsworth ripped off the layer of black shiny tape, exposing the victim's swollen, bloated face.

'Fuck! What's that in his mouth?' asked one of the SOCOs.

Brady didn't answer. Neither did Ainsworth.

'Oh, Christ! Tell me he didn't choke to death on his own . . .' The last word was left unsaid. The reality too sickening.

Brady's stomach felt as if it had hit the ground.

How? How, after thirty-seven years?

Chapter Nine

'Sir . . .' Brady began. He still wasn't quite sure what he was going to tell his boss. He didn't want to get this one wrong. Not on his first day back. Five months was a long time to be away. A lot of things could happen in that time. Brady was aware that he was not irreplaceable. His sick leave stint had shown him as much. The job had continued – *his job*. DI Adamson had stepped in and seen to that. He had proven to Gates and the team – *his team* – that he could do his own job as well as bearing the brunt of Brady's. Brady wasn't sure where exactly that left him.

'What's so important that it can't wait until I get back on Friday?' Gates snapped.

Brady found himself momentarily lost for words. If he had been expecting his boss to ask how his first day back at work was going after being nearly killed five months ago, he would have been bitterly disappointed. But Brady knew Gates well. Well enough to not expect his boss to give two fucks about his physical or mental state. He was back at work. That was enough. If he couldn't cope, then he shouldn't have turned up. Gates wasn't known for niceties where Brady was concerned.

'Well . . .' Brady began, unsure of how to begin.

'For Christ's sake, Jack. Spit it out! I've been dragged out of a seminar for this call, so it better be important.'

Brady knew he had no choice. He just had to say it. 'Sir, a young white male was found murdered in the Royal Hotel early this afternoon,' he began.

57

'And?' Gates asked. 'Tell me that's not the reason you've rung me?'

This was familiar territory for Brady. Gates had never hidden the fact that he didn't like him. Brady's method of policing, of allowing his gut feeling to override protocol and yet somehow being proven right, often met with Gates' disapproval. However, Brady always managed to hit those much-needed targets and that was what counted.

'No, sir, but . . .' Brady hesitated.

He could hear Gates sighing on the other end of the phone. He then heard him muttering to someone. The irritation in his tone was evident. Brady assumed it was DI Adamson standing with him.

Fuck it! What did he have to lose? His role as DI was already in question. DI Adamson had seen to that.

'Do you remember the Joker killings in the Seventies?'

He suddenly had Gates' attention. 'What?'

'The Joker killings. Seven young men, all murdered within a period of two months during the summer of 1977?'

'I'm acutely aware of the case, Jack.'

Brady knew that he would have been. After all, Gates had just entered the force at the time. But it was clear from Gates' voice that he was not impressed with Brady bringing up the past. It was evident that he was uncomfortable with even the mention of The Joker. The killer had never been apprehended. In fact, the police hadn't even come close to catching him. They had suspects, of course, but none of them were remotely credible. Most of them had been dragged in for questioning to make it look as if the police had a handle on the situation – which they hadn't.

For some inexplicable reason, The Joker had stopped killing after his seventh victim; much to the relief of the police and the public. Or at least, he had stopped murdering in the same manner. Brady was certain that someone with an appetite for sadism and murder like The Joker didn't just wake up one morning and decide that they had had enough. The drive to kill would have become overwhelming. The question that had been troubling Brady was why he had stopped.

He steeled himself. 'This murder is identical to the other seven from 1977.'

Gates didn't say anything. But his silence said enough. Brady kept quiet.

'You're certain?' Gates finally asked.

Brady could hear the scepticism in his voice. Not that he could blame him. Even he was struggling to accept it – and he had seen it with his own eyes. 'Yes, sir. Hands and feet were bound with rope.'

'Gagged?'

'With his own penis,' Brady replied.

Gates did not reply. Brady did not need to see his face to know that it would be hard and inscrutable as he weighed up the magnitude of what he was being told. No one, aside from the investigating team and the police pathologist, knew the details of the case. The mutilation was deemed too awful to be released to the public. Not even the victims' families were aware of the precise nature of their loved ones' death. They had been fed as little information as possible to avoid the details being leaked to the press. And yet here they were, thirty-seven years later, with a victim murdered in exactly the same manner.

And that was what was troubling Brady. He couldn't get his head around the improbability of The Joker suddenly returning. Or of it being a copycat killing.

He sighed heavily before continuing. 'His severed penis had been stuffed into his mouth and his head had been bound with black duct tape. Identical to the Seventies victims.'

'What about—' Gates began.

Brady beat him to it. He knew exactly what he was going to ask. The exact same question had plagued him when he first saw the victim.

'Joker card pressed between the victim's palms. The card is from a 1960s Waddington deck, sir.'

'The same as before?'

'Identical.'

Brady could hear Gates breathing out at the enormity of the situation as he weighed up what to do.

'What's your feeling on this? Copycat? Or . . .' Gates left the question unfinished. Like Brady, unable to accept the prospect that the serial killer had resurfaced after all this time.

'I don't know,' Brady answered honestly. 'If it is The Joker, then the question is why now, after all this time? And if it isn't, then how would someone have found out the details of the original case?'

Brady had wondered if it could be someone within the police. He had to; it was a possibility. He knew that right now his boss would be plagued with the same thoughts.

'I assume that you're already collating information on the original suspects?'

'Yes, sir. The team's busy tracking them down.'

'Good,' Gates answered. 'Who found the victim?'

'The hotel cleaner.'

'You've told her that she's not to divulge any details to anyone?'

'Yes, sir.'

'Same with the rest of the hotel staff who were on duty?'

'Yes.'

'Good. I want no details being leaked to the press. Understand? Until we can establish exactly what's going on, I want as little released as possible,' Gates instructed him. 'I'll finish off here and see you tomorrow. In the meantime, I want to be kept informed of every detail on this case.'

'Will do, sir,' Brady answered.

With that, Gates hung up.

Brady stood for a moment as he tried to get his head together. He understood that Gates had to return ASAP, given the magnitude of the situation. However, it still left him feeling as if he could not be trusted to take charge of what would soon become a high-profile murder investigation. One that, if it followed the Seventies pattern, had the potential to become a killing spree.

Chapter Ten

Sunday: 3:40 p.m.

'Tea. Drink it! I've put three sugars in.'

'Yes, sir,' Conrad answered. His tongue felt more akin to an over-used litter tray. Small grits of vomit were embedded in his tongue.

He still looked ill, the colour not fully returned to his face. Instead, he had an insipid grey pallor reminiscent of the bleak, drizzle-filled skies that so often clung over the North East.

'Come on. Drink!' ordered Brady. 'I need you on your feet.'

Conrad looked up at him. His head bobbed up and down in a feeble acknowledgement. The last thing he shared at this moment was his boss's excitement and enthusiasm. This was the old Jack Brady in front of him. He was on to something. The gleam in his eye said it all. Brady wanted to get moving. And fast. The clock was counting down. And as it did, each minute worked against them. But right now, Conrad couldn't move. His legs wouldn't take his weight and his stomach was curdling at the prospect of drinking anything.

'Bloody drink it!'

Conrad weakly acquiesced, swallowing down the sweet, milky liquid.

After his call to Gates ended Brady had gone looking for Conrad, eventually finding him in the entrance lobby, slouched on a chair with his head between his knees. His explanation? Lunch: the prawn salad sandwich had obviously been dodgy. So much so, it had made its way back up.

'You look like shit, Conrad,' Brady said with some concern. 'How about I get someone to drive you home?'

Conrad visibly winced. 'No, sir, I'll be fine. Just need a minute or two to clear my head.'

'Have it your way. But this isn't the place to be having a hot flush.'

Conrad's face was clammy, the skin a chalky off-white colour. Not good. Brady shook his head at him. 'I'm serious. You look like you don't know whether you're going to shit yourself or hurl.'

The last thing Brady wanted was Conrad sitting here looking as if he had seen a corpse. The place was buzzing with police: uniform, non-uniform and forensic science officers. Then there were the hotel residents and staff who were milling around the conference room, waiting in turn for the police to talk to them.

Regardless of objections, Brady had not allowed anyone to leave the hotel. Names, addresses had to be given. IDs had to be verified. And then statements taken – no matter how long and laborious the process. The problem the police were up against was that most of the hotel's residents comprised a stag party – two coachloads of muscle-pumped, lager-fuelled fun. Most were lucky if they even knew their names.

So far, no one had seen or heard anything unusual. That included staff as well as residents. Everyone was tight-lipped. Or at least that was the way it felt. The one person Brady did want to talk to was the receptionist on duty the night before. She had finished her shift at 8:00 a.m. this morning and no one had seen or talked to her since. Brady had tried calling her – no answer. He had sent DC Kodovesky and DS Harvey to her address to bring her in. He could have left it to them to take a statement. But there was too much at stake. As far as Brady was concerned, she might have been the only person to have seen the killer. Whoever checked into room 212 had had to do so through the receptionist. So it was crucial they talked to her.

63

At this stage, the crime scene was all Brady had to go on. But Ainsworth had given him hope. And he needed it. So far, it had appeared that the murderer had been very careful about leaving any evidence at the crime scene. There were no fingerprints or fibres. Not even hair samples. It was clean. But Ainsworth was dogged and he didn't give up so easily. He had managed to find a partial footprint that had not been completely brushed over. The killer had proven not to be as vigilant as Ainsworth. The print was from a size ten male shoe. They were now looking for a male perpetrator. No surprise there.

The impression marks from the partial shoe print could be crucial physical evidence. A print from a relatively new shoe would only tell them the make, style and size of the item. If the shoe had been worn for a period of time, then it would have what Ainsworth called 'individualising evidence'. In layman's terms, it meant that it would be specific to the person who wore the shoe – equal in uniqueness to a fingerprint. Everyone had their own individual gait and over time, shoe prints became individualising evidence as the wearer encountered different types of damage to the sole.

Brady had already discounted the victim's footwear – unsurprisingly. But what did surprise Brady was the price tag. They were Italian Forzieri black washed leather boots. In other words, designer, which meant expensive. The boots had been found in the hotel room's basic wardrobe. His designer suit and shirt, both Pal Zileri, were hanging above. His up-to-date iPhone had been left on the bedside cabinet, alongside a Gucci dive watch. It was a limited edition and cost more than Brady could afford. Then there was the victim's wallet, found in his suit jacket. It contained over three hundred pounds in notes, an array of fancy gold credit cards and, crucially, a driver's licence. Consequently, robbery had been ruled out.

What worried Brady was that identification was all too easy – the driver's licence, credit cards. Why leave them? Add the mutilated body into the mix and they had a killer who either thought they were incredibly clever, or just didn't care. Brady didn't believe it was the latter. The attention to detail with the body told him as much. If it had been a crime of passion, or as the tabloids would spin, a sex game gone horrifically wrong, then why mutilate the body? It wasn't as if the killer had panicked. The opposite was true. He had taken time with his victim. Binding him, strangling him and mutilating him. And then . . . Brady shuddered, despite the heat. A horrific way to die – tied up, bleeding, gagged. Choking, spluttering, gasping . . . desperate as the killer wraps the duct tape round again and again. Then, the last detail – the Joker card.

The prancing Jester in bold black outline, coloured blue and red against a white backdrop, filled Brady's mind. The red lips curled at the corners of the mouth – laughing, sneering. It was this jeering face that bothered him. Because he knew it was the killer's signature. His unique calling card.

The driver's licence belonged to the victim. Simple. The photo ID matched the victim's bloated face. They had a name. An age. An address.

Why you? Why did he choose you?

Something told Brady that this victim was different from the others. From the first seven killed in the Seventies. A gut feeling, a hunch? He couldn't say. He just knew it. And that worried him. The others were targeted for a specific reason. All a type.

Why change your MO? Unless it's not really you . . .

'Come on, Conrad! Seriously, on your feet. Either that, or give me the car keys. I'll drive myself to the station and send a patrol car down to collect you when you're good and ready.'

Brady knew that Conrad wouldn't let him drive his new sports car – it had the desired effect, and Conrad staggered to his feet. His face paled as the blood rushed from his head to his stomach.

For a moment Brady was worried he was going to keel over.

'Do you want to lean on me?'

'I'm fine, sir,' Conrad said through gritted teeth.

'Right. Give me five minutes. I'll see you at the car,' Brady instructed.

65

Chapter Eleven

Irritated, she watched as the policeman made his way to reception.

'Yes?'

He flashed his ID card. 'Detective Inspector Brady.'

'And?' she asked, without even giving the ID card a cursory glance.

'I need to see the details logged against room 212.'

She sighed, then gave him a pained look as if she had better things to do on a Sunday afternoon than help the police with a murder inquiry. It didn't matter that it had taken place in the hotel where she worked. The fact was, she hadn't been working when it had happened. So, it wasn't her problem. And she shouldn't even be in today. She was covering someone else's shift as a favour.

Her long, thick, dyed black hair swished behind her as she turned to the computer. Red painted acrylic nails tapped irritably on the keyboard as she scrolled down.

'Nah. Hasn't changed since the last time I checked. John Smith. That's it.'

'No address. Credit card details?'

She looked at him as if he were stupid. Her thin lips pursed, about to tell him that she'd had enough of this crap. Police officers asking the same question, again and again. As if she was the daft one. They got the same answer every time: John Smith, no address, no credit card, no personal information.

Joanne hadn't come into work this morning bargaining on the hotel being overrun with police. Where the fuck was Chantelle when you needed her? This was her fucking mess. Always the same. She'd come in and pick up the pieces from that sloppy cow's shift. God knows how she held on to a job here. But she knew how. They all did. Chantelle was doing the boss. That's how her scrawny arse hadn't been sacked yet. Joanne knew that it wouldn't last. They never did.

She looked at him as he cleared his throat.

'Is it practice not to take down the guest's address?'

She sighed. Again. Same questions over and over. 'No.'

Joanne waited for him to let her get on with her job. A dead body in a hotel wasn't great for business, but it could be dealt with without causing too much damage. People died all the time. The odds are that an occasional guest's heart might give out. But a murder was a different story entirely. The hotel had been put in lockdown mode. Hotel guests had decided to check out, to cut their stay short. Who could blame them? But she was the one left trying to keep it all together. Her boss had left for a week's holiday. Flown somewhere hot, Joanne imagined. Lucky bastard. Her mind automatically thought of Chantelle. Had she gone with him? She wouldn't put it past that two-faced cow. But she wasn't booked in for a week's holiday. Then again, this was Chantelle. Twenty-two years old, and with the attitude that life owed her. She'd no doubt ring in before her shift tomorrow, pretending to be ill again. Nothing about that girl was kosher. Fake tan, fake tits and a botoxed face like a slapped trout to match. And Joanne knew all too well that on her wages you couldn't afford such niceties.

She looked at the copper still stood in front of her. Not that he looked much like a copper with that scruffy jacket, black T-shirt and long dark hair. He didn't look like the detectives she watched on TV. They were clean-shaven and wore suits.

He refused to move. Despite her scrutiny.

'Look . . . I wasn't here last night, was I? I just happen to be the fool that's left picking up the pieces. You want to know why all we have is "John Smith" on record, then you need to talk to Chantelle.'

'I wish I could.'

'Yeah? Well, you and me both,' she said. She looked at Brady as if seeing him for the first time. He was a really good-looking bloke. Tall, dark, edgy – she liked that. But there was something about his eyes. Deep dark brown eyes filled with . . . But before she had a chance of putting her finger on it, the moment was gone. His eyes had assumed a professional hardness. An impenetrability.

She looked around the reception area to make sure no other members of staff were within earshot, leaned over the desk towards him. 'Look . . . Between you and me, this happens.'

'Meaning?' he asked.

'Cash, no questions asked. You pay a premium for it. But if you can afford anonymity, then you get it. I can only assume that this "John Smith" was a no-questions-asked transaction. But verify it first with Chantelle. For all I know she just made a mistake.'

Joanne resisted the urge to add: *Another mistake.*

'Where are your surveillance cameras?'

She looked at the copper. She couldn't blame him for asking. It was an obvious question.

'We don't have any cameras. Like I said, some guests want that guarantee. No surveillance cameras and no traceable names or cards. Cash pays for a lot.'

Brady was no fool. Did he really believe that there wouldn't be a hidden camera recording everything that happened in front of the reception desk – and behind, for that matter? Simple answer – no. Madley trusted no one. Staff, guests or business associates. All the same to him. 'You're definitely sure there's no cameras?'

She nodded. 'We've asked the boss to install them for our protection. But he keeps promising and nothing happens. I reckon if he had to spend a night checking that lot in,' she gestured towards the two coaches parked in the front car park, 'he'd think again.'

Brady knew all too well about the stag parties that descended on Whitley Bay for the weekend. They were a major headache for uniform and ate up a significant part of the police budget.

He decided he needed to talk to Carl, the one-eyed Mancunian bartender responsible for the club next door. If Madley wasn't around, Carl would be the one left in charge. And if Madley had surveillance tape, which Brady believed he would do, he needed it.

'Apart from the stag and hen parties, what kind of guests come here?'

Joanne chewed her lip as she thought about the question. 'I dunno. All sorts. Businessmen mainly.'

Brady nodded. 'Are they the guests who pay by cash then?'

'Yes,' she said, her voice low. 'Only a few. But you can tell that they look . . . you know, important. That they wouldn't want their wives or the press finding out what they get up to here.'

'Why the press?'

She paused for a moment before answering. 'Well . . . let's just say that there's been a couple of footballers who have booked a whole floor here for a weekend. Not dead famous, but famous enough, you know? You recognise their faces. And they've got the money to throw around. Then you get the type who look like businessmen. Expensively dressed.'

Brady was stunned. Madley suddenly seemed to have friends in high places; friends that he was taking care to look after. And what better place to give you the anonymity that you needed? A seafront hotel in Whitley Bay. Nothing fancy. Always busy with passing trade from other parts of the country. That in itself gave you anonymity. For this wasn't the sort of place that locals would book for their wedding day. Not with two coachloads of lads or lasses booked in for a weekend away.

'And they party, these men. Hard. Girls, booze, drugs. Anything they want, they get.'

Brady nodded. He was intrigued. Was this the case with 'John Smith' last night? Did he – victim or killer – know the perks this hotel offered? Cash for anonymity. That anything goes – including getting away with murder. Brady thought of the victim's clothes – Italian and handmade. Expensive taste for a twenty-two-year-old.

'Look, promise me you won't say anything. What I've told you is confidential. All right? I'd get shot if my boss knew I'd said any of this. Especially to a copper.' She looked worried. Realised too late that she'd let her mouth run.

'Of course. I won't say a word,' Brady reassured her. He decided to change direction. 'Any other way into the hotel?'

Joanne thought about it for a moment.

'There's two emergency exits that lead out onto the back alley. One's through the kitchen though. The staff would have said if someone had come in that way. Nothing gets past the head chef, including a straying guest. The other one is alarmed. It can't be opened from the outside, only internally. But if anyone did open it, the alarm would go off. Apart from that, the only other way in or out is through the hotel front doors.'

Brady already knew this. But he just wanted to make certain. After he had finished at the crime scene he had taken a look around the hotel. Checked out all the entrances and exits. He still wasn't sure whether the victim had checked into the hotel, or the killer. Who had joined who? One of them had checked in and had requested two room cards. Whether it was the victim or the killer, they'd been expecting company.

'Is your boss around?'

'No. He's away on holiday for a week. Left yesterday afternoon.'

'Where did he go?'

She shrugged. 'I'm the last person he would tell.'

Brady nodded. He could accept that. Anyone other than

Madley and he would have been suspicious. But Madley was too clever to be caught with blood on his hands. It wasn't his style. Still, Brady couldn't ignore the fact that a gruesome, mutilated body had turned up in one of Madley's hotel rooms while he was conveniently out of the country. He would have to do some preliminary checks, such as confirming the flight Madley got on – if he did – and the destination. Did Brady think the murder was connected to Madley? No. But did he think he better cover his own arse and make sure that he looked into every possibility? Hell yes. DI Bentley would be making his own inquiries into Madley. Better that Brady got there first.

'If you hear from your colleague, let her know I need to talk to her. Urgently,' Brady said as he handed Joanne his card. 'And if you think of anything that could be relevant, call me.'

She took the card. But the look on her face told him that she wouldn't be calling anytime soon. That she'd already told him too much.

Brady thought about Madley's check-in system. Cash up front, no questions asked. That could buy a lot. Including murder.

Brady turned to leave, then turned back. 'Just so I'm sure about this,' he paused as he looked towards the stairs. 'That's the only way to the first- and second-floor rooms?'

'Yes. And the lifts are over there.'

Brady turned and looked at them. The two lifts were directly opposite the reception desk.

'No one could get past without you noticing? Correct?'

'In theory,' she smiled, 'in practice, no. Try booking in a coachload of drunken blokes. It's hard enough watching what they're up to, let alone anyone else who wanders in.'

Timing was crucial. 'John Smith' had checked into room 212 at 8:15 p.m. The two coachloads of guests had turned up at 7:49 p.m. It had taken the receptionist a good hour to check everyone in. Whether she would have had time to even take note of 'John Smith' was questionable, given how busy she would have been with the stag party. Brady was also looking into the possibility

71

that the killer could have been another guest who had already booked in. At this precise moment he was prepared to consider anything.

'When you say anyone else wandering in . . .'

'We get drunks coming in. Friday and Saturday nights are the worst. Wanting to use the toilets in the lobby or wanting a drink at the bar. Some even think we're here to order them a taxi home.'

Brady thought about it. He knew that this would not have been the case here. The crime had been meticulously planned and orchestrated. The killer had brought rope, duct tape and his trademark – the Joker card. This wasn't some drunk who had wandered in off the street and somehow got past reception and by chance knocked on room 212. That was easily ruled out. But the possibility that the victim had checked in first and that the killer had somehow walked in unseen and joined him in his room later seemed highly probable. Without security tapes it would be impossible to prove whether or not Brady's hunch was right. His only hope was getting hold of the receptionist on duty.

'Your boss really should get some security cameras put up. Make your job safer.'

'Tell me what I don't know,' Joanne said, smiling.

But it was lost on Brady. He was already heading for the double glass doors, his mind focused on the receptionist from the previous night. They needed to talk to her.

Chapter Twelve

Brady had called in his old team. Wanted the reassurance of knowing that he had people he could trust. He didn't know how this investigation would unfold. That worried him. He wasn't sure whether they were dealing with the original Joker or a copycat murderer. Both scenarios meant that there would be more victims. There was also the possibility that they were dealing with a suspect who was trying to elude the police. Someone who had set the crime scene up to look as if this was either the original killer or a copycat murderer. But why? And how would they have found out the details of the original crimes?

Brady dragged a hand through his hair as he looked at his team. DS Harvey and DC Kodovesky were still busy trying to track down the whereabouts of the hotel receptionist. The remaining four were seated around the conference table, waiting for him to speak. Three were CID and the fourth was Northumbria's police forensic psychologist. They were only a small part of the murder investigation team, but they were at its core. Their roles were crucial when it came to delegating tasks and coordinating the other team members. Brady sorely needed to know that he had people he could rely on; who would follow his instructions without question. At least, that was the team he had left behind five months ago. Whether that had changed remained to be seen.

The rest of the team were being called in from other Area Commands, CID and uniform alike. But Brady was old school.

He liked to know who he was dealing with and if they had an agenda other than working on the murder investigation. He was no fool. A case like this could divide people, each looking for their stake in the end result to secure their own glory. He didn't have time for that. Not when he was the SIO. And not on a violent and sickening case like this one.

And then there were the other victims from the Seventies. Murders that had never been solved. No resolution, no closure for the families involved. News of this new murder would bring it all back for them. Questions would be asked, and again, the police would be held accountable. Or to be precise, as the SIO, it would be him in the firing line.

Brady pushed these thoughts to the back of his mind. He had to. He had to focus on the victim: Alexander De Bernier. It was imperative that Brady knew every minuscule detail there was to know about him. His health, personal history, social habits and personality. This would help the team have a better understanding of what it was about Alexander De Bernier that had made him a victim. Why the offender had chosen him. Brady knew that there would be something about De Bernier that had fulfilled the fantasies and desires of his killer. Understanding that would give them an insight into the offender's mind. The ultimate goal was to figure out the reasoning behind the perpetrator's choice of victim in order to determine *his* next step. Because Brady was convinced that if the old cold case was connected to this recent murder, there would be more. They would have a serial killer on their hands – again.

Brady cleared his throat. He felt uncomfortable. All eyes on him; watching him, waiting for him to say something. Anything. But there was one person in particular who was making him feel nervous, not quite up to the job. Dr Amelia Jenkins. It was the first time he had seen her in five months. They had had a run-in shortly before the Dabkunas brothers had taken him hostage.

At the time when he had seen Amelia at the station, he'd believed Claudia to be dead. Amelia had been furious with him.

And she'd had every right to be. But she had still managed to swallow back whatever bitterness and anger she felt. After all, she may not have shared the sentiment, but she was aware that not only Brady but the rest of Whitley Bay police station were reeling from the news that Claudia was missing, presumed dead.

Brady and the team had succeeded in ending what had become a 'runner'. They had a serial rapist on the streets of Whitley Bay and for a time, it seemed as if they would never catch him. But they did – eventually. And when they did, the team, including Amelia, had celebrated by having a few drinks in The Fat Ox pub. There had always been a frisson between them. So that night, after a few drinks, it had seemed perfectly natural for him to accept Amelia's invite back to hers for a late supper and a bottle of wine. But before he could even make it over to her place Claudia had rung him; sounding desperate, anxious and scared. He had had no choice but to leave. When Amelia had come out of the pub toilets, he was gone. The following day was the last time he had seen her. He hadn't really spoken. Too much in shock. And now five months later, here she was, waiting for him to speak. Waiting to see how well he could hold it together.

Brady forced himself to look at her. To acknowledge her. He flinched when he did. Her dark, almond-shaped eyes took him by surprise. They were cool. Reserved. He watched as she deliberately tucked her sleek, black, razor-sharp bobbed hair behind her ear, never once dropping her gaze. But her face was flushed. Whether the room was too hot, or she felt awkward, he couldn't say. Her red lipstick was deep and bold. Her clothes, sophisticated with a Fifties retro spin. Everything about her was still the same. But *she* was different.

Or was it that she was different with him?

She was still only in her early thirties, with a career that was going somewhere. She had originally worked for the force as a forensic psychologist. But something had happened. Brady didn't know what, but it had been enough for her to quit her role and turn to practising clinical psychology. It was Gates who had managed to persuade her to come back. Supposedly as a favour to him. A one-off. That had been nearly eighteen months ago.

Brady took a moment. The way she had looked at him had unnerved him, thrown him off balance.

'I know Conrad's already briefed you regarding the disturbing similarity between Alexander De Bernier's murder and the Joker killings carried out during the summer of 1977,' Brady said, as his eyes turned to his deputy.

Conrad was still ashen. His mouth, a rigid thin line. His lacklustre eyes were barely focused on Brady. He was clearly ill. But he was refusing to accept it.

Amelia looked at Conrad. Concern filled her eyes when she realised how pale he looked.

For a brief second, Brady felt jealous. Jealous of the fact that she cared so much about Conrad. But Brady had hurt her. Badly. What more did he expect? That they could still be friends? But that was the problem. They had never really been friends. They had danced around their attraction to one another. Ignored it, fought it. Until that night when Amelia had decided to take a risk and Brady had thrown it back in her face.

'Yes, sir. I've brought them up to date,' Conrad answered. He stretched over, picked up a glass and poured himself some lukewarm water from the jug in the centre of the table.

Brady shot him a questioning look. Enough to let Conrad know he was worried about him.

He nodded back at Brady. An acknowledgement that he was fine. Or would be.

'Got something stuck at the back of your throat there, Conrad?' Kenny asked as he tried his damnedest not to smirk. But his deep-set mischievous brown eyes gave him away.

Ignoring him, Conrad took a drink.

DC Daniels, his partner, jumped in. 'Maybe he's choked-up thinking about the victim? Gagging at the thought of him!' Daniels said, flashing a knowing grin at Kenny.

Kenny couldn't help himself. The smirk he had been holding in suddenly erupted into laughter.

Conrad's face remained set. Jaw locked, eyes narrowed and his mouth unsmiling as he stared over at the large whiteboard. Photographs of the crime scene and victim had already been staged. Ready and waiting for them to connect the dots.

Brady looked at Conrad. Typically, he didn't rise to the bait. He sighed inwardly. These two idiots were a liability.

'You two keep this up and I'll personally remove your balls and stuff them in your own gobs if you don't shut up,' Brady threatened. He noted the look of silent anger in Amelia's eyes; she looked more than ready to carry out his threat.

'Sir.'

'Yes, sir.'

He felt like cuffing them around the ears. But he was worried about what he had just heard. He had been away for five months. A lot could happen in that time. Brady looked back at Conrad. He looked unfazed by the comments.

Or did he?

Brady wasn't sure whether Conrad's nonchalant air was genuine. There was a crack in his façade. Whether anyone else could see it was another matter. Brady was sure there was more to Daniels' and Kenny's comments than sick banter. The look in Conrad's eyes told him they had got to him. It was personal.

Shit!

Brady turned back to Daniels and Kenny. Both were in their early thirties. Unlike Conrad, they were not graduates. Nor were they focused on fast-tracking. That in itself was a problem. They saw Conrad as different. A cut above the rest. They were Geordie blokes and proud of it. Their talk revolved around three subjects outside work: football, drinking and women. In that exact order. Conrad couldn't have been more different. Newcastle United, lager and lasses were anathema to Conrad. And he made it known when the conversation got out of hand at work. In fact, Conrad only ever talked about the job.

Anything else was inconsequential. Whereas Daniels and Kenny enjoyed the job, but not enough to let it take over their lives. Irreverent, testosterone-fuelled talk about women dominated a lot of their conversation. Unlike Conrad. And it appeared that they had noted it. Not only that, Conrad never talked about his personal life. It was a closed subject. His affluent background and his current personal status were subjects he never acknowledged. Never discussed – no matter how much Daniels and Kenny goaded him. But it was clear that something had changed. Their attitude to Conrad had shifted from begrudged respect for a senior officer to out-and-out taking the piss. The question was, why?

Brady automatically thought of DI Adamson. Five months under that misogynistic, racist, homophobic dickhead could turn two DCs' casual – and at times politically incorrect – banter into something much more insidious. Brady realised that he could have trouble on his hands. The problem was, he didn't have time for there to be discord within the team. Not now.

Daniels was well-built at five foot eleven – a testament to long hours spent at the gym. Good-looking, in a hard way. Women liked him and he knew it and abused it. He and Kenny were inseparable: best mates on the job, best mates off. Kenny was tall, with short, curly dark brown hair. His face already heavily lined. What he lacked in looks he made up for by being a comedian. Brady would constantly find himself telling Kenny to rein it in. But he knew that Kenny's macabre sense of humour was his way of dealing with the atrocities that they faced. Nor was he unusual. Brady knew a lot of coppers and scenes of crime officers who wouldn't miss the opportunity to come out with a sick one-liner at the expense of the deceased.

But what troubled Brady here was whether Kenny's joke was at Conrad's expense or the deceased's. The last thing he wanted was to be dealing with this kind of homophobic crap. He decided to have a word with Conrad later. Test the water. Because if something had happened while Brady had been away, he needed to know. He wouldn't tolerate any kind of bullying innuendos. 'Right, you two. Give me what you know,' Brady fired out. His eyes flashed with menace as he focused on Daniels and Kenny. He was standing in front of them. Needed to be standing, as his left leg had stiffened up and had started cramping. It was involuntary and painful. But being stood in front of these two morons gave him an edge. Reminded them of the hierarchy here. Brady wasn't their friend. He was their boss. And in the ranking order, so was Conrad – whether they liked it or not. But these two needed that knocking back into them. A reminder that they weren't working for Adamson anymore.

Daniels ran a hand over his hair. 'Well, sir,' he began. He then looked at Kenny for him to take the lead.

Kenny frowned at Daniels not sure what he wanted him to say. His eyes darted over to the whiteboard, as if double-checking the case he was supposed to be working on.

'For fuck's sake! Tell me you two knuckleheads aren't still pissed?'

The conference room, despite its size, stank of stale booze. The odious smell emanated from Daniels' and Kenny's breath. Clung to their pores.

Daniels gave an apologetic shrug. 'Sorry, sir. But this was our weekend off. You're lucky that you could get hold of us,' he said with a knowing smile.

'Yeah,' added Kenny, yawning. 'We had an all-nighter at this strip club in town. Christ! It was blinding! Adamson took us to it a few weeks back. Private membership and all. You might know it?' Kenny suggested as he looked straight at Conrad. His eyes were filled with cruel amusement.

Conrad didn't bite. He looked at Kenny and shrugged. 'Can't say I do.'

'Nah, not your sort of club, is it,' Kenny stated flatly, the smile gone.

'Right!' Brady exclaimed. 'You two pissheads shut your mouths and sober up. One more word of crap and I'll have both your bollocks nailed to your bloody foreheads. And then I'll personally see to it that you're both up on a disciplinary. Are we clear on this? You have a problem with Conrad? Then bloody spit it out now! Otherwise shut the fuck up and show some respect for a superior officer!' Brady caught Amelia's eye. She looked surprised by his outburst. As for Conrad, he didn't look impressed that his boss had jumped in to his defence. But Brady didn't care. It had to be said. He would not tolerate homophobic innuendos and if that embarrassed Conrad, so be it. He would rather have it out in the open than ignore something that could end up forcing Conrad out of the force. And he was too good a copper for Brady to lose.

'It's just a bit of harmless piss-taking, sir,' Daniels muttered as he nudged his partner.

'Yeah,' Kenny agreed reluctantly. He folded his arms and sat back as he looked across at Conrad. 'Bit of banter between grown men. Nothing personal.'

Brady sighed. As far as first days back on the job went, this was the worst one yet.

'Victim? What do we know so far?' Brady asked, the question directed at Kenny and Daniels.

'Alexander De Bernier. Twenty-two-year-old politics student at Newcastle Uni, finishing off a Masters. Fourth year there. Already has a first degree in politics,' Kenny answered.

Brady waited.

Kenny looked back down at the scrawl in front of him that passed as notes and frowned as he searched for something else to say.

'And?' He was in no mood today to be carrying these two. He had fifteen other officers and detectives currently being called in from other Area Commands. In other words, he could afford to lose two. And the way they were acting, it didn't seem like a bad idea.

'Lives in Heaton in a student share,' Daniels added.

Again, Brady waited. Nothing.

80

Conrad stepped in. 'We've contacted his parents. They live up in the north-east of Scotland. A few miles from Elgin.'

'Who informed them?' Brady asked.

'The police there. Seemed more appropriate.'

Brady nodded. A phone call wasn't the best way to deliver this kind of news.

'I've got their statement here for you,' Conrad said gesturing to a file in front of him. 'But neither parent could shed any light on why their son had been murdered. Perfect student. Lots of friends. No enemies. As far as they knew he was well-liked by everyone.'

'Not everyone,' Brady commented.

Conrad shook his head as he looked over at the graphic photos of the victim on the whiteboard. He turned back to Brady. 'Only child. They're devastated, as you can imagine. Can't understand how or why it happened to him.'

'Have you talked to them since they found out?' Brady asked. He wasn't one for second-hand knowledge. Would rather get a feel for it himself than trust someone else's instincts.

'Not yet. But I was planning on phoning them. Explain what we're doing to help find their son's murderer.'

'Good. Do that. And organise transport down for them and a hotel in Newcastle, not Whitley Bay. I want them close, but not on my doorstep. I imagine once they've got over the shock they'll want to be here. Organise a family liaison officer to be with them at all times. I don't want them harangued by the bloody vipers from the press.'

Brady didn't think they would be speeding down the A1 to identify their son. The fact that the victim's photo driver's licence was in his wallet was enough proof of identity. No. They would want to be here to be close to the investigation. To feel as if they were doing something. Anything, to avoid them facing the inevitable – a future without their child.

'Anything else?' Brady asked.

'Girlfriend. Molly Johansson. She's from Johannesburg. She came over to take a Masters at Newcastle. Studying on the same course as Alexander De Bernier. That's how they met, according to the victim's parents.'

Brady nodded. No surprise he had a girlfriend. His driver's licence photo showed him to be handsome. Brady assumed he would have been even better looking in the flesh. Not that he'd looked so hot when Brady had been introduced to him.

'Do they share the same student house?'

Conrad shook his head. 'Not from the details I've got here. They both lived in Heaton but at separate addresses.'

'Has she been informed?' Brady asked.

'I believe his parents were going to tell her. They wanted that, rather than leave it to strangers. From what they've said in their statement, they were close to his girlfriend. Seems that the victim and Ms Johansson had been planning on getting engaged once they had both completed their postgraduate degrees.'

This interested Brady. If the victim had been vulnerable, then that would make him an easy target – or at least an easier one. There was a reason that prostitutes – male or female – were at high risk when it came to being attacked, and even murdered. But this victim was different. He wasn't high risk. He came from a good background and seemingly had everything going for him.

'All right. We need to talk to her. Tell me if I'm wrong here, but why would the victim be spending a Saturday night in a hotel in Whitley Bay when he had a girlfriend he was planning on marrying at some point? Doesn't quite add up.'

'Depends . . .' Daniels began.

Brady inwardly steeled himself for yet another inane comment.

'I know blokes who have a long-term girlfriend but still screw around. You know? It's human nature. They may have the woman they want to marry but that doesn't mean they want the same boring meal every day, if you get my drift. Variety is what keeps you sane,' Daniels said with a grin.

82

'Great to get an inside view of what goes on in that Neolithic brain of yours, Daniels. But not everyone is a serial shagger like you.'

Brady could feel Amelia's eyes on him. He didn't want to look at her, to see what she thought of him. After all, hadn't he stood her up in front of the team? Left her alone at the bar, without a word, to console Claudia. But one thing had led to another and he had ended up in bed with Claudia. It was inevitable. Brady was still desperately in love with her. Perhaps always would be.

He cleared his head. Pushed thoughts of what could have happened with Amelia to the back of his mind.

'It's crucial we talk to his girlfriend. ASAP,' Brady said, looking pointedly at Conrad.

He then turned to Daniels and Kenny. 'You two need to shape up. By the time I get back the rest of the team will be working this case. Don't embarrass yourselves. More importantly, don't embarrass me. Understand? In the meantime, you two will go through all the statements taken from the hotel staff and guests. Check for any priors. Anything suspicious, report it back. CCTV footage is crucial. The hotel receptionist said that they don't have a security system. Check it out. And check out the surveillance cameras along the Promenade. My gut feeling is that the killer walked through the double doors into reception. And then, sometime later, walked back out.'

Daniels made a point of exhaling noisily at the workload he had been given.

'Within the hour this team will comprise fifteen detectives and officers. Use your brain, Daniels. Delegate. It's going to be a long night, so I recommend you two get some coffee to help you sober up.'

Brady mentally prepared himself as he turned to Amelia. He had to; she hadn't yet said one word. It unnerved him. It was as if she had her shrink head on. Observing, analysing and judging.

'Amelia . . .' Brady paused. There was no mistaking the coolness. Her eyes lacked any warmth or familiarity – her whole demeanour was one of professional detachment. 'Could you take a look at the spate of murders in the Seventies that took place throughout North Tyneside and compare them to this one? Charlie Turner, the desk sergeant, will help you locate the files. Have a chat with Charlie. He was a young copper at the time these murders took place. He might have some details or insight that you won't glean from the files on the case.'

'It's filed under what?'

The detached professionalism in her voice stung him.

'The Joker murders.'

Without looking at him, she made a note. 'Is it a cold case?'

'Yes,' Brady replied. She still had her head down. 'I'd be interested to know your take on it.'

She finally raised her head to meet Brady's eyes.

'The Seventies murderer was named "The Joker" by the media,' he explained. 'For good reason. He left a Joker card with each of his victims' bodies. There were seven in total from the beginning of the summer of '77 to the end of it. He mutilated his victims, the injuries identical to those sustained by our victim last night, and then, after suffocating them, he left his calling card. The Joker. His way of playing with the police. The Joker card left with Alexander De Bernier is identical to the ones left with the Seventies victims.'

Amelia looked mildly surprised at this information. 'You seriously think this could be the same perpetrator?'

Brady could feel Kenny and Daniels watching him.

'We have to keep our options open. It could be that the original killer has resurfaced or it could be a copycat killer. There is a possible third scenario. That we have a killer who has chosen to murder Alexander De Bernier in the same manner as the Seventies victims to confuse us. To make us believe it's either the original Joker or a copycat killer.'

Amelia frowned at this suggestion.

84

'I honestly don't know,' Brady responded. 'I'm really hoping you can help us on this by narrowing down the potential suspects and giving us a profile to work with. Why was Alexander De Bernier murdered? What was it about him that made him a victim? And then, why was he murdered in this unique way?'

Amelia nodded at Brady. 'All right. I'll do my best,' she answered. 'Can I have a look at the list of suspects from the original case?'

'Yeah, Harvey will sort you out with those details. From what we've gathered so far the original investigative team didn't really have much to go on. The team was headed by DI McKaley. At the time, he was crucified by the press for not catching the killer. From what I've gathered he's the only surviving member of the investigative team. The others are all deceased.'

'Have you told him?' Amelia asked.

It was an obvious question, and one that Brady would have asked if he had been in her position. What better person to glean information about the Joker killings from than the original SIO? However, it wasn't that simple.

'We thought he was also dead, but then it turned out that he's in a care home in Preston Village, North Shields.'

Amelia looked interested.

Brady shook his head. 'Unfortunately, he has severe Alzheimer's. The care home specialises in patients with advanced symptoms of the disease.'

'Oh . . . I see,' Amelia answered.

She looked as disappointed as Brady had felt when he had found this out. DI McKaley could have been a very useful source. He hadn't written off talking to him – not yet. Despite the nurse's insistence that McKaley point-blank refused visitors.

'Over the course of the Joker investigation, McKaley brought in four suspects for questioning. They were each detained for a short period but were eventually released without charge. If I'm honest with you, I've had a brief look at the case notes and the

85

reasons for bringing them in were fairly tenuous. Out of the four there's now only one of the original suspects remaining. Two of them are deceased. Harold Walters died a couple of years after he had been released without charge. Suicide,' Brady explained. 'Then Roger Sawyer died in the early Eighties. He contracted HIV and then went on to have full-blown AIDS.'

Amelia looked at Brady. 'Am I guessing that these men were all gay?'

Brady nodded. 'Each of them had been charged with obscene acts in public toilets.'

Amelia sighed. 'I understand now why the original investigative team's reasons for bringing them in were tenuous.'

Brady couldn't help but notice Amelia shooting Conrad a look of disbelief.

'The other two suspects?'

'Martyn Jenkins has cancer. Lung cancer. Prognosis doesn't look good. From what I've been told, he'll be lucky if he lasts the next twenty-four hours. He's currently in a hospice in Newcastle.'

'And the fourth?' Amelia asked, frowning.

'Sidney Foster. Left the North East in 1977 after he was released without charge. Can't say I blame him. He moved around for the next twenty years and from what we've gathered he settled down in Cornwall. He's seventy-one now. I can't really see him as a likely suspect but we've got to follow it through.'

'Did Sidney Foster have any other priors than obscene acts in public places?'

Brady nodded. 'He was charged with raping a fifteen-year-old boy in 1977. He was thirty-seven at the time. He was then charged with various sexual offences. All boys under the age of sixteen.'

'I see,' Amelia replied. 'Maybe that's why he moved around so much? Might be worth questioning him.'

'Like I said, we're still trying to track him down,' Brady said. But he had a gut feeling that Sidney Foster wasn't their suspect. Even the fact that he had seemingly disappeared did not raise any alarm bells. There was a huge discrepancy between being charged with rape and actually cutting someone's penis off and choking them to death on it.

'One element in all of this bothers me,' Brady admitted. 'Only the police knew the precise details of the case in the Seventies.' He wasn't quite sure what she was thinking. Her eyes were cool and detached as they held his steady gaze.

'What about the playing card left with each victim? I thought you said that the press called him "The Joker" because of it?'

Brady nodded. Took a moment before he answered her. He needed it. Her air of professional detachment was staring to affect him. It hurt like hell that he had screwed up what had been a friendship between them. But he couldn't blame Amelia for her behaviour. In fact, she was behaving impeccably. There was no edge to her voice and her demeanour with him was professional but by no means frosty. She was simply getting on with her life. And that included getting on with the job at hand – regardless of Brady.

'The card was something that got out,' he explained. 'I don't know the whys or hows of the old investigation. But the method by which the victims were killed was never disclosed. In particular, the mutilation to the victims' groins.'

'They were all male?' Amelia asked.

'Yes. Each one gagged in the same manner.'

'With their own penis?' she asked, curious. Her words were slow and deliberate, cutting through the room like a knife.

'Yes.' He knew this crime was atypical, as did Amelia. Usually they dealt with hate crimes against women – not men.

She didn't respond. Instead, she watched Brady. Scrutinised him for some kind of reaction.

He didn't give her one.

'All right. That's it for now.' Brady watched as Daniels and Kenny scraped their chairs back and stood up. Daniels stretched, while Kenny yawned.

Conrad stood up once they'd left.

'Wait for me in the car, will you?' Brady asked Conrad.

He nodded.

Brady turned to Amelia. She was busy packing her briefcase.

'Can I have a word?' Brady asked.

She looked up at him. For the briefest of moments, her professional mask slipped.

'Look . . . I'm . . . I'm sorry,' Brady begun. It was clumsy and awkward and she knew it. Which made it worse.

'For what?' she asked casually as she made a point of busying herself with packing her briefcase.

Brady didn't answer. Couldn't. She picked up her briefcase and looked at Brady, waiting.

'If that's all?' Her tone was pleasant and non-combative. But it was purely professional. Nothing more.

Brady nodded weakly. He didn't know what else he could say.

He watched as Amelia turned and walked out the room. They had always sparred. That had been part of the attraction. Part of the game they played. But now? This was different. He hadn't known what to expect when he came back to work. But it definitely wasn't this. Five months was a long time to be away. And in that time a lot had changed. He thought of Conrad. He had no idea what was going on with him. Or why Daniels and Kenny had thought it acceptable to take the piss out of him. Something had happened while he had been away. He was certain of it. During that time DI Adamson would have been in charge of them. Not good. Definitely not with two impressionable blockheads like Daniels and Kenny. Their attitude stank. Worse than their foul, stale lager breath and bleary bloodshot eyes from a night on the lash.

Chapter Thirteen

Sunday: 5:38 p.m.

'You OK?'

Conrad nodded. 'I'll live.'

Brady didn't mean that and Conrad knew it.

But Conrad was focused on driving.

Brady looked out the window as the street lights passed in a blur. They were heading to Heaton to question the victim's girlfriend – Molly Johansson. They needed as much information on Alexander De Bernier as possible and what better person to ask than his girlfriend? Most murder inquiries would start with the person closest to the victim. Typically, most murders were acts of blind rage committed by someone the victim knew. A moment's lapsed judgement in a heated argument could end disastrously. But this wasn't what had happened here. At least, he didn't think so.

The murder was too similar to the Seventies murders for Brady to seriously think that the victim's girlfriend could be responsible. But he needed to talk to her and clarify a few things.

Conrad pulled off Coast Road and onto Heaton Road. He then turned right onto Heaton Park View.

'Not bad for student accommodation,' Brady commented as he looked at the large, imposing Victorian houses. Some were detached, others were terraces, but all were in excellent condition, which surprised him.

Conrad parked up outside 1 Heaton Park View.

Brady took in the sight. It was an impressive five-bedroom

Victorian detached house with an ornate gravel driveway leading up to the front door.

'Parents must be paying for this. Can't imagine their student loan covering the rent on it.'

Conrad didn't answer. Instead he cut the engine and got out of the car.

Brady watched him. His silence was unnerving. Not that Conrad was one for unnecessary talking, but this was out of character. He got out the car and joined Conrad.

'Bloody nice street,' Brady said as he looked across at Heaton Park.

Conrad left Brady to it and made his way to the large, dark green panelled door. He knocked twice. It was heavy, authoritative and commanding.

Moments later there was a crack in the door. A pale, blotchy, mascara-streaked face peeked out.

'Detective Sergeant Conrad, I rang earlier?' Conrad introduced himself, flashing his warrant card.

Brady came up behind him. 'Detective Inspector Brady.'

The young woman waited for Brady to show his card before opening the door wide enough to let them in.

'Molly Johansson?' Brady asked as he walked in.

She backed away from him and stood against the wall opposite, arms folded across her white baggy T-shirt. At five foot eleven, she was tall and remarkably thin. Bony even, with long straggly blond hair that was tied up, accentuating her gaunt, hollow features. Her blank blue eyes refused to look at Brady and instead focused on her feet. Her toenails were painted a turquoise blue and she wore a silver toe-ring on her left foot.

'Ms Johansson?' Brady repeated. But it was clear it was her. Her body language and swollen, red-rimmed eyes said enough. 'I am really sorry about your loss. I can only imagine what you must be going through.'

Her eyes drifted up to meet his. Not sure of his sentiment. 'I need a drink.' Her voice was raspy, with a distinctive South African accent.

She turned and walked towards the kitchen straight ahead.

Brady noticed two things about the house. It was massive. The hallway could have acted as a living room in itself. But despite the original features of stained-glass windows, ceiling roses and intricate cornicing, it was most definitely a student house. It was grime-infested. He walked down the tacky-feeling wooden floor into the large kitchen. The brilliant fluorescent light overhead did the place no favours. Dishes were stacked high in the sink. Food-encrusted plates and pans had been discarded across the cluttered worktops. Even more surprising was the empty dishwasher stood with the door wide open. Then there was the rubbish everywhere. Empty cans, half-empty take-out containers and bottles of various sorts littered the worktops and the floor around the overflowing, filthy bin. The place had enough rubbish to fill a landfill. Even the smell that lingered in the kitchen was more akin to a garbage dump on a sweltering hot day. Brady could feel the sole of his boots sticking to the floor, reminiscent of playing in a punk band in his youth, in Mingles Whitley Bay on a Friday night. At least then it was so damned dark, you didn't know what you were standing on, or drinking out of.

Brady assumed there was some kind of guerrilla warfare going on in the student house. Someone had obviously forgotten to do their share and it had descended into all-out war.

Molly's eyes caught Brady's. She shrugged it off. 'Not my mess,' she said, unapologetic.

Brady watched as she picked up a dirty wine glass. She then went to the fridge and took out a new bottle of Chardonnay. He noticed her fingers trembling as she tried to unscrew the cap.

'Let me do that?' Brady offered.

Defeated, she handed the bottle over. He opened it for her and handed it back.

Without thanking him, she poured herself a large glass and

took a gulp. Some of it dribbled down her chin. Annoyed, she wiped it away.

'Want one?' Suddenly she seemed aware that they were watching her.

'On duty. Thanks, though,' Brady answered. Not that he could stomach even a coffee, given the state of the place.

Conrad's face said as much. Especially after his run-in with his lunch.

'Do you want to go somewhere more private?' Brady asked.

She shook her head, freeing some more long strands of blond hair. Her white-knuckled hand clutched her wine glass as she took another drink. 'This is as good a place as any.'

Brady wondered how much she had already drunk. He assumed as soon as the victim's parents had told her the devastating news she had hit the bottle. The question was, how many bottles had she hit?

'You share this house?'

She took another gulp as she thought about the question. 'Why?' she asked as she looked at him.

It wouldn't be long before she was slurring and not able to see straight. Brady looked up at the kitchen clock. It was 5:49 p.m. But then again, she had good reason to want to get off her face.

'I just want to make sure you're not on your own tonight,' Brady answered, his voice gentle, paternalistic.

'And why would that bother you?'

Brady took a deep breath. He knew Molly was in shock. Right now she was feeling pissed off with the world. And why not? Her boyfriend had been murdered and she now had two coppers she didn't know from Sherlock wanting to talk to her. And it was clear she was in no mood for talking.

'Because you've received some distressing news and I want to make sure that you're not on your own,' Brady explained.

'Yeah? That's nice of you.' She took another gulp.

'Molly . . . You don't mind if I call you Molly?' Brady asked.

She shrugged as she reopened the bottle of wine and poured

herself another liberal measure. 'We were going to get married. You know? After uni we were going to get engaged and then in a few years' time, get married. Alex had it all planned – even the date of our wedding.'

Brady kept quiet. He knew now wasn't the time to be direct. She would see it as confrontational. Molly was looking for a fight and it didn't matter who with. It was easier to let her talk her way through it.

'Why the fuck would he do that? Why?' she asked as she wiped aggressively at the tears spilling down her reddened cheeks.

Brady looked across at Conrad, who seemed at a loss.

'You mean, why was he at the Royal Hotel last night?' Brady ventured.

She stared at him as if he might have the answer.

'We were hoping you could tell us that.'

She knocked back another large gulp of wine.

'Molly?' Brady repeated.

'I don't know,' she answered reluctantly. 'I don't know why he was in a hotel last night. I can only imagine.'

'He didn't say anything to you?'

She shook her head.

'When did you last see him?'

She raised her eyes and looked at Brady. 'Why?'

'We just need to know Alexander's whereabouts yesterday. Anyone he met, talked to on the phone. Had arrangements to meet, even.'

Molly Johansson answered. 'I last saw him sometime yesterday morning.'

Brady could see that she would be seen by some to epitomise a certain type of youthful beauty. Her pale, eggshell skin, her painfully thin body and angular features were very heroin chic. He wouldn't have been surprised if at the age of fifteen she had been on the front cover of *Vogue*. She had that arrogant haughtiness about her, accompanied by the height

93

and looks. She seemed an equal match for Alexander De Bernier.

'Did you have a fight?' Brady asked. His felt there was more to this than she was revealing. She seemed angry. Not at Brady, although he was on the receiving end. She was angry with her boyfriend. And Brady needed to find out why.

Her blank eyes suddenly sparked, then faded. 'Just the usual . . .' she shrugged.

'What's the usual?'

'Work. He was committed to his job.'

'I thought he was studying for a Masters in politics?' Brady asked.

'We both are . . .' she paused, realising.

'But he worked?' Brady pushed, not wanting to lose her.

'Yes. He had an internship with an MP. He wanted to be a politician. His aim was to be in the House of Commons in ten years' time. And Alex would have done it. People believed in him. He was good. Good at what he did . . .' She stopped.

'So the argument was over his commitment to work?'

Molly Johansson gave a half nod. 'I guess so. I can't really remember now. It just seems so inconsequential.' Her voice trailed off as the tears melted down her sculpted cheekbones.

'Where did he go after he left you?'

'I don't know. He stayed over here on Friday night. Then he left in the morning. I assumed he had gone home. But . . . I . . . I honestly don't know. He never answered my calls, or my texts. I was worried. Rang around all our friends. Nobody had seen or heard from him all of yesterday. And then his parents called me two hours ago to say . . .' Molly stopped. Looked at Brady, then Conrad, before taking another drink.

'Did Alexander have any enemies that you know of?' Brady asked.

Molly laughed. It was as abrupt and sudden as it was cold and bitter. 'Alex? Fuck no! Everyone loved Alex. He was so charismatic and so fucking good-looking that everyone just adored him.' As if surprised by her own outburst, she dropped her gaze to her wobbling wine glass.

But not before her eyes betrayed her. Brady had seen the flash of pure anger in them. She was furious with her boyfriend. It didn't matter that he was dead. Brady wasn't quite sure exactly what was going on. But one thing he was certain of, she knew more than she was letting on.

'Who was he doing his internship with?' Conrad asked.

Molly Johansson turned to Conrad, as if surprised that he was there. She took a slow, deliberate drink before answering. 'The MP, Robert Smythe. We both worked as interns for him.'

Brady noted that Conrad seemed to recognise the name.

'Could Alexander have been working for Robert Smythe yesterday?' Brady asked.

She shook her head. More loose strands fell out of the twisted knot of hair. Some fell down on her shoulders, other strands clung resiliently to her damp cheeks, giving her a drunken, dishevelled look. Not that she cared. Brady could see that the last thing she was bothered about was her appearance. She needed a tissue for her face. It bothered him that he didn't have one to give to her. Tears slid down onto her top lip. As if she read his mind, she swiped at it with the back of her hand, which she then wiped on her black leggings.

'Why not?' Brady continued.

'Smythe was going to Brussels for a political conference. Said he was leaving early this morning and would be away for five days.'

'And you have no knowledge of why Alexander would be in the Royal Hotel last night?'

Again, Molly shook her head.

'Nor who he might have been meeting?'

At this, more tears came. 'I already said so. I don't know who he was fucking meeting do I! That's the point. He shouldn't have been meeting anyone.'

'I'm sorry,' Brady said, his voice low. But it was too late.

95

She glugged back the rest of her wine and then used the heel of her hand to wipe her snotty nose. She then opened the bottle of Chardonnay.

'Why don't you let me make you a coffee?' Brady suggested.

She made a point of pouring a large glass for herself and then turned, glass in hand, to look at Brady.

'Why don't you just leave? I've told you everything I know. Shouldn't you be out there catching whoever killed him? Well?'

Brady didn't answer. But his expression said enough. It was understanding and apologetic.

'Anyway, here's to fucking Alex,' she said as she raised her smeared glass, ignoring Brady. 'You fucking cheating bastard!' She gulped back a couple of mouthfuls in an attempt to stop the tears.

'You OK, Mol?'

Brady turned. A young man was standing in the doorway of the kitchen. Twenty-something, with wild, shaggy blond hair with a tinge of red, and a woolly, reddish-brown goatee.

'Fucking A, Jamie! I'm on my way to getting shit-faced. Oh yeah . . . Meet Inspector Holmes and Watson here,' she said as she waved her wine glass at them.

'Detective Inspector Brady and Detective Sergeant Conrad,' Brady said.

'Great. Well . . . Jamie Scrafton,' she said as she jerked her head towards him, 'he's one of my housemates.'

'You staying with her tonight?' Brady asked him. He was a good-looking bloke with kind eyes.

Jamie nodded. 'Yeah. I'll keep an eye on her.'

'Did you know Alexander well?' Brady ventured.

'Nah. Saw him around when he was here with Molly. But that was it. I'm studying architecture and they're taking politics. Kind of hung out in different places if you get my drift. But he was a really nice guy. Can't believe someone would do that to him. You know? Like . . . kill him?'

'Look, if there's anything you think of, call me. I'll leave my

96

number for Molly with you as well. Just in case she thinks of anything relevant.'

'Sure, glad to help, man,' Jamie said as he took the card with Brady's contact details on. 'Really hope you get the bastard who did it.'

Brady nodded at him. 'Molly?'

She was slouched against the worktop now, her eyes heavy and glazed. Brady couldn't tell if it was from crying or too much booze.

'I'll no doubt need to talk to you again. But in the meantime, if you think of anything, Jamie has my card. OK?'

Whether she heard Brady, he wasn't sure. But she didn't answer him.

'Roll me a cigarette, will you, Jamie?'

'Come on, Mol, you don't smoke,' Jamie objected.

'Haven't you heard, hon? My cheating fucking boyfriend's been found dead in some cheap hotel in Whitley Bay! Alexander De Bernier, destined for great things, murdered in some sordid hotel room. So yes, I don't smoke. So fucking what?' she slurred, her voice raised.

'OK . . . OK . . . I'll roll you one.'

Jamie looked at Brady and Conrad and gave them an apologetic shrug. 'She's not normally like this. She's just in shock.'

'You're a good mate,' Brady said, patting Jamie's shoulder. He walked past him and out into the hallway, followed by Conrad.

'What did you think?' Brady asked him once they were in the car.

'Well, she's drunk. Not surprising really after the news she's received.'

'I don't mean that. I'm interested in the fact that she was certain he was cheating on her. If the victim's injuries weren't so similar to the Seventies murders, I'd be hauling her in for questioning.'

'You really think she could be capable of killing her own boyfriend?' Conrad asked, surprised.

'Her? Yeah. In the right mood, anyone's capable.'

'Can't blame her for being upset, sir. She's just found out her boyfriend was more than likely meeting someone in a hotel to have sex.'

Brady shook his head. 'This wasn't a one-off. This wasn't the first time De Bernier met someone for sex. This was a regular occurrence. He was having an affair, Conrad. She said as much. Question is, who with?'

Conrad turned the engine on, put his foot on the accelerator and smoothly pulled away.

'What makes you so sure?' Conrad asked as he looked at Brady, frowning when he saw Brady's expression.

'You all right, sir?'

'Yeah,' Brady muttered. But it was a lie. His leg was giving him jip again. He felt in his inner jacket pocket for painkillers. He had had the foresight to bring a bottle. The pain necessitated prescribed painkillers. He flipped the lid off the small bottle, popped two into his mouth then swallowed them back dry. He then leaned back against the headrest. Eyes closed, he waited for the burning white pain to ease. Not that it ever entirely left, but on a good day he could get it down to a dull background noise. Not today. It was the first time since they had pinned and bolted his leg together that he had been so active on it. And he had one hell of a headache. One that seemed to be worsening as the hours slipped by.

Conrad kept quiet.

'She knows something, Conrad. She bloody knows something.'

'Do you want me to turn round and go back?'

'No. Leave her for now. We won't get anywhere. But I guarantee she's holding something back. What about the victim's house?' Brady asked.

'Going there now, sir.'

Brady closed his eyes. 'Good.'

98

Chapter Fourteen

Sunday: 6:49 p.m.

Brady used his fist to repeatedly bang on the door. He had been knocking for five minutes. Another minute and he would kick the door down. He knew there was someone inside. The thumping music and upstairs bedroom light was a giveaway.

'Coming! For fuck's sake, what's your problem?' yelled a male voice on the other side as he released the deadlock.

A twenty-something dishevelled-looking man poked his head out from behind the door.

'Police!' Brady flashed his warrant card. It was enough. The guy knew they were serious.

Without thinking, he tried to close the door.

Brady threw himself against it, ramming it open.

'Fucking hell, man!' the young man protested as he backed away with his hands out in front of him. 'I haven't done anything.'

'Nobody said you had,' Brady answered as he weighed up the short, scrawny male trembling in front of him, dressed only in a pair of boxer shorts. 'I heard that student life was hard but I didn't realise that it meant the choice between beer and clothes.'

'I was in bed,' he replied sourly.

'Explains why it took you so long to answer the door to the police, then.'

The student scratched his head, making his hair even messier. 'I was up all night. OK? It's not against the law is it?'

Brady looked at Conrad and shrugged. 'Depends what you were getting up to, doesn't it?'

'We haven't got any weed here. All right! Talk about a fucking police state!'

Brady wasn't here to do a drugs search. He didn't have a warrant and had no evidence. Add to that, he didn't have the time or inclination to even be bothered about the student's recreational habits. Not when he had a murder victim on his hands.

'Your housemate, Alexander De Bernier. We want to see his bedroom.'

The student scratched his head again, confused. 'What?'

'Alexander De Bernier?' Brady repeated.

'Yeah . . . Shit, course I know Alex. But he moved out of here two weeks back. Paid to the end of the lease even though he had four more months to go. Said we could rent his room out if we wanted.'

'He's moved out?' Brady said as he shot Conrad a 'what the fuck' look.

'Yeah. Like I said, two weeks back.'

'Where?'

'Christ! I don't know. Alex and I weren't close. What about his girlfriend? She'll know.'

'Seems she believed he was still living here.'

'Shit, man! That sucks,' the guy said. It seemed clear that he thought Alex had met someone else. 'Why would he fuck around on that, eh?'

'And he definitely didn't leave a forwarding address for any mail that might come here?'

'No.' He shrugged. 'Have you tried the uni? They'll have a record of his new address. Or his parents?'

Brady looked at Conrad. The expression on his face told Brady that both had this address on file.

Fuck!

'Can we see his bedroom?'

'Sure. No one's moved into it yet.'

He started leading them up the stairs when he suddenly stopped and turned back. 'What's Alex done anyway?'

Brady looked up at the scrawny young man. 'He's been murdered.'

'Fuck me! You're not serious?'

'His bedroom?' Brady asked, ignoring his question.

He looked around the room. Even empty, it was still a dump. It stank of damp. Not surprising, given the fact it was on the top floor of the old six-bedroom Victorian house. The walls were painted a subtle light blue. It was the only piece of information Brady had about the victim. For this was recent, showing that it had been Alex's choice – or his attempt at improving the room, not that it did. The paint only added to the overall bleakness. The carpet was a Seventies statement of swirling diarrhoea browns and yellows.

'Where are you, Alex? Where did you go?' Brady muttered to himself.

Conrad cleared his throat. He was standing in the doorway. 'He's in the morgue, sir.'

'Hah bloody hah! Since when did you become a stand-up comic?'

Conrad didn't answer.

'I want to know where he went when he packed up here. And why he never told his parents or his girlfriend. What was he hiding, Conrad? Eh? What the bloody hell was he hiding?'

Brady sighed. He pushed his hand through his hair as he thought about it. It didn't make any sense. His eye suddenly caught something wedged between the carpet and the chipped skirting board under the window. He walked over and bent down. It was a business card for a discreet members club in Newcastle. Brady had heard of it, but for obvious reasons had never been. It was an exclusive members-only club for the moneyed in society. Brady turned it over. The back was blank.

Why would you have this card, Alexander?

'What do the victim's parents do for a living, Conrad?'

'Both retired lecturers. Why?'

'Wealthy?'

'Not from what I've gathered. They're comfortable. But that's it.'

'And from what we've learned so far about our victim, he was by no means affluent?'

'No, sir.'

Brady only had to take a look at the student share that Alexander had been living in for the past eleven months to see that.

'So tell me, why was he wearing Italian designer clothes? The Gucci watch? He had three hundred quid in his wallet, tucked in beside numerous gold credit cards. Tell me how a Masters' student could afford all that?'

Conrad shrugged. 'He's racked up a lot of debt, sir? Students do that. It's not unusual for them to get carried away with bank loans and credit cards.'

'And what would a twenty-two-year-old student be doing with a business card for a members-only club in town?'

'Can I?' Conrad asked, curious. Brady handed it over.

Conrad's eyes gave him away. His face may have been typically impassive, but his eyes showed a flicker of recognition. He quickly attempted to regain control but he was too late.

'How do you know the club?'

Conrad seemed reluctant to explain.

'For fuck's sake, this is a murder investigation. If you know something about this club, bloody well spit it out!'

Embarrassed, Conrad avoided Brady's eyes. 'It is a gentleman's club like you said, sir. Private members only. Been established for years. Some members' families have been in the club since it first opened in 1890. Most members are old money. Some nouveau.'

'And? How do you know it?' But Brady already knew the answer. He understood why his deputy was stood there wishing the floor would open up and he would disappear into the bowels of student housing hell.

'I'm a member,' Conrad answered, his voice barely audible.

'Right,' Brady replied. It was all he could think of to say. He wanted to ask the obvious question. How the hell are *you* a member? But there was a lot about Conrad that he didn't know. He was sure that the ribbing Conrad had received from Daniels and Kenny was partly to do with this class difference. They were Northern working-class lads and proud of it. They wore it as a badge of honour. Conrad was the opposite of them. His background was something he kept very private. As was his sexuality. But now it seemed that both Daniels and Kenny had taken a keen interest in Conrad's personal life. And not in a good way.

'And Alexander De Bernier?'

Conrad looked at Brady. 'He's not a member.'

'You're sure about that?'

'Yes, sir. I'm sure. He was a bartender there.'

'What?'

Conrad dropped his eyes. His face was crimson. 'I've been trying to place his face. I was sure it was familiar. And now . . . this card. I realised where I recognised him from.'

'You kept that bloody quiet!'

Conrad awkwardly shuffled his feet, not sure how to respond. 'I . . . I hadn't seen him there for nearly a year. I assumed he had quit.'

Brady dragged his hair back from his face as he absorbed Conrad's admission.

'Sir . . .' Conrad began.

'Shut up! I'm trying to get my head round this.'

Brady focused momentarily on the Victorian sash window. Droplets of condensation trailed down the glass, pooling onto the mouldy wooden windowsill. Outside, the street lamps threw out a burnished orange haze. The street below was quiet. It was a Sunday night. Most of the students around here would be sobering up after a weekend of drinking and smoking whatever was on offer.

Fuck! Fuck! Fuck!

He couldn't stop thinking about what Conrad had just admitted.

He needed to still his mind. Stop the panic taking hold. He could feel his guts twisting and knotting. He had to get his head around this and figure out what the fuck he was going to do.

'Who else knows that you're a member of this club?' Brady forced himself to ask. His voice was hoarse. The words were strained.

'No one.'

'Daniels and Kenny? DI Adamson?'

'No.'

'Then what the fuck was that all about back in the Incident Room? Daniels and Kenny were cockier than usual. Seemed to think they had something on you. Are you sure it's not this?' Brady said gesturing at the card.

'I'm certain,' Conrad replied, unable to look Brady in the eye.

'Then what the fuck was it about?' Brady demanded.

Conrad remained silent. He kept his eyes averted from Brady's. His face was cold and impenetrable.

Brady didn't need Conrad to admit it. It was his business what he got up to in his private life. Not that Conrad had ever intimated anything, let alone said anything to him. But he knew, all the same. Had caught snippets of private conversations when Conrad had thought he wasn't within earshot. Had put two and two together. Not that he had a problem with it. But what hurt was the fact that Conrad now had an opportunity to just come out and say it. He should have known that Brady would support him. That he would back him up against any form of prejudice from other colleagues.

'You do know that if something is going on at the station and you feel you can't handle it, you can come to me?'

Brady waited until Conrad felt forced to say something.

'Nothing is going on.'

Brady looked at him. Conrad's eyes still avoided Brady's, his cheeks now flushed a deep crimson.

'Have it your way, Conrad. But I'm not an idiot. You know something?' Brady asked, unable to hide his hurt. 'I'm not the one who has a problem with it. Who you sleep with is your business. But it becomes my business when dickheads like Daniels and Kenny start in on you. It's your choice as to whether you see that.'

Conrad looked at him. His jaw was clenched, his eyes narrowed and filled with indignation. It was rare to see Conrad angry. But he looked as if he wanted to knock seven bells of shit out of Brady.

'I didn't say you had a problem with "it", sir,' Conrad replied, his voice thick with derision. 'Now if you wouldn't mind, I'd rather drop the subject.'

Brady held Conrad's hostile gaze. He was tempted to push him. Hard. To just get it out there. Acknowledge it and move on. But he knew from the look in Conrad's eyes that he had already gone too far. It was obvious that Conrad wasn't ready to disclose his personal life – especially not to him. Whether Conrad liked it or not, Brady had known for some time. But if Conrad wanted to keep things on a professional footing then that was fine with him. He decided to let him fight his own battles with the Daniels and Kennys of this world. That was his choice. Conrad had made that perfectly clear.

Brady walked out of the room, then turned and looked back. Conrad hadn't moved. He was still standing in the room with his back to the door, rigid, with clenched hands by his side. 'I trust you on this, Conrad. But—' Brady paused, waiting for a reaction. Nothing. 'If you've lied to me. If you actually know the victim in a personal capacity . . .' He left it unsaid. Brady then turned and left the suffocating, damp, cold room. Conrad remained there: back straight, head held high, fists balled, trying his damnedest to keep it together.

Chapter Fifteen

'What do you mean she's gone?' Brady exploded.

'Just what I said. Look, Jack, it's not my fault.'

'I didn't say it bloody was, did I?' he snapped. But he felt like telling DS Tom Harvey that it *was* his bloody fault. And then some.

Brady sighed as he massaged his temples. Why could nothing be bloody straightforward? It felt like he'd never left the job, or his team. His desk was as overrun with inconsequential crap as ever. An in-tray that was in a permanent state of disarray. Files and papers toppled over one another, spilling onto his large wooden desk. He couldn't quite figure out how, on his first day back, he had such a backlog of paperwork waiting for him. He picked up his red Che Guevara mug and took a hit of much-needed caffeine. He would have preferred a cigarette. He winced. The coffee was cold. He wanted that cigarette.

'Jack? You still there?' Harvey asked when Brady made no attempt to talk to him.

Brady resisted the urge to disconnect. It would have been petulant. He was better than that. But he was struggling to be civil. Conrad had not spoken to him on the drive back to the station. Brady realised that he might have pushed him too hard. And now he had Harvey on the phone telling him his investigation had come to a sudden and abrupt halt.

'Where else would I be? I'm not the one on a fucking plane to fuck knows where!' Brady growled.

His head was pounding. The painkillers he had knocked back had made no difference. The smell of the victim's body cooking in that infernal heat had kicked it off. And the news that Harvey had just delivered was the punch that left him feeling as if someone had taken a baseball bat to his head.

Harvey held his tongue. Waited a moment before he took a chance. 'Look, how were we to know that she would disappear?'

'Oh, let me think. It's your job to be suspicious?'

'Jack—'

Brady cut him off. He didn't have time for excuses. 'Her parents are certain that she's taken her passport?'

'Yes.'

'But she didn't say where she was going?'

'No. From their reckoning she must have got home from work this morning, packed a bag, took her passport and left. They were out. Didn't return from an overnight stay at a hotel until late afternoon. At some wedding they said.'

'That's it? That's all we have?'

'Well, she left them a note saying she was going on holiday for a week with the girls and that she'd be back next Sunday.'

'And what good's a bloody note, eh? Shall I pass that onto DCI Gates? It's OK, sir. Don't worry we haven't got the key bloody witness in our murder inquiry. Yes, the murder inquiry that's going to send the press into a feeding frenzy. No. But what we do have is a note to her parents, kindly telling them she's fucked off on bloody holiday! He'll have my balls nailed to my desk as soon as he finds out.'

Brady breathed out, exhausted. Rant over.

Harvey didn't say a word. He knew not to point out that he and Kodovesky couldn't have foreseen that the receptionist, Chantelle Robertson, would decide to have an unscheduled holiday just before some poor bugger had been found at the hotel where she worked; dead, and with the added bonus of a gender realignment job.

'And tell me again why it's taken you—' Brady paused as he checked the time on his laptop screen, 'four bloody hours to get me this information?' It was just after 7:30 p.m. Five and a half hours since he had first walked into the crime scene. Five and a half long, hard, gruelling hours and still he was nowhere close to understanding why the victim had been murdered. The problem was, the victim was too damned perfect. Or was he? Cracks were starting to show. His girlfriend was understandably distraught that he had been murdered. But it was the circumstances in which Alex had been murdered that were causing Molly Johansson so much angst. It was clear in her mind that he had been meeting someone – for sex. And Brady had a hunch that she was right. After all, she knew him better than anyone else.

Or did she?

What interested, or, to be more accurate, concerned Brady, was the fact that Molly didn't know that Alex had moved out of his student house. Or have any idea where he had gone. Brady had called her on the torturous drive back down Coast Road with Conrad. Despite the fact that she was drunk, she still had enough wits about her to understand the magnitude of what Brady had told her. She had been left not with just the acrid aftertaste of Chardonnay in her mouth but the knowledge that her boyfriend had been lying to her. That, for whatever reason, he had decided not to share all aspects of his life with her. He had been duplicitous. And this duplicity worried Brady.

What did the killer know about you, Alexander?

Brady had to find out what Alexander de Bernier was hiding. The money, gold credit cards, the designer clothes and watch all pointed to something. He needed to find the victim's new address. And when he did, Brady was certain that it would be in keeping with this new moneyed lifestyle. But who was paying for it? After all, Alexander De Bernier was a postgraduate student from an average middle-class background.

Brady suddenly remembered Harvey. His silence was heavy on the other end of the phone.

'I asked you a bloody question!' Brady prompted.

Harvey nearly made the mistake of sighing. 'Because no one was home when we first called.'

It didn't appease Brady.

'And why was that, Tom? Because one of them was already on a plane! I get that you waited around for the Robertsons to return home. What I don't get is you two spending an hour having coffee and cake and a nice cosy chat. What did they do? Get the family photos out and show you incontinent Aunty Dora on her ninety-seventh birthday?'

Brady tried to rein in his frustration. Taking it out on Harvey wasn't the way forward – even if it did momentarily make him feel better.

'The note. What else did it say?'

'That she would call them when she landed,' Harvey answered.

'Has she called?'

'No.'

'And why's that, Tom?'

'I don't know. Maybe she hasn't landed?'

'Precisely. Because we don't know where the hell she's flying to.'

Harvey waited. He knew exactly what Brady was going to say next. Wished he didn't. Or to be precise, he wished he could have said that he had already done it, that he had covered that angle. But he hadn't. He and Kodovesky had had their hands full with Mr and Mrs Robertson. The couple had panicked when the police had turned up on their doorstep. Their initial fear was that something had happened to their only child. Relief had quickly evaporated to a fevered state of anxiety about their daughter's whereabouts. More so when they realised that she was possibly the only witness in a murder investigation. Harvey believed them when they said they had no idea where she had gone. And that this was out of character.

'Outbound flights from Newcastle after twelve p.m. Check every passenger list for her name.'

'Will do, Jack,' Harvey quickly replied, hoping that was the end of it.

'Her parents said that she's never done anything like this before?'

'No.'

'And she doesn't have a boyfriend?'

'That's what they said. Not to their knowledge. And the note said she was going with "the girls".'

'And when did you stop being a copper?'

'What do you mean?' Harvey asked, confused.

'She's a twenty-two-year-old girl with a full-time job, living at home with her parents and she just decided to take an unplanned flight hours before a body was discovered in the hotel where she works. And she's the only potential witness, to boot. Of course she's not gone on holiday with the girls! This stinks as bad as the victim's body. If you can't engage your brain then use your bloody nose, Tom!'

Harvey remained silent. It was the safest option.

'I want her flight and destination on my desk ASAP. If we're lucky, and I'm not holding out much hope here given the hours it's taken us to establish that she's left the country, then she might not have landed. Which means that we can request to have her detained as soon as the plane touches down. I also want a list of all her friends. Check out if anyone knew about this and if she has a boyfriend. We don't know if she booked a seat or someone else did it for her.'

'I'm on it,' Harvey replied.

'Yeah. Here's hoping for our sakes that she's still on the plane. Because I for one don't want to be telling Gates that we've fucked up here.'

Harvey kept his mouth shut. Brady was in no mood for excuses. It was his first day back after five months and it showed. Not that Harvey could fault him. First day back on the job and Brady had been thrown into the deep end. Harvey was just relieved that he wasn't the one reporting back to Gates.

* * *

Brady disconnected the line.

Shit . . . shit . . . shit!

It didn't look good and it didn't feel good.

Where have you gone – and why?

The one thought racing through Brady's mind was whether or not Chantelle knew something – or someone.

All he could do was wait. And hope that what his gut was telling him was wrong. That Chantelle Robertson's sudden disappearance was nothing more than coincidence. Brady's problem? He didn't believe in coincidences.

He had already tried Madley. Repeatedly. Every time, it had cut to voicemail. Too convenient. Too bloody convenient for his liking. Madley was the owner of the hotel, which meant that Brady needed to speak with him. Not that he suspected Madley of anything necessarily; it was just another line of inquiry, but one that he had to follow. After all, Brady had to report every decision he made back to DCI Gates. Every breath he took had to be accounted for – Gates had made that clear as hell when Brady had called him after he'd got back to the station. He wished he hadn't. The upshot was that Gates and DI Adamson would be back on duty tomorrow. Gates had made it clear to Brady not to release anything to the press. That he, with his blue-eyed boy Adamson, would deal with the onslaught from the media. In the meantime he had to keep Gates updated until his return. Brady wondered what the hell the shrink had put in her report. She had signed him off as fit to return to work – so why was Gates acting as if he didn't know his arse from his elbow? Or had the details of this murder affected Gates as much as they had Brady? Because he was certain that Gates would be asking himself the same question.

How? How can it be possible that De Bernier was murdered in an identical way to those killed thirty-seven years ago?

Chapter Sixteen

Sunday: 8:11 p.m.

Brady walked into the Incident Room and stopped. He took stock of the large conference room, capable of holding up to thirty officers comfortably if required. He had been here only hours earlier but now it looked, and felt, radically different, having been transformed from a soulless conference room into the hub of a major murder investigation. He was hit first by the noise. The incessant chatter. Small explosions of it throughout the large room as officers and detectives worked at the desks that were dotted around. Some on computers, others on phones. Two detectives were yelling, trading information across the room at one another. Others were caught up in small bursts of conversation; hushed and private. Despite the fact it was Sunday, and early evening at that, the energy in the room was palpable. Everyone was focused on the job assigned them, all working towards garnering as much information as possible about the crime scene and victim. Brady was already thinking ahead to potential suspects, but until he had discussed it with Amelia, he was holding back. He was also waiting for the results of the autopsy. There was one detail that he needed confirmed before he talked to her.

A press release had been issued. Details had been sketchy – intentionally so. Brady had followed Gates' orders to the letter. They still did not know enough about the victim to understand who could have killed him and why. Aside from the possibility that it was the Seventies killer, 'The Joker'. But then, why would he have started again now?

They were still looking for Sidney Foster, the suspect from the original case. The seventy-one-year-old had seemingly disappeared from his two-bedroomed house in the village of Porthtowan on the west coast of Cornwall. The local police had interviewed his neighbours, who were equally baffled by his disappearance. They said the retired engineer lived alone – always had done – and kept himself pretty much to himself. So much so that they had no idea when they had last seen him. The police knew that he had no living relatives in the North East, or anywhere else in the UK. They needed to find him. He was, as Gates had reminded Brady when he updated him, a key suspect in the Seventies, and consequently now too. But Brady was certain that Sidney Foster's disappearance was just a coincidence. He still had the same instinct which was telling him that Foster had nothing to do with the original murders or the recent one.

The phones were now ringing incessantly as a result of the press release. An appeal had been made for information regarding the missing suspect, Sidney Foster, and Alexander De Bernier's murder. However, that came at a price. An appeal to the public cost time and labour. Most of the information reported amounted to nothing. But it still had to be verified on the off-chance that it led to something of importance to the case.

Brady didn't know whether it was the pulsating glare of the overhead fluorescent light or the buzzing noise it made that had upped the level of the pounding in his head. All he knew was that the Incident Room felt chaotic and claustrophobic. There was nowhere to hide in here. It was bustling with activity. There were at least fifteen people working on various tasks. Four of them consisted of Brady's team – his old team. But the dynamics weren't the same anymore. Not one of them had looked at him when he had walked in. Intentional or otherwise, their attitude towards him had changed. Whether he could attribute that to the five months they had been reassigned to DI Adamson while he had been on sick leave, he couldn't say for sure.

He could feel a knot in his stomach at the thought of DI Adamson. He wasn't entirely sure whether the return of Adamson tomorrow would see him unceremoniously kicked off the case. Brady walked over towards the two sash windows, aware that eyes were on him. He could feel them burning into him. Then the whispers. Low and questioning, and damned obvious. After all, he had just returned after being held hostage and tortured by ex-militia types. Brady was certain that was what interested them. Speculation about whether he would actually return to active duty would have done the rounds. Wagers would have been placed. Who won, who lost, Brady had no idea. But he knew this station well enough to know that his colleagues would have gambled on the likelihood of him returning in one piece. And now that he had quelled that conjecture, natural curiosity would take over as to whether he really was fit enough, physically and psychologically, to be back at work. Let alone to be acting as Senior Investigating Officer of a murder inquiry of this magnitude.

Brady exhaled slowly as he stared out of the large window at the residential street below. It was quiet. Unusual for a Sunday evening. The burning ochre sun had faded hours ago and been replaced by a crisp, cloudless dark night. The day had been glorious; unusually hot, with dazzling skies and a sea reminiscent of warmer climes. As if to balance the ledger, the night would be bitter and biting; a reminder that it was still March.

Brady suddenly felt cold. The chilled darkness taking hold of him. He had a job to do. One that he didn't relish. But it went with the territory.

'Ready, sir?'

Brady nodded without turning.

'You up to this?'

'Yes,' Conrad replied, 'over the worst, I reckon.'

'Good. Because you'll need a strong stomach.'

★   ★   ★

Brady tried not to gag. The smell was noxious. And it was every-where, burning his eyes and his nose. A sickening combination of overpowering antiseptic cleaner and the gaseous smell coming from the victim's body.

'You all right there, Jack?' Wolfe wheezed as he looked over at him.

Brady nodded.

'What about him?' Wolfe puffed, his voice raspier than usual, his eyes now on Conrad.

Brady turned to Conrad. He was typically pale and thin-lipped. Not an unusual look for the morgue.

'Yeah, he's good.'

'In my medical opinion he doesn't look so good,' Wolfe disagreed.

'Your medical opinion, my arse! Your patients are bloody lucky they're already dead!'

'Why the hell do I put up with you, laddie?' Wolfe asked with a wry look. His soft, well-educated Scottish lilt betrayed his affection for Brady. Despite having lived in the North East for the past thirty years, Wolfe's Edinburgh roots had never left him, his accent a constant reminder he was from north of the border.

'Because I'm the only person with a pulse that can stand being around you.'

Wolfe shook his head at him. 'See what I have to put up with, Harold?'

Brady automatically looked across at Harold; a tall, gaunt-looking young man with long reddish-blond hair tied back in a ponytail and a red goatee beard plaited into two strips. He was the anatomical pathology technician. In other words, Wolfe's assistant. Not that Wolfe ever used him. Harold's job comprised of standing silently while Wolfe carried out the autopsy. His other job would be to move whichever cadaver was requested from one of the thirty body refrigerators in the hospi-tal onto the mortuary slab. Wolfe, being the compulsive obsessive type, would not allow Harold, or anyone else for that matter, near his work. He would be the one who would weigh stomach contents, organs and the like. Harold was a glorified hospital porter.

Harold didn't flinch at Wolfe's remark. Nor did he look at Brady. Instead, his acne-marked, permanently flushed face remained focused on the deceased's body. If he had heard Wolfe, he didn't show it. Brady turned back to Wolfe. The pathologist had already forgotten Harold and was now focused on the victim's body. Wolfe was a short, bald, overweight man in his late fifties. His large, jowly face spoke of a man who liked his vices a little too much. A heavy smoker and a drinker with a rather robust appetite, who had no intention of letting the gruesome nature of the job get in the way of his pleasures. Despite his short stature and expanding waistline, Wolfe was always impeccably dressed. He wore tailored suits, silk shirts and matching ties. And he never failed to be seen without a silk handkerchief in his breast pocket. However, in the morgue he was suitably attired in a white surgeon's gown and skull hat with white rubber boots. His delicate, chubby hands were covered in white latex gloves. To anyone's eye he looked like a surgeon. But Wolfe's job as the Home Office pathologist was to find evidence that could help the police prevent another murder. To prevent another dead body ending up on a morgue slab waiting to be cut open.

Wolfe was the best Home Office pathologist in the force, but it came at a price; a high one. He had a drink problem. One that would begin at lunchtime and follow through to the next day. He wasn't a raging alcoholic. Instead, he was a functioning one. He turned up at work on time; showered, dressed and breathing a combination of Listerine and stale booze. It wasn't a secret. Even Chief Superintendent O'Donnell was aware of Wolfe's indiscretions, but chose to ignore it. Wolfe was too valuable to let go. He had an unerring nose for finding crucial evidence on a body. Evidence that ultimately led to convictions.

But Wolfe was not as infallible as everyone believed – himself included. Eleven months ago, he had scared himself, and Brady.

The deceased had been a sex-trafficked victim. Not that they knew it at the time. But the body had the tell-tale signs. She had been branded – her skin burned with initials and a scorpion symbol – and brutally raped. Wolfe had slipped up. For once his liquid lunch had proven too much and he had missed some key evidence. At the time, Brady had thought it would have shaken Wolfe enough to make him consider quitting. Not the booze – the job. But he hadn't. Nor had he quit the booze. Somehow he had managed to keep hold of his position – because until that one fuck-up, Wolfe had been faultless. As far as Brady's superiors were concerned, the pathologist walked on water. He delivered where others failed. But his time was numbered. He was part of the old school. The old guard that were being driven out, slowly but surely. Soon, there would be no place for Wolfe. He had the tolerance of a rhinoceros when it came to drinking. But it was starting to show. It had been five months since Brady had seen Wolfe and in that time the booze had significantly affected him. That, and the twenty a day. Ironic for a man who dealt with the deadly effects of cirrhosis of the liver and lung cancer. Even more ironic given the fact he had asthma and was at least five stone overweight.

Brady stood up straight and clasped his hands behind his back. He was trying his best not to react to the carnage lying in front of him. Unlike Wolfe, he didn't have the stomach for this. He turned and glanced at Conrad. Still grim-faced. Brady didn't know whether it was the sight of the victim's mutilated body that made him look like he wanted to puke or if it was being in the same room as Wolfe. For some reason, Conrad and Wolfe didn't quite see eye to eye. But Brady knew that the enmity was more on Wolfe's part than Conrad's. And Wolfe had a knack of letting you know if he didn't like you. Needless to say, Wolfe didn't have a lot of friends.

Brady looked down at the bloody mess before him. He could feel his stomach writhing, objecting to the odious smell coming from it.

'You don't look so grand, laddie. You want Harold to fetch you the bucket?' Wolfe asked.

The 'sick bucket' was always on stand-by for new coppers or for the particularly gruesome autopsies, where the bodies had been left to fester for weeks, allowing eye-watering bodily gases to build. As was the case with this body. It had been left to cook too long and the unbearable heat had sped up the decomposition process.

Brady swallowed hard. Forced himself to remain in the room. 'No . . . I'm fine.'

'Aye, sure you are! You look as green as your laddie behind you,' Wolfe pointed out. He turned to Harold. 'Fetch the sick bucket.'

Harold did as instructed.

'Down there, Harold. I guarantee one of them will end up using it.' Wolfe wheezed, gesturing towards the two grim-faced detectives.

Brady ignored Wolfe's snide comment. He was too busy wincing as he looked at the gutted, gruesome thing that was the victim. His ribs had been forced apart and his organs removed. A pool of black blood swilled around in what was left of the empty carcass. It was a shocking sight. And then there was the distinct, unforgettable odour that was putrefaction. Brady had been around the morgue enough to know that once dead, bacteria would escape from the body's intestinal tract, finding its way into the corpse. It would then begin the process of literally breaking it down. Thirty-six hours after this process had begun, the neck, abdomen, shoulders and the body's head would begin to turn a discoloured green. This would be followed by bloating – caused by an accumulation of gases produced by the bacteria.

'How long has he been dead?' Brady asked as his eyes rested on the victim's head. Even to Brady's unskilled eye, the body had considerably bloated.

'From the body's rate of cooling, the degree of rigor mortis and the partially undigested food in his stomach, he'd been dead for approximately fourteen hours before he was discovered.'

'Time of death would be after eleven p.m. then?' Brady asked.

Wolfe nodded. 'Roughly. Give or take an hour.' He paused for a moment as he looked at the body. 'The reason it looks as if he's been dead for longer than he has is because the decomposition was exacerbated by intense heat in an airtight room.'

'Is that bloating on the victim's face, or has it been caused by strangulation?' Brady asked. Despite being repulsed, he forced himself to look at the bulging eyes and protruding tongue.

Wolfe shook his head. 'It's the gases inside that's causing the tongue and eyes to bulge forward like that. Like I said, the heat sped up the breakdown of the body. If he had been left there for another twenty-four hours who knows what kind of mess he would have been. We would have been scraping him up off the bed. Not for the fainthearted, that's for sure. Eh, Conrad?' Wolfe laughed wheezily as he turned his attention to Brady's deputy.

Brady looked at Conrad. He was clearly not amused.

But Wolfe was right. If the room had been booked for two nights, instead of one, then the maid would have respected the 'Do Not Disturb' sign on the door. The body, left to fester for another twenty-four hours, would have literally melted in the heat. Death was not for the fainthearted. It was an ugly, messy affair. And the longer it was left untreated, the uglier it got.

Brady held his breath as he tried not to react. Wolfe had performed most of the autopsy already, which accounted for the nauseating smell. The internal organs still had to be put back into the chest before the deep Y-shaped incision which worked from the shoulders down to the groin could be stitched up and the body put back together. But first the internal organs would have to be individually weighed and documented. The slightest detail noted.

'Have you established cause of death?' Brady asked.

'Well . . . this was an interesting one. You see the damage to the neck?' Wolfe said as he pointed at the mottled bruising around the victim's swollen, blackening neck.

Brady nodded stiffly.

'The victim was choked. The ligature marks are consistent with that of a rope. The injuries on the ankles and the wrists are consistent with rope burns like these . . .' Wolfe traced his finger over the raw flesh on the victim's throat. 'But strangulation wasn't the cause of death, despite the fact the hyoid bone, the thyroid, and the cricoid cartilages are fractured. The damage clearly indicates that he was asphyxiated. But he was suffocated, not strangled to death. I found small particles of black fibres embedded in the airways and lungs. I've sent them off to be analysed, but I guarantee they'll match the duct tape that was wrapped around his head. It's consistent with when someone is smothered to death by a cushion or a pillow. Fibre traces always show up in the lungs. Imagine you're fighting for your life, trying to breathe, it's only natural that you'll breathe in loose fibres from the object restricting your airways,' Wolfe said. 'I'm sure you came to that conclusion yourself, given the condition the victim was found in.'

Brady nodded. 'Yeah, but sometimes they fool you.'

'Hah! Don't they just,' Wolfe laughed. It got the better of him and he ended up coughing and spluttering as he tried to steady his breathing. Instead of abating, it worsened.

Worried, Brady watched as his lips started to turn blue. He was bent over now, gasping.

'You all right, Wolfe?' Brady didn't wait for an answer, but walked hurriedly over to him. 'Shall I call for help?'

Unable to speak, Wolfe shook his head. Embarrassed, he fumbled around his pockets. Brady realised he was searching for his becotide inhaler.

Finding it, Wolfe sucked on it at least six times. Brady was counting. Each time he held his breath to allow the medicine to decrease the inflammation in his lungs.

It was a sobering moment for Brady. He waited, arm on his friend's back as he remained bent over, attempting to breathe.

'You're a silly old fool. You know that?' Brady chided affectionately once Wolfe had got his breathing under control.

Wolfe shook his head. 'Other way round,' he wheezed.

'You know how many people died last year from asthma attacks?' Brady said, frowning.

'What? Are you my doctor all of a sudden?' Wolfe said, straightening up. Tears mingled with sweat streaked down his jowly, crimson face. He walked over to the sink, pulled out some paper towels from the dispenser and delicately dabbed at his face.

'Twelve thousand people in 2012. That's a lot of deaths. Two a day.'

Wolfe stopped dabbing his face and looked at Brady.

'What's this? You looking for a new job as a government health advisor?'

Brady shook his head. Partly in irritation, partly affection. 'I care, you old fool. Someone has to.'

'Well . . . I'm fine. As you can see. It's this poor laddie here that you should be focused on. Not me. Poor big bugger. Physically in his prime. Lungs and heart in excellent condition – as you would expect. Other organs were healthy. Apart from the fact they were in an advanced state of autolysis.'

Wolfe's keen eyes noticed Conrad's bemused expression. 'It's a process of self-digestion. The body's enzymes begin to go into meltdown after death. Autolysis can be speeded up by extreme heat, as in this case here. Or slowed down by extreme cold.'

Brady smiled at him. But there was a sadness there. Wolfe was deflecting. He had had a serious asthma attack. He knew from old that they were regular occurrences. What worried him was the frequency and severity of these attacks.

'So, as I was explaining before, this poor laddie was strangled first. He then had his penis hacked off. Quite a messy job. I counted at least twenty cuts and puncture wounds to the groin area. The penis was also significantly damaged. It was covered in stab wounds,' Wolfe said, staring at the mutilated groin.

'Intentional?' Brady asked. It was a rhetorical question. The evidence too damning.

Wolfe looked at Brady as if he had lost his mind. 'Yes, without a doubt. He wanted to hurt. These stab wounds and punctures occurred before death. I would also hazard a guess that these injuries happened before his penis was sliced off.'

'He was tortured?' Brady asked.

'Exactly,' Wolfe answered as he stared at the victim. He then looked up at Brady. 'You do know that these injuries here are consistent with—' He let the words hang, heavy and ominous.

Brady felt physically sick. And this time it had nothing to do with the repellent smell and physical condition of the body. It was the gut-wrenching reality of what Wolfe had just said. Or to be precise, what he had left unsaid.

'Jack?' Wolfe began when Brady didn't respond to his question, 'you do know about the previous murders? Mind you, I doubt you were even born when they happened. But happen they did. Nasty and brutal. Just like this one. No. *Exactly* like this one.'

'Yeah . . .' Brady croaked. His throat suddenly restricted. 'I know about them. And I thought this one looked similar to the others.'

'Not similar. They're virtually identical. I've already had a look at the old pathology reports on the seven victims from 1977.'

'What about . . . ?' Brady didn't need to spell it out.

'Semen?' Wolfe asked.

Brady waited.

Wolfe shook his head. 'That's the only difference between this and the first seven. Definitely no traces of semen at the back of the victim's throat, unlike the earlier murders.'

Brady felt like he had been punched. He breathed out slowly. It didn't make any sense. The murder was practically identical apart from that crucial difference; the murderer had not ejaculated in the victim's throat prior to gagging him and then binding his head in black duct tape.

Why?

Brady stared at what was left of the victim. Then it hit him. The crucial difference between the Seventies and now was the radical advances in forensic science. Traces of the murderer's semen on the victim would have been too easy. The police would have had his DNA and if the killer had been charged with any other crimes, they would have had an identity. The man responsible for the Seventies killing spree would be all too aware of the exponential leaps in forensic technology. The same with a copycat killer. The result was the same; it made Brady's job even more difficult. He had been counting on traces of sperm being recovered from the body.

'Shit!' Brady muttered.

'That's one word for it, laddie,' Wolfe said with a raised eyebrow. 'I wouldn't want to be in your shoes right now.'

In anticipation, Brady had had the evidence retained from the Seventies cold case sent to the lab. A shirt that one of the victims had been wearing had been contaminated with blood and semen. Brady was hoping that they'd be able to ascertain a DNA sample from the old stains. But he would have to wait. He had been told that it could be at least four days before he heard back, despite the price he was paying to have it expedited.

The police laboratory had long gone. Draconian budget cuts had resulted in all forensic evidence being outsourced to the cheapest private laboratory. In instances like this, there was no one Brady could ring to ask a favour. And definitely not on a Sunday. He had no choice but to wait. The DNA evidence would be crucial. It could lead them to the Seventies murderer, which in turn, could point them in the direction of Alexander De Bernier's killer. However, Brady wasn't sure whether they would be able to get anything conclusive from it. All he could do was hope. Wolfe looked at Brady. '*Mortui vivos docent.*'

Brady frowned at him. 'Tell me how "the dead teach the living" helps me right now?'

'It's all there, Jack. On the body. You've just got to want to see it,' Wolfe said as he looked at the victim.

Brady followed Wolfe's gaze. He stared long and hard at the disembowelled body laid out grotesquely on the slab before him. He wanted to see it. That wasn't the problem. The problem was, no matter how hard he looked, it didn't make any sense to him.

Chapter Seventeen

Sunday: 11:08 p.m.

His phone rang. For the briefest of moments he thought it was Claudia returning his call. No one else would ring at this hour. Disappointment told hold when he looked at the caller. It was a mobile number he didn't recognise.

He clicked 'answer' and waited.

'Detective Inspector Brady?'

'Yeah.'

'It's Joanne. The receptionist from the Royal Hotel.'

'I remember.' Brady leaned back in his chair and closed his eyes. He was fucked. All he wanted to do was go home and crawl into bed. Forget about how shit his first day back had been. Hope that tomorrow would be better. He sighed. 'It's late, Joanne. What can I do for you?'

'It's what I can do for you. There's someone who might be able to help you with last night.' She paused, as if considering whether or not to tell him.

'Go on,' Brady said as he held his breath. He was up against a dead end. And that scared him shitless.

'Well, I've heard that Chantelle had some trouble checking in those two coaches of guests last night. They'd got really rowdy and were basically being knobs, if you get my drift. So she called for backup.'

'Who was that?' Brady asked.

'Carl. Bartender who runs Mr Madley's club next door. He came and worked that shift with her.'

Brady breathed out as he absorbed the information. He had already had feedback from Harvey and Kodovesky regarding Chantelle Robertson's sudden departure. She had boarded a Thomson flight at Newcastle Airport bound for Malaga at 15:30 p.m. It had landed three hours later. Harvey and Kodovesky had been just too late. Otherwise, she would have been held by airport security. The Spanish police had been notified that she was wanted for questioning, but they had no idea where she had gone once she had landed. She had booked a return flight. No accommodation. And Brady did not have the luxury of time to wait around until she decided to show up at Newcastle Airport next Sunday. That was, if she did decide to come back. Right now, Brady was sceptical. He had no idea why she had disappeared. Her story of going on holiday with the girls had been fabricated. Nor had she been booked on the flight with a potential boyfriend. She had bought her ticket at the airport, and as far as Harvey and Kodovesky could tell, she had travelled alone. Brady could request the airport's security footage to see if she had company, but right now, he hadn't decided whether to expend time and energy looking through security tapes. The murder team were already stretched.

Another concern was Martin Madley's whereabouts. Brady had confirmed that Madley and two other men had boarded a flight yesterday afternoon at Newcastle Airport. Worryingly, it was to the same destination as Chantelle Robertson. Brady had tried to ring Madley again. Still no response. It wouldn't have surprised Brady if Madley had a villa in Malaga. But would he be able to trace it? Madley was no fool. He covered his tracks and his assets well. If Madley had some luxurious Spanish retreat, Brady doubted he would actually register it in his own name. Tax evasion being one of many reasons.

Brady thought it was obvious that Chantelle Robertson had flown out to join Madley. But why would Madley want his hotel receptionist with him? Brady had already done the maths. Her flight had been booked at 12:40 p.m., forty minutes after the

126

victim's body had been discovered by the maid. It wouldn't have surprised Brady to find out that Madley had been informed before the police. Forty minutes later, Chantelle Robertson was at the airport booking a flight to Malaga.

Coincidence? No.

'Thanks, Joanne. That's really helpful.'

'Yeah, well, I thought you'd want to know.'

And she was right. Brady wanted to know why Carl the bartender had forgotten to mention this when questioned. Brady and his team had spent hours going through all the statements taken from staff and residents alike. All Madley's staff had been interviewed – apart from Chantelle – including the ones who worked in the Blue Lagoon next door. A photograph of the victim had been shown to everyone questioned. There was a chance that he had been drinking in the club before ending up in the hotel room. Seemingly he hadn't. But then, apparently, Carl had not been completely truthful with his version of events either.

All thoughts of Claudia and returning home disappeared. There was one place he needed to be, regardless of the time – the Blue Lagoon nightclub. Brady grabbed his coat and phone and left without a word to the rest of the team. He had told them to knock off at midnight unless any significant leads came in. They'd reconvene in the morning at 8:00 a.m. In the meantime, they had his number.

'Didn't expect to see you here,' Brady said.

Carl looked at him.

'The place is dead,' Brady clarified. It was an understatement. Then again, uniformed presence next door, accompanied with police tape sealing off the premises, could do that for business.

Carl shrugged. Non-committal. 'I work when I'm told to work.'

Brady expected no less. Carl was the bartender for the Blue Lagoon nightclub. But in reality, he was Madley's sentinel. His personal look-out, who watched everything and everyone. He was a barman, receptionist, bouncer and Madley's most loyal employee. With good reason. The Mancunian bartender had lost his eye working for Madley, the result of a hard punch from a handful of keys hidden in a clenched fist. Some angry, loud-mouthed pisshead had lost his temper and had decided to take it out on the wrong guy. But Madley looked after his own. Carl had received the best private medical care possible, no expense spared. Whether Madley had seen to Carl's attacker afterwards, Brady couldn't say for sure. But he had heard that he had been dealt with in a manner befitting his crime.

Brady liked Carl. Liked his attitude. He wasn't intimidated by anyone – including Brady. Carl may have only been in his early twenties but he had an ease about him that placed him as older than his years. He was a handsome kid. Even after the loss of his eye. Never short of female attention. Tall, physically fit, with tousled curly dark blond hair and designer stubble – throw in the fact that he was always impeccably dressed and it was fair to say he had 'presence'. And he knew it. He was a young Madley in the making.

'Coffee?' Carl said as he walked over to the state-of-the-art stainless steel ECM Heidelberg Barista espresso coffee machine.

'Rather have a scotch,' Brady replied. He hadn't realised how much he needed one until now. It was late. He was tired. And he was no further forward in the case.

Molly Johansson had been no help. And Alexander De Bernier was proving not to be what he had expected. Instead, one word stood out – duplicitous. The alarm bells weren't ring-ing in Brady's head – they were screeching. Then there was the missing link – the receptionist who was on duty last night. Chantelle Robertson.

His head was pounding. His primary concern was that whoever had killed De Bernier would strike again. In the Seventies, The Joker had waited just seven days after he killed his first victim before murdering the second one. By the end of his killing spree his cooling-off period had dropped to less than twenty-four hours. The prospect of this happening again terrified him.

'Thanks,' Brady said when Carl put the double measure in front of him. 'Where's the boss?' He knew the answer but he just wanted to make sure that they were reading the same script.

'Spain. Golfing holiday.'

Brady nodded. He'd heard exactly the same from the receptionist. Not the destination, just the holiday part. But Brady needed to talk to Madley. He just needed to make sure that Madley hadn't pissed off any business associates. It wasn't that long ago that an undercover copper had been dumped, mutilated and bleeding out, in the Gents of the Blue Lagoon. It had transpired that Madley had made a serious enemy of some powerful people. They'd wanted him to join forces with them, or alternatively, let them buy him out. Madley had refused, not liking the 'business' they dealt in. Human trafficking and sex slavery to be precise. The price? A copper left for dead as a warning in his place of business, bringing with it the police.

'What's your take on what happened next door?'

For the briefest of moments, Carl looked thrown by the question. 'I dunno. You tell me. You're the copper.'

Brady stared at him, trying to glean whether he really knew anything. That was the reason he was here. Hoping that Carl would throw him some scraps of information. Anything. If there was one person who would have noticed something unusual, out of character, it was Carl.

'Where were you last night?'

Carl looked amused. 'What? I'm a suspect now?'

'I assume you're looking after things while Madley's away.'

Carl shrugged. 'Maybe.'

Brady persisted. 'What hours did you work yesterday?'

'The graveyard shift,' Carl answered.

'Very droll. I just need to know if you saw anything. Or anyone acting suspiciously.'

'I've already told your lot. I didn't see anything.'

Brady nodded. Took a mouthful of scotch. He savoured the burning in his mouth as it slid down the back of his throat. It wasn't a single malt. It was a blend; scratchy and raw. Nonetheless, he appreciated the numbing sensation that followed the brash taste.

He considered his options. He needed information. And he knew Carl, despite his pretence, was holding something back. The problem was that Carl could be an obstinate bastard at times.

Two more swigs and the scotch was gone. Brady placed the glass down on the bar and looked Carl in the eye. 'Let me level with you. A serious crime took place in the Royal. At a guess, it happened late last night or in the early hours of this morning.' Brady lowered his voice as he continued. 'One person checked into that room: John Smith.'

Carl waited.

One theory was that the victim had checked into room 212 under a pseudonym. Another was that it was his killer who had checked in. Brady was looking into both. 'But two people were there. One left the room alive. That's the one I'm interested in.'

'I can see why,' Carl replied.

'You worked the hotel front of desk last night. Why?'

It took Carl a moment to answer – as if he was distracted, or thinking of a reply. 'You lot know what trouble we get down here on weekends. Our clients tend to be stag and hen parties by the coachload. They come from all over the place. Birmingham, Glasgow – you name it. And they come looking for one thing. To escape. Get drunk, get laid and then get out of Dodge. But at times they can be too much for the receptionists that work here. Sexual harassment and all that. So Mr Madley asked me to look into it.'

Brady nodded. It was a good enough answer. Plausible even. And it matched with what he had already been told.

'What about Gibbs and that wiry little runt from the East End that your boss is so fond of?'

'They're both accompanying Mr Madley.'

Madley had assumed that the 'heavies' Gibbs and Weasel Face were with Madley. It matched with the flight bookings to Spain yesterday afternoon. And if he had them with him, he meant business.

He knew Carl was lying about the front desk situation. Something else was going on. But he wasn't here to find out what. Brady was only interested in finding De Bernier's killer.

'You know I still can't get hold of the receptionist on duty last night?'

Carl didn't look too surprised.

'By all accounts she took a flight to Malaga early this afternoon.'

Carl didn't react.

'Did she mention it to you last night?'

'No.'

'Seems odd, don't you think? The flight was booked around midday. I wonder why she would suddenly decide to go to Spain. By all accounts, her parents had no idea. She came home, got her passport, packed a suitcase and she's gone. No explanation. Nothing. And she's scheduled to be back in at work for eight tomorrow morning.'

Carl shrugged. 'She never mentioned it to me. Maybe she'd had enough of Whitley Bay? Opted for the sunshine instead.'

Brady waited. It was clear that Carl was not going to offer anything else on the subject. He took out a photograph of the victim. Slid it across the bar towards Carl. Watched as he picked it up.

'Don't recognise him.'

'Look again.'

Carl made a play of scrutinising the photograph of the victim, then shook his head. 'No. Definitely didn't see him.'

The photograph would be on all the front pages tomorrow morning and across the news headlines, even though Brady had tried his best to stop the speculation. He'd followed Gates' orders and kept his mouth shut. Fed the press the usual crap, that the police were busy investigating a suspicious death. That if the public had seen anything suspicious or had any relevant information to contact the police. The details of the murder had been vague, but word would get out. No matter how hard Brady tried to keep the press at a distance, they had a way of sniffing out a story. He had already had Rubenfeld, a hard-nosed hack with the *Northern Echo* – and Brady's snitch when there was something in it for him – on the phone. Brady could hear him salivating at the thought of a front page story. Brady wasn't throwing him any scraps. He couldn't. The reason was simple: the headlines would incite public hysteria. He thought of the press cuttings he had read from the Seventies murder cases. The press had dined out on The Joker for years afterwards. He had never been caught. No resolution. No punishment meted out. Nothing. He had just disappeared.

Until now.

'Look, Carl,' Brady paused, 'you've got a choice. Give me something, then I'll back off. Don't, then I'll keep coming back. And each time, I'll bring backup to re-interview every member of staff. Then I'll pick apart the hotel next door, this nightclub and your boss's offices upstairs. I know that Madley won't be best pleased to have the police poking around. Not when all you have to do is tell me what you know.'

It was clear from Carl's expression that he didn't like being threatened. Who did? But Brady had no choice. Carl knew something. He had to. Otherwise, why was Brady standing here?

Carl nodded. His expression was cold, eyes hard as nails as he stared at Brady. 'All right.'

'Go on,' Brady instructed.

'Some girl came in after half ten. Drunk and hysterical. She had a taxi waiting for her outside.'

'What did she look like?' Brady asked, not wanting to jump to conclusions. But he already had a good idea who Carl was talking about.

'Tall, thin, blonde. Good-looking, if her face wasn't so messed up from crying. She had mascara running down her cheeks and smeared lipstick across one cheek. Not a good look. Her accent wasn't from around here. Sounded South African.'

Brady recognised the description: Molly Johansson.

'Why had she turned up?'

'Claimed her boyfriend was in the hotel. That she knew he was here. She wanted us to check our records. See what room he was in so she could "chop his cheating balls off!" Her words. Verbatim.'

Brady resisted the urge to grab hold of Carl's suit jacket and shout in his face that he was a fucking idiot for not mentioning it earlier. Somehow he reined it in. 'What did you do?'

'I told her to go home and sober up. That we weren't in the business of revealing the identity of our clients. Regardless of whether they claimed to be the wife, the girlfriend or the boss. That client confidentiality matters.'

'Did she do as you asked?'

'What do you think? She refused to leave. Said that she'd wait for him at the hotel bar. That he would have to leave at some point. I said that we didn't want a scene and she assured me there wouldn't be one.'

'You didn't see her leave?'

'No. The taxi left. She went and paid it. Came back in and went to the toilets. Sorted her face out and then headed for the bar. Last time I checked, she'd gone. I imagine she'd given up waiting and ordered a taxi.'

'What time was it when you noticed that she had gone?'

Carl shrugged. 'Before midnight.'

Brady couldn't hide the incredulity he felt.

'What?' Carl asked.

'You didn't think that was significant in any way?' Brady did his best to keep his voice controlled. It was proving difficult.

'She was some young, drunk, girl mouthing off that her boyfriend was in one of our rooms screwing someone else. How does that figure in a murder investigation?'

Brady shook his head. 'For a smart bloke, you can be exceptionally fucking stupid!'

'Do you know how many fights I have to sort out? Girls claiming their boyfriend's just shagged some lass in the toilets over there?' Carl gestured towards the Gents. 'Loads. Take the hotel next door. People come here wanting privacy. If they want to bang someone else other than their missus, that's their prerogative. It's not for me or you to moralise. Life's shit. Straight up. So if people want to fuck around, have a shag-fest right under my nose, I look the other way. Not my business. That's what I'm paid to do. '

'Since when did you turn so cynical?' Brady asked.

'I was born that way.'

Brady resisted the urge to tell Carl what he thought of him. There was one final question. 'You definitely didn't give her the room number?'

'I already said no.'

'Was there any point when you left the reception area?'

Carl gave it some thought. 'Yeah, a couple of times. I had to check on the club here. I also got Stu the chef to make me a steak sandwich. So, yeah . . .'

'Chantelle Robertson was left on her own then?'

Carl sighed, seeing where Brady was taking this.

'Could she have given the room number to her?'

'Bit hard if the guest was registered as "John Smith". Chantelle's a sweet girl but you've got to spell things out for her, if you get my drift.'

'All right,' Brady continued, trying to keep his voice level, 'say Chantelle checked her boyfriend in. So she'd seen him, yeah? He's a good-looking bloke. Or at least he was. If the girlfriend had a photo on her phone, which I'm sure she would do, and she showed it to her, then Chantelle would recognise him. I'm sure there's not many blokes who walk in the Royal looking like him. He'd be memorable. Especially to a young woman.'

Carl stared at Brady. 'Like I said, Chantelle isn't exceptionally smart.'

134

'Thanks for the drink,' Brady said and then turned and walked towards the front doors.

'No problem.'

'Carl?' Brady said, turning back.

'Yeah?'

'Tell your boss I need to speak with him. It's a matter of course, given what's happened here. But also tell him I want Chantelle Robertson on a flight back to Newcastle ASAP.'

Carl did not react.

Brady left it. He turned and made his way out of the club.

Once outside he stood for a few moments, letting the chilled spring air cool his temper down. He had bigger problems than his overwhelming desire to go back in there and lay Carl out cold. He needed Molly Johansson brought in for questioning. Three reasons: firstly, she had lied; secondly, she had a motive; thirdly and the most crucial detail of all, she could be placed at the crime scene. Or in the vicinity. It was good enough for Brady to consider her a credible suspect.

What about The Joker? The original killer?

Maybe she knew about the earlier murders? Read old newspaper articles. Found about his signature – the Joker card.

But how the fuck could she know about the way he killed his victims?

Brady thought of the crime scene. The first thing that had struck him was that there hadn't been a struggle. The victim hadn't put up a fight. Which meant he had willingly allowed himself to be restrained. It implied that he trusted whoever had bound his hands and legs. He knew them.

The victim's girlfriend was clearly upset when Brady had visited her. Angry was a more accurate description. Was it possible that she had suspected her fiancé of having an affair and had followed him last night? Could she have killed him?

Brady attempted to silence the thoughts that hit him like pellets, disabling him.

He wanted Molly Johansson brought in for questioning. Now.

Brady steadied himself. It was too late to interview her tonight. He was too tired to think straight. He couldn't risk the chance of screwing this up. He would wait until the morning. From the amount she had been knocking back, he knew that she would be in a comatose state right now and he didn't believe she'd be going anywhere. A patrol car knocking at 6:00 a.m. to bring her in would be good enough.

The majority of the team had already gone home, including Conrad, but a few had stayed to cover the nightshift. Just in case. For a moment Brady was undecided as to what he should do. It was nearly 1:00 a.m. He didn't want to face Claudia, didn't have the energy. He knew that she would have been drinking. Would still be drinking. Meaning that she wouldn't be in a good state – mentally or physically. The beat-up old leather couch under the leaking window in his office seemed really appealing. He desperately needed a few hours' sleep, just to get his head together. After all, DCI Gates and DI Adamson would be returning later today. He would have a lot of answering to do.

MONDAY

Chapter Eighteen

Monday: 1:39 a.m.

Brady had gone straight home. It was after one in the morning and he was mentally and physically exhausted. He needed a few hours' sleep and then he would be back at his desk first thing.

He opened the door, hoping that Claudia would be asleep. He was too tired to deal with anything else right now. But she wasn't. He could hear the mumbling of some Sky arts programme coming from the living room.

He breathed in deeply as he mentally prepared himself.

'Hey,' he said as he walked into the living room.

She didn't even look up at him.

'I haven't woken you, have I?' Brady said softly as he knelt down beside her.

She was lying on the sofa, staring blankly at the flickering TV screen.

'Claudia?' Brady whispered as he stroked the unruly curls back off her forehead.

It was unusually clammy.

'Claudia?' Brady asked again as he gently tilted her face towards him.

Her dull, lacklustre eyes stared back without any recognition.

Then he noticed something lying on the wooden floor beside her limp, outstretched arm.

He didn't need to pick up the small plastic bottle to know that it was empty. Alongside it was a bottle of single malt. Two-thirds gone.

Shit! Shit! How many? How many tablets were left?

Brady tried to remember when he had last taken some. He breathed out. Tried to stop himself panicking.

Fucking remember!

Then it came to him. Four. There would have only been four left. He had picked up the repeat prescription on Saturday morning and still had the bottle in his jacket pocket.

Thank fuck . . .

He had been careless. He hadn't thought. Hadn't realised she would go through his things looking for his prescription painkillers. If she had taken the full bottle . . .

Stop it! She didn't. She's fine . . . But if she had . . . she would be dead.

'Claudia?' Brady asked, scared.

Nothing. Her eyes were lifeless. Her frail body slack and limp.

He pressed his lips against her forehead and then held her against his chest as he tried to figure out what to do. He could take her to hospital to have her stomach pumped but then she would be on suicide watch. The doctors would intervene. Check her medical history. Find out what had happened to her five months ago. Her parents would be notified. Claudia wouldn't want that. She would hate him if this got out. It was just a desperate attempt at scaring him. That was all. He had left her for the first time in five months. What did he expect? She had panicked. Brady should have come home earlier. Or at least, he should have checked up on her.

She fucking took prescribed painkillers! Washed down with two-thirds of a bottle of scotch. What more do you want?

Brady blinked back the tears. It was only four tablets. That was all.

'Baby? Can you hear me?' Brady asked, as he cupped her lolling head in his hands.

Claudia mumbled something. He could see a flicker of recognition in her eyes.

'Jack?' she mouthed. It was barely audible. But it was enough. Enough for him not to take her to hospital.

'I'm here now,' he answered. 'I'm here with you.'

Tears slipped down his face as he stroked her pale cheek. He didn't know what he would do if he lost her. He couldn't imagine his life without her.

'Come on,' he finally said. 'Let's go sort you out.'

He scooped her weightless body up in his arms and carried her upstairs to the bathroom.

He needed to put his fingers down her throat. Force her to vomit the tablets and scotch back up. Just to be sure. Then he would put her in the shower. Cold water would help bring her round. Then coffee. Lots of it. Gone were thoughts of sleep. Or of the ongoing investigation. All Brady had on his mind was Claudia.

He lay with her in the darkness. Held her to him. Tight. Secure. She was breathing gently. Asleep now. It was after four-thirty in the morning. He had spent the last few hours forcing her to be sick. He had then held her shivering body against his as he sat with her on the floor of the shower cubicle as icy cold water hit them both. Finally she had come back to him – just. Embarrassed. Apologetic. Crying. Pleading that it was an accident. That she hadn't intended to harm herself. She had had a headache. That was all. She had only taken four tablets.

Brady hadn't argued that there had only been four tablets in the bottle to take. The question that tortured him was what if there had been more.

Exhausted, she had finally fallen asleep. But first, he had made Claudia promise she would never do this again. Even if it was, as she claimed, just an accident.

Chapter Nineteen

Monday: 7:30 a.m.

Brady had showered and changed. He had also downed two cups of unadulterated black coffee. It was as strong as a kick in the bollocks from a mule. And it had the desired effect. He had also taken some painkillers to silence the deafening pounding in his head from lack of sleep and was now at his desk. The early hours felt surreal. Daylight made him question whether Claudia's overdose attempt had actually happened. It dispelled the fear. The doubts. The recriminations. Brady had lain all night with her on his chest, his arms around her, scared to fall asleep in case she stopped breathing. He was in no doubt that he was responsible for what had happened to Claudia both five months ago and last night.

He had left Claudia a note. It was honest. In it, he told her that she'd scared the hell out of him. That they had to talk. He needed to know if she needed help. Not just his help. Professional intervention. He couldn't lose her. He had come close to it. Too close.

Brady exhaled; slow, deliberate. He had to get his head together. It was his second day back on a major murder investigation. He had to put all thoughts of Claudia to the back of his mind – for now at least.

A patrol car had been ordered to pick up Molly Johansson at precisely 6:00 a.m. There was a reason that police raids always happened early in the morning. It was the element of surprise. No one expected someone to be kicking their door down at that time of the morning. Nine times out of ten, the suspects would be lying in bed scratching their nads, completely unaware. No time to hide.

Brady had a briefing scheduled in thirty minutes. The team had been here since 6:00 a.m., prepping themselves for the day ahead. He was eager to get the briefing over with and interview Johansson, who was currently being held in an interview room. She had kicked up a fuss – understandably – but Brady expected no less. He stared at the open files laid out on his desk, steeling himself for the day ahead. He had been renewing his knowledge of the Seventies serial murders. He wanted something to throw on DCI Gates' desk when he returned. Something that would knock the smug smile off DI Adamson's face. Other than his fist.

There was an abrupt knock at the door.

'Yeah?' Brady called out as he looked up.

Conrad opened the door and walked in. 'Brought you something. Reckon that you wouldn't have eaten last night. Not after spending the evening in the morgue.' Embarrassed, he placed a greasy paper bag on Brady's desk. 'Bacon, two fried eggs in a stottie. Fresh from the canteen.'

Brady looked at him, genuinely surprised. He had forgotten this about his deputy – his unique ability to look out for him. To take care of him when he failed to do so himself. And he was right, Brady hadn't eaten since yesterday morning. A lot had happened to get in the way of his appetite. 'Thanks, Conrad.'

Grateful, he picked up the greasy bag. 'Two fried eggs?' Brady asked, as he took the stottie out the bag.

'Yes, sir. And with runny yolks.'

Brady broke into a grin. 'Shit, Conrad! Only you would think of that,' he said, touched by the sentiment. It may have been a small gesture, but Brady couldn't remember the last time someone had actually taken time to consider his likes and dislikes. 'You'll make someone a good wife one day. You know that?' Brady joked. But as soon as he had spoken the words, he could see that he had hit a raw nerve. Brady thought back to the conversation in Conrad's car yesterday evening. It was not what had been said, it was what had *not* been said.

Brady shook it off. He hadn't meant anything by the joke. He took a bite of the stottie, making sure the bag was placed directly below in case of any spillage.

'What time did you get to bed?' Brady asked between mouthfuls.

'About one-ish. You?' Conrad asked taking a seat.

'About the same time,' Brady answered. But it was a lie – and he was sure it showed. It wasn't the best look for his second day back on the job. Let alone for the day DCI Gates would be marching into his office demanding to know what the fuck Brady was doing about the Joker-style murderer they had on their hands. Gates would want to know if the original killer had resurfaced or if they had a copycat murderer to contend with. Either way, it would mean that the body count would go up. But right now, Brady just wasn't so sure that they had a serial killer on their hands.

Admittedly, he'd brought the victim's girlfriend in for questioning. Was she a suspect? Simple answer – yes. Could she have killed her boyfriend? Again, yes. Jealousy and betrayal were powerful driving forces. Combine them with alcohol, and it could be fatal. But did he really believe she could be responsible? Brady would answer that once he had interviewed her. But it was Molly Johansson that had made him think that this was more about the victim than the Seventies Joker murders. What troubled Brady was, why set the murder scene up to look as if Alexander De Bernier had been killed by the original Joker murderer, or even a copycat killer? Why go to all that effort to try and fool the police? It didn't make sense to him.

Unless it was a clever attempt at getting away with murder.

Brady looked at Conrad. It was clear something was troubling him – but Brady knew if he asked him outright, Conrad would clam up.

'You had a chance to have a look at these?' Brady said, gesturing at the files on his desk.

Conrad nodded. 'Took them to bed with me last night.'

'You need to get out more,' Brady said, as a smile played at the corners of his lips.

Conrad didn't reply. But his reaction told Brady that something wasn't right. He was being overly sensitive, which wasn't like Conrad.

'You all right?'

'Fine,' Conrad said. The finality of his tone and his expression made it quite clear that he didn't want to talk.

It was clear to Brady that something was wrong.

'So . . .' Brady began, changing the subject. 'What do you think?'

'I honestly don't know. De Bernier is physically very different from the Seventies victims. If it was the same murderer, why change his type? It doesn't make sense.'

Brady nodded his agreement through a mouthful of bacon and egg.

'Sir?' Conrad said, gesturing to his chin.

'Yeah . . . thanks.' Brady picked up the paper bag and used it to mop up the egg yolk.

'You know the seven young men were roughly the same age as our victim?'

Brady nodded. 'Between the ages of nineteen and twenty-two.'

'Yes, sir,' Conrad agreed. 'But there is one other difference with the MO . . .' Conrad faltered.

'Go on,' Brady instructed.

'All the earlier victims were gay,' Conrad stated.

Brady considered Conrad's comment as he wiped the remnants of the stottie onto the paper bag before screwing it up and throwing it into the wastepaper bin. It was one he had considered himself. But from the statements taken at the time and the reports about the victims' lifestyles, nothing definitive stood out to say these young men were definitely gay. If anything, the original case notes detailed the victims as typical young men who had been drinking in town and had somehow been picked up by The Joker and driven to the remote locations, where they were then murdered and left until found by dog walkers and joggers.

'How so? Admittedly, all seven victims had traces of sperm in their mouths and at the back of their throats. But that doesn't make it consensual, or make these men gay. I know McKaley's suspects were gay but as for the victims . . .'

He could feel his headache starting to ratchet up a gear. It was too early in the morning to be having this conversation. And if he was brutally honest, he could not see where Conrad was going with it. 'Explain to me what you saw that I didn't that suggested the Seventies victims led a high-risk lifestyle? If they were gay and had been picked up by the Joker for casual sex, then surely McKaley would have released a statement warning the public that there was a murderer targeting young, gay men looking for sex?'

Conrad did not answer.

'Conrad?' Brady was starting to get irate. Conrad's reluctance to speak was not helping the dull, nauseating pain in his head. 'Is this to do with the victim? You admitted that you recognised him from this gentleman's club in Newcastle. Is there more to it than that?' he asked, worried.

Brady could feel the bacon and egg curdling in his stomach. If he was honest, he didn't want to know the answer. He had tried his damnedest to downplay what Conrad had admitted yesterday – that he recognised the victim. But why hadn't he informed Brady at the outset? The victim's photo driver's licence was recent. Surely Conrad would have recognised him from that? For some reason it was the business card for the members-only gentleman's club that had sparked that cognitive leap. Not that Conrad had voluntarily admitted it. The flicker of recognition when he saw the card was what had given him away.

Conrad frowned at his boss. His eyes flashed with mild irritation that Brady could even ask the question. 'No. I just recognised him as a bartender there. I've never even talked to him.'

Brady sat back. He weighed up what Conrad had just told him. He had one choice – accept it. Otherwise he would have to take Conrad off the investigation; and that in itself would ignite speculation, creating a fire of controversy that would run wild throughout the station. And from what Brady had witnessed, there was already enough speculation about Conrad on the job to last him a lifetime. The upshot was, Brady trusted him. Always had. But there was one question going through his mind: had Conrad only told him this detail because Brady would have eventually found out? It was a given that they would look into every aspect of De Bernier's life – including his jobs. Would Conrad be on a members list for the club? Undoubtedly, yes. Conrad had had no choice but to divulge this personal information before the team got their hands on it. Brady would have to carefully consider how he would play this hand. His loyalty was to Conrad and if that meant excluding his name from the list of members that the team would be privy to, then Brady had no other option.

Brady stared hard at his deputy. It was getting to 7:34 a.m. 'Go on. Tell me what DI McKaley missed at the time. And make it fast. I've got a briefing to give and I also have one hell of a headache that you happen to be making a damned sight worse. Get to the point.'

'It was where these victims were picked up, sir,' Conrad explained.

Brady was none the wiser. 'I don't understand. What did I miss? I know there's the Pink Triangle in Newcastle but these victims were not found anywhere near there.' He leaned forward. 'Look, the first thing I questioned was the common denominator between these victims. They were all murdered in different locations. DI McKaley states in each murder report that he believed the victims had been picked up as they were making

147

their way home from a night out in town. That he believed they had been offered a lift and then . . .' Brady faltered, 'well . . . you know the rest.'

'May I?' Conrad questioned as he gestured towards the rest of the files.

'Help yourself,' Brady said. He watched as Conrad placed each of the seven victims' crime scene photos in front of him.

'This victim, Derek Thompson, was found close by Byker Bridge. On one of the secluded paths leading off from it. Ideal location, because there's lots of cover there. Overgrown bushes to hide behind,' Conrad paused and looked at Brady to see if he was getting his drift. 'But McKaley never made an issue of the locations. Apart from the obvious, that they were ideal places to take someone and murder them without being interrupted.'

Brady waited, still unsure.

'This victim here, William Humphries? Found in Leazes Park. Again, nothing was made of the area where the body was found.'

Brady still wasn't certain that he understood what Conrad was getting at.

Conrad's face flushed scarlet. 'All these locations are well-known gay cruising areas, sir. They're very popular now and I'm sure they would have been as popular in the Seventies.'

Brady sat back. He was silent for a moment. 'You're certain?'

'Yes. One hundred per cent,' Conrad answered as his face coloured even more.

Brady was about to ask how he knew but stopped himself. Conrad looked pained enough as it was without Brady making the situation worse for him. It was Conrad's business. Brady had made it clear that if he wanted to discuss anything that he was there for him.

'All right. So your theory is that the unknown suspect cruised these areas? He knew that gay men would be there and he effectively hunted them? Picks up a young man who fits his type and goes off somewhere more private and . . .' Brady stopped. He didn't need to repeat what he had done to his victims. They had both spent long enough looking at pictures of the mutilated bodies the killer had left at the crime scenes. 'So why the hell wouldn't McKaley and his team have known that at the time? Why didn't he acknowledge that the victims were gay? That gay men were being targeted?'

'Firstly, the murderer didn't go off somewhere more private. They were picked up by the killer exactly where they were murdered. They would have been there looking for sex. They wouldn't have been picked up as they made their way home after a night out in Newcastle as McKaley suggests.'

Brady was surprised at Conrad's assertion. It didn't make sense to him. 'So, why did McKaley choose to ignore such crucial evidence?'

'Do you really want my honest opinion?' Conrad asked.

'Go on,' Brady instructed.

'From what I've heard, McKaley was an extreme homophobe. He wanted promotion and thought this case would bring him it. But he didn't want his name or reputation tarnished by heading a serial murder investigation into the mutilation of gay men. He presented the victims to the press and public as young heterosexual men targeted by some perverted homosexual. Gives it a better spin for the media, rather than young gay men looking for casual sex who end up murdered as a consequence. The press and the public wouldn't care about the victims. Not back then. It's only recently that there has been a change in the public and media's attitude towards gay people. And there's still a huge amount of intolerance out there.'

Brady frowned. 'Where the hell did you hear all that about McKaley?'

'Let's just say he had a really nasty reputation when it came to gay men. He beat one of the gay suspects to within an inch of his life. Nobody did anything to stop him. And there were at least four witnesses.'

'Christ, Conrad! Are you sure you've got your facts straight on this? McKaley worked right here. People I worked with in the past worked with McKaley. You're not suggesting that they covered up for him?'

'It happened in one of the holding cells in the basement,' Conrad answered factually, ignoring Brady's question.

The look in his eye told Brady that he was serious – deadly serious. 'Who told you this?'

'Martyn Jenkins, one of the men arrested back then. A call came in from his niece late last night. He was really distressed and wanted to talk to us. Before . . . before it was too late. He recognised Sidney Foster's name on the ten o'clock news last night. Put two and two together when he saw the report on De Bernier's murder.'

Brady was incredulous. 'I was told by his doctor that he couldn't be interviewed because he was critically ill. That he had a very limited time left.'

Conrad nodded. 'That's correct. I talked to his niece at around ten forty-five last night. She insisted it was urgent. That he wanted to talk to the police ASAP. She said he was worried that he didn't have long and he needed someone to listen to him. By all accounts he was very distressed so I went straight there and stayed with him until he fell asleep at twelve-thirty. Then I went home and reread all of McKaley's files on the Joker case.'

Brady ran a hand back through his hair in disbelief. 'Why didn't you think to tell me?'

'I did try to call you. You didn't answer your phone.'

Brady suddenly remembered seeing the missed call from Conrad when he had been chatting to Carl in the Blue Lagoon. Once back home, he had forgotten about it; too busy dealing with Claudia.

Brady sat back as he thought about the magnitude of what Conrad was saying. He was already aware that physically De Bernier could not have been more different from the Seventies victims. De Bernier was taller and more muscular than the earlier victims who had all been under five foot eight and slightly built. Again he wondered whether his murder had been staged to fool the police. To have them chasing their own tails, looking for the original Joker or a copycat murderer when the actual killer was sitting back watching them make a fool of themselves.

Brady finally spoke: 'So I take it Martyn Jenkins was the one McKaley beat up?'

Conrad nodded. 'Yes, sir. Left him with four broken ribs, a broken arm and a ruptured spleen. Not to mention the damage to his face.'

Stories like this weren't unheard of, but Brady was staggered to hear about McKaley acting in such a manner. As far as he knew, the retired detective had had a distinguished and impeccable career.

'How did he get away with it?'

'Said that Martyn Jenkins had fallen down the steps to the basement when being led to his cell. No one asked any questions. But Mr Jenkins said that a crowd had gathered and had cheered McKaley's "faggot beating", as he called it. Said he was trying to "straighten the queer out and if that meant beating the shit out of the queer fucker then he would," verbatim, sir. Mr Jenkins said those words are etched on his mind, like the scars on his body.'

Brady found himself regretting eating the bacon and fried egg stottie. He felt physically sick when he thought of what McKaley had done – and got away with. 'Did Jenkins report it?'

He knew from the look on Conrad's face that it was a naïve question.

'No. He had been arrested for having sex with a man in the Gents in Grainger Market in Newcastle. He didn't feel he had the right to lodge a complaint. Nor did he believe that anyone would do anything. Let's just say the police in those days saw him as subhuman.'

'I see . . .' Brady replied, voice low. 'But why did he want to talk to us now?'

'Because he wanted to make sure that history wouldn't repeat itself. That this wasn't going to end up becoming some homosexual witch-hunt like McKaley's investigation. He said that McKaley even laughed as he kicked him in the balls, telling him that the victims deserved to have their penises cut off and stuffed down their throats. That if he had his way, he'd congratulate the murderer for dealing with queers in such a befitting manner.'

'Shit! I . . . I don't know what to say . . .' Brady said, shaking his head.

'There's nothing to say, sir. I just wanted to tell you that McKaley was a homophobic bastard who didn't give a damn about the investigation he was heading. One other thing,' Conrad added, 'The Seventies victims were—'

'Physically different to our victim,' interrupted Brady

'Yes, sir. Also, De Bernier wasn't picked up or found in a gay cruising spot. Unlike the earlier victims, he was heterosexual, as far as we know.'

Brady sat back and clasped his hands around the back of his head. 'So . . . in your opinion De Bernier wasn't murdered by the same killer? But all eight victims were killed in exactly the same way. None of it is coincidence, Conrad. Only the police and the original killer knew the details of the murders. Even the Joker card left cupped in the palms of De Bernier's hands was identical to the others. It was from a 1960's vintage Waddington deck. Now how the hell would a copycat murderer know that detail?'

'The press? Didn't they nickname him "The Joker"?'

Brady sighed. Frustrated. 'Yes, but they didn't know the make or the year of the deck. All they knew was that it was a Joker card.'

'I see,' Conrad answered.

Brady thought about what Conrad had told him. 'For what it's worth, if you're right, then it changes things. It changes the motive. It makes the Seventies case about gay killings. What does that say about the murderer? If he was gay too, perhaps that he hates himself and the urges and desires that consume him. If you're right, then he actively sought out his victims in gay cruising spots. Gained their trust enough to tie them up. Because, like De Bernier, none of the seven earlier victims put up a fight. He then has oral sex, forced or otherwise, and mutilates their groin – the object of his hate and simultaneously the object of his desire. It both attracts and repulses him. Finished, he chokes them and wraps duct tape around their mouths, securely gagging them and continues wrapping the tape over their noses, eyes, until the head is completely covered. He removed their sexual organ and hides their faces. Both parts of the body that attracts him.'

Conrad nodded.

'And our victim? Don't you see that as a hate crime?'

'Yes, sir. I'm just not convinced it's the same killer. And it's nothing to do with the fact that our victim didn't have traces of semen in his throat. I think that's down to the murderer being aware of DNA evidence.'

Brady was still waiting to hear if forensics had found anything on the bedding or pillows. But as yet nothing had shown up. Which suggested to him that perhaps the killer was not interested in sex. Perhaps De Bernier had been murdered for personal reasons, unlike the sexually motivated Seventies murders. The victim's girlfriend immediately came to mind. Molly Johansson had a motive. She was also seen at the hotel on the evening when her fiancé was killed. What were the odds?

Brady pushed his chair back and stood up. 'Well, we'll soon be able to see whether your theory is correct.'

Conrad looked at Brady, puzzled.

'I've had Molly Johansson brought in for questioning.'

'What has she got to do with her boyfriend's murder?'

'That's what I am about to find out.'

Conrad was unable to disguise his surprise at this news.

153

'Trust me, I have good reason to bring her in.'

Brady thought about what Martyn Jenkins had said to Conrad. 'I appreciate you taking the time to talk to Mr Jenkins. I'm sure he would have felt unburdened disclosing what he did to you. And I appreciate you telling me about McKaley. I know this must be difficult for you.'

As soon as he said it, he regretted it.

The flash of anger in Conrad's eye said it all.

'Fuck it, Conrad! I'm not McKaley. All right? And I never will be.'

'I never said you were,' Conrad replied. But his tone had an edge to it.

Before Brady had a chance to say anything else, Conrad was already walking out the office. He knew that the attack on Jenkins by a homophobic SIO had deeply affected his deputy – more than he wanted to admit.

Chapter Twenty

Monday: 8:10 a.m.

Brady looked around the Incident Room. It was crammed. Some faces he recognised, others he didn't. This was his murder team. It comprised fifteen detectives and officers, male and female, but mostly male. All watching and waiting for Brady, filled with pent-up frustration. Agitated that he hadn't finished the briefing so they could get on with the job at hand – finding Alexander De Bernier's killer.

He winced inwardly as he looked at the whiteboard. The mutilation of the victim's groin still made him want to puke. Still made his testicles shrivel upwards into nothing. Brady's mind was filled with questions as he forced himself to continue looking at the graphic images of the faceless body. His eyes moved to various photographs of the crime scene. It again confirmed there had not been a struggle, that the victim had known their killer. This fact was glaringly obvious. Nothing had been knocked over. The pillows and cushions were still on the bed. Blood was the only sign that something had happened. An ugly blight upon the magnolia backdrop of the hotel room.

He then looked at the crimes scene photographs taken of the others in situ. The seven young men who had suffered the same fate as De Bernier, thirty-seven years earlier. Brady sighed. He still couldn't get his head around it. The murders all looked as if they had been committed by the same hand, the knife wounds uncannily identical. Could he explain it? No, not yet. But there was no denying that the first seven victims were a type. That the recent victim did not fit into that type concerned Brady. The crime scene and the killer's signature suggested the same perpetrator. The MO said something entirely different. Unless . . . Brady stopped himself. He would need to hear Amelia's opinion first.

He turned to the room. 'Anyone?'

No one spoke. Not that this surprised him. They were equally confounded, all looking to him for answers. The problem was, Brady had none.

Brady glanced around the room. And waited. The team automatically shifted their gaze so it wouldn't be in a direct line with his.

He sighed. Heavily. Looked back at the whiteboard, at the flurry of scrawled words barely legible to anyone else's eyes but his. He had furiously scribbled what they knew so far. And that wasn't a lot.

'The victim?'

Brady could feel the nervous energy in the room mounting. No one wanted to say it. Everyone thinking it. *Which victim?* Because up there on the whiteboard, they all looked identical: mutilated bodies, faceless heads bound in black tape.

Brady turned from the photos of the victims and looked at Daniels and Kenny, sitting side by side. Both slouched as low as physically possible, trying their damnedest to look inconspicuous.

'Daniels? What do we have so far on De Bernier?' Brady asked. He could see Daniels wince at the question. He nervously ran his hand over the stubble that covered his scalp, then shifted forward and sat up straight. Finally, he cleared his throat as he scrabbled through his notebook.

Brady waited. He had given Daniels and Kenny a list as long as his arm late yesterday afternoon. Admittedly it was 8:10 a.m. on a Monday morning. But he and the team had had all last night to try to find some much-needed answers. As well as the two hours they had already clocked in this morning.

'We've checked the calls made to and from the victim's mobile phone. Including texts. There were numerous calls from the mobile number that belongs to the victim's girlfriend. Throughout the Saturday she bombarded him with calls and then texts. He didn't answer her calls. Nor any texts.'

'Any other calls or texts made to De Bernier's mobile that day?'

Daniels shook his head as he looked back down at his notes. 'No, sir.'

'Check with the mobile company. For all we know he deleted texts that he received or sent.'

Brady looked around the room again. Still silent. No one wanted to talk. They had three potential killers: the original Joker, a copycat killer or a murderer who wanted De Bernier's death to suggest that either of the first two were behind it. But they were no further forward in establishing which of the three scenarios they should prioritise.

They still had no word back on the suspect from the Seventies case. It seemed that Sidney Foster had simply disappeared, taking with him his vintage 1977 red Ford Capri car. A call had been put out on his car but there had been no sightings of it. As yet, no DNA evidence had been found at the crime scene. If it had, it would have made Brady's job a hell of a lot easier. He would've known whether Foster was actually responsible.

'Sir? There's something else,' Kenny ventured, nervously breaking the tension.

Brady turned to him. Kenny shot Daniels a look. But from the expression on Daniels' face it was clear he had no intention of speaking.

Kenny looked back at Brady standing there, waiting. In no mood for any more surprises. 'The victim's girlfriend . . .' Kenny faltered at the expression on his boss's face.

'Go on,' Brady instructed, steeling himself.

'She continued texting him up until ten forty-five p.m. Some of them are . . . well . . . quite concerning.'

157

'How?' Brady questioned. The time element had caught his attention. Wolfe, the Home Office pathologist, had said that the time of death was sometime after eleven p.m. 'Just to be clear, all communication from her definitely ended at ten forty-five p.m.?'

'Yes, sir. But there was a barrage of unanswered texts between eight p.m. and ten forty-five p.m. Each one escalating in anger. The last one reads—' Kenny looked down at his notes, 'yeah, here it is: "Fucking bastard. I know where you are and who you're with. I'm in the bar downstairs waiting to cut your fucking cheating dick off!"'

Brady steadied himself. The room was suddenly bristling. He had already told them that he had Molly Johansson in custody, waiting to be interviewed. He caught Conrad's quizzical eye. It was clear everyone in the room believed he had been privy to this knowledge prior to the briefing.

He looked at Kenny. His eyes darted nervously back down to his notes. His expression was deadly serious. He knew he and Daniels had fucked up in a big way by not informing Brady immediately.

Brady decided he would deal with them afterwards. Now wasn't the time. Humiliating them in public did him no favours. After all, he could count on one hand how many people he trusted in this room. Most would do anything to further their careers. Jobs were at an all-time premium. Coppers were being re-interviewed for their own job. Some didn't even have that luxury, finding themselves competing for a lower level rank. Less pay, less responsibility and one step closer to the dole queue. Brady would not make it public that he had two fuckwits on his team, simply because it made him look as if he didn't know what the hell was going on with his own murder investigation. Which was true, apparently. But it was something that he didn't want to share.

Chapter Twenty-One

Monday: 8:19 a.m.

Brady now needed Dr Amelia Jenkins' opinion. He was at a loss. He had a few ideas, but nothing concrete. The case was a conundrum. Every way he looked at it, he had three potential directions. He could not ignore that the original suspect from the Seventies had disappeared. Could Sidney Foster have come back to the North East? Could he have murdered De Bernier? But why? Alex was physically different from the victims in the past. And he had a girlfriend, unlike any of the earlier victims. That made him very different from the original Joker's 'type'.

The problem Brady had was in coming up with a watertight explanation, one that he could take to DCI Gates when he showed up. He was struggling. He also knew Gates would not be impressed that they still had no word on the whereabouts of the retired engineer – *or* paedophile.

Brady had since discovered that another serious allegation had recently been made against Foster. That a twenty-five-year-old man had gone to the police alleging Foster had groomed him from the age of eight years old and had then sexually abused him until the age of fifteen. When asked why he hadn't come forward earlier, the victim had claimed that he had been too ashamed to disclose what had happened. Brady felt there was a correlation between Foster's sudden disappearance and the allegation that had been made. His gut told him that the fact they couldn't track him down was just coincidence and had nothing to do with the murder. Whether Gates would accept that was another matter entirely.

He looked across at Amelia, hopeful that she could shed more light on the similarities between the cold case and the current murder investigation. She was sitting with her hands folded in front of her, composed, relaxed, but very much on the ball. She had been intently watching everything that had unfolded in the briefing. Nothing got past her. Not that Brady would expect it to. After all, she was the police shrink. She waited for him to speak. Her sleek bobbed hair fell against her pale cheek. Dark eyes focused on her notes in front of her. He watched as she unconsciously tucked the stray hair behind her ear.

'Dr Jenkins?' Brady asked as he turned to the whiteboard. Unlike Daniels and Kenny, he didn't need to spell it out for Amelia. She knew her job; knew what he was asking from her.

She followed his gaze, her eyes slowly taking in the carnage on the whiteboard.

Brady turned back to her, expectantly. Her eyes met his. Cold. Brady's expression remained impassive but inwardly he felt as if he had been punched in the guts.

She cut free from Brady's gaze and looked down at the open file in front of her. She nodded, as if to herself, before beginning: 'The signature marks left at all the crime scenes, or should I say on all the victims, are identical. That should concern us.'

'Why?' Brady asked. He knew the answer, but it was for the benefit of the rest of the team.

'Simply put, this signature is the calling card of one person. It is a trademark. A unique message left behind by the murderer,' Amelia answered.

Brady nodded for her to elaborate.

'As you've already pointed out, rope was used as a method of restraining both the Seventies victims and De Bernier. Could it be pure coincidence? Yes. But what is not coincidental is the fact that the handcuff knot used to restrain the Seventies victims was also used on Alexander De Bernier. I don't know if any of you are familiar with knots but this particular one is not that common. That's one example of the murderer's signature. Also, this perpetrator is not just interested in killing his victims. He has his own unique style. He binds them, strangles them until I imagine they start to lose consciousness and then he waits,' Amelia said as she looked around the conference table, 'waits for them to regain consciousness so they are fully aware of it when he mutilates them. We know that there were no traces of semen found in the victim's throat or on his body this time around. But we are still waiting to hear if any traces were found on the bedding or pillows.'

Amelia turned and suddenly addressed Brady. 'What about biological evidence from the Seventies cases?'

'Traces of sperm and blood were found on one of the victim's T-shirts. But whether the lab will be able to get anything from that after so long, I don't know. I've had the T-shirt sent off, so we've just got to wait. It would make our lives a hell of a lot easier if they did manage to extract DNA from what was left. Here's hoping that the advances in forensic science work in our favour.'

Amelia nodded in agreement. He again noted there was no intimacy in her eyes. Whatever history they had, professional or personal, she had wiped it clean.

'We may not have matching DNA samples from the old case and this new murder to confirm it's the same perpetrator, but as I was explaining, we do have the perpetrator's signature. Details of which were only known to the police and the killer.'

'Like what?' Hamilton asked.

Brady looked at him. He was young. In his early twenties. This was no doubt the first time Hamilton had heard about the Joker murders. And the first time he had met Dr Amelia Jenkins. His keenness to prove himself as competent and worthy of being part of the murder investigation was driven by his desire to impress the forensic psychologist. Brady knew the young lad stood no chance with her. He was most definitely batting out of his league. Even if Amelia liked younger men, Hamilton was still very much a boy. He had a lot of maturing to do, lacking the cynicism that so often came with the job. That, Brady noted bitterly, would come later. A few more years on him, and Hamilton would lose his idealism. The belief that you can actually make a difference to the world. Brady just had to think of the Seventies serial murder case left to rot in files on the third floor of Whitley Bay police station, the mutilated victims' bodies either cremated or buried, long gone and forgotten – until now. Defeatism got to them all eventually. It was hard for it not to. Not when a killer was still on the loose, thirty-seven years after his crimes – and might even have killed again.

'Well, a perpetrator's signature can include posing or branding victims in a particular way. With these eight victims, all were left sitting half upright, hands bound behind their backs, legs restrained at the ankles, heads bound in black duct tape and their severed penises stuffed in their mouths. If you look at these close-ups of the victims' groins you can see that they've all been repeatedly stabbed. This torture and disfigurement of the victims' bodies is another part of the killer's signature. Some perpetrators will take items of clothing, jewellery or even body parts as keepsakes. Again, this would be that individual's signature. Something unique to them that goes beyond just the act of, say, raping or killing.'

'Like the Joker card?' Hamilton suggested.

Amelia nodded. 'Exactly.'

This was one of the troubling aspects of the murder. Brady still couldn't figure out how De Bernier's killer could have known such details from the Seventies case, unless they were the same person. Or . . . Brady stopped himself. He found it difficult to accept that someone within the police could be responsible. But he knew that they had no choice but to follow it up. Regardless of Molly Johansson. He had to investigate all the possibilities.

'What does the signature say about our killer?' Brady asked.

'The signature, as you know gives us clues about the perpetrator's past, personality and emotional and mental state. The psychological driving forces behind any crime can tell us a great deal about the perpetrator. Here,' Amelia said as she pointed to Alexander De Bernier's mutilated groin, 'is the main signature – sadistic torture. Now this can be a sign of underlying emotional issues, such as anger and self-hatred. This is very much the case here. Our perpetrator feels the need to gain control over his victims. They were all males between nineteen and twenty-two years old. All white, with dark hair.'

'Tell me about The Joker,' Brady said.

Amelia looked at him. Held his gaze for a moment longer than was comfortable. Or at least, comfortable for him.

'In 1977 he would have been roughly in his early twenties. He would have had a history of mental illness and I suspect you will find that he had been institutionalised. He would have spent time in a young offenders' institute or in and out of mental hospitals from as young as fifteen. Up until then he would have been seen as a social deviant. Destructive, angry; a social misfit. He would have started hurting and torturing animals early in his youth. He likes inflicting pain and, consequently, lacks any empathy with his victims. I expect he would have been tested for antisocial personality disorder, psychopathy and aggression.'

'Is he a psychopath?'

'Well, psychopathy is a personality disorder in which the individual typically exhibits amoral and antisocial behaviour. The other common traits are: diminished empathy and remorse, disinhibited behaviour, pathological lying, failure to accept responsibility for their own actions. They also lack the ability to love or to establish meaningful, personal relationships; suffer from extreme egocentricity and can have superficial charm and can be cunning, manipulative and very intelligent. I wouldn't be surprised if our killer shows some or all of these traits.'

'Why? What would have made him this way?' Brady questioned.

Amelia shrugged. 'Nature or nurture? Most likely he was genetically predisposed to commit these sadistic acts,' she said as her eyes drifted back to what their unknown perpetrator had actually carried out. 'But typical contributing factors can be abuse as a child, whether emotional, physical or sexual. More than likely to have happened at a young age and continued up until his teens.' Amelia paused for a moment as she looked around the table. 'Jeffrey Dahmer, a serial killer also known as the Milwaukee Cannibal, was neglected as a child and later in life was diagnosed as suffering from borderline personality disorder. He raped, murdered and dismembered seventeen young men between 1978 and 1991. Many of his later murders involved necrophilia, cannibalism and preservation of body parts. Including penises, and all of the skeletal structure.'

'Shit!' Daniels cursed. 'That's one sick bastard!' Sitting beside him, Kenny looked equally as disgusted.

'Don't worry, Daniels, I don't think you're his type,' Amelia said.

Daniels didn't look impressed with her comment. But a look from Brady made him keep his mouth shut.

'Do you think that's what we're dealing with here? A British equivalent to Jeffrey Dahmer?' Brady asked.

Amelia weighed up the question before answering it. 'Yes. You potentially could have a series of murders again. Just like in the summer of 1977. And like Jeffrey Dahmer, he might start getting more and more extreme.'

'And he's gay?' Brady asked. He already knew the answer but he wanted the rest of the team to hear it.

Amelia nodded. 'Most definitely.'

Brady looked around the team. None of them looked too clever. Not surprising, given the topic of conversation early on a Monday morning.

★　★　★

'I'm sorry, how can you be so sure that the murderer responsible for either the serial killings in the Seventies and the one committed on Saturday evening are gay? Heterosexual men are known to commit sexual acts on other men. It's a dominance thing. Just like when men rape women. It's rarely about the sex act itself, it's primarily about humiliating the victim.'

Brady looked at the muscle-bound forty-something detective sergeant who had asked the question. He had a square jaw and a sneering mouth. He recognised him as one of DI Bentley's men, brought in from North Shields station. He was sitting with his thick, bulging arms crossed, clearly not accepting her words.

Amelia looked at him. If his rancorous attitude bothered her, she didn't let it show. 'I agree with you. Look, I'm well aware of the myth around male rape that all perpetrators are homosexual. And that the reverse is true, that heterosexual men make up the majority of perpetrators who assault or rape other men. But I can assure you that this isn't the case here. Yes, the victims were specifically targeted because of their sexuality. But their murderer was not some homophobe on a rampage. Anything but. He himself is homosexual. But the rage and disgust he takes out on these young men is really what he feels about himself. He despises his sexual attraction to men, which is why he so violently mutilates their groins. He not only severs the penis, he humiliates the victim by gagging them with it. That's after he's ejaculated in their mouths. Then he smothers them in black tape, hiding their identity. Faceless and genderless, he leaves them to suffocate to death. It doesn't take a psychologist to point out the significance of that.'

The DS looked even less convinced. 'So, what you're saying is that the victims were all gay as well as the murderer?' he asked, raising an eyebrow at her. 'What do you know about their backgrounds that was overlooked by the investigators at the time?'

Again, Amelia seemed untouched by the sarcasm in the detective sergeant's voice. 'Simple. The choice of crime scenes. The Seventies murders all took place in isolated areas. Ideal for what the suspect planned to do with his victims.' She paused for a moment as she briefly looked at Brady. No sooner did she catch his eye, than she broke away and turned to Conrad who was next to her.

Something passed between them. Nobody else in the room had noticed. But Brady had. And it hurt. He felt excluded from whatever intimacy they shared. It was clear that Conrad had shared whatever was troubling him with Amelia. That one fleeting look spoke volumes.

Brady knew what she was going to say. Realised that Conrad had told Amelia about McKaley's refusal to acknowledge that the crime scenes were gay cruising spots. However, Amelia was an obvious choice to confide in. If anyone could see a pattern, it would be the team's forensic psychologist.

Amelia began again, her words slow and deliberate – mainly for the benefit of the belligerent DS. 'At the time of the Seventies investigation, no one made the connection that where the bodies were found could be crucial to the investigation. It was assumed that they were just ideal locations to carry out a crime at night. But that couldn't be further from the truth. These locations, Brunton Lane, Leazes Park, Heaton Park and the others,' Amelia gestured towards the whiteboard and the crime scene photos, 'all are known among the gay community as cruising areas. If you're gay and you want to meet like-minded men for casual sex, these are the places to go. I would suggest that the Seventies suspect knew where he could pick up young gay men. All of them appear to have been consensually tied up. Which makes me think that the killer is someone who you would trust. Someone who comes over as non-threatening. Especially if you weren't particularly strong, like these victims. Or else why would you allow yourself to be put in such a vulnerable position?'

Brady was waiting for Daniels and Kenny to make some puerile remark. It didn't come. They both were remarkably contrite for a change. He assumed that they both knew they were in for a bollocking once the briefing ended. Instead it was Harvey who spoke.

'Wouldn't their build mean that it would be easier to over-power them? To tie them up against their will?' Harvey asked, frowning at Amelia.

Brady studied Tom Harvey. He was the oldest member of the team and a long-standing friend. He was a detective sergeant with no intentions of rising through the ranks, considering the politics to be too bothersome to be worth it. He always spoke as he found. Still unmarried and fast approaching his late forties, he had made some desperate choices when it came to dating. He had tried every dating website out there and had still failed. For a detective, he was lousy when it came to choosing women. He currently had a twenty-two-year-old Thai girlfriend. At least, that's what he believed. That jarred with Brady. Not that Harvey would listen to him. He was still waiting for her to come over to the UK – despite the bitter fact he had already paid her £5,000 for the privilege. At least, that was the amount he had told Brady. Brady was certain he had parted with a heftier amount of cash than that. But Harvey would not, or could not, see that he was being played. The middle-aged fool really thought she was inter-ested in him – not his wallet. He was an average-looking bloke. His light brown hair was cropped short to disguise the flecks of grey that were becoming more and more dominant. It wouldn't be long before Harvey was covering up with Grecian 2000 in an attempt to reclaim his misspent youth, and keep his twenty-two-year-old internet girlfriend. Brady noticed the tell-tale nicks on his strong, square jaw. Razor cuts. Whether it was the murder investigation, or more likely, his girlfriend's latest demand for money, Harvey's mind hadn't been on the job at hand.

And he looked worried. Deep lines were etched into his forehead. His puffy, blood-shot eyes told Brady he'd had a few too many drinks last night. But the bags under his eyes were permanent. As was the ever-expanding waistline. Brady thought of Harvey's main pleasure in life – drinking. He had an unquenchable thirst and a knack for being the last one standing at the end of a heavy session, still wanting more to drink. Brady studied his earnest face. He was certain that there was a slight jaundiced hue to his skin. Maybe it was the overhead fluorescent lighting, or maybe the heavy sessions in the pub were catching up with him. Brady made a mental note to talk to him, just to check that he was all right. He had a lot of time for Harvey. He had gone up through the ranks with him. Brady had initially worried that his promotion to detective inspector would rankle with Harvey. But, it hadn't. Harvey was a better man than that. He had wished Brady well, and meant it.

Amelia shook her head as she looked at Harvey. 'No. There was no evidence of struggle. If someone was attempting to tie you up, you'd fight back. There's no physical evidence of this on any of the bodies. Including De Bernier's.'

'And if Alexander De Bernier's killer is the same person, and that's a big "if", why wouldn't this murder have taken place in the gay pick-up areas like the original crimes?' Harvey asked.

'Why the hotel? Because that would give the murderer privacy. Why not the locations used in the Seventies? Because these spots are so well-known now, unlike then, that they are the last place you would go to commit a crime. Too many cars and people cruising by to see what's on offer.'

It was DC Kodovesky's turn to question the forensic pathologist. 'I don't understand. Are you saying that this is the same person? The same killer from thirty-seven years ago? How could that even be possible?'

Brady knew he was going to have to call an end to the briefing. The same questions were being raised as the team tried to get their heads around the murder – or murders. They were getting nowhere, and fast. He took a much-needed drink of water. He had a hell of a lot to get through today, once the briefing was over. There were still a few areas he needed to cover. But then the murder team had to get to work. In particular, delving into De Bernier's personal life. They still didn't know where he had relocated. Or how he could afford such expensive designer clothes and accessories. Bank accounts had to be accessed to find out what money De Bernier actually had and where he had sourced it. Brady was certain there was more to him than they initially first suspected. He was hoping that the victim's girl-friend would have some of the answers.

He looked at Kodovesky. In her late twenties, she was one of the youngest members of his team. Her long black hair was always worn scraped back into a tight knotted ponytail. It was a harsh look. But it suited her. Her clothes were professional, yet practical: a black polo neck top, black pinstriped trousers and low-heeled black boots. She never deviated from this dress code. For good reason; the same reason she never wore make-up on the job or a skirt. Kodovesky was making a state-ment. She was a pragmatist. And as such, she was all too aware that she worked in a male-dominated police force. Women did make it through the ranks. But they were still the rarity; the one example that could be cited to prove that equality existed in a predominately testosterone-fuelled environment. One where the size of your bollocks still counted. The bigger, the better. Consequently, Kodovesky chose to downplay the gender card. Her air of detachment was simply self-preservation. She had a lot to prove, despite being better at the job than most of her male peers.

She was clean-cut and career-obsessed. Two words interested her – fast-tracking. Like Conrad, she did not socialise with other coppers. She kept her head down, did what was asked of her and more, and then went home. Brady could guarantee that she would always be the first one in and the last one out, and admired her dogged tenacity. She knew where she wanted to be, which was giving out orders behind the DCI's desk.

Amelia looked at Kodovesky and nodded. 'Good point and one that I've been struggling with. The problem we have here is that even though the MO has changed, with a physically different type of victim, and a radically different crime scene choice, the signature is identical,' she said. She then looked around at the rest of the faces. 'I'm sure you're all aware that the modus operandi is the methodology of the crime. Meaning the procedures and rules that the suspect follows. You can see that with the first seven victims the perpetrator was consistent with his type of victim and choice of crime scene. But an MO can evolve over time and change as a result of the suspect's experience. This can then have an impact on the planning and execution of the crime and even the choice of victim.' Amelia stopped for a moment, allowing the room to register what she was saying. 'If this is the same suspect, then it would be a given that he would have evolved and changed over thirty-seven years.'

'Why now? Why start again?' Kodovesky asked.

It was a question that was on everyone's mind. Including Brady's. He had done nothing but think about it from the moment he walked into the crime scene. But he had already reached a conclusion. He was curious to know whether Amelia had reached the same one.

'And you say "he", are you certain the suspect is male? I can understand the Seventies murderer being male . . . but with De Bernier, maybe it was his girlfriend. Especially given the threatening text she sent him,' Kodovesky said as she looked from Amelia to the crime scene photos of the victims on the whiteboard. 'Women may commit less than ten per cent of murders but surely that doesn't rule them out. They're still driven by the same forces as male murderers. And his girlfriend did have the motive. She also threatened to . . .' Kodovesky paused, embarrassed to point out the obvious.

Amelia stepped in. 'To chop his penis off because she suspected he was cheating on her?'

Kodovesky nodded, her cheeks unusually flushed. 'Yes. There's the infamous case of Lorena Bobbitt who cut off her husband's penis because he was abusive and unfaithful. But this is a practice that has been going on for centuries.'

Brady was impressed with what he was hearing. She had actually put some thought into the case.

'You're absolutely right,' Amelia replied. 'Lorena Bobbitt was not the first woman and nor will she be the last to cut off an adulterous partner's straying anatomy. It may surprise you,' Amelia said as she turned to the rest of the room, 'that there has been a culture of cutting off penises throughout the centuries. Whether as a punishment for a criminal act or as personal vengeance. It was a practice prevalent in South East Asia. Particularly during the Seventies, when there were over one hundred cases reported of Thai women cutting off their husbands' penises.' Amelia paused for a moment.

Brady could see Harvey wincing at what he was hearing. Even Daniels looked grim for once. Then again, monogamy was not a practice Daniels subscribed to.

'In case any of you were wondering, the reason for this sudden spate of penis mutilations was the same reason that Lorena Bobbitt gave as her defence. They were objecting to their husbands' practice of keeping a second wife,' Amelia explained. She looked around at some of the wry smiles from some of the males in the room. 'This was acceptable in traditional Thai culture but these extra-marital relations were not supported by the law, which enforced monogamy. Some women were not even sentenced. Even Lorena Bobbitt was acquitted. And I'm sure the men in here will want to know that the police found John Bobbitt's penis and that surgeons managed to successfully reattach it to the extent he went on to become a porn star.'

There was a ripple of laughter around the room. Brady noticed that there were two people who remained taciturn: Conrad and Kodovesky.

Brady waited until the noise gradually died down. It was time to wind it up. But he had one last question.

'If we are seriously considering that it's the same suspect, where has he been for thirty-seven years?' Brady asked, looking directly at Amelia.

She looked at him, not surprised by the question. 'Prison, or a psychiatric hospital. The first seven murders were committed over a relatively short period during the summer of 1977. Then they stopped as abruptly as they started,' Amelia answered. 'So, that means that something stopped him.'

Brady nodded. He looked at the rest of the room. 'Which means that we need to be considering all recently paroled serious offenders. There are four bail hostels in the North East and we have one right in Whitley Bay – Ashley House.' Brady turned to Harvey and Kodovesky. 'I want details on every person in those bail hostels.'

'Sir,' Kodovesky answered. There was a keenness in her eye. She had something to work with, which was more than they had when she had first walked in.

'Same applies to psychiatric hospitals. Not just restricted to this area. I want a list of patients recently released across the UK. If our suspect was in his early twenties when he committed these crimes,' Brady said as he gestured at the whiteboard, 'that would make him now in his mid-to-late fifties, which narrows the search down considerably.'

'There is another possibility, of course. What if this is a copycat?' Amelia said.

Brady nodded. 'That makes our search even more time-consuming and difficult,' he said. But he had already thought about this. He could see from the blank faces in front of him that the rest of the team hadn't quite caught on to the problem. 'If this suspect,' Brady gestured towards the Seventies crime scenes, 'was detained, which would account for the sudden end to his killing spree, what if he talked to someone? Shared a prison cell or a ward with a like-minded inmate? Someone younger than him perhaps? Someone he shared every intimate detail with. Including even the vintage Waddington Joker cards. What if someone else is now copying the original killer? If that's the case, we're in trouble. Without the identity of the original Joker, it makes it virtually impossible to find out who could be copying him. And right now we're running out of time. The Joker killed his second victim seven days after the first. Today's Monday. De Bernier was murdered on Saturday. You do the maths.'

Brady left it at that. The heavy silence in the room was claustrophobic as everyone weighed up the enormity of the situation.

Chapter Twenty-Two

Monday: 10:08 a.m.

He didn't waste any time, just headed straight for the aisle. This was the first step. Perhaps the most crucial. He had planned everything meticulously.

'Can I help you, sir?' an elderly assistant asked him, suddenly appearing by his side.

James David Macintosh turned slowly to the assistant in the orange B&Q apron. He shook his head. 'No . . . I know exactly what I'm looking for, thank you.'

Dismissed, the assistant walked off to help another shopper at the end of the aisle.

Macintosh studied the array in front of him. He could feel the excitement stirring in his stomach, slowly awakening . . . A delicious sensation, that made him feel alive.

He smiled as he indulged himself. His mouth watered with anticipation as he chose the one that reminded him of the axe that he had swung repeatedly into his psychiatrist's skull.

He could feel himself buzzing. The adrenalin building as he relived the skull exploding open. The shock on his face. The realisation as the axe came down. Heavily. Slowly. Beautifully.

He could smell it. Taste it even. The blood. *His blood.*

He touched the blade, gently, reverently, as he imagined swinging the axe. Bludgeoning *his* face. *His skull* . . .

He swallowed. It would be better this time. So much better than before.

Chapter Twenty-Three

Monday: 10:40 a.m.

Brady's head was still pounding. He had already taken painkillers but they had had no effect. Whether it was dealing with Claudia throughout the early hours of the morning or the stifling atmosphere in the Incident Room, he couldn't say. But his head felt like it was going to explode from the tension. To make matters worse, he was now sitting in an interview room with Alexander De Bernier's parents.

To be fair, Conrad was with him. Neither of them wanted to be here. But they had no choice.

The victim's parents had chosen to ignore the request to wait at the hotel they had been booked into in Newcastle. Brady had told the liaison officers assigned to them that he would visit later this afternoon. However, they'd wanted to come straight to the station instead of checking into the hotel.

He couldn't blame them. Alexander was their only son. Their only child. And he was gone. Someone had murdered him in a profoundly cruel way. Brady's main concern was minimising the gruesome details of their son's death. There was no need to distress them more than necessary.

'So . . . how? How did he die?' Francis De Bernier asked. His voice boomed around the room, deep and assertive as he directed this question straight at Brady.

Brady looked at him. It was clear that he wouldn't take any bullshit. He was a large man – over six foot four – with curly silver hair and a heavily lined face. He was in his early seventies, his wife in her early sixties. Both looked exhausted. The strain of the devastating news had evidently taken its toll. But Francis De Bernier was clearly doing his best to hold it together. To act like he was in charge. Clinging to an old-fashioned sense of manhood. And he was succeeding – just.

Brady swallowed. His throat felt raw and itchy. The dry air in the room wasn't helping. Nor was the fact that Molly Johansson was in the adjacent interview room waiting for him to question her. It felt wrong to be here offering lame words of comfort to the victim's parents when he could be solving their son's death.

'Well?' Francis De Bernier asked.

Brady could see his large hands trembling on the table in front of him. He could obviously tell that his son's death had been particularly nasty. Why else would the SIO in charge of the case be stalling?

'He was suffocated,' Brady said reluctantly.

'Oh . . .' was the only response that came from Jacqueline De Bernier. Her brown watery eyes turned away from Brady to her husband as a thin bony hand fluttered up to her neck.

'I am so sorry,' Brady offered. But the words hung pointlessly in the brittle air.

Francis De Bernier's eyes bore into him. It was clear that he didn't believe his son had just been suffocated; his sharp eyes told Brady he knew there was more to it than that. But out of respect for his wife he didn't challenge Brady.

'What else? What else can you tell us?' Francis De Bernier continued.

Silent tears were now falling down Jacqueline De Bernier's pale face. Whatever she felt or wanted to say, she kept it to herself. Her short, white hair was immaculately styled. Her clothes tasteful and chosen with care. She was wearing a black suit with flat black pumps. The only make-up she wore was bright red lipstick.

Like his wife, Francis De Bernier was also smartly dressed in a tan linen jacket with a pale blue shirt and tan linen trousers. Dark brown brogues finished the look. But his hair was ragged.

'At this precise moment, I'm afraid there's not a lot I can share. But I can assure you that we are doing everything in our power to find whoever did this to your son,' Brady replied, carefully. Very carefully.

He never liked situations like this. No one did. It was difficult when faced with a murder victim's grieving loved ones. They knew the victim intimately. Their likes, dislikes. What made them laugh or cry. All Brady and the team had was a body. A decaying body that someone had decided to butcher. Nothing else. They had to build a picture up of who the victim had been in life. But they would never know what he was really like. Nor could they ever feel the pain and anguish that would eat away at the victim's loved ones. Burying its way deep into their bones, so that every joint ached when they were forced to move on with their lives. To continue existing without them.

Jacqueline De Bernier dropped her hand down from her neck and let it rest on top of her husband's. Something unspoken passed between them. Her swollen, tear-filled eyes remained on Brady.

'Why do you have his fiancée here?' Francis De Bernier asked. His tone told Brady he wouldn't accept anything less than the truth.

'We want to question her in relation to your son's murder,' Brady answered honestly.

Francis De Bernier shook his head as he held Brady's sympathetic gaze. 'She didn't do it. That girl loved Alexander. Adored the ground our boy walked on. As he did her. I suggest that you look further afield for the killer.'

Brady struggled to reply. He sorely wished that Conrad would step in and help him out. But he knew it wouldn't happen. He was the SIO and as such, it came with the territory that he should be the one to reassure and offer words of comfort to the victim's parents. Not that he felt like he was doing either.

'It's purely a preliminary line of inquiry. Molly Johansson will hopefully be able to help us get an idea of who would want to harm your son.'

Brady noticed Mrs De Bernier visibly wince when he said the word 'harm'.

'When you release Molly, please ensure that she is driven to our hotel. I'm sure the poor girl must be in a dreadful state.'

'I will,' Brady assured him. *If* he released Molly.

'Why? Why would someone do that to Alexander? Why?' Jacqueline De Bernier asked suddenly.

Her voice surprised Brady. It was strong and clear and didn't seem to belong to the tearful, petite woman sat in front of him.

'I honestly don't know. But as soon as we do, you will be the first to be informed.'

'He was just a young man. And a good one at that. He had his whole life ahead of him. He had big plans. Wanted to be a Member of Parliament. And our boy would have done it.' Francis De Bernier paused for a moment as he collected himself. 'We were very proud of him, DI Brady. Very proud. Don't let us down. Or him.'

With that, he scraped his chair back and stood up before turning to help his wife to stand.

'Thank you,' Francis De Bernier said as he stretched his hand out to shake Brady's.

It was a firm, hard grip. One that told Brady that he sincerely hoped Brady would deliver – for the sake of his wife. And for his own peace of mind.

Chapter Twenty-Four

Monday: 11:51 a.m.

Brady splashed cold water over his face. Repeatedly. He needed to clear his head. His next job was crucial: interviewing the victim's girlfriend. Brady seriously doubted that the threatening text and her presence in the hotel the night De Bernier was murdered were just coincidence. Dripping wet, he lifted his head and looked at himself in the mirror. He was exhausted, but was all too aware that DCI Gates would be descending on the station with the press biting at his heels. Brady needed to be on the ball for when he finally showed.

The door to the Gents opened. Brady turned to see Harvey walk in, red-faced and flustered.

'Christ, Jack! Don't you answer your bloody phone?'

'Not when I'm in the Gents I don't,' Brady answered.

'Next time, make an exception for me, will you? I've been running all over the station looking for you,' Harvey panted as he bent over slightly to catch his breath.

Brady pulled out a paper towel and dried his face. He scrunched it into a ball and threw it into the bin.

'Are you not going to ask me what it's about?' Harvey asked, looking up. His face was even more flustered.

'Chantelle Robertson?'

'How the bloody hell did you know?' Harvey asked, incredulous.

Brady shrugged. He wasn't about to tell Harvey that he had had three missed calls from the receptionist he had talked to yesterday at the Royal Hotel. He had returned the call and she'd told him that Chantelle Robertson had rung in sick that morning. Joanne the receptionist had explained to Brady that she had taken great delight in telling her that she was lying. And that she was wanted for questioning by the police. Chantelle had then hung up.

'She rang her parents this morning and they insisted that she ring me. Seems that it was nothing more than coincidence, her disappearing like that. Some bloke she's having a fling with had asked her to his villa in Spain for the week. She didn't want her parents to know about it because he's married and they would go apeshit if they found out. And she didn't want work to find out either. Seems she's screwing the boss,' Harvey said, winking. 'Lucky bastard, eh?'

Brady ignored Harvey's enthusiasm. He did not find the idea of Martin Madley sleeping with a twenty-two-year-old employee all that entertaining.

'Upshot is, she pulled a sickie at work so no one would guess, and left her parents a note saying that she was going away with the girls. Poor lass was beside herself when she heard what had happened.'

Brady leaned back against the sinks and waited for Harvey to finish.

'She remembered checking in a "John Smith". Her description matches our victim.'

'Why did she remember him?' Brady was curious. 'John Smith' had checked in around the same time that the two coach-loads of men on a stag weekend had turned up.

'Paid cash. And he gave her a tip. Fifty quid.'

'Why?' asked Brady, frowning.

'Why what?'

'Why did he tip her?'

'How the fuck would I know, Jack! Maybe he wanted to shag her?' Harvey suggested.

Brady breathed out slowly. He wondered how the hell Harvey kept his job, let alone had made it to detective sergeant.

'Is she coming back?' Brady asked, not holding out much hope since Harvey had been left in charge of Chantelle's return to the UK.

'Well . . . I did ask and she got so upset. Said she didn't have the money to fly back. I did explain that we really needed to take a statement from her . . . but . . . You know I can't stand it when women cry, Jack. It makes me uncomfortable. So I said it could wait until she got back on Sunday. She told me everything she knew anyway.'

Brady cursed inwardly. 'Did she say anything about Molly Johansson turning up?' he asked, ignoring Harvey's excuses.

'Yeah . . . yeah she remembered her. Said that Molly came back once the bloke who was working the reception desk with her had left.'

Brady thought of what Carl, Madley's look-out, had told him. He hadn't been certain whether Molly had talked to Chantelle Robertson when she was on her own.

'And?'

'She showed Chantelle a photo of the victim on her phone. Chantelle said she didn't say anything but it must've been clear that she recognised him. Molly begged Chantelle to ring the room, to tell him that someone was in reception asking for him. Gave her a sob story and the lass fell for it. Like I said, there's nothing disingenuous about her.'

'Shit!' Brady muttered as he ran a hand through his damp hair.

'What's the problem? No one answered when she rang and the girlfriend thanked Chantelle and went back into the bar. She didn't see her after that.'

'I bet she bloody didn't.'

'I don't understand. What's the big deal?'

'I don't know who is stupider, you or that bloody receptionist! When she called him, the receptionist would have had to key his room number in. Molly Johansson would have known that. Christ, Tom! She would have seen the room number.'

Harvey looked at Brady and shrugged. 'I'm not a bloody receptionist, am I?'

'You're a fucking detective. It's not rocket science!' Brady retorted. 'Jesus Christ!'

He breathed out. Tried to calm himself down. Getting pissed off with Harvey wasn't going to help matters. 'You're a bloody big lummox at times. Do you know that?' Brady said, the edge gone from his voice. It was his way of apologising for exploding at him.

Harvey shrugged. He still looked aggrieved that Brady had briefly lost it with him.

'Did you ask if she noticed anyone coming into the hotel after ten that night?' Brady asked. They knew from the post-mortem that the victim was killed approximately around eleven.

Harvey took a moment to answer. Whether he was choosing his words carefully or actually trying to recall the conversation, Brady couldn't say.

'I did, and she said that it was a typically chaotic Saturday night and fairly rowdy because of the stag party that had booked in. She said the bar was really busy and noisy and anyone could have come in through reception and taken the lift or stairs without her noticing.'

'What about later that evening?'

Harvey shrugged. 'Same answer.'

'Do you think she was hiding something?' Brady asked.

'No. Her taking off like that was just coincidence, Jack. Nothing more, nothing less,' Harvey answered. 'I'm not a fool. Regardless of what you might think, I can still tell when someone's lying to me.'

Brady kept quiet, even though Harvey's internet Thai girlfriend came to mind. But that was his choice and he had the right to make a mess of his personal life. His professional one was a separate matter entirely.

In any case, right now, Chantelle Robertson was not his biggest concern. It was the victim's girlfriend, Molly Johansson.

Chapter Twenty-Five

Brady was gathering as much information as he could about the victim. He wanted as much as possible before he interviewed Molly Johansson. So far, it was making interesting reading. Troublingly so. Conrad had updated him on the victim's bank statements. Alexander De Bernier had over two hundred thousand pounds in a high-interest savings account. Brady knew he hadn't won the lottery, so they needed to know where he had sourced that kind of money. It had been paid into the account over a period of ten months. Cash. In varying amounts. Small payments in the hundreds and a maximum payment of ten grand.

'What do you think, sir?' Conrad asked as Brady studied the bank statements.

They had reconvened in his office to go over what they had to date.

Brady looked up at Conrad. His expression said it all. 'What's the going rate for a bartender in that gentleman's club of yours, Conrad?'

'It wouldn't explain even a small percentage of the capital he has there,' Conrad answered.

Brady looked at him. Conrad looked perplexed. 'What is it?'

'I don't know, sir,' Conrad replied, 'there's something about this that doesn't feel right.'

'Tell me something I don't bloody know!'

'Do you think he earned it?' Conrad asked.

'Doing what, for fuck's sake? There's over two hundred grand in this account,' Brady replied, exasperated. 'What students do you know earn that kind of cash? Unless he's a card reader at poker tables I can't figure out how he's got this kind of money. And I wouldn't fancy my chances at the casino in town. If one of the other players, let alone the staff, realised what he was up to, he'd have been found dead in a back alley long before now.'

One thought had hit Brady. Hard. He needed more evidence before he seriously considered it. But it was the only logical explanation he could think of.

'Seems there's a lot we still don't know about De Bernier,' Brady said as he looked at the figures on the printout.

'Do you think he could have been murdered because of the money?'

The question did not surprise Brady. He expected no less from Conrad. It was one of the first thoughts that had crossed his mind.

'What if he was blackmailing someone?' Conrad asked.

Brady nodded. 'Exactly what I was thinking,' he said as he picked up his coffee. He took a slug. It was cold and bitter. He grimaced as he swallowed it down. 'The problem we have is why he was murdered in an identical way to the Seventies victims. That's what I'm not getting.'

Conrad didn't answer him.

'Come on, let's get this over with,' Brady said. 'Maybe his girlfriend will be able to shed some light on his financial affairs.'

Chapter Twenty-Six

Monday: 2:17 p.m.

Molly Johansson looked as bad as Brady felt. It was clear that she had one hell of a hangover. She looked like shit – she was sweating so much that the stuffy, claustrophobic interview room was becoming unbearable. The room was filled with a nauseating mixture of stale sweat and alcohol. Throw into the mix the rancid vomit splattered on her clothes, and it was understandable why Brady was struggling to concentrate. Not the best working conditions. The room was small and hot. There was no fancy air conditioning in the station. Nor were there any windows in the interview room.

Her bloodshot, puffy eyes darted nervously around the room. Anywhere but at Brady, or Conrad sitting stiffly beside him.

'I . . . I . . . honestly can't remember . . .' she mumbled, eyes looking apprehensively at the camera in the corner of the ceiling.

Brady sat back and folded his arms. It was heading into mid-afternoon. But he had all day if need be. And at this rate, it would take all day. He knew that she would break before he did. And he also knew that he wouldn't let her go until she talked. The threat she had texted to the victim was a good enough reason not to release her until she had explained herself. Brady was pretty sure she hadn't killed her boyfriend. That she simply didn't have it in her. But he wanted her version. That, and he needed to know who she suspected her boyfriend of seeing. Until then, Molly was going nowhere.

Brady's eyes dropped down to the printed list of the texts Johansson had sent De Bernier. The phone company had confirmed that the texts had been sent from her phone. He looked back up at her. Her blond hair was pulled back into a tight knot emphasising her clammy, pale face. She was dressed in a baggy white T-shirt and grey leggings. Her bony white arms were covered in blotches and angry wheals where she had been scratching and squeezing her skin. Brady had put it down to nerves. Understandable. She had threatened to cut off her boyfriend's dick the same night someone actually did. Bad luck didn't even cover it. But Brady didn't understand her reluctance to talk.

Brady looked over at the duty solicitor. He simply shrugged at him. His way of telling Brady there was nothing he could do. His client simply did not want to talk. That was her privilege. Perhaps not a good idea, given the evidence that had been presented to her. But it was still her choice to sweat it out.

Tim Cowan was in his mid-to-late thirties and had worked at the station for the past five years. Brady liked him. Got on with him most of the time. Sometimes the job got in the way. Aside from that, he was a guy that Brady would happily have a pint with. The reason Brady liked him was because he was a realist and the job, as so often was the case, had made him cynical. Spend long enough dealing with the dregs of society, and your view of the world shifts – radically. Tim Cowan was no idealist. He did the job purely for the money. Most of the time he was called in, it was to represent some drug- and alcohol-addled scum who'd decided to rearrange someone's face simply because they didn't like the look of it.

'Molly?' Brady began.

Startled, she looked up at him with the frenzied eyes of a wild animal backed into a corner.

'You can make this easier on yourself if you just tell me what you know.'

Molly looked at him as if trying to comprehend what he was saying.

Conrad coughed. 'Sorry,' he mumbled. He then coughed again. Before he knew it, he was in the midst of a coughing fit.

It was no surprise. The air was dusty and dry. And rank. Brady could feel it catching in the back of his own throat when he breathed.

Conrad's coughing escalated. His face turned puce as he tried and failed to get it under control.

'Go get some water,' Brady ordered. His head was still pounding and Conrad's persistent barking wasn't helping.

Conrad did as he was told, scraped his chair back and left the room.

Tim Cowan raised his eyebrows at Brady. The look in his hazel eyes suggested he would like to follow suit.

Brady breathed out. Tried to relax. To not let the cloying air get to him. Nor the reluctance of the suspect to talk. He watched as Tim Cowan started to shuffle the papers in front of him, a clear sign that he was going to ask for the interview to be postponed until he had had another chance to have a talk with his client. Not that Cowan had fared any better than Brady. Apparently she had refused the right to a solicitor. When told that she had to have legal representation, she had refused to even tell him her name.

Whether she was still drunk, Brady wasn't sure. However, from the state of her, he wouldn't be surprised. Or she could still be in shock. After all, it wasn't every day that you got dragged out of bed by two burly officers and brought in for questioning. Not the morning after you were informed of your boyfriend's horrific death.

'Look, Molly . . . let's start again, shall we? Believe me when I say I want to let you go,' Brady said.

She looked at him. Her eyes filled with uncertainty. Unsure of whether he was trying to trick her.

Brady continued, his voice low, trusting, 'But first you need to help me understand. You see, there's things about your boyfriend that we still don't quite get.'

187

When Brady had requested the victim's bank and credit card statements he had hoped that he had changed his personal details. But he hadn't, which meant they still did not know his new address. Frustratingly, neither did his girlfriend. Brady needed to know exactly what kind of life De Bernier led. Clearly, it was one that had placed him in the hands of a sadistic murderer.

Brady looked at Molly in front of him. Painfully thin and terribly nauseous. The dark circles under her darting eyes added to her air of overall malaise. Her limp T-shirt had started to cling to her. The damp patches under her armpits had deepened. She was terrified. Of what? Brady had no idea. He thought back to last night. The change in Johansson was remarkable.

'All right,' Brady continued, 'you said you had an argument with the victim on Saturday morning? Is that correct?'

She nodded. Barely.

'And that's why he never returned any of your calls and texts? Because of the argument?'

Again she nodded.

'What was the argument about?'

She looked at him wearily and shrugged. 'I . . . don't remember . . .'

'I don't believe you,' Brady fired back.

She looked stung.

'I don't believe you, because of all these texts you sent him,' Brady stated, shoving the printed sheet towards her.

Molly refused to look at them. Brady knew why – because she remembered texting every single word.

'If you can't remember, take a look,' Brady insisted.

Still she refused.

'What's wrong? Don't want to be reminded of what you sent?' Brady asked. He suddenly leaned in close. 'Doesn't look good, does it? All those threats? Not now they've been carried out!'

Molly looked as if Brady had just slapped her. Wide-eyed, she stared at him, trying to gauge whether he was serious.

Brady ignored the polite rap on the door. He was too busy trying not to lose his temper with the petulant young madam sat in front of him who had the misfortune to believe that she was somehow immune from being charged.

'I'm not messing around here, Molly. I've dealt with worse than you. If you want to wait this out, then go for it. But I'll charge you with the murder of your boyfriend,' Brady threatened her, just as a surprised-looking Conrad walked back into the interview room.

He sat back down quietly.

'You've got nothing on me,' she answered. Her voice was suddenly defiant.

'What about the last text you sent the victim? Sent at ten forty-five p.m., shortly before he was murdered. Remember what you said?' Brady asked. But he didn't give her a chance to answer. 'I do. You said, quote: "Fucking bastard. I know where you are and who you're with. I'm in the bar downstairs waiting to cut your cheating dick off!"'

She shook her head. 'So? I was angry. That's not a crime. We'd had an argument. That's all.'

'You see, that's where you're wrong. That argument gave you a motive to kill him,' Brady pointed out calmly. He waited a moment to allow her to absorb the magnitude of her situation.

She shrugged. 'I thought he was seeing someone else. That's why I sent that text. Nothing was meant by it. Not really—'

Brady didn't give her a chance to continue. He'd had enough bullshit. 'Then tell me why you were at the Royal Hotel on the night in question?'

She shook her head. 'I . . . I wasn't . . .'

First lie. Brady knew that it was hard enough when you were telling the truth to be consistent; to be able to relay the events in the same way each time. But when a suspect starts lying it is almost impossible to get all of the details to match the previous version. Molly Johansson had just started to talk and she was already inventing. As soon as she opened her mouth, out came the first lie. All he'd have to do was sit back and wait to hear something change when he asked her to retell the story again and again. There'd be a subtle change; something different would come into play. It was all about waiting. About giving the suspect enough rope to let them hang themselves.

But Brady didn't have time to play mind games. He knew she was lying. Had the evidence to substantiate it.

'I've got a reliable witness that places you there. Drunk, hysterical – you walked into reception demanding to know which room your cheating boyfriend was in. Sound familiar? They wouldn't tell you, so you took off to the toilets to sort yourself out. You then went into the hotel bar and waited. Waited for what exactly?'

The look in her eyes told Brady he had her. Molly crossed her arms in front of herself, her nails anxiously digging into the flesh.

'What happened? Did you confront him? Did you carry out your threat? Did you cut his penis off as a punishment for screwing around on you?'

'No . . . Don't be stupid.'

'I'm not the stupid one here, Molly. I'm not the one whose boyfriend was found—'

'Sir!' interjected Conrad.

It worked. It had stopped Brady from adding 'with his penis stuffed down his throat'.

He breathed out slowly. He needed to get a grip. He had come dangerously close to losing his temper and, perhaps, losing the case. Details of the mutilation had not been released. And Brady had made a point of not informing the victim's parents. Some things were better left unsaid. There was also the possibility that it would be leaked to the press. The last thing the police wanted was a public frenzy – not again.

Molly Johansson looked at Brady with red-rimmed watery eyes. She wiped her nose with the back of her hand as she waited for him to finish whatever he was going to say.

Instead, he pushed the box of tissues he had brought in her direction.

She took one. Blew her nose. Another to wipe her tear-filled eyes.

'Ready?' Brady asked. 'Because if you don't talk I'll have no choice but to charge you with your boyfriend's murder.'

Not that he had any intention of doing any such thing. But it had the desired effect.

Molly nodded, defeated.

Brady imagined that last night after he and Conrad had left she had gone on a self-pitying bender. Two blows had hit her hard. The first was that her boyfriend, soon-to-be fiancé, was screwing someone else. The second, that his infidelity had got him killed.

'Right, I want you to explain to me what happened on Saturday. How did you know Alex was going to be at the hotel in question?'

She looked at Brady. There was no resistance or defiance in her eyes. Instead, she had the look of someone whose fate was sealed.

'Am I in trouble?' she asked, biting her bottom lip. Tears started to well up again. Spilling silently down her face.

Brady ignored the tears. 'Depends on what you tell me.'

Molly took a breath. And then she began, her voice unsteady, eyes focused on nothing in particular. 'I knew he was seeing someone . . .' She paused, chewing her lip, then looked at Brady. 'You can tell. We'd argue about it and he'd claim I was paranoid. Messed up in the head and the like . . .' she shook her head as more tears welled up. 'But I loved him. You know? I just hoped it would pass. That he'd just get it out of his system. I mean, she's like twice my age.' She stopped and reached for another tissue to wipe her nose.

Brady decided to just let her talk. To get it all out. She was going nowhere. Neither was he.

'I knew he was meeting her that night. He started the argument. Thought I was stupid. That I didn't realise that he was trying to pick a fight to give him an out. We were meant to be going to a party that night. It was that morning when he checked his phone that his attitude changed. I knew he had a text. Even though he acted like he hadn't. I asked him who he was texting when he thought I wasn't looking and he gave me his usual answer of "no one". I knew he was lying, so when he went to get a shower I had a look. I knew something was up. He was too cagey and off-hand with me. He always locked his phone but I had watched him enough times to figure out the password. But when I accessed it, he'd obviously deleted the text he'd had and the one he sent. There were a couple of numbers on his phone that had no contact details. I assumed they were other girls he had been seeing. Or ex-girlfriends,' she said resignedly.

Brady was still waiting for this information from the mobile phone company. He was expecting something on his desk by the end of the day. The team were also busy tracking down friends and students on De Bernier's Masters course in case they knew something that might help. But so far, it seemed that despite the victim being popular and well-liked, nobody actually knew much about his personal life. They knew he had a girlfriend and shared a student house in Heaton. After that, they had no idea about him; not the money, his old job as a bartender at the gentleman's club, or where he had moved to two weeks prior to his murder.

Embarrassed at her next admission, Molly Johansson looked down at her hands. 'So, I had a good look through his phone. I couldn't find anything. No texts. He must have deleted everything she sent to him and vice versa. So I decided to have a look though his online history. He'd recently closed down a browser for a page on the Royal Hotel, showing the availability for that Saturday night. That's when I realised that she must have texted him about arrangements and asked him to sort out a hotel. Or at least said that she had chosen a hotel. I was devastated. I didn't know what to do.' Molly paused.

Brady waited for her to get her thoughts together and continue.

'After his shower, I challenged him. I demanded to know who had texted him. Told him I wasn't a fool, that I knew he was seeing someone. That was when he lost it. Said that he didn't like me prying on him, asking him who was texting whenever his phone went off. He accused me of being fucked in the head. That all he was doing was putting in late hours for Robert Smythe. For us. That he was working hard to get his career established so that we could get married. That whenever a text or email came in, it would be connected with the political campaign he was working on. But I knew it wasn't. You know? Intuition? You know when someone's cheating on you. It's a feeling you can't shake off. Anyway, he stormed out and that was the last I saw or heard from him . . .' she faltered, realising the magnitude of what she had just said.

'I tried ringing and texting, but he ignored me,' Molly shrugged, her eyes now focused on the tissue paper she was absentmindedly twisting between her long fingers. 'So . . . I got mad. Had a few too many drinks, as you do. And I guess it clouded my judgement. You see? He just kept ignoring my calls and texts. So I decided to confront them. Him. At the hotel. Make a scene. Shame her. Get her to leave him alone. Threaten her face to face that I would tell her husband. That would have scared her off. She had too much to lose if he found out.'

Brady shot a glance at Conrad. He face may have been impassive, but Brady knew that he was transfixed by every word.

She suddenly looked at Brady, fearful. 'I didn't do it,' she stuttered as tears fell down her face. 'I . . . I just wanted them to end it. I . . . I loved Alex. I really did.'

Brady nodded. 'I understand that,' he replied. It was time now to start directing the interview. He had questions that needed answering. He exhaled slowly. Looked at her and then spoke. 'What did you do?'

'Nothing,' she shrugged. 'Apart from make a fool of myself.'

Brady waited for her to fill in the gap.

Eventually she continued. 'I . . . I got a taxi from Heaton to the coast. To the hotel. I went up to reception and asked if my boyfriend had checked in. There was a male and female receptionist. The guy was abrupt and shut me down. Said it wasn't company policy to reveal who had checked in. So I decided to wait it out. I went into the bar. Had a couple more drinks and watched until he left. Then I asked the woman, who had been really friendly, if she could help. I showed her a photo of Alex. She didn't say anything but I knew that she recognised him. Just the look on her face. She looked so sorry for me. That's how I knew she had checked him in. So I took a chance and explained what I thought he was up to and asked if she could ring his room. Let him know that I was in reception. That I needed to talk to him. She was really nice. She said it was breaking the rules and she'd get into trouble if anyone found out, but she did it for me. Said she'd been there before herself. But he didn't answer the phone. She let it ring, but nothing.' Molly paused for a moment, as if remembering what had happened.

Brady watched her. She looked exhausted. No surprise. But he still needed a lot more from her before she could be released.

She suddenly focused on Brady, as if reading his thoughts. She gave a weak half-smile. 'I noticed his room number. When the receptionist dialled it. Room 212. So I went back to the bar and had another drink and waited until the lobby was too busy for her to notice me going into the lift. It was really crowded that night. Some stag party, they said.'

Brady nodded.

'I did go up to the room. Banged on the door. Shouted for them to come out. But they didn't. He didn't.'

'What time was this?' Brady asked. He wasn't surprised that no one had reported a disturbance on the second floor. It would easily have gone unnoticed amidst the noise and drunken revelry of seventy or more lads on a stag weekend.

She shrugged. 'I'd had a lot to drink. But I'd say sometime after ten-thirty.'

'The last text you sent at ten forty-five, was that before or after you went up to his room?' Brady asked. It wasn't worth reading the text to her. She knew which one he was referring to.

Uncomfortable with the reference to the text, she dropped her gaze. 'Before I went up to his room but I . . . I wish I hadn't . . . You know? I . . .' her voice faltered as she wondered about the consequences of that text. Weighed up what would have happened that night if she had not attempted to confront them.

She looked back up at Brady, chewing her bottom lip. 'I know who did it. I know who killed him.'

'Go on,' Brady said.

'Sarah Huntingdon-Smythe. The wife of the Conservative MP Robert Smythe.'

Brady didn't visibly react. But it didn't mean he wasn't shocked. He had seen the politician on the news and at various functions. He was a very good-looking man in his late fifties, who could have passed for ten years younger. He had a look about him that reminded Brady of a younger Rutger Hauer. Brady was also aware that Chief Superintendent O'Donnell was on personal terms with him.

'You do realise what you are claiming?' Brady questioned as he leaned in towards her.

He needed Molly to be aware of the seriousness of her allegation.

'Of course I am.'

Brady didn't say anything.

'She heard me banging outside the hotel room door. I was screaming that I knew she was in there. That if she didn't end the affair I was going straight to the press.'

Brady nodded at her, despite the fact that he didn't accept a word of it. The problem was, Molly Johansson was clueless about crucial details involving the murder. The key one being that De Bernier was killed in a way identical to the Joker killings of the Seventies. That in itself ruled out the hypothesis that it was some love tryst gone awry. That Sarah Huntingdon-Smythe had panicked when her young lover's girlfriend had threatened to expose them and that she had then killed him. This murder was planned and executed to precision. The killer had a motive for murdering De Bernier.

Could Sarah Huntingdon-Smythe have been sexually involved with Alex, though? Perhaps. At this stage of the investigation, Brady conceded that anything was possible.

'Tell me why you believed that your boyfriend was having an affair with this woman?' Brady asked, curious to hear her reasoning.

Molly Johansson took a moment before answering Brady. She then nodded, as if decided on the answer. 'Alex and I were both politics students,' she began.

Brady nodded.

'Last summer we got the opportunity to work with Robert Smythe. An internship of sorts. We didn't get paid for it. But it wasn't about that. It was about gaining invaluable experience. Alex was determined that he would get a permanent position out of it as a political aide to Robert. They got on very well, you see. I imagine if . . .' she stopped, unable to finish the sentence. She looked at Brady, eyes filled with regret. 'What I'm trying to say is that when he finished his Masters I would have been very surprised if there wasn't a job waiting for him with Robert. You see . . . Alex was really good. Charismatic, clever, politically motivated. He had it all. He had the makings of a great politician.'

Brady looked at her. 'Is that what he wanted to be?'

'Yes. That was his end goal. And he would have done it. He would have made it to the House of Commons if . . .'

'So where does Sarah Huntingdon-Smythe come into this?'

Johansson sighed. 'I knew there was something going on. Not at the start,' she said, shaking her head. 'It was only at the end of last year that I really started to notice that Alex was always busy or preoccupied with work. Or at least, that's what he said. Always making furtive phone calls or texts. He'd promise to see me and then break it off at the last minute. And lately, whenever we were invited to social gatherings with the Smythes, I would find Alex talking to her. He would always be so attentive and charming. Even Robert noticed it. I caught him looking at the two of them once and he looked furious. So it wasn't just me who had noticed the intimacy between them. I asked Alex, and he denied it, claiming I was being paranoid. That she was a thirty-five-year-old married woman. Married to his employer, no less. But I didn't buy it. I knew there was something going on between them. Then lately, they started having these really heated discussions. Raised voices and everything. Other people noticed. Including her husband. But the last one was a huge argument.'

Brady leaned forward. Now he was interested.

'When was this?'

'Last Thursday evening. There was a political function that we attended. Then we went back to the Smythes' house with other party members for drinks. That's when I saw them together. In one of the guest bedrooms. Alex had said he was going to the bathroom. But I knew that he was lying. That he was looking for her,' she said, her voice starting to crack. Molly shook her head as her eyes welled up. 'There had been this unspoken tension between them at the function earlier. She kept staring at him. Trying to get his attention. But Alex made a point of ignoring her.'

'You said they had an argument?'

'Yes. I heard her shouting at him that she wanted it to end. For him to leave her life for good. That she never wanted to see him again. She wanted him to quit Robert's political campaign. If not, she threatened that she would see to it that Alex was discredited within the Conservative Party. That he would never work in politics again if he did not end it.'

'If what you're saying is correct, then why would she contact Alex after she ended their affair that night?'

Johansson looked surprised by Brady's question.

'I don't know . . .' A pained look crossed her face. 'Maybe he didn't want it to end?'

Brady sighed wearily. He leaned back as he weighed up the significance of what Molly Johansson had just said.

'Did anyone else see or overhear this?' he asked.

She shook her head. 'No.'

'Are you certain?' Brady pushed.

'Yes . . . I had followed Alex. I wanted to know what was taking him so long. You know, I had my suspicions about them. She wasn't anywhere to be found downstairs so I knew that they must be together. So I went looking for them. That was when I heard raised voices coming from one of the guest bedrooms on the first floor. The door was closed but I could still hear them. She was furious with him. I knew Alex was in there with her. I recognised his voice. It was too low to be able to hear what he was saying. But she was shrieking at him. She really seemed to have lost it.'

'Why do you think she was shouting at him?'

'I assume he wasn't accepting what she was saying . . .' Molly shook her head as tears started to fill her eyes. 'Maybe Alex threatened to tell Robert? Maybe that's why she was screaming at him? Alex could be . . .' She faltered for a moment. 'He could be very determined and single-minded when he wanted to be. Alex never let anything get in his way. Never.'

Brady now understood why Johansson believed that Sarah Huntingdon-Smythe could have murdered her boyfriend. She had just given Brady a motive. If Alexander De Bernier had threatened to expose his relationship with Sarah to her husband, then that would be a good enough reason for her to want rid of him – for good. But the problem he had with Molly's account was that there were no credible witnesses. He just had her word. Which, at this precise moment, didn't count for a lot.

'What did you do?'

'I went downstairs and waited for him.'

'Did you say anything to him?'

She shook her head. 'No, I didn't get a chance. It wasn't the place to talk. On the drive home he said he had a really bad headache and that he was going back to his place. I asked if I could come back with him and he said no. That he wasn't in the mood. That he would drop me home and see me the following evening as planned.'

'Molly?'

She looked at him, unsure of what he was going to ask.

'Was there anything about Alex that struck you as odd lately? And I mean anything?'

'Aside from acting suspicious all the time, and never being around?'

Brady nodded. He waited while she thought about it. But he knew from the expression on her face that there was something.

'It may sound stupid but he got this new plate BMW 4 series convertible. Metallic silver. It even had a private licence plate,' she said, frowning. 'I asked him how he could afford it and he just shrugged it off. Said it was one of the perks of working for Robert's campaign. He needed to drive all over the place for political events and the car was a necessity. Allegedly it came out of the campaign budget.'

'You don't believe that?' Brady asked. It was clear from the look in her eye that it was a crazy suggestion.

'Christ no! All they talk about is the budget. That it won't cover this or that, and that we need to increase donations. So I knew that he was lying to me. Alex had the documentation for the car. He owned it outright. If it had been a company car, he wouldn't have had the registration details.'

'How did you know he had them if you lived at two separate houses?'

'I found them when I was rummaging through the glove box. I imagine he thought they were safer in the car, as it was alarmed, than leaving them in his bedroom. He didn't really trust his housemates. He was always complaining that people would go into his room and take stuff without asking. He even put a padlock on his door, but he was still paranoid that they could get in.'

Brady wondered exactly what it was that De Bernier was hiding in his bedroom that would lead him to put a padlock on the outside. He was now even more intrigued about the victim. Two hundred grand in a savings bank account and now some flash BMW sports convertible that would have cost serious money.

'Do you think the car was a gift?' Brady asked.

'What do you think? Yeah! He got the car three months ago. That was around the time that it was clear he was seeing someone else. And that was when I started to notice the way he behaved around Sarah. We'd go to some political event together and he would always leave me to go and chat to her. I used to have to stand there and pretend that I didn't notice them, laughing and flirting together.'

Brady resisted the urge to ask Molly why she would stay in a relationship where she was certain that her boyfriend was cheating on her. Let alone allow herself to be humiliated by the man she loved. He knew from his own experience that life was not simply black and white. People were human. That made them, by nature, fallible and susceptible to the grey areas in life.

Chapter Twenty-Seven

Monday: 4:38 p.m.

Molly Johansson was now detained in a holding cell without charge. Not that Brady thought she had anything to do with the victim's murder. When questioned, she had no idea about the Joker murders from the Seventies. Not that it surprised Brady, given that she wasn't from Newcastle and hadn't even been born when the crimes had taken place. Johansson had only been in the UK for a year, having spent the last twenty in South Africa. Could she have found out somehow about the killings?

Perhaps. It was highly unlikely. But she did have a motive.

Right now, the victim's girlfriend was the least of Brady's concerns. He was still troubled by the fact that De Bernier's murder was identical to the Joker killings, and wanted to talk to the SIO in charge of the original Joker case – the retired DI McKaley. He would have roughly been Brady's age at the time of the original investigation. Thirty-seven years on and he was some dribbling, obstate, foul-mouthed old man living in a care home off Preston Park, on the outskirts of North Shields. Long hours, bad diets, coupled with heavy drinking and smoking had taken its toll on the original investigative team. The last one standing was ironically enough DI McKaley; known on the force for the long hours he worked, but equally the long hours he would spend drinking in the station bar after his shift ended. Or even during it. Something unheard of nowadays.

McKaley had no surviving family members and had effectively disappeared – hidden away in a nursing home. Brady had been forewarned by the staff of the specialist care home that he was suffering from senile dementia. Brady had no clue what the effects would be on the once highly regarded and feared detective inspector. Not that Brady had any regard for the copper. Not after Conrad had disclosed McKaley's style of policing.

Conrad had insisted on coming. Whether it was to have some closure for Martyn Jenkins, Brady couldn't say. But Conrad was in no mood for arguments. He wanted to see McKaley in person.

McKaley was still an indomitable figure of a man, even at the age of eighty. He was just under six foot tall and two hundred pounds in weight. Brady imagined if he did kick off with the nurses that he would be difficult to control. But despite McKaley's physically healthy appearance, it was his mind that had radically deteriorated.

'Who the fuck are you?' McKaley fired at them again as globules of spit dribbled down his white, bristly chin. His narrowed, suspicious, watery blue eyes darted from Brady to Conrad.

'DI Brady, Mr McKaley,' Brady repeated for the tenth time.

'Never heard of a DI Brady,' McKaley spat. 'Where's Jones and Trevors?'

Brady could see that he was clearly agitated. They had been there for ten minutes and were no further forward. He also wished that Conrad had not insisted on coming. McKaley kept staring at him, eyes filled with disgust.

'I don't know where they are, Mr McKaley,' Brady replied.

'Sir to you, you fucking dick!' he shouted.

'Sorry, sir,' Brady answered, wishing he was anywhere rather than in this sterile, impersonal room with a single bed, a set of drawers and a matching wardrobe. It stank of a combination of antiseptic and the unmistakable odour of stale piss.

'Where's Jones and Trevors?' McKaley demanded as he looked at the closed door again. His white, gnarled knuckles gripped the arms of his chair as he waited with agitation for them to make an appearance.

'I'm sure they'll be here soon, sir,' Brady answered.

He was uncomfortable but was trying his best to appear relaxed. He was here on the off-chance he could glean some information from McKaley that could help with the current investigation. But he was doubtful that McKaley would even remember it now and if he did, that he would actually have anything significant.

'Who are you?' McKaley asked again.

'Sir, I'm here to ask you some questions about a case you worked on,' Brady repeated for the tenth time.

McKaley's trembling hand patted down his remaining white tufts of hair as he stared at the closed door.

'Sir? I haven't got much time. This is important,' Brady began.

'Trevors? Trevors?' McKaley shouted out.

'I'm sure he'll be here in a minute, sir,' Brady placated him. 'Sir. The Joker killings, do you remember them?'

McKaley suddenly leaned forward as he stared hard at Brady. 'Watch the way you talk to me, you fucking dick!'

'We need your help, sir. We were hoping that you would be able to answer some questions for us,' Brady persisted.

'Fags. You know that? All fags,' McKaley suddenly stated with disgust. 'Did us a favour, he did. They all deserved to have their dicks cut off. Disgusting fucking homos. Shouldn't be allowed. Sick fuckers. Had one on my team. Snivelling fucking poof. Soon got rid. Private talking-to in the Gents sorted him out. Don't know how long it was before he could use his dick again. If at all!' McKaley said, laughing. His deep, throaty laugh filled the room.

Brady could feel Conrad bristling beside him.

'Did you ever narrow a suspect down?' Brady asked as he ignored Conrad. He was struggling to rein in his own anger.

McKaley stopped laughing and looked at Brady as if seeing him for the first time.

'Suspect? What suspect? Trevors! Where the fuck have you got to?' McKaley shouted out. Disgruntled, he looked towards the door again.

'The Joker killings. Can you tell us anything about the suspects?' Brady doggedly continued.

McKaley's eyes flashed with disgust. His pale wet lips were downturned as he shook his head. 'Pulled them in. All of them fags. Taught them some respect. Fucking poofs.' McKaley paused as he leaned even closer in to Brady. 'Between you and me he did society a favour. They were an abomination. Should have been drowned at birth. He sent a message out loud and clear, I can tell you! Stopped the faggots hanging around those pick-up places looking for sex. Scared them shitless and drove them underground. Some six feet under!' McKaley confided as he gurgled throatily.

Conrad suddenly stood up. 'We're wasting our time, sir.'

'What's your problem, you little prick? You one of them?' McKaley leered.

Brady watched Conrad. He looked as if he was about to say something. But he didn't. He held back whatever retort he wanted to ram down the homophobic, vile old man's throat.

Instead it was Brady who said it: 'If you weren't so sick, you old fuck, I would take great delight in knocking seven bells of shit out of you. Remember Martyn Jenkins? What you did to him?'

McKaley looked confused. He shook his head, at a loss as to why Brady was shouting at him.

'Martyn Jenkins?' Brady asked. 'You don't remember, do you? He remembered you all right. You evil bastard. And yeah,' Brady said as he gestured towards Conrad. He ignored the expression of shock followed by horror on Conrad's face as it dawned on him what Brady was about to disclose. Before Conrad could intervene he said it: 'He's gay. So what? He's the best copper I've ever had the privilege to work with and one of my closest friends. I would trust him with my life,' Brady said as he tried to control the rage he felt inside. It was clear that McKaley had had no interest in solving the Joker killings. That to him, the victims who had been so horrifically tortured and then murdered had deserved it.

204

Conrad stood there, rigid. His eyes were filled with rage as he stared at Brady. 'You had no right,' he said in a strained voice. 'No right to tell him that.'

'Get out, you fucking fag! Go on. Get out of my room before I kick you out!' McKaley shouted at Conrad.

Conrad ignored McKaley, still staring in disbelief at his boss.

'For fuck's sake, Conrad!' Brady exploded. He couldn't believe the way Conrad was looking at him, as if he were the enemy. His eyes filled with hurt at what he felt was Brady's betrayal.

Brady shook his head in frustration. 'When I have to deal with the homophobic rants of pricks like McKaley or the sick shit that's being bandied around the station about you then it becomes my business. I respect and value you and always have done. The fact that you're gay makes no difference to me. Never has done. You know that. And it shouldn't to anyone else. So yeah, I'm more than prepared to tackle any bullying regarding your personal life. Whether you like it or not. I'm not just your boss, Harry. Sometimes you should remember that.'

'I mean it! Fucking get out, you poof, before I kick the shit out of you,' McKaley spat as he attempted to get up from his chair. 'And take your snivelling fag lover with you!' he added, turning with disgust to Brady.

Brady clenched his fists as he resisted the urge to punch the retired copper. He knew if he did, it would make him no better than McKaley. But he would have felt a hell of a lot better for it.

Instead Brady walked out, leaving Conrad still standing there.

'You all right?' Brady asked, regretting his outburst in front of McKaley. But he couldn't help himself. It had been left unsaid for too long.

Conrad nodded as he started up the car.

But Brady wasn't convinced. He watched as Conrad reversed out of the car park, thinking over what had just happened. It was hard to believe that McKaley had once been a copper. That he had shared the same rank as Brady. Worse, that McKaley had a reputation that was still fiercely protected.

Brady stared out at the road. He wished that his DS hadn't been there to witness McKaley's vile, venomous tongue. He knew that Conrad was having a hard enough time back at the station with the likes of Daniels and Kenny without experiencing the homophobic rants of some old, twisted son of a bitch.

'Thank you,' Conrad said, low. 'For . . .' He left the sentence unspoken.

The words were barely loud enough for Brady to hear. But he heard them.

Brady turned to him, surprised.

But Conrad kept his eyes on the road ahead.

Brady didn't know how to respond. So he switched the conversation back to work. The job. Anything other than acknowledging the awkwardness between them.

'Sarah Huntingdon-Smythe . . .' Brady began. 'I'll need you to verify her alibi for Saturday night when we get back.'

'Do you really think there's any truth in Molly Johansson's accusation that she was having an affair with De Bernier?'

Brady shrugged. 'Honestly? I'm not sure. All I know is that Johansson is convinced of it.'

'You don't think Johansson was lying? Trying to throw us off?'

Brady thought about it for a moment. 'No. I reckon she's genuine, Conrad. Doesn't mean that what she believes is fact. But I don't get the feeling that she was lying to us.'

Chapter Twenty-Eight

Monday: 7:18 p.m.

Charlie Turner, the desk sergeant on duty, had warned Brady when he returned that Gates was around. Turner had described Gates as: 'Marching in with a face like a slapped arse.' Not a good sign. Brady knew he was looking for him. Word was out that he wanted to talk to Brady – ASAP.

So far Brady had succeeded in avoiding Gates. It might have been early evening but it felt like his day was just beginning.

Suddenly the door opened and Conrad walked in.

Brady wasn't surprised to see him. He was expecting news on Sarah Huntingdon-Smythe.

'So, does she have an alibi for Saturday night?' Brady asked.

Conrad shook his head. 'I haven't checked yet, sir.' Before Brady had a chance to question him, Conrad continued, 'We've managed to trace a text that was deleted from the victim's phone on Saturday night. It was sent at ten thirty-two p.m.'

Brady frowned. 'What did it say?'

Conrad looked down at the notes in his hand. 'First rule, no talking. Second rule, blindfold yourself. Third rule. Face-down, ready to be bound and gagged.'

'Shit!' Brady muttered. 'Read it out again.'

'First rule, no talking. Second rule, blindfold yourself. Third rule, face-down, ready to be bound and gagged,' Conrad repeated.

'Do we know who sent it?'

'No sir, we're still trying to trace the number.'

Brady sighed heavily.

'It's definitely not Molly Johansson's mobile number?'

'No,' Conrad answered.

The news did not surprise Brady.

'So, that means that someone else other than his girlfriend was with him at the hotel that night. Someone who instructed him to blindfold himself. Which he did with his own tie. And then he waited for them to come in and bind and gag him,' Brady said as he shook his head. 'Christ!'

'How do you think they got into the room if he was blindfolded?' Conrad asked.

'A duplicate key maybe?' Brady answered. But that wasn't what worried him. What troubled him was the text. A text that detailed exactly what the victim had done before he was tortured and murdered.

Brady was tired and hungry. Worse still, it looked like he would be here for hours. He had a mountain of files on his desk. Old case notes from the Seventies investigation and information on all the recently paroled serious offenders in bail hostels and bedsits in the North East. Then there was the list of mentally ill patients recently released throughout the UK in the last few months. The NHS was seriously underfunded and mentally ill patients were now expected to travel hundreds of miles for medical attention. The upshot was that Brady could not afford to be lazy. It would have made his life easier if his search was limited to psychiatric hospitals in the North East, but then there was always the chance that the killer would slip through his fingers. Brady couldn't afford that. Not with any murderer, but in particular, not with this one.

If it was the original Joker or a copycat killer, Brady feared that De Bernier's death was just the beginning. That the sadistic killer would strike again, and again – reminiscent of the spree of killings committed by serial killer David Berkowitz, also known as Son of Sam, during 1976 to the end of the summer of 1977.

Six victims were left dead and a further seven wounded. As the body count increased, Berkowitz continued to elude police and taunt them with letters promising further murders. The press went hysterical and it gained international coverage. But unlike David Berkowitz, The Joker was still continuing to elude the police. This case was proving to be one hell of a headache. Amelia had made their task nigh-on impossible. If this was the original Joker killer, then as Amelia had said, he would probably be in his mid-to-late fifties. Even early sixties. But if this was a copycat killer, someone the Seventies Joker had divulged his method of murders to, then it was an entirely different ball game. It could simply be anyone. However, Brady was working on the assumption it was someone who knew De Bernier. Someone the victim was willing to meet in a hotel room for sex. At least, that was Brady's assumption, given the text that the victim had received.

Brady checked the time. It was later than he realised: 8:43 p.m. He was waiting for information on the phone that had sent the text to the victim before he went to see Gates. If Molly Johansson's accusation that Robert Smythe's wife was having an affair with his political aide was true, then there was a strong possibility that she would have texted or called the victim's phone.

These were serious allegations against a prominent politician's wife. Brady knew that this would not go down well with either DCI Gates or Detective Superintendent O'Donnell. He had no choice but to question Sarah Huntingdon-Smythe. But he would have to play this one very carefully.

As for Molly Johansson, Brady had released her without charge on condition that she remained in the area in case he needed her for further questioning.

A loud rap at the door broke his thoughts. 'Yeah?'

Conrad walked in.

'Tell me something positive for a change,' Brady said, hoping that Conrad had details on the phone.

Conrad closed the door behind him. 'Good news, DCI Gates has gone home. Bad news, he wants you in his office first thing.'

'Shit,' Brady muttered. 'What about the number that sent the text?'

Conrad shook his head. 'Sorry sir, still trying to trace it.'

Brady sighed.

'At least you don't have to report to Gates until the morning. Buys you some more time, sir,' Conrad stated.

'Have you seen the amount of information in these files, Conrad?' Brady said wearily. 'This lot will take me all night to get through.'

'I thought you had it run it through HOLMES, sir?' Conrad asked, surprised that Brady was going through it himself.

'I did. It didn't see a connection with any of the ex-inmates detailed here,' Brady answered. 'Not even a maybe.'

'Maybe that's because there isn't a connection. Saves you a lot of time if you accept that's the case,' Conrad suggested.

As soon as the investigation opened, Brady had entered the details of the murder into HOLMES 2, AKA the Home Office Large Major Enquiry System. It was his role as SIO to ensure that every detail of the case was inputted into HOLMES 2. It was a system used across the UK police force for serious crimes. The computer system was designed to carefully process the masses of information it was provided and cross-reference the details from other forces throughout the UK, making sure no vital clue or similar crime was missed. All relevant information that came through to the Major Incident Room where the rest of the team were working was entered into HOLMES 2 – whether it was information from members of the public, or something that one of the team had learned; if relevant, it would be added. HOLMES 2 effectively replaced the role of countless officers who would spend weeks trailing through information while the culprit simply disappeared. It also eliminated human error. No clues were missed, regardless of how nebulous. Its role was to help the SIO direct and control the course of the inquiry.

But it was adding to Brady's headache. It was coming back with no concrete direction. Not that he had expected it to. There were no other similar murder cases in the UK, apart from the obvious – the Seventies Joker killings.

And now Brady had to face going through the files in front of him to try and see something more than the nothing HOLMES 2 had given him. There was something that the specialist police database couldn't replace and that was when a copper got a hunch. That was why he was preparing to do an all-nighter. He had no choice. He could have given it to any one of the team to go through, but it was too important for him to run the risk of someone screwing up and not seeing something that Brady would consider important. He thought of McKaley. If the old bastard had actually done his job then Brady might not have been in this position. And maybe . . . just maybe De Bernier would not have been found tortured and mutilated. And very dead.

'So,' Brady said as he looked at Conrad, 'what have you brought me? Apart from whatever was left in Sainsbury's?' He had already spotted the bag in Conrad's hand.

Conrad somehow found a space on the desk and placed it down. 'Chicken and salad and tuna mayonnaise. Threw in a couple of ready salted crisps to add some texture for you.'

'Thanks,' Brady muttered. 'Sounds like shit.'

'Be grateful I even went out. It's pouring.'

Brady looked over at the window. It was pitch black and pissing it down. He wondered where the day had gone. He looked at the files on his desk distractedly. He had been hoping that McKaley would have had something, anything, that would help him narrow down his search. Despite Johansson's allegation, he had to keep his options open until they had evidence. However, the visit to the retired DI had not gone quite as Brady had hoped. It still left a bad taste in his mouth. He was also angry with himself that he had put Conrad in such a humiliating position. And for what? There was no gain. Just the bitter, twisted homophobic rants of an old man who had once had the power to exert his ignorant and cruel prejudices over others.

Brady looked back up at Conrad. 'OK, we've got dinner sorted. Question is, do I have to arm-wrestle you for the chicken salad?'

Suddenly Brady's phone vibrated. He looked at it and saw it was a text from Claudia. He had tried ringing her earlier but she hadn't answered. He had assumed that after last night she had spent most of the day sleeping. So he had left her a voicemail simply saying that he was worried about her. That she had scared him last night and she needed to call him back.

He picked up the phone and read her message.

Sorry. Don't worry I'm fine x

For a moment Brady forgot Conrad was still there. He smiled as relief coursed through him. He felt hopeful. It was a new feeling. One he hadn't been expecting. But maybe everything would be all right.

'Sorry, Claudia,' Brady explained.

Conrad looked uncomfortable at the mention of Claudia's name. 'Is she all right?'

'I think so.' Brady could feel his eyes starting to smart from the sudden relief. He willed himself not to get emotional. Especially not in front of his deputy.

'Right,' he said, changing the subject. 'Your choice. Tuna or chicken?'

'I'm sorry, sir. I . . . I have some personal problems I need to sort out,' Conrad apologised. He looked as awkward as he sounded. His cheeks were flushed and his eyes broke away from Brady's surprised expression. 'I . . . I was just coming in to update you on what I have so far.'

'Oh . . . right,' Brady answered, not quite knowing what to say. He wanted to ask Conrad if everything was all right, but found himself unable to bring the subject up. Conrad looked uncomfortable enough for the both of them. It was clear that he didn't want to talk about whatever he was going through.

'I have done a fourteen-hour shift. And, I'll happily put in eighteen tomorrow but I . . .' Conrad faltered, unable or unwilling to explain himself.

Brady accepted that the hours he put in were basically unheard of these days. Not that long ago a murder team could continue working the job and claim overtime. Not now. Hours were regulated. What happened to an investigation when you had clocked off was anyone's guess. The first few days were crucial in any murder investigation. The SIO in particular needed to be on the ball while the killer was still within reach. Every nuance, every potential lead and Brady wanted to know.

'What about Amelia? Is she still around?' Brady asked. He could do with all the help he could get to go through these files. If anyone could see something that could be promising, it was her. He also wanted a chance to clear the air with her. Explain what had happened that night when he had left her standing at the bar.

Conrad cleared his throat. 'She left at exactly six p.m. She waited to hear what updates we had and then went home. Said she'd be back at eight a.m. tomorrow.'

'What? So I take it I'm the only one who's still working on this bloody case?'

'There's still five other members of the murder team in the Incident Room working through. Or so they said,' Conrad answered. He realised it wasn't the answer that Brady wanted.

'So why didn't Amelia at least give me an update before she left? I mean, fuck it! She is meant to be the forensic psychologist on this case. And in case nobody's noticed, we don't actually have a profile. Or has that passed everyone's attention? Because that's why I'm bloody well sat here having to scour through this lot,' Brady ranted. He slowly breathed in as he tried to control his mounting frustration. Second day back on the job and it felt as if his team were bailing on him. Kenny and Daniels had kept out of his way all day, fearful of a repeat of the bollocking he had given them after the briefing. Harvey and Kodovesky had kept their heads down as well. Brady had no idea what he had done to piss Kodovesky off but he knew Harvey was still smarting from Brady losing it with him over the Chantelle Robertson business.

'So, why's our forensic psychologist rushed off? A hot date, is it? Or is she moonlighting for that deadbeat DI Bentley at North Shields?' Brady asked, assuming the latter.

Conrad's embarrassed expression said it all.

'She's got a date? On a bloody Monday night in the middle of a crucial murder investigation?' Brady asked, unable to disguise his surprise.

'From what I gather, sir. Yes.'

'Fuck me!'

'No thank you,' Conrad answered, trying to make light of the situation.

It was lost on Brady. He was still reeling from the fact that Amelia had moved on. What had he expected? To come back five months later and for everything to be as it had been between them before . . . He stopped himself. He didn't want to think about it. Not again. Then there was Claudia. Their relationship, not that it could be called one, was proof that things could never be the same again.

'I have that information you requested, sir. But as far as I can see there's nothing else that we can do tonight. Apart from read through those files,' Conrad said, attempting to change the subject. He knew mentioning the files was taking a risk. The last thing he wanted was to be taking half of them home with him.

'You've managed to track her down?' Brady asked.

Conrad nodded. 'Sarah Huntingdon-Smythe is at a medical conference in London. She travelled down last Friday and returns tomorrow. She was shocked when she heard the news and said that she would be more than happy to help in whatever way she can. She also implied that she didn't know him that well. She said that he just worked for her husband. Contrary to Johansson's suspicions, she said that she did not know him in a personal context. But it seems like she couldn't have killed De Bernier.'

Brady looked at Conrad. 'How do you know?'

'She's staying in the Covent Garden Hotel. I rang the reception desk and they put me through to her room. They also confirmed that on the night of the murder she had dinner at seven p.m. in the hotel restaurant. Sarah Huntingdon-Smythe said that herself when I talked to her.'

Brady nodded. He'd wanted to make sure. If Conrad had rung her on her mobile she could be sitting in her luxury, four-storey Victorian home in Tynemouth claiming to be in London.

'Covent Garden Hotel. Very nice,' Brady said.

'You've stayed there, sir?' Conrad asked, not picking up the subtle sarcasm.

'I've never bloody been, Conrad. I'm a copper on a modest salary. I probably couldn't even afford afternoon tea there, let alone stay the night. Christ! I can't even imagine what it costs.'

Conrad answered without thinking: 'The Covent Garden loft suite would set you back nearly two thousand pounds.'

'I see,' Brady muttered. Why did it fail to surprise him?

The colour on Conrad's face deepened.

Brady couldn't give a damn what Conrad did in his own time. He knew that he came from a moneyed background. It was a given that he would have stayed in hotels like the Covent Garden. But Brady still didn't understand why Conrad was in the north of England of all places. Or bloody Whitley Bay. He could understand why he joined the force. He would make detective chief superintendent one day. He was liked from above, and he had connections. Both useful arsenal when climbing the corporate ladder.

'Husband's money is it?' Brady asked, unable to hide the cynicism from his voice.

'No, sir. She's a heart surgeon at the Freeman hospital. She's internationally recognised as an expert in infant heart surgery.'

It wasn't the answer he expected. Maybe he was getting too old and cynical. It wasn't like him to automatically assume a woman did not have her own money behind her. Claudia was an excellent example. When they had been married, she was the high earner. It jarred that he could make such a presumption. But to be fair, he would be the first to admit he had his prejudices. Mainly about politicians. Or to be accurate, right-wing politicians. He was old-school Labour. Not that there was such a party anymore. New Labour had seen to that. Brady also had an innate dislike of the privileged set. Perhaps it was because he had had to fight so hard to get where he was in his life. No background or education to speak of, and no money to buy in favours. And he definitely didn't like them together. Politics and money were a dangerous combination.

He would talk to Sarah Huntingdon-Smythe tomorrow when she got back from London. It was better face-to-face than over the phone. Conrad had already alerted her to the situation. And as he pointed out, she was in London when the victim was murdered. Distance itself ruled her out, regardless of Molly Johansson's belief that she had been with the victim that night. But Sarah Huntingdon-Smythe had known the victim, even though she claimed she didn't. Molly Johansson had overheard her having a heated conversation with him, one that included threatening to destroy his burgeoning career in politics. This interested Brady – a lot.

Chapter Twenty-Nine

Monday: 9:39 p.m.

There was still a mountain of files to get through. He took a slug of lukewarm coffee. It wasn't great, but it would do. It had enough of a kick to wake him up. He had to go through every released inmate's record in front of him. Just in case. On the off-chance that their killer was there. He couldn't sit back and wait to talk to Sarah Huntingdon-Smythe in the hope that, despite the problem of her location on the night of the murder, she was De Bernier's killer. However, Brady still needed to talk to her. He would have to inform Gates tomorrow morning. He knew it would be tricky. Her husband Robert Smythe was not only a prominent politician, he was also a powerful business-man who had connections everywhere – including within the police. He knew that he would have to tread carefully. Even more so, considering he would have to interview him as well. Alexander De Bernier had been Robert's junior political aide, after all.

There was a sudden knock at his door.

'It's open.' He looked up, surprised to see Daniels stood there.

'I've gone through the CCTV footage from that night, sir. I think you might want to see what I've found.'

'See?' Daniels asked, pointing at the screen in the viewing room.

'Yeah. Just. Rewind and freeze it, will you?'

Brady stared at the grainy image. He turned to Daniels. 'The time's ten thirty-one p.m. Alexander De Bernier was murdered shortly after that. I want to know who the Audi is registered to, ASAP.'

'Yes, sir,' Daniels answered. Only part of the licence plate was visible, which would make his job time-consuming. But he was all too aware that his boss was not in the mood for details. All he wanted was the information.

Brady had also made a mental note of the limousine pulling up outside the hotel at 7:31 p.m. on Saturday night. Four well-dressed men had got out the limo, each with an overnight bag. Brady had watched as they headed in the direction of the hotel entrance. The limousine had then pulled away. Brady had scrutinised the hotel's check-in list and he knew that four men had not checked in at around that time. He made Daniels fast-forward the tape to the following morning. At 11:31 a.m. the same limousine pulled up outside the hotel and sat idling until the four men it had dropped off returned.

Brady had left Daniels with the task of finding the owner of the Audi R8 while he went back to his office. He needed to make a phone call. One that had to be done in private.

It was now 10:37 p.m. It would be 11:37 p.m. in Spain. He had no choice but to ring Madley – again.

He was surprised when Madley answered.

'Yeah?'

'I assumed you were dead,' Brady said.

'I'm on holiday, Jack. You should try it sometime.'

'I wish I could. Unfortunately, I'm trying to clean up a mess that was left behind in one of your hotel rooms.'

'Shame. You'd like it out here. Sun, sea and ice-cold beer. It would do you the world of good, getting away from that job.'

'Is that an invite?' Brady asked. He knew the answer. The last person Martin Madley would want in his luxury villa was a copper. It didn't matter that Brady was a friend, a childhood friend at that, he was still working for the opposition.

'No.' The delivery had an unmistakable edge to it.

Brady imagined Madley sitting in some exclusive restaurant somewhere. Dressed impeccably, as always. Dark Armani suit, crisp white shirt casually left open at the neck, and handmade Italian shoes. He would have a whisky, twenty-year-old single malt at that, in his left hand, every so often swirling the golden liquid around in the crystal tumbler as he spoke. His dark eyes, menacing and dangerously intelligent, would be watching for trouble.

Madley was the same age as Brady. His frame was slighter than Brady's, but that meant nothing. Madley could take anyone down – including his hired bodyguard, Gibbs. Madley's long-standing henchman was an imposing figure with thick, knotted, black and silver dreads and a large diamond drilled into his front tooth. The Afro-Caribbean stood at six foot four and was built like a brick shithouse. Even at forty-six years old, his fists were legendary. That said, Madley would still be able to floor him.

Brady knew that Gibbs and Weasel-Face, Madley's other henchman, would be behind him. On guard the whole time. It might be a holiday for Madley, but his men were expected to work – regardless of the luxurious setting.

'So, what do you know about what happened on Saturday night?' Brady asked. He didn't expect an answer. At least not a straight one.

'Isn't it your job to inform me?' Madley suggested.

'Stop pissing around, Martin. I'm serious.'

'Like I said, you need a holiday, Jack. You sound stressed. Sure you didn't return to work too soon after what happened to you?'

Brady sighed heavily. He was getting nowhere, fast.

'So I take it you know nothing about it?' Brady asked.

'Why was he killed?'

'I was hoping you could tell me that.'

'Difficult, when I was in Spain the night the kid was murdered.'

Brady knew that there was no point in continuing. Even if Madley knew anything, he was clearly not going to talk.

'Chantelle Robertson?' Brady asked.

'What about her?' His voice was cold.

Brady realised that he had hit a nerve.

'Bit young for you, don't you think?'

Madley had never struck Brady as someone interested in having some young glamour girl on his arm. But then again, Madley lived by a different set of rules to Brady.

Madley laughed. It was hard and insincere. 'I thought you knew me better than that.'

'Why's she over there with you then?'

'Who's to say she's here?'

'Come on, Martin. I'm not stupid, all right? Why is she there and who invited her?'

'Paul. He's owed a few days off so I agreed to her flying out. Keeps him busy.'

Paul, AKA Weasel Face: a scrote from the East End of London. Madley kept the wiry, snake-eyed little runt on a tight leash for good reason. He was trouble. It wasn't the Glock 31 semi-automatic that he carried around under his cheap, synthetic suit. No, it was his small, hungry, darting eyes that warned people off. He was like a coiled spring. Always on the edge, pumped full of adrenalin, waiting for trouble.

Brady couldn't understand why Madley kept him on. He was a liability. A dangerous one at that. But Madley obviously had his reasons.

'You seriously expect me to buy that? You don't allow your staff to fraternise with one another. Never mind shag each other.'

'He did me a favour. I owed him.'

Brady wasn't buying it. 'Don't fuck me around. '

Madley laughed. Cold, insincere and menacing. 'What is it with you, Jack? Always poking your nose in where it doesn't belong.'

'I'm a copper. That's what I do.'

'And I'm a businessman who likes to keep my affairs private.'

'Bit hard when you have the police crawling all over your hotel,' Brady answered.

Madley didn't respond.

'Look, I'm not a fool. I've heard that you have some kind of business providing certain clients with whatever they want. No questions asked.'

'Maybe you should be more careful who you listen to,' Madley replied.

'Maybe you should be more careful who you employ. Did you have to fly her over to make sure she didn't talk?'

Madley's silence said it all.

'I imagine that the murder victim is the least of your problems. But it's my problem. And right now what troubles me is that there's no security cameras in your hotel and the one person who checked the murder victim in, and perhaps the last person to see him alive, is sunning herself in your villa, not giving a damn.' Brady knew that Madley would have cameras hidden throughout the hotel. He was a shrewd businessman. He would be keeping very discreet tabs on the comings and goings at his hotel, especially when dealing with rich and powerful clients. Madley liked to be in control. He also liked to be one step ahead. Would he have security tapes that he could use as leverage if the need ever arose? Without a doubt.

Madley still did not comment.

'You want to tell me why a limousine pulled up outside your hotel on Saturday night at seven thirty-one? From what we can make out from the CCTV footage along the Promenade, four well-dressed men with overnight bags got out of the limousine and headed towards the entrance of your hotel. Who were they and why were they not checked into the system? I know they went into the hotel because the limousine disappeared and then returned the following morning. The exact same four men can be seen walking from the direction of your hotel entrance and back to the limousine.'

'I don't know what you're talking about,' Madley answered. There was an unmistakable edge to his voice.

'Martin, don't piss me around. I'm trying to keep you out of this. Remember, someone was murdered in your hotel and we're still looking for a suspect. If you really want the police turning up on your grounds over in Spain to haul Chantelle Robertson's arse back here then that's your call. I can only assume that you're worried that she'll talk about whoever those four men were. I'm certain they won't want their names brought into a murder investigation. Let alone the press getting hold of their identities.'

Brady waited. He knew Madley was mulling this over.

'All right. But this goes no further,' Madley finally said.

'Go on.'

'You're right. Four men did turn up. They're regulars. They pay a high price for anonymity and discretion. They're not on the hotel system because they want absolute privacy. If their identities got out to the press they would have a lot to lose.'

'What do they get up to?'

'None of my business. Or yours.'

'I don't believe that you don't have hidden cameras recording the goings-on in your hotel. You're a clever man, Martin. I know for a fact you would make sure you had something on them.'

'That's none of your business, Jack. Focus on your murder investigation. These men had nothing to do with it. I can personally assure you of that.'

'Then why not let your receptionist be interviewed?'

'Because I don't trust her to keep her mouth shut,' Madley replied. 'I had to take the precaution of removing what could be a threat to my business and other peoples' lives.'

Brady breathed out. He knew that Madley would not give him any more than he had. But at least it explained the sudden disappearance of Chantelle Robertson; nothing more than Madley covering himself.

From what, though?

222

Brady accepted he would probably never find out. It was better that way for both of them.

'How's Claudia doing?' Madley asked suddenly.

The abrupt change in conversation took Brady by surprise.

'I take it, not good,' Madley said, when Brady failed to answer.

'No . . . she's fine,' Brady replied. But it was clear from his voice that she was anything but.

'You were always a lousy liar, Jack. Even as a kid,' Madley said, the hardness momentarily gone.

Brady couldn't help but notice the concern in Madley's voice. It was a rare occurrence. One that told Brady he should be worried. Whether he liked it or not, he had to face reality. Claudia was far from fine.

'Let's catch up when I get back, yeah?' Madley suggested.

'Yeah, sounds good,' Brady answered, half-heartedly. He knew it would not happen. Gone were the Monday night poker sessions. And the late-night drinking sessions in the Blue Lagoon. Things had changed. Their differing careers more apparent than ever. Madley would always be there if Brady was in trouble. That went without saying. And vice-versa. But other than that, Madley had made it quite clear that Brady was no longer welcome in his newfound milieu. He had worked hard at distancing himself from his rough, crime-ridden background. Madley's associates were now powerful businessmen and politicians alike, and as such, it went without saying that Brady was not welcome.

Brady listened to the dull tone, realising that Madley had disconnected the call. He looked around his office. The shadowy glow from the desk lamp gave the room a bleak, soulless, empty feeling. The rain continued to pelt mercilessly at the windowpane. It struck him that he had never felt so alone.

He got up and stretched his stiff legs. His left one was aching. Again. He limped over to the window and looked out. The dark street was deserted. No surprise. It was cold, miserable and lashing it down. He decided that he would stay for another hour and then he would go home. Pick up an Indian take-out from Spice Junction and a couple of bottles of wine from the Tesco Express on Park View Road in Whitley Bay.

First, he needed to rethink the Seventies case. He knew that it was crucial. After all, it was no coincidence that De Bernier had been murdered in an identical way to The Joker's victims. Amelia had made an astute point when she had said that the reason The Joker had stopped killing was not out of choice. He had been prevented from killing. In other words, he had more than likely been locked up. And the answer could be staring him in the face. The files in front of Brady could hold a lead that had somehow been missed. Something so minor, so minuscule that it had fallen below the radar. He trusted his gut. And right now it was telling him to keep looking, to keep poking around until he hit something.

Despite Brady's best intentions, it was after 1:00 a.m. before he even realised it. He had found himself completely absorbed in the task at hand. He had gone through all of the case files of the recently released psychiatric patients. Some of it was beyond disturbing. But he hadn't found anything that stood out. Nothing that he could say tied into the Seventies killings – or the recent murder.

He was nearly halfway through the paroled serious ex-offenders when something – or someone – stood out. He was an ex-offender who had been paroled two weeks ago and rehomed in Ashley House, a bail hostel in Edwards Road, Whitley Bay. Adrenalised with too much caffeine and newfound optimism, Brady had wanted to call Amelia. Let her know. But he had resisted. The idea that she could still be with someone had stopped him short. He couldn't call Conrad either. He had made it very clear that he was off-duty. If he was having a tough time personally, then the last thing he needed was his boss calling him into work at all hours. For all Brady knew, the job could be starting to have a negative impact on Conrad's relationship. Brady decided to deal with it on his own. He trusted his instinct.

There was something about this paroled offender's history that troubled him. He looked up his probation officer: Jonathan Edwards. He would call him in the morning. Let him know he needed to talk to this particular ex-offender. A diagnosed psychopath who had been in and out of psychiatric hospitals and then a significant stint in prison, a parole board had decided to release him two weeks ago. HOLMES 2 hadn't picked up on this particular offender because his criminal history did not match the Seventies killings. But there was something that had caught Brady's eye. Something Conrad had said about the killer's choice of victims. The choice of victims and the way they'd been killed were interlinked in a way Brady had not seen before. It had made him rethink the possibility that this parolee could actually be him – *The Joker.*

TUESDAY

Chapter Thirty

The house was in darkness when Brady crept in, which had come as a relief. It had meant that Claudia had gone to bed – something that should have struck him as odd. But at the time, he had not even questioned it. Punch-drunk with tiredness, he climbed the stairs. He passed the guest bedroom – now Claudia's room. The door was closed. Without thinking any more of it, he headed straight for bed.

Four hours later and he was dragged out of unconsciousness by his BlackBerry relentlessly buzzing. He had set the alarm for 5:30 a.m. It was now 5:40 a.m. He had fifteen minutes to get shaved, showered and dressed. And in between that, down two cups of coffee to shake off what felt like a hangover.

Brady stood in the shower, letting ice-cold water hit his body. His mind kept replaying the previous day's events. He was making sure he hadn't missed anything. That he had played everything by the book. He had to face DCI Gates this morning and he wanted to go in knowing that he hadn't fucked up in any way. What troubled him was the MP, Robert Smythe. He knew that Gates would be less than impressed when he heard the news that Brady wanted to interview his wife – then him. But he had no choice. Robert Smythe was the victim's employer. And his wife had been accused of having an affair with Alex. Even of murdering him.

Brady scrawled a note to Claudia, apologising for getting home so late and with the promise that he would make it up to her. He then left it alongside a coffee on the granite worktop. He had ground Italian coffee beans and left a pot of fresh coffee for when she woke up. He had thought about taking the note and coffee upstairs to the guest room and leaving it next to her, but decided against it. He was sure she wouldn't thank him for waking her at this hour. And anyway, he was expected at the station.

'Sir,' Conrad greeted him as he walked into Brady's office.

Brady looked up. Conrad looked nervous, as if he was expecting a bollocking.

'It's after nine-thirty. You're late,' Brady informed him.

'Er,' Conrad began, apprehensively.

'You haven't hit my bloody car trying to park your Saab, have you?' Brady demanded. He had opened his window to get some fresh air into his office and had heard someone making a dog's dinner of attempting to park in the congested street a few minutes before.

His car was his pride and joy; a black 1978 Ford Granada 2.8i Ghia. It was his only connection to his brother Nick and it meant everything to him. Nick was four years younger than him and had relocated out of the North East as soon as he could. He was based in London but worked throughout Europe. Nick was ex-SAS and hired himself out as a bodyguard; at least that was what he told Brady. And it was a story he stuck to – religiously. Brady rarely saw Nick. He had made some powerful enemies in his line of work and as such he kept a low profile. Even his phone calls were becoming more and more sporadic. His excuse was that his type of work made it impossible to maintain regular contact. Brady sorely missed him. But there was nothing he could do. It felt as if he was losing everyone connected to his past life.

The Ford Granada was Brady's connection to the past – to his brother. The car had been bought as a project for them both to work on. But it was Nick who had turned it around. He had a flair for fixing things, ever since he was a young kid. It had been nothing but a rusty shell when they had bought it, but now it was a work of art. His younger brother had spent months working on it on the odd weekends, slowly and steadily rebuilding it to beyond its former glory.

Brady waited for Conrad to say whether he had damaged it.

'No, sir,' Conrad answered.

'Well, what then? You look like you're about to tell me that I've been bloody sacked or something,' Brady said, frowning.

'It can wait,' Conrad replied.

'I've got five minutes, come on. What is it that you've heard? Has Gates said something? Shit! He's not handing the investigation over to that two-faced, snivelling shit Adamson, is he?'

Before Conrad had a chance to answer, Brady's phone rang. 'Give me a minute, yeah?'

Conrad nodded and turned to leave.

Brady waited until he had left the office before answering the call. He couldn't help noticing that Conrad looked on edge. He made a mental note to have a private word with Conrad later, but he had other more pressing things to worry about now.

'Detective Inspector Jack Brady,' he answered.

'Hi, it's Jonathan Edwards, Inspector.'

'Thanks for returning my call so quickly. I appreciate it,' Brady replied.

'No problem. What can I do for you?'

Brady mentally prepared himself. There was a good chance his hunch would lead nowhere. But he was prepared to take the risk.

'I'm interested in a recently paroled offender residing at Ashley House,' Brady began. 'It's an ex-offender by the name of James David Macintosh.'

'Are you sure?' Edwards asked.

'Yes,' Brady answered. 'I'm sure. Can you confirm his whereabouts on the evening of Saturday, fifteenth March?' He could feel his blood pounding in his ears as he waited to hear whether or not he was onto something.

Brady could hear the probation officer breathing out slowly.

'Is this to do with the murder on Saturday in the Royal Hotel?'

'Can you answer my question, please?' Brady replied.

'Sorry . . . Yes . . . I mean no. No, I can't confirm his whereabouts. He broke his curfew. He was supposed to sign back in to Ashley House at seven p.m. at the latest. He didn't return until after midnight.'

'Did he say where he had been?'

'No. All he said was that he had been walking around and hadn't realised the time.'

It was enough for Brady. He needed James David Macintosh brought in for questioning.

Chapter Thirty-One

There was a knock at the door, followed by Amelia walking in.

Brady looked up, surprised.

'Why didn't you call me about this?' Amelia asked.

For the briefest of moments Brady could see the hurt in her eyes.

'I had to run it by Gates first, otherwise I would have done,' he assured her. But it was a lie. He had been too busy to even think about informing Amelia.

Brady hadn't seen Gates, so he had had no choice but to brief him over the phone about Robert and Sarah Huntingdon-Smythe. Then there was James David Macintosh, who had now been brought in and was waiting to be questioned. The investigation had taken a sudden turn with the entrance of Macintosh, and Gates was holding a press conference to appease the media. One that Brady had not been invited to attend. Gates had given him the same old crap as to why Brady shouldn't be holding it. That his time was too valuable. That Gates needed him actively working the case, not courting the press. Brady couldn't care less. The last thing he wanted was to be caught up in PR. Or to be the face that the press could demonise if the investigation went belly-up.

'I don't understand. You seriously believe James David Macintosh could be a suspect?'

'Take a seat and I'll explain,' Brady offered, trying his best to be congenial. He realised that he was at fault. He should have contacted Amelia immediately, rather than letting her hear it from Gates.

Amelia sat down opposite Brady.

'I'm sorry, I should have informed you. Remember you said that the Seventies murderer might have been forced to stop killing? That it wasn't necessarily voluntary? I spent most of last night going through recently paroled ex-offenders and James David Macintosh jumped out at me.'

Amelia listened intently, without saying a word.

'Have you had a look at his background?'

Amelia nodded. 'Just now.'

'Well, surely you can see why I've called him for questioning? He broke his curfew on the same night the victim was murdered. He did not return to Ashley House until after midnight and no one can account for his whereabouts.'

'Yes, I can see that might make you suspicious. But what else do you have?'

'Macintosh has been locked up for thirty-seven years. I don't believe that it's a mere coincidence. At the end of the summer of 1977, a serial killer suddenly stopped in the midst of a killing spree. You yourself said that the sudden departure from killing would not be the suspect's choice. It would have been taken away from him. In other words, he must have found himself locked up. But locked up for an unrelated crime. Otherwise the original investigative team would have made the connection,' Brady explained.

'But the operative word here, Jack, is "unrelated",' Amelia replied.

Brady nodded. He understood why she was finding it difficult to see Macintosh as a suspect. 'I know. But let's start with his childhood. Raised in Jesmond to a father who was in the army. From all accounts he was a patriarchal bully who regularly beat his wife and child. He was a heavy drinker, which fuelled his insufferable rages. From a very early age James started exhibiting signs of social deviance. He was repeatedly reprimanded at school for misbehaving. One account is recorded

234

of him urinating into a milk bottle and drinking it in front of his shocked classmates and teacher.'

'I still don't see the connection,' Amelia cut in.

'I was building up to it. Pointing out how his background ties in with your profile. That he tortured animals as a child. Progressively got worse the older he got. Threw both his pet guinea pigs onto a bonfire he had built – alive. His father died of a sudden heart attack when he was fourteen years old and that was when his violence and depravity escalated. He replaced his father and began terrorising his mother.'

'But he was at Cambridge University when the Seventies murders occurred. He was living there, not in the North East.'

Brady nodded in agreement. 'But he spent most of 1973 in St Nicholas psychiatric hospital in Gosforth where one doctor diagnosed him as a psychopath. He missed the first year of his degree and had to start a year later. His psychiatrist at the time had said that he was an exceptionally intelligent young man with the propensity to become a killer.'

'Yes, I know,' Amelia replied, still not convinced.

'And when you say he left the area, that's not quite true. At the beginning of the summer of 1977 when he was coming to the end of his third year, Macintosh voluntarily admitted himself back into St Nicholas, stating that: "He felt peculiar and could not trust himself around the other students. The male students." He was diagnosed by his new psychiatrist as battling with homosexual urges. Distressed by his attraction to the same sex, he was one of twenty-nine patients studied in the UK who underwent homosexual aversion therapy. In other words, he willingly received electric shock treatment.' Brady paused for a moment as he shook his head. 'The conclusion of these studies were damning. The fact that they defined same sex attraction as an illness, one that could be treated by electric shock therapy to get rid of homosexual desires, understandably had a negative long-term impact on the individuals who took part. Including Macintosh.' Brady stopped talking.

The whole idea of what Macintosh and other patients suffered at the hands of these so-called doctors made him feel physically sick.

'The most common treatment from the early 1960s to late 1970s was behavioural aversion therapy with electric shocks. In electric shock aversion therapy, shocks were administered while the patient watched photographs of men and women in varying stages of undress. The aim was to encourage avoidance of the shock by moving to photographs of the opposite sex. It was hoped that arousal to same sex photographs would reduce, while relief arising from shock avoidance would increase interest in the opposite sex. Each treatment lasted about thirty minutes. We know from Macintosh's medical records that he also regularly received ECT which was more commonly used for treatment of severe mental illnesses, including, as in the case of Macintosh, homosexuality.' Brady paused for a moment to collect his thoughts. The idea of an electric current being passed through someone's brain to produce an epileptic fit – hence the name, electroconvulsive – because they had homosexual desires was anathema to him. 'It has been known to leave patients with short-term and in some cases long-term memory loss. Some patients also claimed that their personalities had changed for the worse and the outcome of the treatment was disturbing.'

Amelia waited, curious to see where Brady was going with his theory.

'Finally, he was also subject to discussions of the evils of homosexuality. Quite a lot for a twenty-two year old to experience.'

'I'm not disagreeing with you, Jack. But I honestly can't see where you're taking this.'

'All right, he underwent all this treatment because he was gay. Why? Because he didn't want to be gay. Understandable, given his background, which was discussed in detail in sessions he had during his time at St Nicholas.' Brady knew that Amelia hadn't read the transcripts from these sessions, because they had not been included in Macintosh's medical and criminal records. These transcripts were private conversations between Macintosh and his psychiatrist.

'I'm aware of his criminal history. And I also knew that he had undergone various aversion therapies. But I haven't read anything connected to these sessions you're talking about.' Amelia faltered, at a loss.

'But you're aware that he murdered his psychiatrist?' Brady asked.

'Of course. From what I read it was a horrific crime scene.'

Brady nodded. He felt sick as he thought about the notes he had read. Macintosh had used an axe. First his psychiatrist and then . . .

Brady swallowed as the bloody crime scene photos filled his mind.

'How did you get his medical files expedited so quickly? It is the NHS after all.' It took him a moment to register what Amelia had said.

'Yeah, sorry . . . I know someone who works at the hospital. It pays to be nice to people. You never know when you're going to need them,' Brady answered.

'You're lucky. Ordinarily it could take days to access someone's records. Police or not.'

Brady leaned forward. 'So? Interested in his history now?'

'I was always interested. But I'm still curious to understand why you think he is a suspect. He was locked up in a psychiatric hospital from the beginning of the summer of 1977 to the end. How could he have possibly committed seven murders?'

It was a fair point. 'Because he was there as a voluntary patient. Meaning he wasn't kept under lock and key. He paid for a private room so he wasn't kept on a main ward. Effectively, he was free to come and go. I also checked and he had a car, giving him the means to get to and from the crime scenes.'

'All right, say for argument's sake that you're right, and he *was* able to commit these crimes. The question now is, why?'

'I was waiting for you to ask me that. Like I said, his father was an extremely violent alcoholic with a sadistic streak in him. Whether it was years in the army, I couldn't say, but he had an absolute hatred for homosexuals. Something about James incited his father to outbursts of homophobic abuse and violence. Whether he suspected his son was gay from an early age, I don't know. But he had his own extreme aversion therapies.' He looked at Amelia. He had her full attention. 'His father would beat him, calling him obscene names. He would make his son undress in front of him and humiliate him. He would take a cut-throat razor to James' penis and threaten to cut it off. He said he would have no qualms in cutting his own son's penis off and choking him on it.'

'Oh God!' Amelia muttered as she covered her mouth with her hand; the magnitude of what Brady had uncovered making her momentarily lose her cool.

'Sir?' interrupted Conrad.

Brady and Amelia both turned round.

'Sarah Huntingdon-Smythe is here to talk to you. She says she hasn't got much time as she has an important appointment later this afternoon.'

'What time is it?' Brady asked Conrad. He had lost track, too absorbed in getting as much background information on James David Macintosh as he could. He had dedicated his entire morning to chasing up people for medical records. It had felt like he was getting nowhere until he had ended up getting put through to an ex-girlfriend of his from ten years ago. She had recognised his name and, luckily for him, hadn't hung up. She had left to travel to New Zealand. As far as he had heard she had ended up emigrating there. Eight years and one divorce later, she found herself back in the North East, with a senior role in management at St Nicholas's psychiatric hospital. If it hadn't been for her, he would never have uncovered the crucial psychiatric transcripts on the suspect. She had gone through countless shelved boxes of abandoned medical files to look for them.

When Brady had picked them up she had told him that she had regretted ever going to New Zealand. He wasn't quite sure what she meant by that, but she had given him her number.

'It's twelve thirty-nine.'

Brady sighed. He had a hell of a lot to do and not a lot of time to do it in. The case was suddenly shooting off in different directions.

'Sir? She really doesn't want to be kept waiting,' Conrad insisted.

'Fine,' Brady said, pushing his chair back and standing up. 'Let's get this over with. But I don't see why she's come into the station.'

'Because I rang her yesterday. We wanted a statement from her. Remember, sir? Molly Johansson implicated her in his murder? Said that they were having an affair?'

'I know all that, Conrad,' Brady snapped, not in the mood for a history lesson. 'But we have a witness at the hotel she was staying at who verified that she was at dinner on Saturday evening and was in the hotel on Sunday morning, which places her in London on the night of the murder. We have rather more pressing matters at this precise moment than jumping up and running because some politician's wife has snapped her fingers.'

'Surgeon. She's an eminent heart surgeon,' Conrad reminded him.

The look on Brady's face told him he did not need reminding.

'Detective Inspector Brady,' Sarah Huntingdon-Smythe greeted him as Brady walked into the room, followed by Conrad.

Brady took a seat across the table from her. The room still had a lingering smell of stale vomit from when they had interviewed Molly Johansson yesterday. But now there was also a subtle smell of expensive perfume and skin cream.

It didn't feel like yesterday to Brady. It felt like weeks ago. So much had happened since.

'I appreciate you coming in, Mrs Huntingdon-Smythe,' Brady began.

She shot him a smile of white, perfect teeth. 'Please, it's "Ms", not "Mrs", but feel free to call me Sarah.'

'Thank you, Sarah,' Brady began. 'My colleague, DS Conrad here, informed you yesterday about the sad news regarding your husband's political aide?'

'Yes, tragic,' she replied.

Brady looked at her. She was a handsome women in her mid-thirties. Tall, fashionably thin, with an air of refinement about her. Her short black hair was scraped back from her gaunt face. She wore no make-up that he could tell, adding to her overall air of androgyny. She was dressed elegantly and conservatively in a dark grey trouser suit and a light grey wool V-neck jumper under the jacket. Her dark brown eyes were filled with curiosity as she looked at Brady. He imagined that this was the first time she had given a statement to the police. And also, her first experience of a police interview room.

Brady found himself staring at her slender long hands. She wore no jewellery. But what intrigued him was that there was no wedding ring on her finger. A tell-tale white band told him that she had recently removed it.

She caught him looking. Momentarily self-conscious, she placed her right hand over her left one.

'How long have you been married to your husband?' Brady asked.

'Why?' she replied, her face expressionless.

'Because Alexander De Bernier's girlfriend is claiming that you were having a sexual relationship with him.'

She laughed at the suggestion. 'That's preposterous!'

'Why?'

She gave Brady a look which implied he was an imbecile for asking such a question.

'I have been married to my husband for ten years. In that

time I have been nothing but faithful. Have you met Robert?' she asked, with an edge to her voice.

Brady wasn't an idiot, despite what she thought. He knew she was trying to intimidate him. But he wasn't intimidated by anyone; least of all, some jumped-up Conservative politician. Or his wife.

'No. Not yet,' Brady answered.

'Well, when you do you'll see why I would have no inclination to have a scurrilous affair with my husband's junior aide. Robert means everything to me.'

Brady wasn't buying it. The missing wedding ring said it all.

'Your husband is older than you?'

For a moment Sarah's cool composure was lost as her eyes flashed with irritation. 'Yes. I am thirty-five and my husband is fifty-nine. However, I don't see why the age difference between us could be relevant to a murder inquiry.'

'I was just curious,' Brady answered, ignoring her icy glare.

She turned to Conrad. 'Look, I came here to be of some help. Out of respect, really, for Alexander. I was so shocked by the news . . .' She faltered as her eyes dropped to her hands.

'I am sorry, Ms Huntingdon-Smythe. I assure you that we do appreciate you making the time to come in,' Conrad appeased her.

'Thank you. At least one of you has good manners.'

'How well did you know Alexander De Bernier?' Brady asked, ignoring the jibe.

She turned back to Brady, her face cold and impassive. 'Not very well. He worked for my husband. Perhaps you should ask him about Alexander?'

'I plan to, as soon as he gets back from Brussels,' Brady replied. However, this was something he still had to run past Gates. Robert Smythe was a powerful politician and Brady had to tread very carefully. 'Do you know why the victim's girlfriend would suggest that you were having a relationship with him?'

'Haven't you already asked that question?' she asked haughtily.

'Yes, but you failed to answer it.'

She gave Brady a hard, cold look. 'I have no idea why that silly girl would say such a thing. As far as I remember she spent all her time trying to bed my husband.'

Brady didn't react, despite her best attempt. 'Does your husband have a habit of sleeping with his junior aides?' he enquired.

'What man wouldn't if it is offered to him on a plate? I am not a fool, detective. Robert is no exception. I am aware of his indiscretions but, aside from that, we have a good marriage. Sometimes one has to compromise for the sake of equilibrium,' she answered simply.

Brady looked at her. She was an enigma. There was no bitterness or malevolence when she delivered the news that her husband had sexual relations with his interns. The cool, detached manner and her acceptance of the status quo within her marriage was remarkable.

'Johansson said that she witnessed you and her boyfriend talking intimately—' Brady was forced to stop as she cut him off.

'If by "intimately", you mean Alexander apologising to me for the spectacle that his imbecilic, drunken slut of a girlfriend was making of herself by flirting shamelessly with my husband? Then yes, you could say we were talking "intimately".'

'She never mentioned that she was attracted to your husband,' Brady replied.

'Infatuated, detective.'

'Molly Johansson claimed that last Thursday evening she overheard you and the victim arguing in one of your guest bedrooms. Is that correct?' Brady asked, not expecting an answer. Or at least a straight answer.

'Yes. That is correct,' Sarah answered.

Brady could not figure her out. She was composed and dignified, an unmistakable air of imperiousness about her.

'Can you explain to us what the argument was about?' Brady asked.

242

'Of course. I had a private word with Alexander about his girlfriend's unacceptable behaviour. I told him in no uncertain terms that I had had enough. That if it did not end, then I would have no choice but to get Robert to sack her, and him. He was understandably upset, but I am afraid that it had gone on long enough.'

Brady nodded. 'Do you think your husband was sleeping with her?'

She gave Brady a condescending look. 'I have no idea. If he was, then that is his business. However, Robert understands that there is one thing I cannot abide, and that is public indiscretions of any sort. I may be tolerant of my husband's foibles but I am no fool.'

Brady could feel the frustration building. He was getting nowhere with her.

'Is there anything else that you think could be pertinent to our investigation?' he asked, deciding it was time to end what had fast become a farce.

'No.'

'I appreciate you coming in, Ms Huntingdon-Smythe,' he concluded as he stood up. 'My colleague DS Conrad will see you out.'

Brady left the interview room, not quite sure what had just happened. He couldn't place his finger on it but there was something about her that jarred with him. He thought of her accusation that Molly Johansson was trying to bed her husband. But before he had a chance to think it through, he walked into a flustered and out of breath Daniels.

'Sir? I've . . .' Daniels gasped, trying to get his breath back. 'You need to take a look at this,' he said, clutching some papers. 'It's to do with Robert Smythe.'

Chapter Thirty-Two

It took Brady a moment to absorb what Daniels had just said. He felt as if he'd been punched in the guts, by a blow he had not been expecting. 'Shit! You're not serious?

Daniels' face was deadly serious.

Brady looked again at the printout in his hand. He reread the name the phone was registered to, and then the words: *First rule, no talking. Second rule, blindfold yourself. Third rule. Face-down, ready to be bound and gagged.*

He shook his head. *How? How the hell could it be?* He looked at Daniels. 'You're certain this text came from a phone registered in Robert Smythe's name?'

'Yes, sir. But it's his business phone,' Daniels replied.

Not that it made a difference to Brady. It had still come from a phone registered to Smythe.

'And the white Audi R8 that we saw pull into the hotel car park at ten thirty-one is definitely registered to Smythe?'

Daniels nodded. 'His own private car, sir.'

Brady pushed his hair back from his face as he absorbed the enormity of the situation. 'Fuck!'

He looked at Conrad. 'I need to talk to Gates. We need Robert Smythe in custody.'

Conrad nodded but he still looked unsure. 'Do you think DCI Gates will sanction it?'

'Shit, Conrad! He's got no other choice. Has he?'

*   *   *

'Sir,' Brady greeted Gates as he walked into his office.

Gates looked up from his desk.

Brady noted that he didn't look in the mood for surprises.

He was roughly the same height and build as Brady, but he was physically fitter despite the ten-year age difference. He worked out religiously. He was a man who liked to feel in control. Everything about him was regimented and exact. His dark hair was cropped short. His face, clean-shaven at all times, regardless of the hours he had put in on the job. Gates kept a tight rein on his feelings, no matter what the situation was. But Brady wasn't sure how he was going to handle this news.

'Sir, we've now got information back on the victim's phone.'

Gates gestured for Brady to take a seat, his heavily lined, pockmarked face as dispassionate as ever.

Brady did as instructed. It gave him a moment to prepare himself for the next blow he was about to deliver. He knew for a fact that Gates would not be expecting this – no one would.

'A text was sent to the victim's phone at ten thirty-two p.m. Here it is,' Brady said as he handed over the sheet of paper with the text printed on it.

'Shit!' He looked up at Brady. 'Is this correct?'

'Yes, sir,' confirmed Brady.

Gates sighed heavily as he reread the words:

First rule, no talking. Second rule, blindfold yourself. Third rule. Face-down, ready to be bound and gagged.

'The other text explains how the murderer gained access to the victim's room, sir.'

Gates looked at the text that Alexander De Bernier had sent at 8:39 p.m. '212 vase?' Gates read out.

'The victim's room number was 212 and on the second floor I noticed a large, ornate Chinese vase. I assume De Bernier placed the duplicate room key card under the vase. That text went to the same number that sent the instructions of what the victim had to do.'

Gates shook his head as he reread both messages. He then looked up at Brady. 'Do you know who sent the texts?'

Brady nodded. Apprehensive.

'Well?' Gates snapped.

'Robert Smythe, sir. The politician,' he added. Not that he needed to. There was only one Robert Smythe.

It took Gates a moment to absorb what Brady had just said. 'You're absolutely certain?' he asked, his voice filled with disbelief.

'Yes, sir. It's from his business phone.'

'Have you talked to his secretary?'

Brady nodded. 'She confirmed that on the night of De Bernier's murder Robert Smythe was at a political dinner.'

'I see,' Gates replied as he clasped his hands together. It was clear from the look in his eyes that he did not for one second believe that the politician could be responsible for the murder.

Brady sighed inwardly. The worst was yet to come. 'But she did say that he left sometime between nine p.m. and ten p.m.'

Gates frowned. 'Go on.'

'Well, sir, she was adamant that anyone could have picked up her employer's business phone. That he had a habit of leaving it unattended.'

Gates nodded, relief etched on his face. It was evident that he did not want to make an enemy out of Robert Smythe or affect his chances of promotion.

'But . . .' Brady paused as he readied himself. 'His white Audi R8 was spotted on CCTV camera pulling off from the Promenade and into the Royal Hotel car park.'

'What time was this?' Gates asked abruptly.

'Precisely ten thirty-one p.m.'

'And this is definitely on the night he attended a political dinner?'

'Yes, sir. But as I said, his secretary and other witnesses have said that no one saw him after ten p.m. The political dinner was held at the Grand in Tynemouth. A five-minute drive from Whitley Bay. At ten thirty-one his car pulls up outside the hotel where De Bernier is waiting and at ten thirty-two a text is sent from Smythe's business phone instructing the victim to blind-fold himself.'

Gates sat back as he weighed up this new information. 'I take it Robert Smythe's still in Brussels?'

'Yes. He's due back home on Thursday.'

Gates narrowed his eyes as he looked at Brady. 'We need him to return to the UK ASAP.'

'Sir,' Brady said as he pushed his chair back and stood up.

'You interviewed his wife, I take it?'

'Yes, sir.'

'Did she mention any of this?'

'No, sir. Not at all. She was at a medical conference in London on the night of the dinner and De Bernier's murder. She hasn't seen Smythe since she left on Friday morning for London. Witnesses have placed her at the hotel on both the evening in question and the following morning.'

Gates nodded. Disappointed.

Brady realised he was checking to see whether Smythe could have an alibi for his whereabouts after he left the dinner. His wife would have been the obvious cover. However, she'd been in London.

'When did Smythe leave for Brussels?'

'He took a flight from Newcastle on the morning following the murder.'

Gates breathed out heavily. He looked up at Brady. 'One thing,' he began.

Brady looked at him expectantly.

'This is not to get out. Understand? It's an extremely delicate situation and until we are absolutely certain Robert Smythe's involved in De Bernier's death I want no details released to the press.'

'Understood, sir.'

Chapter Thirty-Three

Tuesday: 3:14 p.m.

Brady was back in his office. He had instructed Robert Smythe's secretary that he needed the politician to return home on the next available flight, otherwise he would be going over to arrest him on suspicion of murder.

It had had the desired effect. Smythe was coming back to the UK on a flight early the following morning.

Brady thought of the victim's parents. Forty-eight hours after the news of their only son's death and they were holed up in a Newcastle hotel with two family liaison officers: DC Somerfield and DC Leighton. They had reported that the parents had positively identified the victim as their son. Not that there had been any doubt in Brady's mind. But it was a given that they would have resisted accepting the news. At least until coming face-to-face with the harsh reality in the morgue.

The family liaison officers had told Brady that the press had somehow got hold of the whereabouts of the parents and were now camping outside the hotel in the pursuit of exploiting their grief for the sake of public interest. Or naked voyeurism, to be precise. Gates had thrown the press a few more scraps to keep them happy. But it wasn't much. Now that the body had been officially identified, the victim's name had been released. Brady was already anticipating the crank calls they would receive from the public. Sifting through information that typically led them nowhere was one of the hazards of a high-profile murder case like this one. Gates had not released the fact that the victim had

248

been mutilated in an identical manner to the Seventies killings. That in itself would spark a media-induced hysteria, elevating the local crime to national news. The last thing they needed was the press following their every move. Not that it wasn't already happening on a small scale. But as soon as word leaked out about the disquieting similarity to the Joker case, then all hell would break loose. Old wounds would be reopened, not just for the original victim's families, but also for the police. Brady thought of McKaley. Some things were better left in the past.

Brady rubbed the stubble on his chin as he thought over their potential suspect – Robert Smythe. Someone who had enough power and influence behind him to force Brady out of a job if he'd got it wrong. But there was no disputing the text that Smythe had sent De Bernier. It clearly suggested that the politician was involved in a sexual relationship with his junior aide. One where the victim trusted the older man to bind and gag him. This wasn't a typical murder. It had been premeditated – unlike the usual murders that the police dealt with, the result of an argument escalating to murderous levels. The problem for Brady was still the link to the Joker killings.

How? And why?

If Smythe really was responsible, then how would he know details of the original murders that only the investigative team were privy to? It didn't make any sense. As to why the murder was a copycat killing, Brady felt that this was to confuse the police. To throw them off the scent of the actual killer. But Brady still wanted to know what had happened to the original Joker.

Where are you? Who are you? And why did you suddenly stop killing?

Macintosh came to mind, as well as Sidney Foster – one of the original suspects who was still missing. No one had seen the retired engineer, despite his face being plastered all over the tabloids and across the BBC news. Brady wasn't sure now whether his disappearance was coincidence. If details of De Bernier's murder had been released before he disappeared,

Brady could have understood it. After all, Foster had been subject to DI McKaley's form of questioning during the original investigation. It would be no surprise that he would go into hiding, since he would be the obvious suspect. But Sidney Foster had not been sighted for a couple of days before the victim was murdered. *Why not?*

He now had three suspects for the new killing: James David Macintosh, Robert Smythe and Sidney Foster. As to the original killings, James David Macintosh or Sidney Foster were still plausible suspects in Brady's mind. But which one was responsible for which crimes? Brady readied himself for his next move: questioning the only suspect he had in custody – Macintosh.

'What did you think of Sarah Huntingdon-Smythe?' Brady asked.

Conrad shrugged. 'Difficult to say.'

'Two coffees, one black and one with milk,' Brady ordered as he handed over the correct change. 'Do you want something to eat?' he asked Conrad.

Conrad shook his head as he looked at the paltry leftovers from the lunchtime rush.

They were in the basement cafeteria, taking a fifteen-minute break before interviewing James David Macintosh. Brady was in dire need of caffeine. Lunchtime had come and long gone, along with his appetite.

'Thanks,' Brady said as he absentmindedly picked the coffees up. He handed the milky one to Conrad.

'Tell me, that story about Molly Johansson flirting with her husband, do you believe her?' Brady asked as they headed towards the cracked, red laminated table by the window.

'Why not?' Conrad asked.

'I'm not doubting her when she says that her husband has his "indiscretions", as she called them. I just—' Brady stopped himself before he said it. He knew it sounded ludicrous.

'What, sir?' Conrad asked, frowning.

Brady pulled out a chair and sat down. He looked up at the barred window. The day outside was typically grey and overcast. It did nothing to lift his mood.

'Sir?' Conrad repeated.

He shook his head. 'Nothing about the outcome of this investigation would surprise me, Conrad. Nothing.'

Out of the corner of his eye, Brady saw Harvey come into the canteen. He was clearly looking for him.

'Jack,' Harvey said when he strode over. His dark M&S suit was immaculate, as was the shirt, though his bloated, blotchy face told a different story. His eyes were red-rimmed and bloodshot. But, apart from that, he looked remarkably pleased with himself.

Brady could see the disapproval on Conrad's face. Whether it was Harvey's sudden intrusion, or his over-familiarity with a senior ranking officer that rankled, Brady couldn't say.

'What the hell happened to you?' Brady asked, frowning.

Harvey shook his head. 'Worked until one a.m. on this,' he gestured at the file in his hand. 'Then back in at five a.m.'

'What is it?'

Harvey pulled out a chair and collapsed. 'I need a strong coffee and a full English if anyone's going over to order,' he said, looking straight at Conrad.

Conrad didn't bite.

'I have two minutes before I interview Macintosh. Tell me what you've found out and not what you're about to put in your stomach,' Brady said, too tired for Harvey's bullshitting.

'Shit, Jack! You think I wanted to work like some lackey? No. But I did it,' Harvey answered.

Brady could feel the frustration building. But he kept it in check and waited.

'There you go,' Harvey said throwing the file down on the table. 'See for yourself.'

Brady opened it up. It was details of the victim's recent travel. He quickly looked over the three-page document. It didn't take long for him to do the sums. 'Fuck,' Brady muttered.

'My sentiments exactly,' Harvey replied.

Brady passed the file to Conrad.

'Holidays to the Caribbean, Dubai and Thailand. Skiing trips to Aspen. What student do you know who could afford all that?' Brady asked. But it was a rhetorical question. The answers were clearly printed out in black and white. 'All paid for by other people's credit cards.'

Brady shook his head as he turned and looked at Harvey. He was impressed. He couldn't believe that Harvey had managed to pull this off. Maybe he had misjudged him. Brady was aware that the Chantelle Robertson fuck-up would have hit him hard. Or more likely, it was the verbal punch from Brady that had shaken him. Whatever it was, Brady wasn't complaining. 'How did you get this?'

Harvey shrugged casually. 'I worked a paper trail. That's all.'

Brady could understand why Harvey would question the extravagant and luxurious holidays. But putting together a comprehensive list of who had accompanied Alex on trips as well as who paid for them was another matter entirely.

For a moment Brady thought Conrad was going to be civil towards Harvey. Even compliment him for his hard-earned endeavours. He didn't. Harvey may have been of the same rank as Conrad but that was where the similarity ended.

'Sir,' Conrad said. 'These two names.'

Brady looked at him. Conrad's expression worried him. His eyes were narrowed as he looked back down at the document in his hand. His jaw was clenched, lips set in a thin line. Something was clearly wrong.

Brady gave him a quizzical look. He had not had a chance to scrutinise the information yet. 'Go on.'

'Robert Smythe is here.'

'Where?' Brady asked.

'R. Smith, sir,' Conrad stated.

Brady frowned at him. As did Harvey.

'I assume it's the alias he uses on his credit card and bank details,' Conrad explained warily.

252

'Why?' Harvey asked, clearly not convinced.

'Because it gives him anonymity. I imagine he would feel more secure conducting his financial affairs that way.'

Harvey looked at Conrad as if he were barking mad.

'He doesn't necessarily want to advertise that he's a politician. People may not know what he looks like, but they would recognise the name. How many Smythes do you know around here?' Conrad asked Harvey.

Harvey shrugged. 'I can't say.'

'Well, R. Smith is definitely Robert Smythe. I checked up on the politician's address earlier and it matches with this one,' Conrad explained. 'Eight Priors Terrace, Tynemouth.'

Brady took the document from Conrad and scanned down the list of names that the credit cards were registered in. He was not surprised to see R. Smith's name listed. His transactions were the most recent. Luxury stays in Dubai, Aspen and numerous weekend trips to Kinloch Lodge in Skye and Kinfauns Castle Hotel in Perthshire.

Brady sighed, the meaning of Conrad's revelation starting to dawn on him. 'The other name here?' he asked, looking at Harvey.

It was lost on Harvey. Brady turned to Conrad. He nodded tensely, understanding what Brady was getting at.

Brady cursed. 'Tell me that this isn't the Malcolm J. Hughes I think it is?'

Conrad's expression said it all.

Brady could see from the information that Harvey had collated that the victim had had no reason to work since he gave up his bar job in the exclusive members club a year before. Since then he had had two very wealthy men funding his luxurious lifestyle. But why? An answer came to mind. One that he didn't like. One that was connected to the text sent from Robert Smythe's business phone. A text that clearly stated that the victim was involved in a sexual relationship – a sadomasochistic one at that. Not that Brady had a problem with it. As far as he was concerned, two consenting adults they could do what the fuck they liked. But not when it came to murder.

'Sir . . .' Conrad faltered, not wanting to be the one to deliver the next piece of damning news.

Brady looked at him. It was clear he wanted to say something, but was unsure of Brady's reaction.

'There was another number that had been in regular contact with the victim's phone. The phone company came back with the details earlier. I didn't think it was significant at the time, thought it was just connected to De Bernier's role as a political aide for Smythe, but now I realise that it could be important.'

'Go on,' Brady instructed.

'The number has been traced to a Malcolm J. Hughes.'

Brady knew Malcolm J. Hughes. Not personally, but he knew of him. Everyone did. As a well-known philanthropist and a local hero, he was constantly in the press. It was down to a generous donation from Hughes that a much-needed hospice had remained open in Newcastle. He was one of the most prominent businessmen in the North East, with a chain of successful hotels throughout the UK and he had shares in more companies than Brady could imagine. But he was a Geordie born and bred who had made good. And Hughes was proud to let it be known that he gave back to the community.

'So what is his phone number doing on some twenty-two year old's mobile phone?'

'Your guess is as good as mine,' Conrad answered.

But the look in his eye was enough. It told Brady that he was thinking the same thing. Brady sighed heavily. He was starting to feel nervous. He didn't like where this could be leading. Malcolm J. Hughes was a powerful figure. The media adored him, as did the public. Brady would have to tread very carefully.

'We need to talk to him,' Brady after some consideration.

'Sir?' Conrad said, clearly uncomfortable with the implications.

'We need him to explain why he's been in regular contact with a twenty-two-year-old student and crucially, why the hell he's been taking the victim on luxurious holidays to the Caribbean and fuck knows wherever else. I know he's a philanthropist but this smacks of something other than philanthropy.'

Brady turned to Harvey, who been listening. 'I assume Hughes used his private jet for these excursions with De Bernier?'

Harvey looked at Brady. 'I'll check into it.'

'Shit!' Brady muttered to himself. He picked up the sheets of paper again. His eyes darted over the information, looking for something, anything that would give him more cause for bringing Malcolm J. Hughes in. Not that he didn't have enough already. But it wasn't exactly incriminating.

'There's definitely no phone record between Hughes and the victim on the night in question?' Brady asked Conrad.

'No, sir. The last communication between them was on the Friday, fourteenth March.'

Brady felt as if the investigation was running away from him. Spinning out of control. The problem was not that they didn't have any suspects. It was the fact that they already had three key suspects; one of whom Brady was about to interview. And now there was a fourth. And two of the suspects who were involved with the victim were powerful men – bringing them in for questioning came at a price. It would make Brady even more enemies than he already had. And there were plenty. If Hughes and Smythe genuinely had nothing to do with De Bernier's murder, then Brady was running the risk of losing his job over this one. He was acutely aware that neither of these public figures would appreciate the police delving into their personal affairs and kicking up a fuss about their *questionable* relationship with the victim. But it was clear that both these men knew the victim well – perhaps too well. Brady was sure De Bernier was murdered for a specific reason. He wasn't just in the wrong place at the wrong time. Nor was this a copycat killing or The Joker striking again. It was personal.

Brady's eyes continued scanning over the information until he finally found what he wanted.

'Is this correct?' Brady asked, his expression darkening.

Harvey nodded. 'Yeah, seems De Bernier owns an apartment down on the quayside in Newcastle.'

'You're fucking with me, Tom.'

Harvey frowned. 'No. Did a land registry check against his name and this came back.'

Brady couldn't believe it. 'Do you know how much those apartments cost? They start at a quarter of million and then some.'

Harvey didn't answer.

'Shit! There's no way he could afford this. When was it registered in his name?'

'Two weeks ago, I think,' Harvey answered.

Brady looked at Conrad. It made perfect sense.

'Explains why he moved out of his student share, then.'

'So, what? Is he some kind of high-class rent boy?' Harvey asked as he looked from Brady to Conrad.

'At a guess, you could be right. But until we've talked to the two men involved, we can't say.'

'Fucking hell! Malcolm Hughes – a fucking fag! You wouldn't know from looking at him, would you?' Harvey blustered, suddenly shocked at the revelation.

Brady was mindful of Conrad next to him. He could see his clenched jaw out of the corner of his eye.

'Tom!' Brady chided.

'What?' Harvey asked, frowning. 'A fucking politician. I can believe that! They all went to those public schools didn't they? I mean they were educated in the art of bumming! But blimey! Hughes, I can't believe it. I mean, Christ! He's a normal bloke. A Geordie. Big Newcastle United fan. Sits in a box up there with the other directors. Shit!' He rubbed the coarse stubble on his chin as he absorbed this information.

'Firstly, we don't know the nature of Hughes' relationship with the victim. Or even that of Robert Smythe. We have to keep an open mind here and not jump to dangerous conclusions. So whatever you're thinking, keep it up here,' Brady said tapping his forehead, 'because I don't want to hear it, all right?'

Harvey didn't answer.

Brady realised that Harvey was genuinely devastated. The disappointment in his eyes said it all. Hughes was a local legend. The press adored him, as did the public. The man was meant to have been happily married to the woman of his dreams for the past ten years and had two young children to show for it. He would bring them to every public event he hosted. They looked like the perfect family. But then, Brady was more aware than most that looks could be deceiving. That there was no such thing as the perfect family. Perfection was an illusion. Something that could not be sustained.

Brady looked at Harvey: 'What I do want you focusing on is the purchase of that apartment on the quayside. I need to know everything about the transaction. And I mean everything. Someone bought that apartment for him. I want to know who it was. If I'm right, it's already narrowed down to one of two men. I need you to find out which one.'

Harvey nodded. 'Will do. As soon as I get something to eat.'

'I mean now, Tom. I need that information before I risk getting my balls chewed off by Gates for bringing in Hughes for questioning. I need as much as I can get on him first. Clear?'

'Come on, Jack, have a bloody heart will you? I've been work-ing flat out since five a.m.'

Brady didn't answer. But it was clear from his expression that he was more than serious.

Harvey sighed heavily. He got up and reluctantly walked over to the counter to get himself a sandwich to eat at his desk. He'd have no choice but to head back to his office and start finding out who paid the cash for the apartment.

Conrad waited until Harvey was well out of earshot. 'Sir,' he began.

Brady waited, noticing that Conrad's face had reddened.

'I wanted to ask you about Claudia. If you've heard from her today?'

Brady stared at Conrad, not quite believing what he was hearing. 'What?' he asked, confused.

'Claudia?' Conrad repeated awkwardly, his voice starting to crack.

'I know who the hell she is! Christ! Conrad, we've got a hundred other things to be doing right now and one of them isn't talking about my personal life. Understand?' Brady demanded. He pushed his chair back and stood up.

Conrad cursed inwardly. He realised that it had not been the most opportune moment to bring up his boss's relationship with Claudia. Inwardly kicking himself, he watched Brady leave the canteen. It had not gone to plan. He just didn't know how to bring it up. It was clear that Brady was clueless. The problem was, he didn't want to be the one to tell him. Neither did Conrad want to be around when Brady finally found out. He might have been totally preoccupied with the murder investigation, as was Brady's way, but at some point he would have to take stock of his personal life. Or at least, what was left of it.

Chapter Thirty-Four

Brady was starting to feel out of his depth. Worryingly so. The clock was ticking and he had officers scrabbling around trying to piece together Robert Smythe's relationship with De Bernier. Nearly everyone who had attended the dinner Robert Smythe had been at on the Saturday had been questioned. No one stood out as having cause to hurt De Bernier, let alone murder him; there was no one apart from Smythe who might have sent the text. As for when the MP left the function, no one could say one hundred per cent what the actual time had been. Every person interviewed had been clear that they had not seen the politician after 10:00 p.m., which meant Smythe didn't actually have a watertight alibi for when the victim had been murdered.

Then there was the problem of Malcolm J. Hughes. It appeared that powerful people were difficult to get hold of – even for the police. Conrad had left multiple messages with varying secretaries and personal assistants, but so far, nothing. The mobile number registered to Hughes had also been disconnected. No surprise really. The victim's face and news of his sadistic murder was now dominating the news. Brady imagined that Hughes would be scurrying around trying his damnedest to get rid of any evidence that connected him in any way to De Bernier. Brady was still waiting to hear back about who had bought the apartment on the quayside in Newcastle.

It seemed that the investigation had turned into a waiting game. The victim's girlfriend Molly Johansson may have no longer been a suspect but he now had four others: James David Macintosh, currently held in custody waiting to be interviewed; the retired engineer, Sidney Foster, who was still missing; the entrepreneur, Malcolm J. Hughes, and finally the politician, Robert Smythe, who was still in Brussels, booked on a flight back the following morning. Brady could have insisted he returned immediately but the last thing he wanted to do was get heavy-handed. Not with such a high-profile figure. Not that Smythe's status bothered Brady. It was more the friends he kept – such as Detective Chief Superintendent O'Donnell. Detective Superintendent O'Donnell had apparently talked to Smythe and had the politician's word that on his return, he would do everything to help the police. The information had had the desired effect – it was a clear warning to Brady to tread very carefully where Smythe was concerned.

Brady was getting ready to interview the only suspect he had in custody: Macintosh.

Brady looked at Jonathan Edwards, the suspect's probation officer, who had accompanied him to the station. At this point, Macintosh had refused the right to be represented by the duty solicitor. Confident in his innocence. So Edwards had offered to sit in the interview with him.

They were sitting in the interview room waiting for Macintosh to be brought up from the holding cell.

Edwards cleared his throat.

He looked uncomfortable. Brady couldn't blame him. After all, he would have questions to answer. Mainly why he didn't report Macintosh when he broke parole.

Edwards might be easily convinced. But it took more to allay Brady's suspicions than an ex-prisoner's word that he had 'lost track of time'.

'Honestly, I can vouch for James. Apart from breaking his parole this one time, his behaviour has been exemplary,' Edwards stuttered.

Brady resisted the urge to advise him not to get so easily sucked in by his clients. That the men Edwards dealt with on a regular basis would not think twice about slicing his throat open and watching him die. Brady included Macintosh in that.

Brady did not reply. There was no need. Edwards knew he was in the wrong.

Brady watched as the probation officer nervously pushed his designer glasses back up onto his nose. He was genuinely worried. He had allowed the lines to become blurred. Macintosh was his client and he should have reported him for breaking parole. Simple.

'You don't mind if I take my top off? It's rather stuffy in here,' Edwards said as he removed his black wool cardigan.

Damp sweat patches had stained under his arms. Whether it was nerves, or the extra weight he was carrying, Brady couldn't say. Edwards looked remarkably ill at ease. Then again, mused Brady, he did have Edwards' client in here on suspicion of murdering a student at the weekend. That wouldn't look good in front of the parole board, or on his CV.

Brady looked up as the door to the interview room opened and Macintosh was brought in. He watched as Macintosh sat down opposite him.

Brady was waiting for Macintosh's DNA sample and finger-prints to come back. He had not needed to request a sample of either as they already had his details on the database. It was currently being tested against the biological evidence found at the crime scene to see if it was a match. Ainsworth had perse-vered and somehow had found minuscule traces of semen on the bedding in the hotel room. But the lab were being typically tardy. Brady had paid more to expedite the findings but it didn't feel as if he were getting value for money. Even though it wasn't him paying for it out of his own pocket, he still felt it. He had to account for every penny overspent from his ever-decreasing budget. Every uniform and non-uniform officer called in from other area commands to work within the murder investigation team had to be paid. Every decision he made cost money.

Brady tried not to think about what would happen if Macintosh's DNA sample came back negative. It meant the suspect would walk. Other than DNA evidence placing him at the crime scene, Brady had nothing on him. He looked across at Macintosh. Relaxed and smiling, Brady was certain about one thing; despite Macintosh's seemingly agreeable personality, he knew this man was a cold-blooded killer. He didn't need to read Macintosh's criminal records, he just felt it lurking behind his disarmingly friendly eyes. It was there, so much so, it was almost palpable.

Brady studied Macintosh. He was not what Brady had expected. But then, murderers never are what you expect them to be. Not in the flesh. He was tall and physically fit. Evidence that he had spent a good amount of time in the prison gym. He still bore a resemblance to his younger self and was still an unnervingly handsome man. He was remarkably calm, unlike his probation officer. Then again, thought Brady, Macintosh had nothing to lose; unlike Edwards, whose decision-making process would be called into account. For he had chosen not to report the fact that his client had broken his parole on the same night as a murder had been committed.

James David Macintosh studied DI Brady studying him. He knew that the detective didn't like him. Could see it in his eyes.

'So there's nothing else you would like to tell me about Saturday night?' Brady asked.

Macintosh smiled as he shook his head. The smile was false. He knew that Brady could see it. He was shrewder than most. Most definitely not a fool like Edwards. He had been so easily duped. Persuaded that he was a redeemed man. But Brady was different. He liked the DI.

Macintosh laid his hands out on the table. Relaxed. Confident, but not arrogant. He had nothing to hide. His shirt was open, giving him a casual but professional look. He knew that he looked good for his age. He was nearly sixty but looked as if he had just hit his fifties. Life had been good to him inside. He had spent thirty-seven years in Frankland Prison, Durham, a facility housing some of the UK's most high-profile and dangerous criminals.

Recently a long-term inmate there had been murdered by his cellmate. His murderer had found out that he was a convicted paedophile and had decided to mete out his own form of justice. He had waited until after midnight before sitting on his cell-mate's chest and slicing his neck open with a shiv – a homemade scalpel made from plastic cutlery and a razor blade. Then he had gouged the man's eyes out. Satisfied that justice had been carried out, he had gone back to sleep.

Macintosh knew this character well. He had found him distasteful and unimaginative. Unlike him. He smiled as he thought of what he had done to his psychiatrist. He had swung the axe repeatedly into his skull until his brains had covered the blade. The walls. The floor. And the bath. His features gone. Hacked into bloodied pieces. He had left his psychiatrist in the bath. Floating in the water where he had found him bathing. The only difference was that the water was red.

'I'm really sorry, DI Brady,' Macintosh said slowly. 'As I've already explained, I went for a walk and somehow lost track of the time. When I realised how late it actually was I returned and apologised to Ronnie, the key worker who was on duty that night. That was just after midnight. It was stupid of me, I know. I was just finding it so difficult coping with some of the other residents in Ashley House. It can be quite difficult at times, despite the likes of Jonathan's intervention,' he said, turning to Edwards and smiling appreciatively.

He turned back to Brady. The smile had gone. 'I really wish I could have been more helpful. I understand how difficult it must be, an investigation of this magnitude,' he said as his eyes held Brady's gaze. Macintosh smiled again in an attempt to disarm him. But he could see that it hadn't worked.

He tried again. 'But I'm sure that you'll find whoever did this to that young man. What was his name again?' Macintosh's voice quivered just for a moment as he tried to hold in his anger. Furious did not come close. He did not like being accused of something he had not done. His murders had been beautiful. They had purpose. His victims meant something to him. And they knew it. He let them know it.

'Alexander De Bernier,' Brady answered.

Macintosh nodded. But it meant nothing to him. He stared at DI Brady, trying to glean something. Anything. But his face was unreadable. 'I suppose you can't tell me what happened to the victim, can you?' he asked. His mouth watered as images flashed through his mind of what he had done to his young men. Beautiful young men.

'No, I am not at liberty to say. Unless you already know?' Brady challenged him.

Macintosh smiled indulgently. 'I'm afraid I have no idea what happened to . . . this Alexander De Bernier.'

'What about the series of murders that took place here in 1977?' Brady asked, as he held Macintosh's gaze.

Macintosh shook his head. 'I'm afraid I have no idea what you are talking about, DI Brady? Do you, Jonathan?' There was no anger or irritation in his voice, simply puzzlement. He was good. He knew he was good. Because he knew exactly what the detective was talking about. After all, he had chosen each of the victims. Carefully, deliberately. He had taken them and enjoyed them. Then . . . then he had destroyed them so they would never touch him again.

'Seven men were killed during the summer of 1977. I'm surprised that you don't remember? It was all over the news. The press nicknamed him The Joker at the time,' Brady explained.

Macintosh knew that the detective was studying him for anything that would give him away. A look in his eye. An involuntary twitch or tapping of the hand. But he was better than that. He had read Sigmund Freud, Carl Jung and the rest. He understood psychology better than DI Brady could ever have imagined.

'Again, I'm sorry to disappoint you, DI Brady. I have no memory from that time. You see, during that year I was a patient

264

in a psychiatric ward where I was given electroconvulsive therapy for severe depression. Some suffer memory loss as a result. I, sadly, am one of those unfortunates.'

'Convenient, don't you think?' Brady asked.

Macintosh remained poised and relaxed as he gave Brady a disarming smile. But inside, he could feel the anger rising. He didn't like being challenged. 'I don't follow.'

'It's a shame you don't remember, because it appears that he's come back,' Brady replied.

As soon as he said it, Macintosh understood what he meant. His blue eyes narrowed and turned cold. An involuntary, automatic reaction to hearing something he didn't like. Jack Brady suddenly reminded him of his psychiatrist. He had betrayed him. Caught him out. Just like the detective was attempting to here. But it wouldn't work. Not a second time. He had confided in his psychiatrist about his father.

His nasty fucking bastard of a father who had repeatedly threatened to cut off his cock and shove it down his throat if he didn't do what he was told. Bastard! Bastard! Fucking old, evil bastard. He had taken a knife to him. To his cock. Stroked it, caressed it with a knife and cut it. Again and again . . . while he screamed and screamed.

When he had shared this information, he had forgotten that his killings were all over the news. 'The Joker', as the press had coined him. He liked it. It fitted. But in that moment when he revealed his deepest, darkest memories to Dr Jackson, he realised he had said too much. He had seen it in his eyes. The realisation, followed by horror. Then fear. Fleeting, but there all the same. So he had broken into his office and had read his follow-up notes on the session. Dr Jackson had predicted that he was in no doubt that Macintosh was a psychopath who would kill. The psychiatrist would never have believed what would happen next – that he and his family would be the target of his rage.

Macintosh smiled as he looked at the detective. He was imagining what it would be like to hurt him. And those close to him.

265

Chapter Thirty-Five

'Shit!' Brady cursed. He didn't know why he was so surprised. He already knew that the lab results would come back negative. The forensic evidence recovered at the hotel room by Ainsworth and his team did not match Macintosh's DNA. Macintosh had told him in his own way that De Bernier had not died at his hands – but that he had killed the seven young men in the summer of 1977. Then he had abruptly stopped, because he had gone on to kill his psychiatrist and was subsequently locked up. Macintosh was clever. He had covered his tracks well.

'But we'll have to release him,' Conrad said.

Brady looked at Conrad. He knew they had no choice.

The DNA evidence also eliminated Sidney Foster – the suspect from the original case. His DNA was still on file from when he had been convicted of rape. Three convictions; the most recent less than a decade ago. He was still missing. Not that Brady cared. After all, he was no longer a suspect.

But it was not just Macintosh's DNA that did not match; neither did his shoes. The partial print had come from a size ten and Macintosh was a size twelve. Brady had nothing on him. Apart from the uneasy feeling that he had been looking into the eyes of a killer.

For all the good it had done him, he had gone to Gates after the interview and asked him if they could extend the time they held Macintosh until Brady had secured a warrant to search his room at Ashley House. Just in case there was something there that could tie him to the first seven murders. A trophy that he had kept from one of the victims: letters, diaries, drawings – anything that connected him. But Gates had out and out refused, still furious over the fact that Brady was pursuing two distinguished public figures as credible suspects. No matter what Brady had said, it had no effect. Gates would not listen to reason. They had nothing on Macintosh. Brady's gut feeling, as Gates had pointed out in no uncertain terms, was not enough to hold him. So Macintosh would walk.

'Look sir, it's not as if he was responsible for Alexander De Bernier's murder,' Conrad pointed out.

'But he's responsible for the others, Conrad. I just need more time to prove it.'

Brady dropped his head into his hands as he thought about Macintosh. He was still waiting for the lab to come back to him on the blood and semen stains on the T-shirt from one of the Seventies victims. He needed that DNA evidence – now. Macintosh may have been eliminated from the De Bernier's murder investigation, but as far as Brady was concerned that didn't stop him being a suspect in the Seventies case. He was certain that the DNA evidence would conclusively tie Macintosh to the original Joker killings. He dragged his head up to find Conrad standing awkward and uneasy in front of his desk.

'You think I'm crazy, don't you?'

'I . . . I wouldn't say that,' Conrad began, 'it's just the evidence doesn't seem that compelling to me. I mean, the murders that Macintosh was charged with at the time were so radically different from the Joker killings that it seems unlikely they were committed by the same person. Unless they had an extreme personality disorder.'

Brady sighed wearily. He was tired. Too tired to explain to Conrad why Macintosh murdered his psychiatrist, his wife and children in a way that bore no relation to the seven murders that preceded it. Brady knew the reason why McKaley's team never caught Macintosh. It was because he was too damned clever. The same reason that the police database HOLMES 2 did not see a connection between the murders. Simply because the murders were so radically different. That was what Macintosh had wanted. He did not want any crossover between himself and the Joker killings. That was a part of his identity, his marred psyche, that he did not want known. Brady assumed that he had planned to continue his sadistic killings of young men, if he had not been caught by the police for his psychiatrist's murder. Brady was also convinced that Macintosh had murdered his psychiatrist because he had realised that he had unintentionally revealed his identity as The Joker. Brady had reread the transcripts – in particular, the last one before the psychiatrist had been murdered. He was certain that it wouldn't have taken Dr Henry D. Jackson long to have made the connection that his patient was responsible for the local killings. The details of Macintosh's childhood abuse were too similar to the fate suffered by the seven young men.

'Trust me here, Conrad.' But it was clear from the look in his eye that he did not. That he couldn't understand how Brady had come to conclude that Macintosh had killed in such different ways.

'Forgive me for speaking out of turn here,' Conrad began, 'but I've read his files. The murders were . . .' he faltered.

'Horrific?' Brady said.

Conrad nodded as he sat down across from Brady. 'I understand the time-frame element. I can see why you think there's a connection. That the seventh victim was murdered thirty-six hours before Macintosh's last session with Dr Jackson. Then that evening Macintosh had followed his psychiatrist home and—' He stopped.

Brady raised his eyebrows at him. 'What? Hard to accept that the man we're releasing back onto the streets of Whitley Bay actually committed such an abhorrent crime? That the handsome, courteous gentleman that we just interviewed, who chatted so casually with you at the end of the interview about your time at Cambridge, could have killed in the way he did?'

'Yes,' Conrad replied.

They both knew that Macintosh's crime had been so shocking that the Joker killings were briefly forgotten by the press.

Brady nodded. But after Macintosh had butchered his psychiatrist, the Joker killings had stopped. Bang. Right in the midst of a killing frenzy. And why? Because Macintosh had been arrested and charged with the brutal killing of an entire family. In one week, the Joker had murdered two young men, three days apart – showing that his cooling-off period was radically lessening. Then, thirty-six hours later, he had ended his psychiatric treatment for good.

'How did he know I studied at Cambridge?' Conrad asked, concerned.

Brady shrugged. 'Christ knows. Your manner? The way you talk?'

Conrad looked uneasy.

'Don't worry. I don't think he'll be coming after you,' Brady said, shaking his head at his deputy. But Conrad's grim expression told Brady that he didn't find the idea amusing. And Brady knew why.

Macintosh had taken an axe with him when he followed his psychiatrist home to the leafy, expensive suburbs of Jesmond. He had watched and waited. When darkness fell, he had broken in. Then he had set to work. The police who had attended the crime scene had reported that they had never seen anything so bloody and horrific in their time on the force. Dr Jackson's body had been found floating in a blood bath. His wife had been found in their master bedroom. Her heavily pregnant body had been splayed and then tied face-down to the bed. He had begun by chopping her hands and feet off. That, by comparison to what followed next, was civilised. Brady shuddered at the thought of what he had done to her. Then, the two children. Twin boys. He had killed them with a merciless swing of the axe.

The three-year-old girl had been the anomaly. For some reason he had taken her – alive. The police had caught him – forty-eight hours later – with the girl. Brady did not even want to think about what Macintosh had done to the child. Needless to say, when the police had tracked him down to a remote cottage in the wilds of Northumberland, they had been too late. A few hours earlier, and then it might have been a different story.

Macintosh had pleaded insanity.

Who wouldn't?

However, Newcastle County Court had found him sane. Thirty-seven years later, and he had been paroled. This was the part that Brady didn't understand. It left him feeling nervous.

'I want him under surveillance,' Brady instructed.

'Who?' Conrad asked.

'Macintosh.'

Conrad was visibly taken aback. 'Why, sir?' he asked, puzzled. 'He's in a bail hostel, under strict curfew.'

'So strict that he broke his parole?'

Brady accepted that they didn't have the resources to put him under twenty-four-hour surveillance. But he could not shake the feeling he had about Macintosh. The problem he had was that there was nothing – yet – to substantiate his hunch. But it was the *yet* that worried him. The look in Macintosh's eye for that split second had told Brady that his long stint in prison had not rehabilitated him. That he was still a cold-blooded killer. He just hoped for Edwards' sake that he knew what he was doing, allowing Macintosh to remain on parole. If it had been Brady, he would have had Macintosh back inside without a second's hesitation. He had broken his parole. Simple. And Brady sure as hell didn't believe Macintosh's bullshit about walking to Blyth on the night in question; the same night Alexander De Bernier was murdered. Brady had a bad feeling that Macintosh was preparing to kill – again.

270

Chapter Thirty-Six

Harvey had come looking for Brady. Had found him in the Major Incident Room. His expression had told Brady that it wasn't good news. At least, not for Malcolm J. Hughes. The sickening disappointment was written all over Harvey's face. Any thoughts Brady had regarding · Macintosh's release quickly evaporated.

'Shit, Jack! This is one fucking mess!' Harvey moaned.

'Outside,' Brady ordered. Whatever Harvey had found out, he wanted to hear it in private.

'Go on,' Brady instructed, once they'd left the room.

'First blow is that Sidney Foster has been found.'

Brady looked at Harvey. 'Where?'

'In some wooded area not far from Porthtowan.'

Brady realised he was dead. 'He killed himself?'

Harvey nodded, surprised. 'How did you know?'

Brady didn't answer. 'How did he do it?'

'Car exhaust fumes. Closed all the windows and gassed himself. It was a car from the late Seventies so . . .' Harvey shrugged.

Brady knew why. Someone had made an allegation to the local police that he had been abused by Foster from the age of eight. It was enough to destroy his sedate lifestyle and chase him out of the small Cornish village that he had spent thirty years in. Brady imagined that there was more than one victim. That once it got out into the local press more would come forward. It just took one person to break the silence on paedophiles like Foster. Not that Brady could say he felt sorry for him. He saw him as a coward. He had preyed upon young boys who were voiceless and powerless and when he was threatened with exposure he had taken the coward's way out.

'What's the second blow?' Brady asked.

'Malcolm J. Hughes.'

Brady waited.

'He owned the quayside apartment. Purchased it two years back,' Harvey said.

It came as no surprise. Phone records indicated that whatever relationship Hughes had with De Bernier had begun two years earlier when the victim was working at the gentleman's club. No surprise that was where he would have been introduced to the entrepreneur and philanthropist. Brady imagined there would be others like Hughes and Smythe – at least in the early days. Not now. It appeared that the victim had become more selective over time. Lucrative business. Or at least it was, until someone had decided to end it for him.

'Hughes transferred the property into De Bernier's name two weeks ago,' Harvey said, shaking his head, not quite believing it. 'It means what I think it does, right?'

'Yeah, I believe it does,' Brady answered.

Harvey looked wounded. Brady accepted that once this got out Harvey wouldn't be alone in feeling so cheated by Hughes' behaviour.

'What now, Jack?' Harvey asked.

'You and Kodovesky bring him in for questioning.'

'You're not serious, are you? Can't someone else do it? I . . . I've spoken to him, Jack. It would be awkward—' Harvey stopped.

'Get a grip, Tom. He's a suspect. No more, no less. He's not bloody Gandhi and he doesn't walk on water. What he does do is fuck around on his missus. Ordinarily, no big deal. But you're right, it is awkward – for him. Because when the press find out about his bit on the side, then the shit's going to hit the fan big style.'

'You really think he was having a sexual relationship with De Bernier?' Harvey asked, not really wanting the answer.

Brady raised his eyebrows.

'But you've got no evidence. Maybe it's innocent. Maybe he just liked the kid. You know?' Harvey suggested, floundering.

'I can guarantee you that in a few hours I'll have evidence that Hughes was paying the victim for sex. The apartment, the holidays? The cash in the victim's bank? Regardless of what you think, Tom, Hughes is not some benevolent benefactor. His relationship with the victim was based on something else entirely.'

'Has Gates said anything about you bringing him in?' Harvey questioned.

The look in his eye told Brady that Harvey didn't want to get it in the neck when he walked into the station with Hughes in tow.

'Let me worry about Gates, while you concentrate on finding our suspect.'

Harvey nodded reluctantly. 'What do I say to his wife?'

'Tell her to get a good divorce lawyer!'

'I'm serious. Come on, Jack.'

'So am I . . . Oh for fuck's sake,' Brady said, exasperated, when he saw Harvey's worried expression. 'Tell her . . . I don't know. The usual crap. That we need him to help us with our inquiries. Keep it ambiguous. It's his fucking mess, so he should be the one that does the explaining. After he's explained it to us first.'

Harvey looked uncomfortable with the prospect of dealing with Hughes' wife, let alone Hughes himself.

'Where does he live?' Brady asked, curious.

'Darras Hall,' Harvey replied, dejectedly.

'Figures.' It was no surprise that the entrepreneur resided in what was known as millionaire's paradise, a few miles outside of the idyllic village of Ponteland, Northumberland. There was a reason why most of the players from Newcastle United owned properties there.

'I suggest you take a drive out there and sit it out. He'll show up. He has to. He lives there.'

Harvey looked crestfallen.

'Come on, Tom. Could be worse. You could be ramming down a door in Shields looking for some scrote high on ketamine who wouldn't think twice about shoving an infected needle into your neck if he got half a chance.'

Harvey didn't look convinced.

Conrad approached them.

'Ready?' Brady asked.

'Yes, sir,' Conrad answered.

'Where are you off to?' Harvey asked.

'The victim's flat.'

Forty minutes later, Brady was standing in De Bernier's luxurious apartment overlooking Newcastle quayside. It looked like some New York warehouse conversion. Huge open-plan rooms, exposed wooden beams and sandblasted brickwork. It was breathtaking. Then there was the pièce de résistance – the enormous floor-to-ceiling wall of glass that overlooked the Tyne river. Below, the bustling quayside was lit from all angles. Straight ahead was a stunning view of the Gateshead Millennium Bridge, lit up in neon blue, arcing gracefully over the Tyne river.

'Bloody hell!' Brady muttered to himself as he took in the majestic views. This took serious money.

Conrad shot him a questioning look. One that reminded Brady that the victim had paid a high price for this penthouse apartment.

'Right, you start in here and I'll go search his bedroom.'

It didn't take Brady long. 'Conrad?' he called out.

'Take a look at these,' Brady said as he pointed to a collection of homemade DVDs. 'I found them hidden under the flooring in that walk-in wardrobe,' he said, indicating a room large enough to be another bedroom.

'How did you know he'd have something hidden?' Conrad asked.

'Because this guy was smart. He played people. He got what he wanted out of them. Holidays, cars and this penthouse apartment. You have to ask yourself what De Bernier offered in return. Sex, sure. But would that in itself have been enough to have banked over two hundred grand in a savings account? I reckon the holidays and the sports car were gifts. Expensive gifts at that. But this place?' Brady said, looking around him. 'No. I think he changed the rules of the game. And in order to do so, he needed to have something on these men. If it was me? I'd secretly film them, making damned sure their faces were identifiable. He could sit on those films and let the value increase until he decided to cash in his assets.'

Brady walked over to the DVD player. 'Reckon these might give us an idea as to how De Bernier made his money,' he said, thinking of the entrepreneur who had signed the apartment over to the victim.

'Do you think he could have been blackmailing Hughes?'

'I don't know,' Brady shrugged. 'We'll have to ask him when we get back to the station.'

Brady put one of the films in and pressed play.

'Fuck! That looks painful,' Brady winced, as he watched the victim engaging in various sex acts with an unidentifiable older male.

After a few minutes he fast-forwarded the film. Then suddenly paused it. 'Shit!' He turned to Conrad.

It was clear Conrad recognised him too. He looked as shocked as Brady felt.

'We need forensics here. I want the place searched. I need Jed to analyse whatever material we have on the victim's laptop and desktop computer,' Brady said, as he absorbed the magnitude of what they had just found. 'Christ, Conrad! I had a feeling that this could be the case. But to actually see it . . .'

Conrad looked worried. 'You know this could cause a lot of damage if it got into the wrong hands?'

'Already has,' Brady said, stopping the film and taking it out of the DVD player.

He put another DVD in and fast-forwarded it. 'Fuck!' He cursed again when he recognised the man having sex with the victim. He paused on the image of his face. There was no question as to his identity.

Brady turned to Conrad and breathed out heavily. 'Reckon Harvey's going to need a drink tonight after he's witnessed this.'

Brady stopped the DVD. He had no choice but to take these findings to Gates. He knew that his boss wouldn't be happy with what he had found. Not at all.

'Reckon I've got the perfect job for Daniels and Kenny tonight,' Brady said.

'Sir?' Conrad asked, unsure of what he meant. But he realised as soon as he saw the mischievous look in Brady's eye.

'It will take hours to go through these DVDs,' Brady said, trying hard not to grin at the thought of the two most sexist blokes in the station having to sit through hours of hardcore gay porn.

But it was crucial that the films were analysed. Brady was certain that they were behind the victim's newly acquired assets.

Chapter Thirty-Seven

Brady was preparing himself for his interview with Malcolm J. Hughes. Harvey and Kodovesky had brought him in while he and Conrad had been searching the victim's apartment. It seemed that Hughes had heard the news about De Bernier, and had been expecting the police – not that he acknowledged the countless calls that had been made to his secretary and PA. He had told his wife that the victim was a bartender at the gentleman's club he belonged to, and as a member he needed to give the police whatever information he knew about the victim. It was bullshit. But his wife bought it.

The station was buzzing at the news that Hughes had been brought in for questioning. That, and the evidence on film of his sexual relationship with the victim. However, Brady's summoning of Hughes had also attracted Gates' attention, who was on the warpath. Brady had managed to keep his head down and out of firing range. But he knew that couldn't last forever.

Brady was now waiting on news from Jed, the police forensic computer analyst. He wanted this information before he interviewed Hughes. But he was being made to sweat. Budgets had been radically slashed, resulting in their only full-time computer geek inundated with work. Jed had heard it all. SIOs would dump software on him and expect a miracle overnight. It didn't happen. It couldn't. There were not enough hours in the day for Jed to even get close to managing his workload.

Brady had cajoled Jed into looking at De Bernier's laptop. He firmly believed there would be something incriminating on the hardware and Jed was the only person he knew who could find it – and fast. The victim had not struck Brady as a computer geek. He did not believe De Bernier would have any encrypted files on his laptop. Brady was simply looking for some emails. Messages that he assumed would have been deleted for fear of the victim's girlfriend gaining access into his private email account. Not that Brady could blame him for being paranoid. Molly Johansson had admitted that she regularly checked the victim's phone if it was left lying around, on the off-chance she would find an incriminating text or email proving he was having an affair. To be fair to her in turn, she had not been unfounded in her suspicions. The victim's homemade DVD collection had shown that – not that Brady would be telling her about it. Some things were better left unsaid. Unless the press got hold of it.

Brady still had Rubenfeld, the hard-nosed hack and snitch, chasing him for a story. Something to head the front page of the *Northern Echo*. Brady had refused to take his calls and Rubenfeld was starting to get pissy about it. Not a good move, because at some point Brady would need him. Ordinarily he kept Rubenfeld sweet, but the nature of the investigation and the high public profile of the two main suspects had forced him to stonewall the journalist.

Brady's BlackBerry rang.

'Did you find it?' he asked, his voice tense.

Jed sighed. 'Yeah. I found it all right. You owe me, Jack. Again.'

'Fuck!' Brady exhaled, relief coursing through him. 'Anything, name it and it's yours.'

Jed laughed. 'You couldn't afford it!'

'Who did he send it to?' Brady asked, as he leaned his elbows on his desk and massaged his temple. He had expected this. It was true to form.

'Some politician. Robert Smythe. Sound familiar?' Jed asked.

'Yeah,' Brady answered, breathing slowly out.

278

Shit. Shit. Shit.

He had expected it, but the reality still hit him hard.

'What did it say?' It was a rhetorical question because Brady already knew the answer.

'Let's see . . . Looks like he's blackmailing this guy over some films he's made. Yeah . . . From what he saying here, they're fairly incriminating.'

'Sounds about right,' Brady answered. 'What's he asking for?'

'Wanted to meet up and discuss "options" regarding his political career,' Jed replied.

'When?' Brady asked. The answer was crucial.

'When what? The email was sent?' Jed asked. 'Thursday, thirteenth March at nine oh-seven a.m.'

'No. When did he want to meet up?'

'Saturday evening just gone. Says here that he wanted to meet up at a hotel.'

Brady breathed out. 'Shit!'

'Hey, don't feel the need to thank me for busting my balls to retrieve this for you,' Jed replied.

'Yeah, thanks, mate. I really do owe you one. Can you send it to me?'

'Sure. You want me to go through what else he might have on here?'

'If you can, that would be great. But right now, that email is all that I want.'

As Brady disconnected the call there was a loud knock at the door.

'Yeah?' he called out as he leaned back in his chair. He was exhausted. It felt like he had been getting nowhere and suddenly . . . Brady rubbed his tired face with the palms of his hands. He suddenly realised that he hadn't eaten for hours. But at least they had got somewhere. And soon he would have Robert Smythe on UK soil, preferably handcuffed.

Conrad walked in. 'Hughes' brief is kicking off. Wants his client interviewed ASAP.'

Brady looked up at him and massaged his temples. He was tired and at this precise moment Hughes was the least of his concerns.

'What's wrong?' Conrad asked, concerned.

Brady sighed heavily. 'Jed went through De Bernier's laptop and found a deleted email from last Thursday morning blackmailing the politician with the DVDs he had secretly filmed.'

Conrad looked stunned. 'Smythe was being blackmailed?'

Brady nodded.

'Robert Smythe killed his political aide because he was blackmailing him?' Conrad asked, incredulous.

'Unless we're having completely different conversations, then yes. That's exactly what I'm saying,' Brady said, more forcefully than he intended. 'And before you ask – yes, the evidence is damning. Enough to haul his arse in now on the grounds that the victim asked to meet him on the Saturday evening at a hotel to discuss how the MP would forward his career in politics. It didn't quite go as he had planned.'

Conrad's face paled. 'You do know how serious this is? If you're wrong . . .' He shook his head.

'I'm not wrong, though. That's the bloody point, Conrad.'

'But . . .' Conrad faltered. He shook his head. 'It doesn't make sense.'

'Which part?' Brady asked.

'All of it,' Conrad replied, nervously. 'I've met him. He . . . he just didn't seem the type to—'

'To what? Murder someone? Show me the "type" and then we can retire. There is no "type", Conrad. You've been doing the job long enough to know that, surely?'

Conrad didn't answer him.

'Sit down, will you? You're starting to make me feel nervous,' Brady said. He waited until Conrad had pulled out a chair and was sitting opposite him. 'Until we actually hear from the suspect himself, we can only speculate as to motive. But I would suggest the victim blackmailing him is a good start. In his email,

De Bernier threatened to go to the press with the film footage if Smythe didn't do as he asked. Something of that magnitude would destroy his career. And his marriage. I can't imagine Sarah Huntingdon-Smythe accepting that little indiscretion so easily.'

Conrad shook his head. 'I understand the motive, but what about the signature? The MO? It doesn't make sense. Even you believed it was the same killer from the Seventies murders. How could he have known the details from the original investigation? They were never released to the public.'

'I know,' Brady replied. 'And that was the part that I struggled with. How did he know? How could he know?'

Conrad looked expectantly at Brady.

'Let's start with why he would copy the Seventies murders.' Conrad waited.

'Smythe's from around here and of an age, late fifties, where he would remember the crime. What if he decided that murdering De Bernier that way would throw us off? That we would end up chasing our own tails trying to look for the original killer? Why else kill in exactly the same way as the Seventies murders? I mean, the first thing we would do is narrow down who knew the suspect and who had a relationship with him. It was a given that we would end up talking to Smythe. The man's not a fool, he would have known that,' Brady said. 'What we established with the first seven victims was that they did not know their attacker. Smythe could have been trying to put as much distance between himself and the victim by attempting to make it look like De Bernier did not know his murderer. That it was a copy-cat killing, or even that the original killer had struck again.'

Brady could see that Conrad didn't look convinced.

'I accept that maybe it was an attempt at throwing us off his scent,' Conrad conceded, reluctantly, 'but how could he have known specifics of the murders that were only known to the police?'

'I don't know, Conrad. I honestly don't know.'

'And what about Hughes?'

'Well, I think we ought to interview him. Don't you?'

'Why, if you already have evidence against Smythe?'

'Because until his DNA comes back as negative, he's going nowhere.'

Brady couldn't give a damn about Hughes' reputation or his powerful business associates. All he was interested in was holding people accountable, regardless of whether they believed themselves to be above the law.

Chapter Thirty-Eight

Tuesday: 10:31 p.m.

Brady looked at Hughes. He was finding it hard to hide the disdain he felt. It was clear that Hughes would kick up a fuss about being questioned; that he would no doubt go as high up as Detective Chief Superintendent O'Donnell. But Brady wasn't in the job to make friends.

'So,' Brady said, his voice relaxed. 'Let's go over your whereabouts on Saturday night again, shall we?'

'I'm sorry, Inspector Brady, but this is ridiculous. My client has a watertight alibi for Saturday evening. He could not possibly have murdered this De Bernier,' said Blake Edward Barrington as he shot Brady a contemptuous look. 'We have already been through this.'

Brady returned the look with a casual smile. The Barringtons of this world did not bother him. Even if he was one of the best barristers in the country. Brady saw him for what he was – privileged and pretentious. Barrington was a tall, well-built man with thick curly hair and penetrating brown eyes, dressed impeccably. He had an edge about him. One that told people he was used to getting his own way. It was obvious why he was one of the most expensive barristers in the UK. Hughes had requested Barrington represent him as an attempt at intimidating the police – or to be precise, Brady. It hadn't worked.

It was the first time Brady had met Barrington. No surprise really, since it was the first time a barrister had deigned to represent a client in Whitley Bay police station. But then money could buy anything; including the Barringtons of this world. Hughes had lots of money. Enough to be able to throw it at any problem that stood in his way.

Currently, it was Brady standing in Hughes' way. But no amount of money could make him disappear. Brady sat back and folded his arms as he stared at the philanthropist opposite him. It wasn't his altruism that had found him being questioned in a police interview room. It was his philandering ways with young men. Brady was sure De Bernier wasn't the first, and that he would not be the last. Hughes might have had a short, sharp rap over the knuckles, but Brady didn't think it'd be long before the shock from the blow lessened, and he would go back to cheating on his wife.

Hughes was a short, balding, barrel of a man whose appetites clearly stretched beyond his penchant for handsome young men. His small, indignant eyes looked straight through Brady as if he didn't exist. But he did. As Hughes was about to find out.

'Yes, wives are rather useful when it comes to alibis, aren't they?' Brady said as he stared at Hughes, not giving him a chance to answer. 'So, you admit to having a sexual relationship with the victim?'

Red-faced, Hughes struggled to get his words out. 'I . . . I . . . I've already told you everything. This is tantamount to persecution.'

'I'll put a formal complaint in to Detective Chief Superintendent O'Donnell later,' Barrington advised his client.

Brady ignored Barrington. 'What about the quayside flat that you had transferred into the victim's name?'

Hughes looked uneasy. 'I . . . I don't know—'

'Was Alexander De Bernier blackmailing you, Mr Hughes?' Brady fired.

'Don't answer that,' advised Barrington before Hughes had a chance to respond.

'You see, we found the victim's private film collection. I assume you know what I'm talking about?' Brady asked.

The colour of Hughes' face deepened.

There was a knock at the door. Harvey walked in.

'Jack, you might want this,' he said as he handed Brady a sheet of paper.

'Thanks.' He waited until Harvey had left the room before looking at the lab results. They were negative. It was no surprise. But there was something on the lab results that Brady had not been expecting. De Bernier's blood test results. Brady handed the sheet of paper to Conrad.

Conrad's eyes quickly took in the information. His expression told Brady he was as surprised by the findings as his boss.

Brady turned to Hughes.

'You're free to go,' he said.

'That's it! No apology for wasting my time?' Hughes spluttered, red-faced. 'Believe me when I say this, DI Brady, after this façade your time on this force will be short-lived!'

Brady sighed wearily. He was tired. Too tired for Hughes' bullshitting. He had bigger problems.

'Did you know that De Bernier was HIV positive?' Brady asked bluntly.

It had the desired effect. It shut Hughes up.

'If I were you, I'd think about how you're going to tell your wife you've had unprotected sex with an HIV-infected partner. May be worth having your barrister with you for that little conversation.'

The colour drained from Hughes' face.

Brady had seen the films. He knew exactly what was going through Hughes' head; that he had had unprotected sex with the victim – on many occasions.

'If it's any consolation, I'm sure De Bernier was completely unaware he was infected. After all, why would you want to intentionally damage a prosperous career as a high-class rent boy?'

'What?' Hughes exclaimed, offended.

'Did you think you were exclusive?' Brady asked with a faux-sympathetic look. He solemnly shook his head. 'No . . . until he was murdered, De Bernier had quite a lucrative business on the go. Unfortunately, Mr Hughes, you were one of many.'

With that, Brady got up and left.

'I'll be having a word with your superiors, DI Brady!' Barrington shouted after him.

Chapter Thirty-Nine

Tuesday: 11:21 p.m.

'For fuck's sake, Jack! What did you think you were playing at?' demanded Gates.

He was standing with his back to Brady, looking out the window. Hands tightly clasped together behind him.

'I just thought someone should tell him. At least, for his wife's sake. I'm sure Hughes would have appreciated my humanitarianism,' Brady replied, unable to help himself.

He quickly regretted it.

'Don't fuck with me!' Gates thundered as he spun around.

He was an imposing man at the best of times, but now he looked as if he was ready to jump over his desk and floor Brady. They may have roughly been the same height and build but Brady knew that when Gates was in this kind of mood, he was well and truly capable of knocking him out. Ordinarily Gates kept control, regardless of the situation. Not this time. Brady had obviously pushed him too far. His face was unusually flushed.

Brady could see the vein pulsating in Gates' neck as he decided what to do with him. It wasn't a good sign.

'Sit!' barked Gates.

Relieved, Brady did as instructed. He had been standing in Gates' office for the past ten minutes waiting for his boss to finish bollocking him and let him get on with his job.

Robert Smythe was booked on a flight back from Brussels to Newcastle Airport. He would be landing at five a.m. Brady needed to be prepared. The longer he wasted in Gates' office, the less time he had to get everything organised for Smythe's long-overdue arrest.

'Three bloody days! That's all it's taken you. Three days and you end up causing problems. Why the hell can you not learn to keep your mouth shut and play things by the book? Do you know how powerful Hughes is? Do you, Jack?'

Brady shrugged. He wasn't bothered. The guy was a jerk.

Gates' eyes were filled with cold fury as they bore into him.

'Why do you make my bloody life so difficult? Why can't you take some notes from Adamson?'

Brady could not help himself reacting to the name. Adamson was his nemesis. He was also Gates' protégé.

'I'm this close to handing your investigation over to Adamson,' Gates warned, as he gestured with his thumb and forefinger.

It was close. Even a blind man could tell that.

Brady was about to object but the expression on Gates' furious face told him to keep quiet.

'Step out of line once more and that's it. You're off. And it won't just be me who will want to see you walking the beat in Blyth. I'm sure there'll be a line of people that you've pissed off. Hughes being one of them.'

Brady didn't bother disputing the fact.

'Tell me one thing,' Gates demanded. 'Are you certain that Smythe is responsible for De Bernier's murder?'

Brady was surprised by the question. However, he didn't let it show.

'As sure as I can be without the DNA evidence, sir,' answered Brady. And it was the truth. But there was something that Conrad had said earlier that had been bothering him. And then there were the lab findings. It was enough to make him feel a gnawing disquiet about what he had found out. But with Gates waiting for Brady to trip up, the last thing he was going to do was confide in him. He was just hoping that it didn't mean what he suspected.

288

He shook it off. The evidence against Smythe was damning. It was better to focus on that than to start causing more problems.

'The evidence is indisputable, sir. Jed found blackmailing emails from the victim to Smythe. De Bernier had quite a DVD collection of himself and the politician.'

Gates nodded. He clearly was not happy.

'His car?'

'Impounded for forensic examination.'

'His house?' Gates asked.

'Forensics have already searched it, which is how Jed was able to access the emails on the desktop computer.'

Brady had applied for a warrant to search the MP's premises as soon Daniels and Kenny had spotted the politician's car. The white Audi sports car was only one of five cars registered to him. But that was the one they needed.

'All right, because if you're wrong on this and you arrest Smythe, then, Jack, I give you my word, you'll be signing on at Whitley Bay Job Centre.'

'Sir,' Brady said as his feeling of unease mounted.

WEDNESDAY

Chapter Forty

Brady had spent the night at the station. He had been too wired to go home, so had decided to put his head down on the couch in his office. He had called Claudia to explain. But there had been no answer. If he had not been so focused on what the next few hours would bring, he might have been more concerned. But he had dispelled his unease and had turned his mind to the investigation. Brady knew that once the case was closed he would have to make some tough decisions; he and Claudia would have to be honest with each other and talk. Neither one of them could continue living the way they had been doing. If Brady was brutally honest, he was terrified of losing her – again. It was easier not to think about it and instead focus on the things in his life he could control. Such as Robert Smythe being charged with murder.

He had sent the rest of the team home late last night. Despite protests. They, too, had wanted to stick around. But there was no point. Nothing could be done until they had the suspect in custody. Harvey and Kodovesky had had the privilege of escorting the MP back from Newcastle Airport.

Someone had leaked the imminent arrest to the press. Brady had an idea who, but could not understand why. Now, what should have been a quiet and orderly affair had turned into a feeding frenzy. As soon as Smythe had been arrested, a DNA swab had been taken and had been couriered to the forensic laboratory. Brady was awaiting the results. He had no doubt that they would come back positive, but he just had to wait for the conclusive proof before they charged him with the murder.

'Ready?' Brady asked Conrad when he saw him heading towards him. The atmosphere in the station was jubilant. They were close to charging a suspect with the sadistic murder of a young student. But Brady was finding it difficult to partake in the exultant mood.

Conrad nodded.

'Come on, then.'

Conrad followed his boss down the stairs.

Brady opened the door and they walked into the small room. He nodded at Robert Smythe and then his solicitor, a small-framed, unassuming man in his mid-forties. For some reason, Brady had expected a Barrington equivalent – disdainful, imperious and in your face. But Oscar Stewart was reserved and cooperative – just like his client.

'Right, let's get started, shall we?' Brady suggested, pulling out a chair.

Smythe was adamant about his innocence, despite the indisputable evidence stacked against him. Brady was hoping that the cooling-off period he had had in the holding cells this morning would change his defence. Yet there was something that Brady couldn't quite put his finger on. It was gnawing at him. All the time.

He could see from Conrad's expression that he was not the only who was troubled.

'You understand why you're here?' Brady asked.

Smythe nodded.

He was courteous and civil. The antithesis of Hughes. Brady had heard people say that the politician was an extremely charismatic man. They were right. He looked a lot younger than fifty-nine; tall, slim, tanned, with thick blond hair and handsome features. But this wasn't what had troubled Brady. The sincerity in Smythe's bright blue eyes unnerved him. There was nothing about this man that smacked of duplicity or greed. Let alone murder. His mood was sedate, if not disconcertingly melancholic. Not because he had been arrested and was waiting to be charged. It seemed that Smythe's mournful disposition could likely be down to the fact that his lover had been murdered.

Disquiet crept through Brady, making him ask himself if he could have been mistaken. But the evidence reminded him that this could not be the case. And the suspect could be playing him. This was a man who had spent years courting the press. And the public.

Oscar Stewart cleared his throat. 'Detective, my client has already accepted the evidence you have against him. He would like to state for the record that he did not murder Alexander De Bernier. That he has been set up.'

Brady nodded at the solicitor. He then turned to the politician. 'Who do you think would want to set you up?'

Smythe looked Brady straight in the eye. 'I have done nothing but ask myself that same question, Detective Inspector. But I honestly cannot say.'

'And why would someone murder your political aide?'

He dropped his gaze.

But it was too late. Brady had already seen the wounded expression on his face.

'Because he meant something to me,' Smythe said. He looked back up at Brady, his eyes watery. 'It's easy to sit there and judge someone's life, Detective Inspector. Unless you're caught up in it, it's difficult to understand the choices one makes.'

'You mean your affair with the victim?'

It was clear from the look in Smythe's eye that Brady had touched a nerve.

'Yes. I mean Alex.'

'The credit card in the name of R. Smith registered to your address belongs to you?' Brady asked.

Smythe looked mildly taken aback. 'Yes. Why?'

'The transactions detail luxury holidays, designer clothes and watches and even a BMW sports car. I assume you bought these for Alex?'

Smythe nodded.

'You loved him?' Brady asked.

Smythe looked away. 'Yes,' he mumbled. 'It just happened. I didn't mean for it to, but it did. Sometimes life has a way of knocking you off-course. You don't expect it and before you know it, you can't get out. No matter how hard you try.'

'Is that what happened with De Bernier?'

He nodded, staring down at his hands. 'Something like that.'

'You wanted out?' Brady asked.

Smythe raised his head up to Brady. His eyes told him that he was no fool. That he knew that Brady was trying to trip him up.

'Yes, for the sake of my wife. We . . . we had been trying for a baby for the past five years. And until recently, we had been unsuccessful.'

'Your wife's pregnant?'

'Yes, twenty weeks. Not that you could tell with Sarah. She's not showing yet.'

Brady took a moment to absorb this news. Sarah Huntingdon-Smythe had not mentioned it when he had interviewed her. Nor did she look pregnant. Not that he would know what to expect at that stage of pregnancy.

Smythe saw the flicker of doubt cross Brady's face. 'I was there at the twelve-week scan. I saw him.'

'Him?' Brady asked, curious. He didn't know a lot about pregnancy but he knew that twelve weeks was too early to be able to tell the sex.

'At sixteen weeks Sarah had an amniocentesis,' Smythe explained.

Brady was none the wiser.

'A needle is inserted into the uterus so tests can be carried out for conditions such as Down's syndrome. It can also tell the sex of the baby. That's how I know we are having a boy.'

'So, let me get this straight, if your wife wasn't pregnant you would have left her for De Bernier?'

'I seriously contemplated it, if that's what you want to know,' Smythe answered.

'What about your political career? Surely such a decision would have dire ramifications for your public persona?'

'Yes. You're right. But I had no intention of going public with my relationship with Alex,' he answered, his voice tinged with sadness.

Brady thought about the email that had been sent to Smythe. The blackmail threats and the film.

'Why would your lover threaten to publicly expose your relationship then?'

Brady watched as Smythe wiped his mouth with a trembling hand. He looked at Brady, eyes filled with regret.

Regret for what?

Brady wasn't sure.

'Alex wanted me to leave Sarah. When I explained that I couldn't, not now that she was. pregnant, it changed things between us. He got angry when he realised that I was serious. That he couldn't change my mind. So he lashed out. Tried to hurt me. Threatened me about going public about our relationship, unless I helped his career.' He shook his head. 'I . . . I never got a chance to talk to him about it.'

'So you didn't meet him as the victim had requested on the Saturday night?'

'No. I ignored the email. I decided the best thing to do was let Alex cool down. He could be like that. Hot-headed and impulsive. I had been planning on talking to him when I came back from Brussels. But . . .' Smythe shook his head at the realisation it was too late.

'What about the fact that our computer analyst found a reply to the email, arranging to meet him at the Royal Hotel the night he was murdered?'

Robert Smythe looked genuinely taken aback. 'How? I don't understand. I definitely did not reply to it.'

Brady watched him. He was convincing. If the evidence wasn't stacked so high against him, Brady would have said he was innocent. That someone had, as his solicitor claimed, set Smythe up. But from where Brady was sitting, he could not see how that was possible.

'You understand that the evidence against you is incriminating?'

Smythe nodded as he ran a shaky hand through his hair. His eyes on Brady. 'I know . . .'

'Can you explain it?'

'No,' he answered simply.

'We have CCTV footage of your white Audi sports car pulling into the hotel at precisely ten thirty-one p.m. It is believed that the victim was murdered sometime after eleven p.m.'

Smythe shook his head, surprised. 'That can't be. Someone must have stolen my car.'

'You really expect us to believe that?' Brady asked, frowning. It all seemed too incredible.

'Yes,' he whispered.

'Then why did we find your car parked in your garage if someone had stolen it?'

'Maybe . . . maybe they drove it back afterwards?'

'What? After they murdered Alexander De Bernier? So, for the record, you believe someone stole your car from your garage without you realising. And then returned it. Again without your knowledge. Yet you claim to have been at home?'

Smythe looked at Brady, his eyes filled with defeat. 'I . . . I don't know. All I can tell you is that I didn't drive my car to the Royal Hotel on Saturday night.'

'How could a car thief break into a garage that can only be accessed by a remote controlled electric garage door?'

'I don't know. Honestly, I don't know how they did it. But someone must have broken in and stolen my car.'

'And then returned it.'

Smythe shook his head. 'I . . . I don't know . . .'

'The text that was sent from your business phone. Quote: "First rule, no talking. Second rule, blindfold yourself. Third rule, face-down, ready to be bound and gagged." How do you explain that?'

Smythe winced when he heard the text.

For a moment, Brady was uncertain. Smythe's reaction seemed to imply it was the first time he had heard the text.

'I . . . I didn't send it. Someone must have used my phone.'

'When?' asked Brady. 'At this dinner you were at the night De Bernier was murdered? The Grand Hotel, wasn't it?'

'Yes . . . Yes. A political event. I was there. My secretary and others can vouch for that.'

'We've already talked to them. But the problem I have here is the time-frame. I have witnesses who say you left at nine-fifty p.m. Your car was seen pulling into the Royal at ten thirty-one p.m. The same time the said text was sent. Then the victim was murdered sometime shortly after. But you have no alibi. No witnesses from nine-fifty p.m. to corroborate your story that you went home and went to bed because you were travelling early the following morning.'

Smythe sighed heavily. He looked genuinely scared. He ran a hand over his face as he thought about it. Finally he answered. 'My wife was in London at a medical conference. Ordinarily she would have been at home. But no, I have no one who can verify my whereabouts.'

Brady nodded. He didn't know what else to say. He caught sight of Conrad out of the corner of his eye. He looked as uncomfortable and uneasy with this interview as Brady felt. Either Smythe was an extraordinary actor, or he was genuinely innocent. If the latter were the case, how could that be physically possible?

Brady needed to be certain. He opened the file in front of him and took out photographs of the crime scene.

Slowly and deliberately he placed them down in front of the politician.

Smythe looked down and then quickly averted his gaze. 'I ... can't ... I ...' He faltered, unable to speak. His hand covered his mouth.

For a moment Brady was certain that Smythe was going to throw up.

Oscar Stewart intervened: 'Can my client have a moment to collect himself, please?'

'Sure,' Brady replied. Ordinarily he would have kept pushing the suspect. The end goal was to get a written confession. But Brady knew that with Smythe this would not be the case. He came over as a man of integrity. He would not sign a confession to a crime he was insisting he did not commit.

Chapter Forty-One

Wednesday: 11:39 a.m.

Brady had gone down to the basement cafeteria to get a coffee. The suspect wasn't the only one who needed to clear his head. He had intended to suspend the interview for ten minutes. Thirty minutes later and he was steeling himself for what was to follow. He had no choice but to charge Smythe with the murder of Alexander De Bernier.

'The lab results are conclusive,' Brady repeated for the third time.

But Smythe was not buying it.

'I don't understand,' he said, his voice tremulous.

'The traces of sperm found on the bed sheets in the hotel room match with your DNA sample. The partial shoe print at the crime scene matches the sole of one of your shoes that we found at your home . . .' Brady paused as he shook his head. The forensic evidence was damning. 'The cut-throat razor used to mutilate the victim's groin. To cut off his penis? That was found in your bathroom. It had been cleaned, but the forensic lab were still able to find traces of the victim's blood on the blade.'

Smythe just stared at Brady, refusing to believe what he was hearing.

'Do you want me to continue?' Brady asked.

'Honestly, I did not murder Alex. I didn't do it. You believe me, don't you?' Smythe asked, his voice desperate.

'I'm sorry . . .' Brady said as he shook his head.

*   *   *

The mood in the station was palpable. Everyone was breathing a collective sigh of relief. Gates included. He had even sought Brady out to commend him on the outcome of the investigation. And to pass on Detective Superintendent O'Donnell's praises. Gates had seemingly forgotten that he had seriously doubted Brady's suspicions regarding the MP.

But for some reason Brady did not share in the elation. The team were planning a piss-up in the Fat Ox later to celebrate. Within a short time, they had got a result. Nobody could have guessed that the Conservative politician had murdered his political aide, also his lover, because he was blackmailing him over sex tapes. He had everything to lose. His marriage, his unborn son and his political career. The choice seemed obvious. To get rid of the threat to his status quo.

But there was one problem. Smythe needed to murder his lover in a way that would not implicate him. The Joker killings from the Seventies must have seemed an ideal cover. Brady still had no idea how Smythe knew the details from the original murders. He accepted that perhaps he never would. And as for the Joker card: vintage Sixties Waddington playing cards could be bought on eBay. And it seemed that was the case with Smythe. His desktop computer had been handed over to Jed. It hadn't taken him long to search through the computer's history. He had found an eBay account in Smythe's name and the most recent transaction – a 1960s Waddington deck. The case was tied up so tight that Smythe would have no chance when he went to trial; despite his protests that he was innocent. Everything pointed to him. His compelling pleas of innocence were just the act of a psychopath.

So why did Brady not feel convinced?

Chapter Forty-Two

There was a knock at his door and Conrad walked in.

'Sir, the team want to know when you're joining them at the Fat Ox.'

Brady considered it for a moment. He knew that he should go. Make an appearance. After all, it was his team's hard work that helped apprehend De Bernier's murderer. But he wasn't in the mood. All he wanted to do was go home and have a drink with Claudia. He hadn't seen her in days.

He shook his head. 'Pass on my apologies, Conrad. I'm going home. Claudia will be wondering what the hell has happened to me.'

Conrad's expression changed. He suddenly looked tense. Too bloody tense.

'What?' Brady asked.

'I . . . I'm sorry, sir—'

Brady suddenly stood up. 'What the fuck is it?'

'Claudia . . . She's not there.'

'What do you mean?'

'She's not at your place. She's gone.'

Brady's face darkened as he walked over towards his deputy. 'Where the fuck is she, if she's not at mine?'

Conrad considered his options. He didn't have many.

'Where the fuck is she?' Brady asked.

'She's . . . she's at mine, sir. She . . . she needed time to decide what she wanted to do,' he explained. Conrad dropped his eyes, unable to look at the flash of hurt that crossed Brady's face. It was quickly replaced by betrayal. Then anger.

'How long?'

Conrad didn't answer.

'How fucking long?' Brady repeated. 'If you don't tell me, I swear I'll beat it out of you.'

'Monday. Claudia rang me Monday morning and asked if she could stay with me and . . .' Conrad paused. 'I went around after I finished my shift and picked her up later that evening. I'm sorry . . .'

Brady thought back. It seemed like weeks ago. But the last time he had heard from Claudia was Monday night. A simple text saying that she was fine. And he believed it. Stupidly believed it after what she had attempted to do on Sunday night. Just two nights ago – yet so much had happened in those forty-eight hours that he had lost track of time. And seemingly, his personal life.

'You didn't think to tell me?' Brady hissed. 'That my wife had left me?'

'Ex-wife, sir,' Conrad pointed out.

Brady punched the wall. It was the only way he could stop himself ramming his fist into Conrad's face.

Conrad moved back and waited for Brady to calm down.

'She said she would call you, sir,' Conrad tried in an attempt to appease him. 'Explain what she was doing. I told her that this was between the two of you, that it's not my business. That I didn't want to get involved.'

'Fucking right it's none of your business!' Brady replied as he flexed his bruised and scraped hand. But he knew that Conrad and Claudia had been close – once. He had not realised that she had been in contact with Conrad, during the last five months, let alone confided in him. Then again, there was a lot he had not realised.

Conrad waited for Brady to absorb the information and calm down.

'Sir, she's not well . . .'

'Tell me something I don't know. I've been living with her. Remember?' Brady snapped.

'I know. But now she needs medical help,' Conrad said.

'Says who?'

'She's ill. She's very ill. She needs to be somewhere where she can have access to doctors twenty-four hours. Just in case she . . .' Conrad faltered. He didn't need to say it.

'No!' shouted Brady. 'She's fine! She doesn't need a shrink and she doesn't need to be locked up!'

Conrad persisted. 'Her parents arrived today. I'm sorry. Really I am. They've sorted out some country house in Kent that specialises in dealing with patients like Claudia.'

Brady looked at Conrad. His eyes searched his face.

'Please tell me you didn't contact her parents?'

'I'm sorry,' Conrad said.

Brady felt winded. He could feel the panic rising. Overwhelming him. 'They haven't taken her? Not yet? I . . . I need to talk to her first . . .' he said, trying to keep the desperation out of his voice.

Conrad's expression told Brady that he was already too late. Claudia had already gone.

'Get out,' Brady ordered.

Conrad did not move. 'I want to explain, sir.'

'You've had plenty of time to tell me.'

'I didn't know how to,' Conrad replied.

'No? Seems like there's a lot you don't know how to tell me,' Brady said.

Conrad didn't answer.

'Go on. Get out!' Brady repeated.

Conrad did as ordered.

THURSDAY

Chapter Forty-Three

Brady couldn't face going home, the reality of it too much for him. So he had stayed at work.

He had been sitting at his desk for the past hour. It was now after midnight and the last thing he felt like doing was sleeping. He was too wired. Too raw. He needed something to distract himself. Anything to stop himself thinking about Claudia. About the fact that she had left him. That . . . that Conrad had been party to it. Had known about it since Monday.

Fuck . . . fuck . . . fuck!

Brady took another hit of scotch in an attempt to silence the tortured thoughts racing through his mind. He had solved De Bernier's sadistic murder. But at what cost to his personal life? His wife had gone. Left him. Alone – *again*.

He thought of Conrad. The betrayal he felt was overwhelming. He took another drink. An attempt at numbing the hurt.

His eyes fell on the files in front of him. Something was still gnawing away at him. Chewing him up inside. He wanted to ignore it. Dispel the doubts with the facts of the case. But he couldn't. No matter how hard he tried, he could not silence the uncertainty that he felt. He was certain that Smythe was innocent. But how? And why?

Who would want to set you up, Robert? Who had a motive so powerful that they were prepared to torture and kill a young man in the style of The Joker and then frame you for it?

It was then that it hit Brady. He thought of the press gathered like vultures at Newcastle Airport waiting for their next meal. As soon as Smythe had appeared under arrest, the media had gone wild. Someone had told them. That person had wanted him publically persecuted and vilified.

Brady knew who it was. All he had to do was prove it.

He needed to go over the CCTV footage again. And he needed more of it.

He picked up his phone. He had no choice. He had to call Conrad.

'Conrad?'

'Sir,' Conrad replied uncomfortably.

'I need you back at the station.'

'Give me thirty minutes and I'll be there,' answered Conrad without question.

Brady disconnected the call. He needed to talk to the hotel to get access to their security tapes. Then he would know for certain if his hunch was right.

He searched through his phone for Wolfe's number.

'Laddie, do you know what time it is?' Wolfe answered, disgruntled.

'Sorry, but I need to run something past you,' Brady explained.

'Go on,' Wolfe wheezed.

Brady could hear him lighting a cigarette and inhaling deeply as he waited. Brady could almost taste the cigarette himself. An overwhelming desire to have one consumed him.

'I think the trace of semen that was found on the sheets at the crime scene was planted,' Brady said.

'Interesting,' Wolfe replied. 'But how?'

'That's what I'm hoping you could tell me.'

Brady listened as Wolfe sucked on his cigarette as he contemplated the question.

'Collect it and freeze it until you want to use it, I guess,' Wolfe answered.

'Yeah . . . that's what I thought. Thanks.'

*　*　*

Eleven hours later and Brady had the evidence in front of him. He had studied the CCTV footage again. And again. There was no disputing it.

There was a knock at his door.

'Yeah?' Brady called out. He knew it would be Conrad. He had turned up at the station after midnight and had worked doggedly since then, trying to help Brady piece together Sarah Huntingdon-Smythe's movements.

The door opened. Conrad walked in. He still couldn't quite look Brady in the eye.

'Did you talk to the member of staff who said that she was at dinner that night?' Brady asked.

'Yes, sir,' Conrad answered as he walked towards Brady's desk. 'He apologised profusely. He had made a mistake. They were incredibly busy that night. She had a reservation with a group of other diners from the medical conference she was attending at the hotel but she wasn't at the dinner with the rest.'

Brady sighed heavily. He knew this would be the case. But he just needed it verified. After all, he had seen her climbing into her metallic blue Mercedes-Benz in the underground hotel car park in London and driving away at 3:01 p.m. It was indisputable.

'But she was seen in the Covent Garden Hotel the following morning?'

Conrad nodded. 'Yes, for breakfast at nine a.m. in the dining hall. She ate with four other colleagues attending the medical conference.'

It came as no surprise to Brady. It had taken her six and a half hours to drive from London to Tynemouth. Then another five and a half for the return journey. At 9:38 p.m. the car could be seen passing through the Tyne Tunnel. Then at 12:34 a.m. the same vehicle went back through, heading for the A1 South back to London. A close-up shot of the driver confirmed it was Sarah Huntingdon-Smythe – the politician's wife. The car was also registered in her name.

Brady thought about what he had found on tape. If it had not been for the doubts that kept tormenting him over Smythe's guilt, then he would never have suspected that his wife could have set him up. Without a reason to be suspicious, he would never have looked. Never have scratched beneath the surface to see what ugly truth lay waiting.

CCTV cameras had followed her Mercedes-Benz down Coast Road. She had parked it in Tynemouth Front Street. On foot, she was caught on surveillance camera leaving Front Street in the direction of her home in Priors Terrace.

When Sarah Huntingdon-Smythe had arrived home on the night of the murder, she had waited for her husband to come in and leave, as he always did, his keys and business phone on the hallway table. Unbeknownst to him, she had then texted De Bernier, setting in motion the events of that fateful night. She had been the one who had replied to Alexander's blackmail threat, and had already made the arrangements. She had then deleted the email. Jed had found it. It also explained why Smythe had been adamant he had no knowledge of the email, or the arrangements to meet the victim at the Royal hotel.

Why her? Why suspect the accused's wife?

But it had seemed obvious to Brady. Robert Smythe had said his wife was pregnant and yet the forensics team searching the house had found female contraceptives in her toiletry bag. That was what had got Brady thinking. That little detail. At the time he hadn't even questioned it. But last night it had hit him – what if?

'It was the female condoms or femidoms that Ainsworth's team found. Why would she be using them if she was pregnant? She was quite clear to us when we interviewed her that she didn't cheat. That she was faithful. So why the contraception?'

Conrad waited for Brady to give him the answer.

'She must have inserted one before having sex with Robert as a means of keeping her husband's sperm. She then froze it until the opportunity arose to plant it on the victim.'

'How can you be certain, sir?' Conrad asked.

'The lab have come back. They said that they had found unusually high traces of spermicide in the traces of sperm found on the sheets.'

'Maybe Smythe wore a condom? Maybe he didn't want to leave biological evidence?' Conrad suggested.

'And what? It broke?' Brady replied shaking his head. 'I admit, I had thought that. So I asked the lab to examine the sperm for any form of damage.'

Conrad frowned.

'To see if it had been frozen,' Brady explained. 'I was right. The lab said that some of the sperm had been damaged, consistent with having been frozen and then defrosted.'

'Why?' Conrad asked. 'Why would she do it? She's an eminent heart surgeon. And she's pregnant. Why risk all she had?'

'Because she had already lost everything. There was nothing left,' Brady answered, unable to hide the sadness he felt.

Proving Sarah Huntingdon-Smythe's part in De Bernier's murder had left Brady feeling profoundly empty. Lives had been destroyed. And for what?

Chapter Forty-Four

Conrad frowned. None of it made sense to him. Sarah Huntingdon-Smythe had everything. Even without her husband, she was still the leading surgeon in her field. And she was expecting a baby. As far as Conrad could make out, she had everything to lose and nothing to gain.

'But why set her husband up? Apart from the obvious, that he was having an affair.'

'Not just having an affair,' Brady pointed out. 'It wasn't another woman. She could compete with that. This was a young man. Imagine how humiliated she must have felt. She admitted to us that her husband had his "indiscretions". I assumed that she accepted those if they were with women. But the public shame and embarrassment if the press found out he was sleeping with men . . .'

Conrad looked uneasy at this statement. Brady realised he had hit a raw nerve. He quickly continued: 'And it wasn't just sex. Robert had fallen in love with Alex. She must have found out about the holidays, the money and the expensive gifts that we traced back to the politician's bank account.'

'All right, I can accept all that. But why set him up for murder? That's extreme, don't you think? For a woman with so much to lose?'

Brady shook his head. 'That's where you're wrong.'

'I don't follow.'

'She had already lost everything. Including her husband. Do you really think a baby would have kept him there? Playing

314

happy families? Smythe would have eventually left her for a man. Whether it was De Bernier or someone else. He had been living a lie. He married her to have the right look in the public eye. The problem was, she had had no idea. Not until she confronted De Bernier with her suspicions. And then she had had a rude awakening. I'm sure the victim would have left her with no doubts about her husband's true sexuality. Think of the content of those DVDs.'

Conrad looked at Brady. 'She knew about the DVDs?'

'She had accessed her husband's email account on her laptop. It was taken into custody with the desktop computer when forensics searched the house,' Brady explained. 'Don't ask me how Jed does it, but he managed to find evidence that she had opened up her husband's emails and watched the films that De Bernier had sent him as a blackmail threat.'

Conrad breathed out. He still looked uncertain.

'Don't worry. You'll have plenty of time to ask her questions when we bring her in.'

'I understand the motive for setting her husband up. But murder? She's a doctor, sir. She's taken the Hippocratic Oath.'

'You do remember the blood tests that came back? That confirmed Alex was HIV positive. We saw in the DVDs that he practised unprotected sex with Smythe and Hughes and others.'

Conrad nodded.

'The DVDs date back to last October. So the odds are that he will be infected.'

'Yes,' Brady answered. 'So will his wife.'

'Oh, Christ!' Conrad muttered.

'Four weeks ago she had an amniocentesis. She would have had her blood tested and if she was HIV positive it would have shown. What do you think the ramifications would be for her? Aside from the health ones?'

'Her career would be over.'

Brady nodded. 'Precisely. She'd have to stop doing surgery because of the risk to her patients.'

'So, she went after the two men who destroyed her life?' Conrad asked.

'Yeah . . . Seems that way. Her revenge on her husband was meticulous. Setting him up for the murder of the young man he loved. She used his car to go the Royal Hotel, knowing CCTV cameras would record the car travelling along the Promenade. She took her husband's business phone and used it to text the victim because she wanted him implicated. She took his cut-throat razor and used it to mutilate the victim, then washed it and returned it to their bathroom. She knew there would be trace evidence left on the blade. She took his shoe to the crime scene with the intention of leaving one partial footprint.'

Conrad looked at Brady in disbelief. 'That is remarkably clever,' he said.

'The evidence was difficult to find. Intentionally so. To make it appear as if Smythe had cleaned the room after the murder. The minuscule drop of sperm on the sheets planted so that when forensics did find it, it would place Smythe at the crime scene. Even the partial footprint was made to look as if her husband had been very careful not to leave any forensic evidence at the crime scene. As to why . . .'

Brady felt as deflated as Conrad looked. There was no pleasure in any of this – none at all.

'I assume he had infected her and put their unborn child at risk.' Brady paused for a moment, imagining her horror when the amniocentesis results came back. She would not have been expecting to find out she was HIV positive. No one would. Brady was aware that a significant portion of the population were unaware that they were HIV positive. For most, the symptoms when first infected were assumed to be a nasty bout of flu. It could be up to ten years before the virus made itself known.

'Then there was De Bernier,' Brady continued, as he thought about the motive behind his murder. 'Do you remember Molly Johansson saying she overheard them arguing? That Sarah Huntingdon-Smythe was threatening that she would destroy his career in politics before it had even properly begun if he did not leave her alone? She had wanted him out of her and her husband's lives. She had given him a chance to walk away. But he didn't. So she murdered him. Lured him to the hotel by pretending to be his lover. Requested that he blindfold himself.'

'So he would not know that it wasn't Smythe,' Conrad said.

'Exactly. Then she bound him, giving her physical power over him. All of this being consensual. The victim had no idea who had walked into the hotel room. Or what was about to happen to him.'

'That's the part I still find hard to accept,' Conrad admitted. 'What she did to him.'

'Why? Because she was pregnant or because she was a surgeon?'

'Both.'

'Put yourself in her position. This young, arrogant man who had no real interest in her husband, other than what he could get out of the relationship, came along and destroyed her life. Her unborn baby's life. And what for? Money and power? That's what he wanted. Malcolm Hughes and Smythe will just be a few on a long list. Who knows how many men Alexander De Bernier unknowingly infected? I'm sure that Sarah Huntingdon-Smythe believed that what she was doing was for the greater good. Permanently preventing him from infecting other men, destroying countless more lives than he already had.'

'But how did she know about The Joker's signature?'

'She's a surgeon, Conrad. How difficult would it be for her to get hold of the pathology reports from the first seven victims? Not that difficult. Not if you are as focused and determined as her. At the time, the autopsies were carried out at the Freeman hospital. The same hospital she works at now. It was something Wolfe said when he was carrying out De Bernier's autopsy, that he had accessed the reports on the Seventies victims. Made me wonder how easy it would be to access this material if you're in the profession.'

'But why The Joker? Why copy him?'

Brady had spent most of the early hours asking himself why Sarah had attempted to fool the police first by framing her husband, and then by setting up a murder scene to make it appear as if the original Seventies killer had returned.

'Good question. Hopefully she'll be able to give you a satisfying answer when we interview her. I personally think she did it because the Seventies killings were so shocking. A copycat murder would be a hit with the media. That was what she wanted. Her husband publicly denounced. Did she think we would consider that Robert Smythe could also be responsible for the first killings? Maybe . . . But I am more certain that she believed that she had come up with the perfect plan to frame her husband for his lover's cruel death.'

Conrad was silent for a moment.

'And you're absolutely certain Smythe did not murder De Bernier?'

'One hundred per cent. I looked in the man's eyes, Conrad. He may be many things, but he's not a killer.'

Brady steeled himself for his final job – Sarah Huntingdon-Smythe's interview. He believed she would confess. Why not? She had nothing to lose. She had achieved what she had set out to do. Publicly expose her husband and destroy his political career and good name. The press had already got hold of the sordid affair between the Conservative politician and his junior aide. Someone had tipped them off about his arrest and that he was sexually involved with the victim. Brady knew who the informant had been before he had talked to Rubenfeld. The sordid, sad affair had hit the front page of the *Northern Echo* that afternoon.

All Rubenfeld would tell him was that the tip-off came from an anonymous female caller. He had also received a copy of a DVD. It had been couriered to him. Brady had contacted the courier direct and the sender's details matched Sarah Huntingdon-Smythe's description. Needless to say, the DVD showed explicit scenes of a sexual nature involving Smythe and De Bernier. Brady had wondered at the time why Sarah had not met her husband at the airport. Why she had not been there to support him at the police station. Her absence itself had implicated her.

'I reckon it's time we go and bring her in for questioning. Don't you?' Brady said as he stood up.

Brady felt the need to bring her in personally. She had refused to leave the family home and had only stayed with friends while forensics were examining the property. He knew that she would have no idea that they would be coming to arrest her. Why would she? After all, her husband's sordid life had been spread across all the tabloids and repeatedly discussed on the news. Sarah had got what she wanted – her husband's duplicitous life exposed. And more.

Chapter Forty-Five

Thursday: 2:29 p.m.

Brady banged on the door again.

'What time is it?' Brady asked Conrad.

'Two-thirty, sir,' Conrad answered.

Brady was exhausted. As was Conrad. No surprise, given the fact that they had worked through the night piecing together Sarah Huntingdon-Smythe's movements.

'Maybe she's having a nap?' Conrad suggested. 'She is pregnant.'

Brady shook his head. He had a bad feeling about this. 'I'm going to take a look around the back and see if I can find a way in.'

'Sir?' Conrad asked, surprised. 'Shouldn't we just call for backup?'

But Brady didn't hear him. Or if he did, he was too distracted. He broke into a run.

Brady found the back of the house. He could see that the kitchen window was open. All he needed to do was climb over the yard wall. He looked around for something to stand on to help give him some leverage to swing himself over. Someone had left a washing machine out for the scrap merchants. Brady dragged it over and pushed it against the wall, climbed onto it and then pulled himself up and over. He jumped down, anticipating the pain before he landed.

'Fuck!' he cursed as a bolt of pain exploded in what remained of his left knee. Hobbling, Brady made his way to the open kitchen window. It was large enough for him to squeeze himself through.

'Sarah? Police! Sarah?' he shouted when he was finally inside.

Nothing. Brady tried to ignore the disquiet he felt.

'Sarah? Sarah, it is DI Brady,' he shouted as he walked into the palatial kitchen. He made his way through to the hallway. Again, nothing.

He checked all the rooms downstairs, knowing that he wouldn't find her. He then walked to the front door and opened it for Conrad.

'Nothing downstairs. But her house keys and car keys are on the hall table.'

Conrad didn't say anything. His sombre expression told Brady he had a bad feeling about this as well.

Brady took the stairs two at a time, ignoring the pain in his leg.

'Sarah?' he shouted out again.

Nothing.

He reached the first floor. The door to the master bedroom was wide open.

'Sarah? It's DI Jack Brady, Sarah. We need to talk to you.'

He didn't notice any of the finer details of the house. The antique furniture, oil paintings and highly polished oak floors covered in Persian rugs. All he noticed was the deathly silence that hung in the air.

Something was wrong. The silence screamed at him that something was very wrong.

He turned and looked back at Conrad behind him. Brady nodded at him that he was going into the master bedroom.

He walked in. The ornate four-poster bed was in disarray, sheets and throws pulled back. Scatter cushions and pillows knocked onto the floor. Clothes dumped next to them.

It was then that Brady heard the water.

Drip . . . drip . . . drip . . .

The chilling noise was coming from the en-suite bathroom.

321

Brady walked towards the closed door, dreading what he would find.

'Sarah?' he called out as he knocked. But he already knew it was in vain.

He swung the door open and stopped. Paralysed.

'Oh God . . .' Brady muttered.

It took him a moment to react. 'Call paramedics. Now!' he ordered.

But it would be too late. Sarah's body lay submerged in the bloodied water in the bath in the centre of the large bathroom. He walked over. Her bloodless grey face looked up at him from underneath the water. Eyes open. Blank. Staring at nothing. He felt sick. For a second it was as if he was looking into Claudia's pale, lifeless face. Into her dead, accusatory eyes.

No . . . Claudia . . .

In that moment he knew how close he had come to losing her.

Brady swallowed the sob that was strangling the back of his throat. He could feel the tears burning his eyes.

'Sarah? Sarah . . .' He was too late. The bath was filled with blood. Her blood. Blood from her slit wrists.

He dropped to his knees and leaned over to carefully lift her head out of the water. He held her tight against his chest, one hand clasped around her damp bloodied hair. Sarah's body was cold. Too cold. He closed his eyes as the tears slipped down his face at the unjustness of it all. For a moment he felt transported back to Sunday night and Claudia.

What if . . . Oh God, what if . . .

Then there was only the image of Sarah's lifeless body. Her swollen belly drowned out Claudia. Naked, there was no mistaking that she was with child.

If only . . . If only he'd realised sooner . . .

Chapter Forty-Six

Macintosh had left a message for DI Brady. To others, it would just be a receipt. But Brady would understand.

He had waited until dark. Hidden himself in the Gents toilets in Whitley Bay. He needed to be close. But not too close. Hours he had waited, crouched behind the closed door of a cubicle. He had heard the goings-on. It had made him feel sick. Brought back the images. The memories of the others. But he had resisted making himself known. Doing what he knew was right felt good. It brought him liberation. A momentary lapse from his father's bullying. That voice, drunk and terrifying. It humiliated and debased him. Ridiculed what felt normal. He calmed himself. Silenced the evil, vindictive words with images of past victims and future victims. Of what he had done and what he was about to do.

He had one hand on the doorbell while the other hand held the axe behind his back. He pressed the bell and listened to the faint chime as footsteps approached. His mind was suddenly filled with images of what was to come. Flashes of the blade. Swift. Slicing. Hacking. Smashing bone. Blood. Flesh. Screaming. He could smell it. Smell them. Hear them. He smiled in preparation.

The feeling was intense. It had consumed him. He had stayed with them. Watched them. Lain down with them. Breathed in their scent. Touched them. Stared into their wide eyes. Then he had left. He had no choice. He needed to get a head start. Ahead of the police. But it was Jack Brady he wanted. This was for him. It was his gift. He was certain that when Brady looked at what he had done for him, he would follow. Then they would see.

All he had to do now was wait. He looked in the rear-view mirror at the blur of headlights behind him. She was in the boot of the car. Gagged and tied. No one would ever know she was there.

Chapter Forty-Seven

Brady had managed to grab four hours' sleep on his office couch. A call from Wolfe woke him up from a deep slumber. He had carried out the autopsy on Sarah Huntingdon-Smythe at his request. Brady had assumed she had killed herself because she was HIV positive, and he'd been correct. Wolfe had accessed her medical records, and blood tests taken in her sixteenth week of pregnancy had exposed the infection. Not that he felt good about being right. Blood had also been taken from the twenty-week-old foetus – her unborn son. He was also HIV positive. She had known about it for the past few weeks, giving her time to plan her revenge.

Brady felt no joy that the investigation was over. Nor that an innocent man would not be sentenced for a murder he had not committed. He just felt an overwhelming sadness at the ugly mess of it all. That it had been so unnecessary. Life could indeed deal some cruel hands. It was up to the individual as to how they played that hand. In Sarah Huntingdon-Smythe's case, she had played it very close to her heart.

Brady picked up his phone. He thought about calling Claudia's mobile but decided against it. He didn't know if she would pick up. Or even if she was allowed to take personal calls. Not that he could phone anyone to find out. He had no idea where her parents had taken her. He had rung them – repeatedly. But to no avail. They simply didn't answer his calls.

He was distracted by a knock at his door. Conrad walked in.

'I thought you'd gone home,' Brady said.

'I was just leaving when I overheard a call coming in—'

'Macintosh has gone missing, hasn't he?' Brady interrupted.

Conrad swallowed. 'Yes, sir, I wanted to tell you that he had broken parole. He's been missing since this morning. He didn't show up at Ashley House for the seven p.m. curfew. Then one of the key workers searched his room and it was empty. He had taken everything. Apart from this,' Conrad said, holding out a plastic evidence bag. He handed it to Brady.

It had a receipt in it from B&Q. It was for an axe.

'Shit! Shit! Shit!' Brady cursed.

He jumped up.

'Get Jonathan Edwards' address right now,' Brady instructed.

'Why, sir?' Conrad asked.

'Because that's where Macintosh has gone,' Brady said as he grabbed his coat. 'Come on, Conrad. Move it!' He snatched his car keys and ran for the door.

Brady had looked on in horror and disbelief. As soon as the Edwards' door had been breached by a battering ram, Brady had gone in. He had to. He had to see whether he was too late. He had found them first. Or . . . what was left of them.

Police cars and ambulances now blocked off Queens Road. But it was already over. James David Macintosh had seen to that.

Brady stood outside. He was shaking. But he couldn't stop. He couldn't stop the scenes of carnage playing over and over again in his mind.

'Here, Jack,' Conrad said, offering him some hot, sweet tea.

Brady nodded numbly. He took the drink and cupped it in trembling hands. Not that he could drink it. His body was shaking uncontrollably. He knew he was in shock. And he knew he had every right to be. What he had witnessed was beyond anything he could ever have imagined.

'We've got to find him,' he whispered, his voice hoarse.

'Yes, sir,' Conrad answered.

'You've put a call out on Edwards' car?'

Conrad nodded.

They had to find him. Someone as dangerous and unbalanced as Macintosh would strike again. There was no question about that. The only question was, how soon.

FRIDAY

Chapter Forty-Eight

Friday: 9:03 a.m.

The DNA results from the lab had come back. Brady had forgotten he had paid to have the tests expedited. But they had arrived too late. The lab had managed to get a sample of DNA from the sperm found on the T-shirt of one of the Seventies victims. It did not come as a surprise that it matched Macintosh.

Brady had been right. The paroled ex-offender had been responsible for the Joker killings of the summer of 1977. He had eluded the police in the Seventies and now he had succeeded in eluding Brady.

He couldn't bring himself to think about it. The bitter fact that Brady had had Macintosh in custody. He could have prevented him from killing Edwards and his wife and son. Their three-year-old daughter Annabel was gone. He had taken her, just as he had taken his psychiatrist's daughter after he had slain him and the rest of his family.

Where the fuck have you taken her, you sick fucker?

Brady closed his eyes as he thought about where Macintosh could have gone. There was a national police hunt to find him. And Annabel Edwards. To find her alive. He winced as what he had witnessed flooded his mind. His psyche. He could smell them. Their bodies. The blood.

Brady opened his eyes. He didn't want to see the blood-drenched walls and beds. The house saturated with blood.

Macintosh had brought the axe down on them. Again. And again. And again.

Brady felt sick. Could feel it rising up the back of his throat. He leaned over, grabbed his wastepaper bin and vomited until only bile was left. He sat up, shaking. Eyes watering. He didn't know whether it was from being sick or from the horrific images that filled his mind. That had contaminated him. That had taken over.

He forced them back. He knew the things he had witnessed would never leave him. They never did. Especially images this horrific and as cruel. They stayed – forever.

Brady thought of James David Macintosh.

Where are you, you sick son of a bitch? Because I'll find you . . . and if you've hurt her . . . If you've hurt her the way you hurt the other little girl then I'll . . .

Brady stood up. Fists clenched. It was time to go. The hours were fast running out. He had vowed that he would hunt Macintosh down. Regardless of how long it took.

Acknowledgements

I am eternally grateful, and always will be, to Jenny Brown.

Heartfelt thanks to all at Mulholland Books and Hodder & Stoughton for being such an incredible team. Also, a huge thank you to Keshini Naidoo for her expertise.

Finally, I am truly indebted to my editor, Ruth Tross – thank you for being so fantastic.

If you've enjoyed BLOOD RECKONING,
why not try another Jack Brady book?

Read on for an extract from the
gripping BLIND ALLEY, out now.

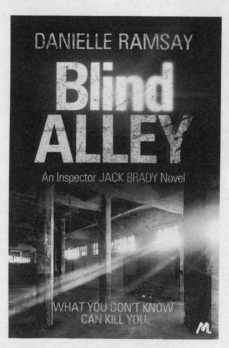

Chapter One

Thursday, 24th October: 10:23 p.m.

He watched her as she came outside. She couldn't see him – he had made sure of that. He sat back in the dark and waited. It was the anticipation of what was about to follow that he savoured more than the event itself. He licked his bottom lip. The location was perfect. Run-down and deserted. If anyone heard anything they wouldn't get involved. People here minded their own business. She couldn't have chosen a better place for what was about to happen to her. *If only she knew . . .*

He smiled to himself. He clenched and unclenched his hands as mentally he walked through the various scenarios he had meticulously planned.

Trina McGuire pursed her bright red lips and sucked on her tab as her cold, hard eyes scanned the shadowy street corners. It was second nature for her. A silver saloon car turned slowly off Saville Street West down onto Borough Road, casting its harsh beam over her. Blowing out smoke seductively, she looked in the direction of the driver. The silver car was now parked directly opposite her with the engine idling. The driver's face was in shadow but she knew he was watching her. Before she had a chance to walk over, he drove off. She was no fool. She was aware that the glare of his headlights had done her no favours. The roots of her long, straggly, bleached-blond hair and the uneven fake-tan smears on her arms and legs would be all too visible.

337

'Fuck you!'

She was getting too old for this game. And she was cold, despite it being mild for late October. She wrapped her thin, bare arms across her low-cut vest top in an attempt to keep warm.

She rested her back against the wall and listened to the dull thump of U2 on the jukebox inside as she smoked. Anything to calm her nerves. She had never known the streets to be so dark and quiet. Business was virtually non-existent. Even the Ballarat pub was empty apart from the hardcore regulars. She shivered again. She could feel the small, prickly hairs on the back of her neck standing up. She didn't know what it was, but something felt wrong. Maybe it was just her nerves getting the better of her, but she couldn't shake the feeling that someone was watching her. She glanced up and down the badly lit street. She couldn't see anyone. *Or could she?*

'Fuck this!' she muttered as she threw away what was left of her cigarette.

She turned on her three-inch red heels, about to go back in.

Before she had a chance to realise what was happening, he had already dragged her into the alley behind the pub where the rubbish bins were kept. A large leather-gloved hand covered her mouth, preventing her from screaming. Panicking, she struggled to get free but it was futile. He had the upper hand. He was at least six foot one and built like a Rottweiler on steroids.

Suddenly his other hand was tearing at her vest top. He found her breasts and started twisting and pulling at them roughly.

She felt physically sick. She wanted to vomit as his hand mauled her. But she knew that no matter what he did to her she had to keep focused. Her mind was racing. She was trying to process what was happening to her and at the same time trying to figure out how to get free.

Was he a punter? No . . . no. She'd been roughed up before but this was different. He was different . . .

338

Then it hit her. The news. It had been all over the news. There was a rapist in the area. *Shit! Shit! Shit! How could she have been so stupid?*

The police had put up photofits of the bloke throughout the local pubs. There was even one pinned by the toilets in the Ballarat. He had attacked three women in the past two months. And from what she'd read in the local paper that evening, the third one had been hurt pretty badly – enough for the poor cow to need reconstructive surgery.

Shit . . . shit . . . shit . . .

Tortured thoughts tore through her mind.

She was confused. She was sure he had only struck in Whitley Bay. She had been relaxed about the story because this was North Shields. How wrong could she have been?

She had to get away from him. Fight . . . Anything to stop him hurting her . . .

She used all her strength to prise his hand from over her mouth. Her long manicured nails snapped and split as she scratched and tore to no avail at the gloved hand. If she could scream it might be enough to scare him off. Desperate, she took her chance and bit as hard as she could through the leather to the flesh underneath.

His reaction was sudden and swift. He raised his knee and rammed it as hard as he could into the small of her back to make her let go.

It had the desired effect.

She was too winded to realise what was about to happen.

The first blow was a surprise. It split her nose clean open. She heard the sickening sound of snapping bones as his fist connected with her face, followed by the hissing of escaping air and blood. She was stunned. She had no chance of protecting herself against what was to follow.

The second punch was harder than the first. It smashed int her face with such force that her left eye socket imploded. H head snapped violently backwards as her teeth ricochete her bottom lip, bursting it open like a swollen dam. Her legs gave way beneath her as everything went black.

Minutes passed as she lay on the ground, her body consumed with a blinding agony. Nothing made sense. All she knew was that she hurt so badly she was certain she would die. Slowly, the hazy fog started to lift. She remembered that she'd been attacked. He had dragged her into the perilously black alley behind the pub. She was aware that she was lying on something cold and hard – the ground. She must have collapsed after he'd punched her.

She could feel the panic overwhelming her.

She looked around in the darkness for him.

Where are you, you bastard? Where the fuck are you?

Her left eye had swollen shut and her right eye was nothing more than a slit. But it was enough to see the glow of a cigarette in the blackness by the large waste bins.

She realised with sickening clarity it was him. That he hadn't finished with her – not yet.

'Where is he?' he asked, throwing his cigarette butt away.

His voice was seamless and flat, devoid of any emotion.

It was this that scared her. It was the voice of someone capable of murder.

Her mind spun as she tried to figure out who he was after.

Realising he wasn't getting anywhere with her, he decided to jolt her memory. He walked over and bent down.

She waited, expecting him to hit her again, but he took her by surprise when he started caressing her bare thin legs with his gloved hand.

She trembled as he touched her gently. He slowly moved his hand further and further up her legs until it was under her skirt.

She tried to struggle, to get his hand away from between her legs. But he had her pinned down.

'I said, where is he?'

He stopped caressing her. His hand had become a ball of ⌐sion, waiting to explode.

⌐he attempted to shake her head.

It wasn't the answer he wanted. He rammed his fist as hard as he could between her legs.

The pain was unbearable. She was certain she would pass out. Instead she retched.

He stood back and watched while she vomited, until eventually only bile was left. His stomach was turning at the sight of her. Vomit combined with blood trailed down the seeping, swollen mess that was her face.

'Nick. Where is he, you fucking slag?'

He was starting to lose his patience.

The question jolted her.

'What?' she mumbled through swollen, bloodied lips.

But the word she uttered made no sense.

Irritated, he bent over her, bringing his face close to hers. She was terrified. The look in his eyes told him he wasn't just going to rape her – he was going to kill her.

'No . . . please . . . no . . .'

But the words were inaudible. The only sound was a gargling, hissing noise.

'I said, where the fuck is NICK, you stupid bitch?'

He rammed a hand deep under her ribs to make sure that she was lucid.

She gasped in agony.

When she managed to breathe again, she mustered all the strength she had and spat at him.

Blood, vomit and spit hit his face. He took a tissue out of his jacket and wiped his cheek. He then took off the jacket and rolled up the sleeves of his shirt.

'Maybe it's time to teach you some manners,' he suggested as he began to unzip his trousers.

She tried to get up but her body refused to move. She willed herself to make a run for it. But something was wrong. Her legs wouldn't work.

Move . . . come on, Trina . . . Fucking move, girl! Move it before it's too late!

Desperate, she tried shuffling backwards on her elbows, dragging herself towards the entrance of the alley.

He was more than ready. He had been anticipating this moment for some time. He took his time stretching a condom over himself. He knew he couldn't take a chance with this disease-riddled bitch. He kneeled down and grabbed her by the legs as she tried in vain to scramble away from him. He leaned over and flipped her onto her stomach.

She groaned in pain at the sudden, violent movement.

Her reaction had the desired effect. It made him even more excited. He pulled up her faux leather skirt, exposing her black thong.

She attempted to struggle but was unable to move under the crushing weight of his body. She felt him yank her thong to one side before he forced himself into her. The pain was excruciating. But it was more the humiliation that hurt. Hot, furious tears slipped down her face as he succeeded in violently thrusting himself deep into her. One hand restrained her head, forcing her damaged face into the hard concrete, while the other held his phone as he filmed what he was doing to her.

She couldn't breathe. Dirt filled her bloodied mouth as she choked and gasped, desperate for air.

She could feel her body beginning to convulse as the lack of oxygen took effect. She prayed for unconsciousness. She was lucky. She blacked out before he started to really lose control.

Once finished with her he felt nothing but disgust and contempt. He gave her lifeless body another hard kick. Nothing. Satisfied, he picked it up and dumped it into the pub's industrial waste bins where it belonged.

Fucking bitch. Deserved everything she got. He had bigger problems than some has-been prostitute. He still had to find Nick Brady. And when he did . . .

He smiled at the prospect. He had what he wanted safe in a plastic bag: evidence that he had dealt with her. He felt no remorse. She was a used-up prostitute who was better off dead. No one would miss her.

He threw the business card with her name scrawled on the back into the alleyway before turning to walk back to his car. He doubted the police would be able to identify her. Not in the condition he had left her in. But he was more than happy to point them in the right direction. After all, he had a job to do and he had to be sure that the police didn't fuck everything up.